THE
SEARCH

Nora Roberts

HOT ICE
SACRED SINS
BRAZEN VIRTUE
SWEET REVENGE
PUBLIC SECRETS
GENUINE LIES
CARNAL INNOCENCE
HONEST ILLUSIONS
DIVINE EVIL
PRIVATE SCANDALS
HIDDEN RICHES
TRUE BETRAYALS
MONTANA SKY
SANCTUARY
HOMEPORT
THE REEF
RIVER'S END
CAROLINA MOON
THE VILLA
MIDNIGHT BAYOU
THREE FATES
BIRTHRIGHT
NORTHERN LIGHTS
BLUE SMOKE
ANGELS FALL
HIGH NOON
TRIBUTE
BLACK HILLS
THE SEARCH
CHASING FIRE
THE WITNESS
THE COLLECTOR
TONIGHT AND ALWAYS
THE LIAR
THE OBSESSION

Series

Irish Born Trilogy
BORN IN FIRE
BORN IN ICE
BORN IN SHAME

Circle Trilogy
MORRIGAN'S CROSS
DANCE OF THE GODS
VALLEY OF SILENCE

Dream Trilogy
DARING TO DREAM
HOLDING THE DREAM
FINDING THE DREAM

Sign of Seven Trilogy
BLOOD BROTHERS
THE HOLLOW
THE PAGAN STONE

Chesapeake Bay Saga
SEA SWEPT
RISING TIDES
INNER HARBOR
CHESAPEAKE BLUE

Bride Quartet
VISION IN WHITE
BED OF ROSES
SAVOR THE MOMENT
HAPPY EVER AFTER

Gallaghers of Ardmore Trilogy
JEWELS OF THE SUN
TEARS OF THE MOON
HEART OF THE SEA

The Inn BoonsBoro Trilogy
THE NEXT ALWAYS
THE LAST BOYFRIEND
THE PERFECT HOPE

Three Sisters Island Trilogy
DANCE UPON THE AIR
HEAVEN AND EARTH
FACE THE FIRE

The Cousins O'Dwyer Trilogy
DARK WITCH
SHADOW SPELL
BLOOD MAGICK

Key Trilogy
KEY OF LIGHT
KEY OF KNOWLEDGE
KEY OF VALOR

The Guardians Trilogy
STARS OF FORTUNE
BAY OF SIGHS
ISLAND OF GLASS

In the Garden Trilogy
BLUE DAHLIA
BLACK ROSE
RED LILY

Anthologies

FROM THE HEART
A LITTLE MAGIC
A LITTLE FATE

MOON SHADOWS
(with Jill Gregory, Ruth Ryan Langan, and Marianne Willman)

The Once Upon Series
(with Jill Gregory, Ruth Ryan Langan, and Marianne Willman)

ONCE UPON A CASTLE	ONCE UPON A ROSE
ONCE UPON A STAR	ONCE UPON A KISS
ONCE UPON A DREAM	ONCE UPON A MIDNIGHT

SILENT NIGHT
(with Susan Plunkett, Dee Holmes, and Claire Cross)

OUT OF THIS WORLD
(with Laurell K. Hamilton, Susan Krinard, and Maggie Shayne)

BUMP IN THE NIGHT
(with Mary Blayney, Ruth Ryan Langan, and Mary Kay McComas)

DEAD OF NIGHT
(with Mary Blayney, Ruth Ryan Langan, and Mary Kay McComas)

THREE IN DEATH

SUITE 606
(with Mary Blayney, Ruth Ryan Langan, and Mary Kay McComas)

IN DEATH

THE LOST
(with Patricia Gaffney, Mary Blayney, and Ruth Ryan Langan)

THE OTHER SIDE
(with Mary Blayney, Patricia Gaffney, Ruth Ryan Langan, and Mary Kay McComas)

TIME OF DEATH

THE UNQUIET
(with Mary Blayney, Patricia Gaffney, Ruth Ryan Langan, and Mary Kay McComas)

MIRROR, MIRROR
(with Mary Blayney, Elaine Fox, Mary Kay McComas, and R. C. Ryan)

DOWN THE RABBIT HOLE
(with Mary Blayney, Elaine Fox, Mary Kay McComas, and R. C. Ryan)

Also available . . .

THE OFFICIAL NORA ROBERTS COMPANION
(edited by Denise Little and Laura Hayden)

THE
SEARCH

NORA ROBERTS

BERKLEY
NEW YORK

BERKLEY
An imprint of Penguin Random House LLC
penguinrandomhouse.com

To Homer and Pancho, and all who sweetened my life before them

BERKLEY and the BERKLEY & B colophon are registered trademarks of
Penguin Random House LLC.

ISBN: 9780593637784

G. P. Putnam's Sons hardcover edition / July 2010
Jove mass-market edition / April 2011
Berkley trade paperback edition / March 2023

Printed in the United States of America
1st Printing

This is a work of fiction. Names, characters, places, and incidents either are the product
of the author's imagination or are used fictitiously, and any resemblance to actual persons,
living or dead, business establishments, events, or locales is entirely coincidental.

PART ONE

Properly trained, a man can be a dog's best friend.

COREY FORD

ONE

On a chilly morning in February with a misty rain shuttering the windows, Devin and Rosie Cauldwell made slow, sleepy love. It was day three of their week's vacation—and month two of their attempt to conceive a second child. Their three-year-old son, Hugh, was the result of a long weekend on Orcas Island in the San Juans and—Rosie was convinced—a rainy afternoon and a bottle of Pinot Noir.

They hoped to repeat their success with a return visit to Orcas, and happily applied themselves to the mission at hand while their toddler slept with his beloved Wubby in the next room.

It was too early in the day for wine, but Rosie took the quiet rain as an omen.

When they were snuggled up together, loose and warm from sex, she smiled.

"Who had the best idea ever?"

Devin gave her ass an easy squeeze. "You did."

"Hang on, because I just had another one."

"I think I need a few minutes, first."

She laughed, rolled and propped herself on his chest to grin at him. "Get your mind off sex, Sleazy."

"I think I need a few minutes for that, too."

"Pancakes. We need pancakes. Rainy morning, our cozy little house. Definitely calls for pancakes."

He squinted at her. "Who's making them?"

"Let the fates decide."

She scooted up, and in a long-standing Cauldwell family tradition they let the balance hang on Rock, Paper, Scissors—best two out of three.

"Damn it," she muttered when he crushed her scissors with his rock.

"Superior skill wins out."

"My ass. But fair's fair—and I have to pee anyway." She bent down to give him a smacking kiss, then jumped out of bed. "I love vacation," she said as she dashed into the bathroom.

She especially loved this vacation, she thought, with her two handsome men. If the rain kept up, or got heavier, they'd play games inside. But if it let up, maybe they'd strap Hugh in the carrier and take a bike ride, or just go for a long hike.

Hugh just loved it here, loved the birds, the lake, the deer they'd spotted and of course the rabbits—all brothers to his faithful Wubby.

And maybe he'd have a brother of his own in the fall. She was ovulating—not that she was obsessing about getting pregnant. But counting days wasn't obsessing, she thought as she caught her sleep- and sex-mussed hair back in a band. It was just being self-aware.

She grabbed a sweatshirt and some flannel pants, glanced back at Devin, who'd gone back to snoozing.

She really thought they'd hit the money shot.

Delighted with the idea, she pulled on heavy socks, then glanced at the watch she'd left on the dresser.

"Gosh, it's after eight. We must've worn Hugh out last night for him to sleep this late."

"Probably the rain," Devin mumbled.

"Yeah, probably."

Still, she turned out of their room for his, as she did every morning, at home or away. She moved quietly, content to let him sleep—a bonus if she could grab her first cup of coffee before she heard the first *Mommy* of the day.

She peeked in, expecting to find him curled up with his stuffed bunny. The empty bed didn't bring panic. He might've gotten up to pee, just as she had. He'd gotten so good with his potty training.

Even when she didn't find him in the little bathroom off the hall, she didn't panic. Since he was habitually an early riser, they'd encouraged him to play for a bit before waking them. She usually heard him, talking to his toys or running his cars, but she'd been a little distracted having vacation sex.

God, she thought as she started downstairs, what if he'd looked in when they were doing it? No, he'd have walked right in and asked what game they were playing.

With a half laugh, she turned into the pretty living room, expecting to see her little boy on the floor surrounded by the toys of his choice.

When she didn't, the first fingers of unease tickled up her throat.

She called his name, moving quickly now, sliding a little on the hardwood floors in her socks.

Panic struck, a knife in the belly.

The kitchen door stood wide open.

SHORTLY AFTER NINE, Fiona Bristow pulled up at the pretty vacation house in the heart of Moran State Park. Rain fizzed along the ground more than pattered, but its steadiness promised sloppy tracking. She signaled her partner to stay in the truck, then got out to approach one of the local deputies.

"Davey."

"Hey, Fee. You got here fast."

"I didn't have far to go. The others are on their way. Are we using the house for base camp or do you want us to set up?"

"We're using it. You'll want to talk to the parents, but I'll give you the basics. Hugh Cauldwell, age three, blond and blue. Last seen wearing Spider-Man pajamas."

Fiona saw his mouth tighten a little. Davey had a boy about the same age as Hugh, and she imagined he had a pair of Spider-Man pj's, too.

"The mother first noticed he was missing at about eight-fifteen," Davey continued. "Found the back door open. No visible signs of forced entry or an intruder. The mother alerted the father. They called it in right away, and they ran around, calling for him, looking in the immediate area."

And tracked up the place, Fiona mused. But who could blame them?

"We did a house-and-grounds search, to make sure he wasn't just hiding." Davey turned back to Fiona with rain dripping off the bill of his cap. "He's not in the house, and his mother says he has his stuffed bunny with him. He sleeps with it, carts it around habitually. We've got rangers on the search, McMahon and Matt are out there," he added, referring to the sheriff and a young deputy.

"McMahon cleared me to call in your unit, and assigned me to base."

"We'll set up and get started. I'd like to interview the parents now, if that's good for you."

He gestured toward the house. "They're scared, as you'd expect—and they want to go out and look for him. You might help me talk them down from that."

"I'll see what I can do." Thinking of that, she went back to the truck, opened the door for her partner. Peck hopped out and walked with her and Davey to the house.

At Davey's nod, Fiona crossed to the couple, who rose from their huddle on the couch. The woman clutched a little red fire engine.

"Mr. and Mrs. Cauldwell, I'm Fiona Bristow with Canine Search and Rescue. This is Peck." She laid a hand on the head of the chocolate Lab. "The rest of my unit's on the way. We're going to help look for Hugh."

"You need to go. You need to go right now. He's only three."

"Yes, ma'am. The rest of my unit will be here any minute. It would help us if I get some information first."

"We told the police and the rangers everything." Devin

looked toward the window. "I need to go out there, look for him. We're wasting time here."

"Believe me, Mr. Cauldwell, the police and the rangers are doing everything they can to find Hugh. They called us because finding him is everyone's priority. We're trained, and your little boy is our only focus now. We're going to coordinate with the police and the park rangers. I need to make sure I have all the information so we optimize our resources. You realized Hugh was missing about eight-fifteen, is that right?"

Tears swam fresh into Rosie's eyes. "I should've checked on him earlier. He hardly ever sleeps past seven. I should've—"

"Mrs. Cauldwell . . . Rosie," Fiona corrected, using the first name to comfort. "You don't want to blame yourself. Little boys are curious, aren't they? Has Hugh ever left the house by himself before?"

"Never, never. I thought he'd come down to play, then I couldn't find him, and I went back to the kitchen. And the door . . . the door was open. Wide open. And I couldn't find him."

"Maybe you could show me." Fiona signaled to Peck to follow. "He's wearing his pajamas?"

"Spider-Man. He'll be cold, and wet, and scared." Her shoulders shook as they moved back to the kitchen. "I don't understand what you can do that the police can't."

"We're another resource, and Peck? He's trained for this. He's been on dozens of searches."

Rosie swiped tears off her cheeks. "Hugh likes dogs. He likes animals. If the dog barks, maybe Hugh will hear and come back."

Fiona said nothing, but opened the back door, then squatted down to take in the view from the level of a three-year-old boy. *Likes animals.* "I bet you can see a lot of wildlife around here. Deer, fox, rabbits."

"Yes. Yes. It's so different from Seattle. He loves watching out the windows, or from the deck. And we've taken hikes and bike rides."

"Is Hugh shy?"

"No. Oh no, he's adventurous and sociable. Fearless. Oh God."

Instinctively Fiona put an arm around Rosie's shaking shoulders. "Rosie, I'm going to set up here in the kitchen, if that's okay. What I need you to do is to get me five things Hugh wore recently. Yesterday's socks, underwear, shirt, like that. Five small items of clothing. Try not to handle them. Put them in these."

Fiona took plastic bags from her kit.

"We're a unit of five. Five handlers, five dogs. We'll each use something of Hugh's to give the dogs his scent."

"They . . . they track him?"

Easier to agree than to try to explain air-scenting, scent cones, skin rafts. The boy had already been gone more than an hour. "That's right. Does he have a favorite treat? Something he likes especially, something you might give him when he's been good?"

"You mean like . . ." Pushing at her hair, Rosie looked around blankly. "He loves gummy worms."

"Great. Do you have any?"

"I . . . yes."

"If you could get the clothes and the worms," Fiona said with a smile. "I'm going to set up. I hear my unit, so I'm going to set up."

"Okay. Okay. Please . . . He's just three."

Rosie dashed out. Fiona shared a brief look with Peck, then began to set up operations.

As her team came in, human and canine, she briefed them and began to assign search sectors while poring over her maps. She knew the area, and knew it well.

A paradise, she thought, for those looking for serenity, scenery, an escape from streets and traffic, buildings, crowds. And for a lost little boy, a world filled with hazards. Creeks, lakes, rocks.

More than thirty miles of foot trails, she thought, over five thousand acres of forest to swallow up a three-year-old and his stuffed rabbit.

"We've got a heavy drizzle, so we'll keep the search grids close and cover this area." As field OL—operational leader—Fiona outlined their sections on the map while Davey listed data on a large whiteboard. "We'll overlap some with the other teams, but let's keep good communications so we don't step on our own feet."

"He's going to be wet and chilled by now." Meg Greene, mother of two and recent grandmother, looked at her husband, Chuck. "Poor little guy."

"And a kid that age? He's got no sense of direction. He'll wander anywhere." James Hutton frowned as he checked his radio.

"He might tire out, just curl up and sleep." Lori Dyson nodded toward her German shepherd, Pip. "He might not hear the searchers calling for him, but our guys will sniff him out."

"That's the plan. Everyone has their coordinates? Radios checked, packs checked? Make sure you set your compass bearings. With Mai in emergency surgery, Davey's solo base OL, so we'll check in with him as we cover our sectors."

She stopped as the Cauldwells came back in.

"I have . . ." Rosie's chin wobbled. "I have what you asked for."

"That's great." Fiona crossed to her, then laid her hands on the terrified mother's shoulders. "You hold good thoughts. Everyone out there has only one thing to do, one thing on their mind: find Hugh and bring him home."

She took the bags, passed them out to her unit. "Okay, let's go get him."

With the others, she walked outside, hitched on her pack. Peck stood by her side, the slight quiver in his body the only sign he was anxious to get started. She and the others spread out to take their assigned sectors, and like the rest of her unit, she set her compass bearing.

She opened the bag holding a little sock, offered it to Peck's nose.

"This is Hugh. It's Hugh. Hugh's just a little boy, Peck. This is Hugh."

He sniffed enthusiastically—a dog who knew his job. He glanced up at her, sniffed again, then looked deep into her eyes, body quivering as if to say, *Okay, I've got it! Let's move!*

"Find Hugh." She added her hand signal, and Peck lifted his nose in the air. "Let's find Hugh!"

She waited, watching him scent and circle, let him take the lead as he prowled and paced. The thin, steady rain posed an obstacle, but Peck worked well in the rain.

She remained where she was, giving him verbal encouragement as he tracked the air and the wet pattered on the bright yellow of her windbreaker.

When he moved east, she followed him into the thickening trees.

At five, Peck was a vet, a seventy-pound chocolate Lab— strong, smart and tireless. He would, Fiona knew, search for hours in any conditions, over any terrain, for the living or for the dead. She had only to ask it of him.

Together, they moved through deep forest, over ground soft and soggy with needles shed from the towering Douglas firs and old-growth cedars, over and around clumps of mushrooms and nurse logs coated with rich green moss, through brambles edgy with thorn. While they searched, Fiona kept an eye on her partner's body language, made note of landmarks, checked her compass. Every few minutes, Peck glanced back to let her know he was on the case.

"Find Hugh. Let's find Hugh, Peck."

He alerted, showing interest in a patch of ground around a nurse log.

"Got something, do you? That's good. Good boy." She flagged the alert first with bright blue tape, then stood with him, scanning the area, calling Hugh's name. Then closing her eyes to listen.

All she heard was the soft sizzle of rain and the whisper of wind through the trees.

When he nudged her, Fiona took the sock out of her pocket, opened the bag so Peck could refresh the scent.

"Find Hugh," she repeated. "Let's find Hugh."

He moved off again, and in her sturdy boots, Fiona stepped

over the log and followed. When Peck angled south, she called her new position in to base, checked in with her team members.

The kid had been out for a minimum of two hours, she thought. A lifetime for worried parents.

But toddlers didn't have any real sense of time. Children of his age were very mobile, she mused, and didn't always understand the concept of being lost. They wandered, distracted by sights and sounds, and had considerable endurance, so it might be hours of that wandering before Hugh tired out and realized he wanted his mother.

She watched a rabbit skitter away into the brush. Peck had too much dignity to do more than spare it a passing glance.

But a little boy? Fiona thought. One who loved his "Wubby," who enjoyed animals? One his mother said was fascinated by the forest? Wouldn't he want to try to catch it, probably hoping to play with it? He'd try, wouldn't he, to follow it? City boy, she thought, enchanted with the woods, the wildlife, the *other* of it all.

How could he resist?

She understood it, the magic of it. She'd been a city girl once herself, charmed and hypnotized by the green shadows, the dance of light, the sheer vastness of trees and hills and sea.

A child could so easily lose himself in the acres and acres of parkland.

He's cold, she thought. Hungry now and scared. He wants his mother.

When the rain increased, they continued on, the tireless dog, the tall woman in rough pants and rougher boots. Her tail of pale red hair hung in a wet rope down her back, while lake-blue eyes searched the gloom.

When Peck angled again, heading down a winding slope, she drew a picture in her mind. Less than a quarter of a mile farther, if they continued in this direction, they'd come to the creek that marked the southeast border of her sector. Chuck and his Quirk searched the other side. Fast water in the creek this time of year, she thought, cold and fast, the verges slippery with moss and rain.

She hoped the little guy hadn't gone too close or, worse, tried to cross it.

And the wind was changing, she realized. Goddamn it. They'd adjust. She'd refresh the scent again, give Peck a quick water break. They'd nearly clocked two hours in the field, and though Peck had alerted strongly three times, she'd yet to see a sign of the boy—a bit of cloth on a bramble, a print in the softened ground. She'd flagged the alerts in blue, used orange tape to mark their progress and knew they'd cross-tracked once or twice.

Check in with Chuck, she decided. If Peck's on the scent and the kid crossed the creek . . .

She didn't allow herself to think *fell in*. Not yet.

Even as she reached for her radio, Peck alerted again. This time he broke into a run, shooting her the briefest of glances over his shoulder.

And she saw the light in his eyes.

"Hugh!" She lifted her voice over the now pounding rain and whistling wind.

She didn't hear the boy, but she heard Peck's three quick barks.

Like the dog, Fiona broke into a run.

She skidded a little as she rounded the turn on the downward slope.

And she saw near the banks of the busy creek—a bit too near for her peace of mind—a very wet little boy sprawled on the ground with his arms full of dog.

"Hey, Hugh, hi." She crossed the distance quickly, squatted down, pulling off her pack as she went. "I'm Fiona, and this is Peck."

"Doggie." He wept it into Peck's fur. "Doggie."

"He's a good doggie. He's the best doggie ever."

As Peck thumped his tail in agreement, Fiona pulled a space blanket out of her pack. "I'm going to wrap you up—and Wubby, too. Is that Wubby?"

"Wubby fell down."

"So I see. It's okay. We'll get you both warm, okay? Did you hurt yourself? Uh-oh."

She said it cheerfully as she draped the blanket over his shoulders and saw the mud and blood on his feet. "Ouch, huh? We're going to fix you all up."

His arms still around Peck, Hugh turned his cheek and sent Fiona a pitiful, bottom-lip-wobbling look. "I want Mommy."

"I bet you do. We're going to take you to Mommy, me and Peck. Here, look what Mommy sent you." She pulled out the little bag of gummy worms.

"Bad boy," Hugh said, but he eyed the candy with interest while he clung to Peck.

"Mommy's not mad. Daddy's not either. Here you go." She gave him the bag, pulled out her radio. When Hugh offered a worm to Peck, Peck gave Fiona a sidelong glance.

Can I? Huh? Can I?

"Go ahead—and say thank you."

Peck took the candy delicately from the boy, gulped it down, then thanked him with a sloppy kiss that made Hugh giggle.

With that sound warming her heart, Fiona contacted base.

"We've got him. Safe and sound. Tell Mom he's eating his gummy worms and we'll be on our way home." She winked at Hugh, who fed the filthy and wet stuffed rabbit, then popped the same candy into his own mouth. "He's got some minor cuts and scrapes, he's wet, but he's alert. Over."

"Copy that. Good work, Fee. Do you need help? Over."

"We've got it. Heading in. I'll keep you updated. Over and out."

"Better wash those down," she suggested, and offered Hugh her canteen.

"Whazit?"

"It's just water."

"I like juice."

"We'll make sure you get some when we get back. Drink a little, okay?"

He did what he was told, sniffling. "I peed outside, like Daddy showed me. Not in my pants."

She grinned at him and thought of Peck's strong alerts. "You did good. How about a piggyback ride?"

As they had at the sight of the candy, his eyes brightened. "Okay."

She wrapped the blanket securely around him, then turned so he could climb onto her back. "You call me Fee. If you need something, you just say, Fee, I need or I want."

"Doggie."

"He's coming, too. He'll lead the way." From her crouch she rubbed Peck, hugged him hard. "Good dog, Peck. Good dog. Return!"

With the pack slung over her shoulder and the boy on her back, the three of them began the hike out of the woods.

"Did you open the door by yourself, Hugh?"

"Bad boy," he murmured.

Well, yeah, she thought, but who wasn't bad now and then? "What did you see out the window?"

"Wubbies. Wubby said let's go see the wubbies."

"Uh-huh." Smart kid, she thought. Blame it on the rabbit.

Hugh began to chatter then, so fast and in the toddlerese that defeated her on every third word. But she got the gist.

Mommy and Daddy sleeping, bunnies out the window, what could you do? Then, if she interpreted correctly, the house disappeared and he couldn't find it. Mommy didn't come when he called, and he was going to get a time-out. He hated time-outs.

She got the picture because even saying "Time-out" made him cry with his face pressed against her back.

"Well, if you get one, I think Wubby needs one, too. Look, hey, Hugh, look. It's Bambi and his mom."

He lifted his head, still sniffling. Then tears were forgotten as he squealed at the sight of the fawn and doe. Then he sighed, laid his head on her shoulder when she boosted him up a bit. "I getting hungry."

"I guess you are. You've had a really big adventure." She managed to dig a power bar out of her pack.

It took less time to hike out than it had to search through, but by the time the trees began to thin the boy weighed like a stone on her back.

Revived, rested, fascinated with everything, Hugh talked

nonstop. Amused, Fiona let him ramble and dreamed of a vat of coffee, an enormous burger and a gallon bucket of fries.

When she spotted the house through the trees, she dug out another gear and quickened her pace. They'd barely cleared the line when Rosie and Devin ran out of the house.

Fiona crouched. "Off you go, Hugh. Run to Mommy."

She stayed down, slung her arm around Peck, whose entire body wagged with joy.

"Yeah," she murmured to him as Devin beat his wife by a couple lopes and snatched Hugh up. Then the three of them were twined together in a tangle of limbs and tears. "Yeah, it's a good day. You're the man, Peck."

With her son safe in her arms, Rosie hurried toward the house. Devin broke away to walk unsteadily to Fiona.

"Thank you. I don't know how to . . ."

"You're welcome. He's a great kid."

"He's . . . everything. Thank you so much." As his eyes filled, Devin wrapped his arms around Fiona and, much as Hugh had, dropped his head on her shoulder. "I can't tell you."

"You don't have to." Her own eyes stung as she patted his back. "Peck found him. He's the one. He'd be pleased if you shook his hand."

"Oh." Devin scrubbed at his face, drew in a couple steadying breaths. "Thank you, Peck. Thank you." He crouched, offered his hand.

Peck smiled as dogs do and placed his paw in Devin's hand.

"Can I . . . can I hug him?"

"He'd love it."

On a deep, shuddering sigh, Devin hugged Peck's neck, pressed his face to the fur. Over the man's shoulder, Peck sent Fiona a twinkling look.

Wasn't that fun? he seemed to say. *Can we do it again?*

TWO

After debriefing, Fiona drove home while Peck sprawled in the back for a quick power nap. He'd earned it, she thought, just as she'd earned the burger she was going to make herself and devour while she transcribed the log onto her computer.

She needed to give Sylvia a call, tell her stepmother they'd found the kid and she wouldn't need her to fill in for the afternoon classes after all.

Of course, now that the hard work was done, Fiona thought, the rain decided to back off. Already she could see a few breaks of blue in the gray.

Hot coffee, she decided, hot shower, lunch and paperwork, and with some luck she'd have dry weather for the afternoon's schedule.

As she drove out of the park, she caught the faint glimmer of a rainbow over the rain-churned sound. A good sign, she decided—maybe even a portent of things to come. A few years before, her life had been like the rain—dull and gray and dreary. The island had been her break in the clouds, and her decision to settle there her chance for rainbows.

"Got what I need now," she murmured. "And if there's more, well, we'll just see."

She turned off the snaking road onto her bumpy drive. Recognizing the change in motion, Peck gave a snort and scrambled up to sit. His tail thumped the seat as they rattled over the narrow bridge spanning her skinny, bubbling stream. When the house came into view, the tail picked up in rhythm and he gave a happy two-note bark.

Her doll-sized cabin, shingled in cedar, generous with windows, grew out of her pretty chunk of forest and field. The yard sprawled and sloped, and held what she thought of as training zones. The sliding boards, teeter-totters, ladders and platforms, tunnels and pass-throughs ranged with benches, tire swings and ramps gave most the impression of a woodsy play area for kids.

Not that far off, Fiona thought. The kids just had four legs.

The other two of her three kids stood on the covered front porch, tails wagging, feet dancing. One of the best things about dogs, to Fiona's mind, was their absolute joy in welcoming you home, whether you'd been gone for five minutes or five days. There lay unconditional and boundless love.

She parked, and her car was immediately surrounded by canine delight while, inside, Peck wiggled in anticipation of reunion with his best pals.

She stepped out to nuzzling snouts and wagging tails. "Hi, boys." Ruffling fur, she angled to open the back door. Peck leaped out so the lovefest could begin.

There was sniffing, happy grumbling, body bumping, then the race and chase. While she retrieved her pack, the three dogs charged away, zipping in circles and zigzags before charging back to her.

Always ready to play, she mused as three pairs of eyes stared up at her with hopeful gleams.

"Soon," she promised. "I need a shower, dry clothes, food. Let's go in. What do you say, wanna go in?"

In answer, all three bulleted for the door.

Newman, a yellow Lab and the oldest, at six, and the most

dignified, led the pack. But then Bogart, the black Lab and the baby, at three, had to stop long enough to grab up his rope.

Surely someone wanted to play tug.

They bounded in behind her, feet tapping on the wide-planked floor. Time, she thought with a glance at her watch. But not a lot of it.

She left her pack out as she had to replace the space blanket before she tucked it away. While the dogs rolled on the floor, she stirred up the fire she'd banked before leaving, added another log. She peeled off her wet jacket as she watched the flames catch.

Dogs on the floor, a fire in the hearth, she thought, made the room cozy. It tempted her to just curl up on the love seat and catch her own power nap.

No time, she reminded herself, and debated which she wanted more: dry clothes or food. After a struggle, she decided to be an adult and get dry first. Even as she turned for the stairs, all three dogs went on alert. Seconds later, she heard the rattle of her bridge.

"Who could that be?"

She walked to the window trailed by her pack.

The blue truck wasn't familiar, and on an island the size of Orcas there weren't many strangers. Tourist was her first thought, a wrong turn, a need for directions.

Resigned, she walked outside, gave her dogs the signal to hold on the porch.

She watched the man get out. Tall, a lot of dark hair, scarred boots, worn jeans on long legs. Good face, she decided, sharp planes, sharp angles blurred by the shadow of stubble that said he'd been too busy or too lazy to shave that morning. The good face held an expression of frustration or annoyance—maybe a combo of both—as he shoved a hand through the mass of hair.

Big hands, she noted, on the ends of long arms.

Like the boots, the leather jacket he wore had some years on it. But the truck looked new.

"Need some help?" she called out, and he stopped frowning at the training area to turn toward her.

"Fiona Bristow?" His voice had an edge to it, not anger so much as that annoyance she read on his face. Behind her, Bogart gave a little whine.

"That's right."

"Dog trainer?"

"I am." She stepped off the porch as he started toward her, watched his gaze skim over her three guardians. "What can I do for you?"

"Did you train those three?"

"I did."

His eyes, tawny, like warm, deeply steeped tea, shifted back to her. "Then you're hired."

"Yay. For what?"

He pointed at her dogs. "Dog trainer. Name your price."

"Okay. Let's open the floor at a million dollars."

"Will you take it in installments?"

That made her smile. "We can negotiate. Let's start this way. Fiona Bristow," she said, and offered her hand.

"Sorry. Simon Doyle."

Working hands, she thought, as his—hard, calloused—took hers. Then the name clicked. "Sure, wood artist."

"Mostly I build furniture."

"Great stuff. I bought one of your bowls a few weeks ago. I can't seem to resist a nice bowl. My stepmother carries your work in her shop. Island Arts."

"Sylvia, yeah. She's great." He brushed off the compliment, the sale, the small talk. A man on a mission. "She's the one who told me to come talk to you. So how much of the million do you need up front?"

"Where's the dog?"

"In the truck."

She looked past him, cocked her head. She saw the pup through the window now. A Lab–retriever mix, she judged— and currently very busy.

"Your dog's eating your truck."

"What?" He spun around. *"Fuck!"*

As he made the dash, Fiona signaled her newly alerted dogs

to stay and sauntered after him. The best way to get a gauge on the man, the dog and their current dynamic was to watch how he handled the situation.

"For God's sake." He wrenched open the door. "Goddamn it, what's wrong with you?"

The puppy, obviously unafraid, unrepentant, leaped into the man's arms and slathered his face with eager kisses.

"Cut it out. Just *stop*!" He held the puppy out at arm's length, where it wagged and wriggled and yipped in delight.

"I just bought this truck. He ate the headrest. How could he eat the headrest in under five minutes?"

"It takes about ten seconds for a puppy to get bored. Bored puppies chew. Happy puppies chew. Sad puppies chew."

"Tell me about it," Simon said bitterly. "I bought him a mountain of chew deals, but he goes for shoes, furniture, freaking rocks and everything else—including my new truck. Here." He shoved the puppy at Fiona. "Do something."

She cradled the pup, who immediately bathed her face as if they were reunited lovers. She caught the faintest whiff of leather on his warm puppy breath.

"Aren't you cute? Are you a pretty boy?"

"He's a monster." Simon snarled it. "An escape artist who doesn't sleep. If I take my eye off him for two minutes, he eats something or breaks something or finds the most inappropriate place to relieve himself. I haven't had a minute's peace in three weeks."

"Um-hmm." She snuggled the pup. "What's his name?"

Simon shot a look at the dog that didn't speak of returning sloppy kisses. "Jaws."

"Very appropriate. Well, let's see what he's made of." She crouched down with him, then signaled her dogs to release. As they trotted over, she set the puppy on the ground.

Some puppies would cower, some would hide or run away. But others, like Jaws, were made of sterner stuff. He leaped at the dogs, yipping and wagging. He sniffed as they sniffed, quivered with glee, nipped at legs and tails.

"Brave little soldier," Fiona murmured.

"He has no fear. Make him afraid."

She sighed, shook her head. "Why did you get a dog?"

"Because my mother gave him to me. Now I'm stuck with him. I like dogs, okay? I'll trade him for one of yours right now. You pick."

She studied Simon's sharp-boned, stubbled face. "Not getting much sleep, are you?"

"The only way I get so much as an hour at a time is if I put him in the bed. He's already ripped every pillow I own to shreds. And he's started on the mattress."

"You should try crate-training him."

"I got a crate. He ate the crate. Or enough of it to get out. I think he must be able to flatten himself like a snake. I can't get any work done. I think maybe he's brain-damaged, or just psychotic."

"What he is, is a baby who needs a lot of playtime, love, patience and discipline," she corrected as Jaws merrily humped Newman's leg.

"Why does he do that? He'll hump anything. If he's a baby, why does he think about humping everything?"

"It's instinct—and an attempt to show dominance. He wants to be the big dog. Bogart! Get the rope!"

"Jesus, I don't want to hang him. Exactly," Simon said, as the black Lab dashed for the porch and through the open door.

The dog came out with the rope between his teeth, bounded to Fiona and dropped it at her feet. When she reached for it, he lowered on his front paws, shot his butt in the air and wagged.

Fiona shook the rope. Bogart bounded up, chomped down and, snarling and pulling, engaged in a spirited tug-of-war.

Jaws abandoned Newman, made a running leap for the rope, missed, fell on his back. He rolled, leaped again, little jaws snapping, tail a mad metronome.

"Want the rope, Jaws? Want the rope? Play!" She lowered it so he could reach, and when his puppy teeth latched on, she released.

Bogart's tug lifted the puppy off the ground and he wiggled and clung like a furry fish on the line.

Determined, she mused, and was pleased when Bogart

dipped down so the pup hit the ground, then adjusted his pull for the smaller dog.

"Peck, Newman, get the balls. Get the balls!"

Like their packmate, Peck and Newman dashed off. They came back with yellow tennis balls, spat them at Fiona's feet. "Newman, Peck! Race!" She heaved the balls in quick succession so both dogs gave chase.

"Nice arm." Simon watched as the dogs retrieved, repeated the return.

This time she made a kissing sound that had Jaws angling his head even while he pulled on the rope. She tossed the balls in the air a couple times, studying his eye line. "Race!" she repeated.

As the big dogs sprinted off, the puppy scrambled after them.

"He has a strong play instinct—and that's a good thing. You just need to channel it. He's had his vet visits, his shots?"

"Up-to-date. Tell me you'll take him. I'll pay room and board."

"It doesn't work like that." As she spoke, she took the returned balls, threw them again. "I take him, I take you. You're a unit now. If you're not going to commit to the dog, to his training, his health and well-being, I'll help you find a home for him."

"I'm not a quitter." Simon jammed his hands in his pockets as once again Fiona threw the balls. "Besides, my mother would . . . I don't want to go there. She's got this idea that since I moved out here, I need companionship. It's a wife or a dog. She can't give me a wife, so . . ."

He frowned as the big yellow Lab let the pup get the ball. Prancing triumphantly, Jaws brought it back.

"He fetched."

"Yes, he did. Ask him for it."

"What?"

"Tell him to give you the ball. Crouch down, hold out your hand and tell him to give you the ball."

Simon crouched, held out his hand. "Give me—" Jaws leaped into his lap, nearly bowling Simon over, and rapped his ball-carrying mouth into his face.

"Tell him 'off,'" Fiona instructed, and had to bite the inside of her cheek as obviously, from his expression, Simon Doyle didn't see the humor. "Set him down on his rump. Hold him down, gently, and take the ball away. When you've got the ball, say, '*Good dog,*' repeat it, be enthusiastic. Smile."

Simon did as he was told, though it was easier said than done with a dog that could wiggle like a wet worm.

"There, he's successfully fetched and returned. You'll use small bits of food and lavish praise, the same commands, over and over again. He'll catch on."

"Tricks are great, but I'm really more interested in teaching him not to destroy my house." He shot a bitter look at the mangled headrest. "Or my truck."

"Following any command is a discipline. He'll learn to do what you ask, if you train him with play. He wants to play—he wants to play with you. Reward him, with play, and with food, with praise and affection, and he'll learn to respect the rules of the house. He wants to please you," she added when the pup rolled over to expose his belly. "He loves you."

"Then he's an easy target since we've had a rocky and short relationship."

"Who's your vet?"

"Funaki."

"Mai's the best. I'll want copies of his medical records for my files."

"I'll get them to you."

"You'll want to buy some small dog treats—the sort he can just chomp down rather than the bigger ones he'd need to stop and chew. Instant gratification. You'll want a head collar and a leash in addition to his regular collar."

"I had a leash. He—"

"Ate it," Fiona finished. "It's common enough."

"Great. Head collar? Like a muzzle?"

She read Simon's face clearly enough and was unsurprised when she saw him considering the idea of a muzzle. And was pleased when she noted his rejecting frown.

"No. It's like a halter, and it's gentle and effective. You'll use it during training sessions here and at home. Instead of putting pressure on the throat, it puts pressure—gentle pressure—on calming points. It helps persuade a dog to walk rather than lunge and pull, to heel. And it'll give him more control as well as put you more in tune with your pup."

"Fine. Whatever works."

"I'd advise you to replace or repair the crate and lay in a very big supply of chew toys and rawhide. The rope's pretty much no-fail, but you'll want tennis balls, rawhide bones, that sort of thing. I'll give you a basic list of recommendations and requirements for training. I've got a class in . . ." She checked her watch. "Crap. Thirty minutes. And I didn't call Syl."

As Jaws began to leap and try to climb up her leg, she simply bent over, pushed his rump to the ground. "Sit." Because she didn't have a reward, she crouched, held him in place to pet and praise. "You might as well stay if you've got the time. I'll sign you up."

"I don't have a million dollars on me."

She released the pup, picked him up to cuddle. "Got thirty?"

"Probably."

"Thirty for a thirty-minute group session. He's, what, about three months old?"

"About."

"We'll make it work. It's an eight-week course. You're two behind. I'll juggle in two individual sessions to bring him up to speed. Does that work for you?"

Simon shrugged. "It's cheaper than a new truck."

"Considerably. I'll lend you a leash and a head collar for now." Still carrying the puppy, she walked to the house.

"What if I paid you fifty, and you worked with him solo?"

She spared him a glance. "That's not what I do. He's not the only one who needs training." She led him into the house before passing the puppy back to him. "You can come on back. I've got some extra leashes and collars, and you need some treats. I have to make a phone call."

She veered off the kitchen to the utility room, where collars and leashes and brushes hung neatly according to type and size, and various toys and treats sat organized on shelves.

It made him think of a small pet boutique.

She gave Jaws another glance as he squirmed in Simon's arms and tried to gnaw on his master's hand.

"Do this."

She turned to the pup and, using her forefinger and thumb, gently closed his mouth. "No." And keeping her eyes on the dog's, she reached behind her, took a rawhide chew toy shaped like a bone. "This is yours." When he clamped it, she nodded. "Good dog! Go ahead and set him down. When he chews on you, or something else he shouldn't, do what I did. Correct, give him a vocal command and replace with what's his. Give positive reinforcement. Consistently. Find a leash and a collar for him."

She stepped out into the kitchen, grabbed the phone and hit her stepmother's number on speed dial. "Crap," she muttered when it shifted to voice mail. "Syl, I hope you're not already on your way. I got distracted and forgot to call. I'm home. We found the little boy. He's fine. Decided to chase a rabbit and got lost, but no worse for wear. Anyway, if you're on your way, I'll see you here. If not, thanks for the standby, and I'll call you later. Bye."

She replaced the phone and turned to see Simon in the doorway, a leash in one hand and a small head collar in the other. "These?"

"Those should work."

"What little boy?"

"Hmm. Oh, Hugh Cauldwell—he and his parents are here for a few days' vacation in the state park. He wandered out of the house and into the forest this morning while they were sleeping. You didn't hear?"

"No. Why would I?"

"Because it's Orcas. Anyway, he's fine. Home safe."

"You work for the park?"

"No. I'm part of Canine Search and Rescue Association volunteers."

Simon gestured toward the three dogs, currently sprawled on the kitchen floor like corpses. "Those?"

"That's right. Trained and certified. You know, Jaws might be a good candidate for S-and-R training."

He snorted out what might've been a laugh. "Right."

"Strong play drive, curious, courageous, friendly, physically sound." She lifted her eyebrows as the pup left his new toy to attack the laces on Simon's boots. "Energetic. Forget your training already, human?"

"Huh?"

"Correct and replace and praise."

"Oh." He crouched, repeated the series Fiona had demonstrated. Jaws clamped on the toy, then spat it out and went for the laces again.

"Just keep doing it. I need to put some things together." She started out, stopped. "Can you work that coffeemaker?"

He glanced to the unit on the counter. "I can figure it out."

"Do that, will you? Black, one sugar. I'm running low."

He frowned after her.

While he'd only been on the island a few months, he doubted he'd ever get used to the casual, open-door policy. Just come on in, complete stranger, he thought, and while you're at it, make me some coffee while I leave you virtually alone.

She only had his word on who he was, and besides that, nobody knew he was there. What if he was a psycho? A rapist? Okay, three dogs, he mused, eyeing them again. But so far they'd been friendly, and about as casual as their mistress.

And currently, they were snoring away.

He wondered how she managed to live with three dogs when he could barely find a way to tolerate one. Looking down, he saw the pup had stopped chewing on his bootlaces because he'd fallen asleep sprawled over the boot, with the laces still caught in his teeth.

With the same care and caution a man might use when easing away from a wild boar, Simon slowly slid his foot back, holding his breath until the pup oozed like furred water onto the kitchen floor.

Passed out cold.

One day, he thought as he crossed to the coffeemaker, he'd find a way to pay his mother back. One fine day.

He studied the machine, checked the bean and water supply.

When he switched it on the burr of the grinder had the pup waking with a barrage of ferocious barks. Across the room, the dogs cocked their ears. One of them yawned.

The movement had Jaws leaping with joy, then charging the pack like a cannonball.

While they rolled, batted and sniffed, Simon wondered if he could borrow one of them. Rent one, he considered. Like a babysitter.

Since the cupboards had glass fronts, he didn't have any trouble finding a pair of bright cobalt blue mugs. He had to open a couple of drawers before he found the flatware, but that gave him the opportunity to marvel. Every drawer was tidy and organized.

How did she do that? He'd been in his house for only a matter of months and his kitchen drawers looked like a flea market. Nobody should be that organized. It wasn't natural.

Interesting-looking woman, though, he decided as he poked around a little. The hair that wasn't really red, wasn't really blond, the eyes of absolutely clear and perfect blue. Her nose tilted up a little on the end and sported a dusting of freckles, and a slight overbite made her bottom lip seem particularly full.

Long neck, he thought as he poured the coffee, lanky build with no rack to speak of.

Not beautiful. Not pretty or cute. But . . . interesting, and the few times she'd smiled? Almost arresting. Almost.

He dumped a spoon of sugar from a squat white bowl in one mug, picked up the other.

He took his first sip looking out her over-the-sink window, then turned when he heard her boot steps. She moved briskly, with an efficiency that hinted at athleticism. Wiry, he thought, as much as lanky.

He saw her shift her gaze down, followed it and saw Jaws circle and squat.

Simon opened his mouth, but before he could yell *Hey!*, his usual response, Fiona tossed the folder she carried on the counter and clapped her hands twice, sharply.

The sound startled Jaws out of his squat.

She moved fast, scooping up the pup with one hand, grabbing the leash with the other. "Good dog, Jaws, good dog. Let's go *out*. Time to go *out*. Pantry, second shelf, canister with mini-treats, grab a handful," she ordered Simon, and clipped the leash on the collar as she headed out the back door.

The three dogs whooshed after her in a flurry of fur and paws.

He found her gnome-sized pantry as scarily organized as the drawers, dug out a handful of little dog cookies the size of his knuckle from a big glass jar. Hooking the mug handles in one hand, he walked outside.

She still carried the dog, with her long legs eating up the short distance to the edge of trees that guarded the back of her property. By the time she put Jaws down Simon caught up.

"Stop." She stopped the pup from attacking the leash, rubbed his head. "Look at the big guys, Jaws! What are the big guys doing?" She turned him, walked a few steps.

Obviously, the pup was more interested in the dogs, currently sniffing, lifting legs, sniffing, than the leash. He bounded after them.

"I'm giving him some slack. Thanks." Fiona took the coffee, drank deep, sighed. "Praise Jesus. Okay, you're going to want to pick a regular spot for your Pooptown. You don't want land mines all over your property. So you consistently take him where you want him to go. Then he'll just start going there. You're the one who has to be vigilant and consistent. He's just a baby, so that means you're going to have to take him out several times a day. As soon as he wakes up in the morning and before you go to bed at night, every time he eats."

In his mind's eye, Simon saw his life becoming a revolving door swinging at the whims of the dog's elimination needs.

"And when he does what he's supposed to do," Fiona continued, "be thrilled. Positive reinforcement—lavish. He wants to please you. Wants to be praised and rewarded. See there, the big guys are going, so he's not going to be outdone."

Simon shook his head. "When I take him out, he spends an hour sniffing, rolling and screwing around, then cuts loose five seconds after I take him back in."

"Show him. You're a guy. Whip it out and pee."

"Now?"

She laughed—and yeah, he thought, *almost* arresting. "No, but in the privacy of your own. Here." She handed him the leash. "Get down to his level, call him. Happy, happy! Use his name, then when he comes, make over him, give him one of the treats."

He felt stupid, making happy noises because his dog shit in the woods, but thinking of the countless piles he'd cleaned off his floors, he followed instructions.

"Well done. Let's try a basic command before the others get here. Jaws." She took hold of him to turn his attention, stroked him until he'd calmed down. She took one of the treats Simon held, palmed it in her left hand, then lifted her right over the pup's head, extended her index finger. "Jaws, sit. Sit!" As she spoke, she moved her finger over his head so he looked up, trying to follow it. And his butt hit the ground.

"Good dog! Good!" She fed him, petted him, praised him. "Repeat, repeat. He'll automatically look up, and when he does the back of him goes down. As soon as he sits, praise, reward. Once he gets that, you try it with just the voice command. If he doesn't get it, go back and repeat. When he does, praise, reward."

She stepped back.

Since the pup wanted to follow her, Simon had a little struggle.

"Make him focus on you. You're the boss. He thinks you're a patsy."

Annoyed, Simon shot her one cold stare. But he had to admit, when the pup's rump hit the ground, he felt a little spurt of pride and pleasure.

He could see Fiona, standing hip-shot, arms folded. Judging him, Simon thought, as he went through the routine again, and again. When her dogs wandered over to join her, sitting like three sphinxes, he felt ridiculous.

"Try it without the motion. Point, use the voice command. Keep eye contact. Point, use the command."

Like that was going to work, Simon thought, but he pointed.

"Sit." And gaped when Jaws plopped his ass on the ground. "He sat. You sat. Nice job. Nice work." As Jaws inhaled the little cookie, Simon grinned over at Fiona. "Did you see that?"

"I did. He's a good, smart dog." Hers went on alert. "Time to get started. Your classmates are coming."

"How do you know?"

"They know." She laid one hand on the closest dog's head. "Here, let Newman smell you."

"What?"

She simply gestured, then took Simon's hand, held it down to Newman. "Newman, this is Simon. This is Simon. Walk with Simon. Walk. I need to set a couple things up. Newman's going to walk with you while you practice leading Jaws on the leash. Stop off and get the head collar, then come on around. Newman'll give you a hand with him."

When she and the other dogs dashed away, Jaws leaped to chase. Newman simply gave him a gentle body block.

"Want to come home with me, big guy? I could use you. Walk, right? Walk!"

In fits and starts, with the big Lab running interference, Simon managed to lead, pull and drag the puppy across the lawn.

If the wiry, almost arresting dog trainer earned her fee, he thought, he might end up with a dog as appealing as Newman.

Miracles happened—occasionally.

AN HOUR LATER, exhausted, Simon sprawled on his own living room couch. Jaws scrabbled at his leg, whined.

"Jesus, don't you ever wind down? I feel like I've been to boot camp." He hefted the dog up and Jaws wiggled and licked and snuggled. "Yeah, yeah. You did okay. We did okay."

He scratched the pup's ears.

In minutes, man and dog were sound asleep.

THREE

With a day loaded with classes, Fiona needed a jump start to the morning. Over sweetened black coffee, she debated the relative fuel ratios of Froot Loops versus Toaster Strudels.

Maybe a combination of both, she considered, as she'd missed out on that fat burger and mountain of fries the day before due to man and dog.

Sexy man, sweet dog, she mused, but she'd ended up settling for frozen pizza at the end of a long day because she'd been too tired to think about actually cooking.

Since she had another long day ahead of her, what was the harm in an extra boost of sugar?

As she debated, she drank the coffee and watched her dogs play outside. She never got tired of watching them. And wasn't she lucky she could make a reasonable living in the company of dogs, and do something important?

She thought of a little boy, warm and safe, and a father weeping with relief with his arms around a very good dog. Now that very good dog pranced around the yard with a stick in his mouth, as proud of that find—or nearly—as he'd been with the kid.

As she watched, all three dogs alerted, then raced around to the front of the house.

Somebody had driven over her little bridge.

Damn it. Her day wasn't supposed to start for nearly an hour. She wanted her solo time, and her Froot Loops/Toaster Strudel combo before she interacted with other humans.

But when she walked to the front door, opened it, her mood took a bounce. She was always ready to interact with Sylvia.

Sylvia hopped out of her snappy hybrid—a compact, energetic woman with rich brown waves bouncing. She wore knee-high boots with skinny little heels under a floaty skirt matched with a gorgeous plummy sweater that had, no doubt, come from her own stock. Huge silver triangles swayed at her ears as she stepped back so her cheerful Boston terrier, Oreo, could jump out after her.

The dogs immediately fell into an orgy of delighted welcome—sniff, lick, roll, run. Sylvia gracefully waded through them and shot Fiona one of her stunning smiles.

"Morning, cutie! We're an hour early, I know, but I wanted some gossip time. Can you spare it?"

"For you I can." Fiona crouched as Oreo raced to give her a quick hello before dashing back to his playmates. "Come on back to the kitchen. You can have some tea while I grab breakfast."

Sylvia's hello included a long, hard hug—it always did—before, with her arm still looped around Fiona's waist, she walked into the house.

"The news about you and Peck finding the little boy is all over the island. You did good."

"Peck was perfect. And the fact Hugh had to pee, twice, didn't hurt. Still, it's pretty amazing how much ground a three-year-old in footie Spider-Man pj's can cover."

"He must've been so scared."

"More wet, cold and tired, really." Fiona put the kettle on, gestured to the cupboard where she kept several options of herbal tea, with Sylvia in mind. "I'm really sorry I didn't call you right away to let you know."

"Don't worry about it." Sylvia waved it off as she settled for cinnamon peach. "I was out and about anyway, checking out some pottery—and naturally left my phone in the car. I have to stop doing that."

She turned, narrowed her eyes as Fiona took a box of Froot Loops out of another cupboard. "You're not having that processed sugar for breakfast."

"Fruit, as in Froot Loops." Smiling hopefully, Fiona shook the box. "There has to be fruit in here."

"Sit down. I'm fixing you a decent breakfast."

"Syl, this is fine."

"It might be, on occasion, if you were ten. Sit," she repeated, and, at home, opened Fiona's refrigerator. "Um-hmm, um-hmm. I can work with this. You'll have a nice egg-white omelet on whole wheat toast."

"I will?"

"And fill me in on the distraction. An interesting eyeful, isn't he?"

"Adorable, and with some training he'll be a wonderful companion."

Sylvia shot Fiona an arched look as she pulled out a small bowl and a tiny container. "I meant Simon."

"Maybe I did, too."

"Ha. He's tremendously talented, and well mannered, if a little mysterious."

"Which one are you talking about?"

"Smarty." Expertly, Sylvia separated the eggs, sealing the yolks in the container before whipping the whites together with a little cheese and herbs. "He has a lovely house on East Sound, is meticulous in his craft, has gorgeous eyes, a strong back, a cute puppy, and he's single."

"He sounds perfect for you. Go get him, Syl."

"I might, if he wasn't two decades behind me." Sylvia poured the egg whites into the skillet she had heating and popped bread into the toaster as Fiona fixed the tea. "You go get him."

"What would I do with him once I got him? Besides that," she added when Sylvia snorted, "men, like dogs, aren't just for the fun times. They're a full-out, long-term commitment."

"You need the fun times so you can decide if you want the rest. You could try, oh, I don't know, the wild and crazy concept of a date."

"I've been known to date. I prefer group socialized events, but I occasionally date. And I occasionally indulge in those euphemistic fun times. And before you give another nudge, just let me say: Pot, kettle."

"I married the love of my life, and had ten wonderful years with him. Sometimes I still feel cheated we didn't have more time."

"I know." Fiona slipped over to rub a hand down Sylvia's back as they both thought of Fiona's father. "You made him so happy."

"We made each other. I can't help wanting that for you." She slid the omelet onto the lightly browned toast on a plate. "Eat your breakfast."

"Yes, ma'am." They sat across from each other at the tiny table, and Fiona took the first bite. "God, this is good."

"And hardly took more time or effort than pouring colored sugar into a bowl."

"You're entirely too hard on the loops of fruit, but this is too good for me to argue."

"Well, while you're eating a decent breakfast, I'll tell you what I know about Simon Doyle." Sipping, Sylvia leaned back, crossed her legs. "And don't bother trying to tell me you're not curious."

"Okay, I won't because I am. A little curious."

"He's thirty-three, originally from Spokane, though he lived the last several years in Seattle."

"Spokane and Seattle. Night and day."

"Pretty much. His father owns and still operates as a contractor in Spokane—with Simon's older brother. He double-majored in art and architecture at USC, then worked as a cabinetmaker before he began to design and build furniture.

He did pretty well for himself in Seattle, won some awards. Had a very hot affair with Nina Abbott—"

"The singer?"

"That's right. Pop star, rock star—I'm not sure where she fits."

"Bad girl of pop," Fiona said over a mouthful of omelet. "She's a little crazy."

"Maybe so, but they steamed it up for a few months after she commissioned him to design several pieces for her house on Bainbridge Island. She's originally from Washington state and has a house there."

"Yeah, I know. I read *People*, watch E! TV now and then. I just . . . Oh, wait. *He's* the one? I remember reading some dish about her and a carpenter. The press mostly referred to him as a carpenter. She's sexy and talented, but there's that little-bit-crazy factor."

"Some people like to shock, I think. Anyway, it fizzled. Still, I expect it didn't hurt him, business-wise. Then about three months ago, he moved here, and Island Arts is very proud, and damn lucky, to be his exclusive outlet in the San Juans."

Sylvia lifted her teacup in toast, then sipped.

"Did you get all that from his bio for Island Arts' Web page and brochures?"

"Actually the bio he gave me was a little thin, so I Googled him."

"Sylvia."

Unashamed, Sylvia tossed her lush curls. "Listen, when I take on an artist I have to know who they are. For one thing, I often have to travel to them to check out their work. I wouldn't want to wander into the den of an ax murderer, would I?"

"I bet you can't Google most ax murderers. Except those already in prison or in the ground."

"You never know. Anyway, over and above his work, I like him. What did you think?"

"Since he was a little pissed that Jaws ate the headrest in his truck—"

"Oops."

"Yeah, and was obviously frustrated with his new puppy-owner status, it might be difficult to judge. On surface observation, and setting aside his physical attributes—"

"And he has them," Sylvia said with a wicked wiggle of eyebrows.

"No question. I'd say he's not used to having responsibility for anyone other than himself, and more used to solo ventures. A lone wolf sort—which you've added to with this morning's data: a private place on the sound of a very small island, his move away from family, his choice of career."

"Sometimes a lone wolf just hasn't found a mate—or his pack."

"You're forever a romantic."

"Guilty," Sylvia agreed. "And proud of it."

"Well, on his side, the puppy's crazy about him. Shows no fear. Right now, the dog is the alpha, which tells me the man has a soft center. It may be small—can't know yet—but it's there. That's also illustrated by the fact that while he's very frustrated and annoyed, he doesn't seem inclined to get rid of the dog. And when given logical options, he accepts. He signed Jaws up for kindergarten, and while I wouldn't say Simon appears to be happy or enthusiastic about it, he did seem determined. So while not especially used to taking responsibility for another, he will take it when he sees no way out."

"I swear, you should have gone into psychology. Or profiling."

"Everything I know, I learned from dogs." Fiona rose to take her plate to the dishwasher, then turned to step behind Sylvia's chair and wrap her arms around her stepmother's neck. "Thanks for breakfast."

"Anytime."

"Have another cup of tea. I'm going to set up for class."

"I'll help you."

"Not in those boots. We're a little soggy from yesterday's rain. Change your very sexy ones for my Uggs before you come out. They're in the mudroom."

"Fee," Sylvia said before Fiona left the room.

"Yeah."

"It's been nearly eight years now, for both of us."

"I know."

"It hit me this morning. Sometimes it does when it comes up on the anniversary of Will's death. So I just wanted to get out of the house—and more, to see you. I want to tell you how glad I am you're here, that I can come by and fix you breakfast, or borrow your Uggs. I'm so glad, Fee."

"Me too."

"He'd be so proud of you. He was proud of you, but—"

"I know he was, and I like knowing he'd be proud and happy with what I've done. With what I'm doing." She let out a breath. "Greg would, too. I think. So much of him's faded, his voice, his scent, even his face. I never thought I'd have to pull out a photo to bring his face clearly into my head."

"Seven years is a long time. You were so young, sweetie. I know you loved him, but you were so young. You didn't have much time together really."

"Almost two years, and he taught me so much. I have what I have now because of what Greg taught me, what he showed me, what he gave me. I did love him, Syl, but I can't remember what it felt like anymore. I can't bring back how he made me feel."

"We loved him, too, your dad and I. He was a good, good man."

"The best."

"Fee, maybe you can't bring back what you felt for him because it's time you let yourself feel for someone else."

"I don't know. Sometimes . . . well, sometimes I'm not sure I'll ever be ready for that."

"Feelings don't always happen when we're ready for them."

"Maybe not. Maybe I'll get a surprise. But for now, I've got enough to keep me occupied. Don't forget the Uggs."

AFTER HER ADVANCED CLASS, a group of six including Oreo, Fiona prepared for her special-skills group, novice level. Most of the students were off-islanders with hopes to earn certifications as Search and Rescue dogs. Some in this larger class would make it, some would not. But she knew every dog and owner would benefit from the additional and more specialized training.

As students arrived, it was socialization time—for canines and humans. Not a waste of time, in her opinion, but a vital step. A dog who couldn't be or wouldn't be socialized would never make the cut. And the ten-minute "mixer" gave her the opportunity to judge how well the dogs and handlers were doing with their at-home training.

She watched, her hands in the sagging pockets of an ancient hooded jacket. "Okay, let's get started. We'll run the basics first."

She ran them through heeling, on then off leash—with mixed results.

"Snitch, Waldo," she said, addressing the dogs rather than the owners. "We're going to need to practice those off-leash skills a little more at home. We're close, but you can do better. Let's try recall. Handlers, step away. I want you to wait until your dog is distracted, then give the command. Let's be firm. Don't forget reward and positive reinforcement."

She deliberately distracted some of the young dogs herself. Petting, playing. Still, the percentage of success pleased her. That percentage faltered on drop on recall as most of the dogs wanted to play when called.

She culled out the worst offenders, assigning the others to work on sit-stay while she did a few one-on-ones.

"There are good reasons you need your dog to stop instantly. There could be danger he doesn't understand. In addition, that instant and complete response shows absolute trust. When you say *Stop!* or whatever word you choose for that command, your dog needs to obey without hesitation. Let's work on this with close proximity. Walk with your dog heeling, off leash, then try your drop command. Callie, can I use Snitch to demonstrate?"

It wasn't the dog portion of the partnership that needed work, but the human, in Fiona's opinion. Callie tended to be hesitant.

In minutes, with a sure, firm tone, Fiona had the puppy heeling like a champ and dropping on command like a soldier.

"I don't know why he won't do it for me."

"He knows he can mess with you, Callie. He doesn't believe you mean it, that you're in charge. You don't have to yell or be angry, but you have to be firm. Your voice, your face, your body language. Convince him you mean business."

"I'll try."

Slightly better, Fiona judged—but she figured it was residual behavior from her own round with Snitch. Unless Callie toughened up, the little golden would walk all over her, and back again.

"Okay, short break for playtime."

It was the signal her own dogs waited for. They joined in the five minutes of chaos, the running, fetching, bounding after balls, rolling in wrestling groups.

"I don't mean to complain."

Fiona added on another layer of patience as Earl Gainer, retired cop and owner of a very clever young German shepherd, began all his complaints the same way.

"What's the problem, Earl?"

"I understand one of your tenets is exploiting the play drive, but it just seems to me we spend an awful lot of time letting all these dogs fool around."

And time, she knew, meant money as well.

"I know it might seem frivolous, but at this age, their attention span is very short. There's a real danger of overtraining. If a dog gets frustrated, simply can't keep up with all the new demands and expectations, he can give up, or revert or rebel. They need time to work off some of that puppy energy—and to continue their socialization with other dogs, other humans. We're going to try a couple new things in the second thirty minutes today."

Earl brightened immediately. "Like what?"

"Let's give them another couple minutes. Kojak has a lot of potential. You know that. He's smart, eager to please. If you stick with this another couple weeks, we'll be into some scent training. Before we go there, we're going to cement the bond, the socialization and the tractability."

Earl puffed out his cheeks. "I heard about what you and your dog did yesterday, finding that boy. That's what I want to do."

"I know, and with your training, your experience, you'll be a great asset. Let's help Kojak want to do the same. He's on his way, I promise you."

"Everybody who knows says you're one of the best in the state, maybe in the Northwest. That's why we're taking that ferry ride twice a week. Well, hell, he's having fun anyway."

"And learning." She gave Earl's arm a pat.

She called her own dogs, sent them to the porch where they sprawled to watch the show.

"Heel your dogs," Fiona called out, and waited for the line to form. "A Search and Rescue dog can and is called on to search in various terrains, rough ground, frozen ground, rock, woods, urban settings. And water. Today, we're going to introduce water."

She gestured to a child's wading pool she'd already filled, then picked up a rubber ball. "Each of you, in turn, will take your dog off leash, then toss this ball into the pool. I want you to command your dog to fetch. Don't worry. I have towels. Earl, why don't you and Kojak go first? Position about ten feet away."

Earl took the ball, got into position. He unleashed his dog, gave him a quick rub, showed him the ball. "Get it, Kojak!" he yelled as he tossed it.

The dog took off like a bullet, made a leap—and a splash. He came up with the ball in his mouth and a shocked look on his face that clearly translated into, to Fiona's mind, *What the fuck!*

But he leaped out again, returned to Earl when his master snapped a finger.

Show-off, Fiona thought, but with a grin, and one that widened as Kojak shook ferociously and soaked his proud and praising owner.

"You see that?" With water dripping from his face, Earl looked over at Fiona. "He did it, first time out."

"He did great."

And so did you, she thought.

Fiona routinely tried to schedule an hour between classes, knowing that a good chunk of that would be taken up by handlers who wanted to talk, ask for advice, get her input on the day's session.

With what she had left, she might be able to squeeze in a quick lunch, play with her own dogs, return any calls that came in during a session.

Since she had forty minutes to herself when the last car bumped over her bridge, she tossed balls, played tug, before dashing inside to grab a couple handfuls of Cheez-Its, then snagged an apple so she didn't feel guilty.

She ate while she checked and answered voice and e-mail, made a few notes for the blog she updated two or three times a week.

The blog, she knew, led people to her website—or vice versa. And that led some of them to her school.

She left herself enough time to empty the pool and go over her lesson plan for the next group. Even as she started to set up, someone drove over her bridge.

So much for quiet time, she thought, then frowned as, for the second time in two days, an unfamiliar vehicle rolled down her drive.

She lifted her hand to shield her eyes from the sun and recognized Rosie and Devin Cauldwell. When the car made the slight turn, she caught a glimpse of Hugh in his car seat in the back.

"Okay, boys, best behavior. Greet."

As the car parked, all three dogs lined up beside it and sat.

Devin got out, dog-side. "Hey, Peck. Hey." When Peck lifted his paw, Devin grinned, then bent over to shake. "Good to see you again."

"Newman," Fiona said as Devin walked down the line, accepting paws. "And Bogart."

"Guess you're a fan of classic movies." He held out a hand to Fiona. "I hope it's okay that we came by."

"Sure it is." She turned toward Hugh, who had his hand in his mother's and looked none the worse for wear in a red hoodie and jeans. "Hi, Hugh. Do you want to say hi to Peck and his pals?"

"Doggies!" Hugh scrambled over to throw his arms around Peck. "Doggie found me. I got lost."

She introduced the boy to the other dogs, who were all treated to a hug.

"I never even thanked you yesterday," Rosie began.

"You were a little preoccupied."

"I— Is that all right?" she asked when the dogs flopped down and Hugh began crawling over them, giggling, tugging on ears.

"They're in heaven. They love kids."

"We've talked about maybe getting a dog. We thought we'd wait another year or two, but now . . ." Rosie watched Hugh, and smiled. "Any recommendations on breeds for an active three-year-old?"

"Obviously I've got a soft spot for Labs. They're great with kids, with families, but they want a lot of interaction. And they need room."

"We have a yard, and a park not far from the house. The way I feel right now? If there's another Peck out there, I want him. Sorry," Rosie added when her eyes watered up. "I haven't quite settled down yet. Ms. Bristow—"

"Fiona."

"Fiona." Rosie reached over to clasp both Fiona's hands. "There aren't words. There just aren't. There's no payment, no gesture. There's nothing we can do that comes close to what you did for us."

"Hugh's playing with my dogs and laughing. That's the payment. That's why we do this."

Devin laid an arm over his wife's shoulders. "We wrote a letter to the organization—the Search and Rescue organization— about your unit, and we're mailing it today with a donation. It's something."

"It's a lot. It's appreciated."

"When we get that puppy, we'll sign up for your classes," Rosie added. "I wouldn't want anyone else to help us train him. Deputy Englewood told us you run an obedience school and train search dogs."

"And we're probably holding you up. But before we go . . . Hugh, don't you have something for Ms. Bristow and Peck? Actually, they said you had the three dogs," Devin continued as Rosie walked Hugh back to the car. "So we got one for each of them."

Hugh came back with his arms loaded with three huge rawhide bones. He dumped them in front of the dogs.

"Don't want?" he said when the dogs simply sat.

"They won't take them until you tell them they can." Fiona moved a bone in front of each dog.

"Get the bone! Get the bone!" Hugh shouted.

Fiona added hand signals so the dogs executed a happy leap, then a stylish bow that had Hugh giggling. "They said thank you very much."

"Hugh picked these out for you." Rosie offered a bouquet of red tulips. "He thought they looked like lollipops."

"They really do, and they're beautiful. Thank you."

"I drew a picture." Hugh took the drawing from his mother. "I drew me and Peck and you."

"Wow." Fiona admired the colorful squiggles, circles and lines. "It's great."

"This is Peck. He's a big dog. And this is Fee, and this is me. I got to ride on Fee's back, and that's Wubby. He got to ride, too. Mommy and me writed the names."

"It's a terrific picture."

"You can put it on your frigedator."

"I will. Thanks, Hugh." She hugged him, breathed in the scent of little boy—wild, innocent and free.

After she waved them off, Fiona went inside to fix the drawing to the front of her fridge, to arrange the lollipop tulips in a bold blue vase.

And was grateful to have a few minutes to compose herself before her first students arrived for the next class.

FOUR

Man's best friend, my ass.

After a furious chase followed by a pitched battle, Simon managed to pry the mallet out of the death grip of Jaws's teeth.

Holding the now slimed and mangled tool while the puppy bounced like a furry spring, Simon imagined giving the dog just one good whack on his bone head. Not that he would, however tempting, but imagining it wasn't a crime.

He pictured chirping cartoon birds circling the pup's head, and little X's in his eyes.

"If only," he muttered.

He set the tool out of reach on the workbench, then looked around—again—at the scatter of toys and bones on the floor of his shop.

"Why are these no good? Why is that?" He picked up a Jaws-sized rope, offered it. "There, go destroy that."

Seconds later, as Simon wiped off the abused mallet, the dog dropped the rope on his boot, then sat, tail thumping, head cocked, eyes bright with fun.

"Can't you see I'm busy?" he demanded. "I don't have time to play every five damn minutes. One of us has to make a living."

Simon turned back to the standing wine cabinet—a thing of beauty, if he did say so himself—of wild cherry and ebony. He used wood glue to affix the last of the trim while the dog attacked his bootlaces. Struggling to focus on the work, Simon shook the dog off, picked up a clamp. Shook, glued, shook, clamped.

Jaws's growls and happy yips mixed with the U2 he'd chosen as shop music for the morning.

He ran his fingers over the smooth, silky wood, nodded.

When he walked over to check the seams on a pair of rockers, he dragged the dog with him through the sawdust.

He supposed Jaws had conned him into playing after all.

He worked for nearly two hours, alternately dragging the dog, chasing him down, ordering himself to stop and walk the dog out to what he'd dubbed Shitville.

The break wasn't so bad, he decided. It gave him a chance to clear his mind, to take in the mild air and the bright sun. He never tired of watching the way the light—sun or moon—played over the sound that formed his narrow link between the island's saddlebags of land.

He liked standing on his rise and listening to the subtle and steady music of the water below, or sitting for a while on the porch of his shop and contemplating the thick forest that closed him in as the sound opened him out.

He'd moved to the island for a reason, after all.

For the solitude, the quiet, the air, the abundance of scenery.

Maybe, in some convoluted way, his mother had been right to foist a dog on him. It forced him to get outside—which was a big part of the purpose of relocating. Gave him a chance to look around, relax, get in tune with what moved around him. Air, water, trees, hills, rocks—all potential inspirations for a design.

Colors, shapes, textures, curves and angles.

This little chunk of land, the woods and the water, the rocky slope, the chip and chatter of birds instead of cars and people offered exactly what he'd been after.

He decided he'd build himself a sturdy bench for this spot, something rustic and organic. Teak, he thought, reclaimed if he could find it, with arms wide enough to hold a beer.

He turned back to his shop for paper to sketch ideas on and remembered the dog.

He called, annoyed the pup wasn't sniffing around his feet as he seemed prone to do half the time so he ended up tripping over the damn dog or stepping on him.

He called again, then again. Cursing while a messy brew of annoyance, guilt and panic stirred up in his belly, Simon began the hunt.

He looked back in the shop to see if the dog had backtracked to wreak destruction, around the building, in the brush and shrubs while he called and whistled. He scanned the slope leading down to the water, and the skinny lane leading from the house to the road.

He looked under the shop porch, then hiked to the house to circle it, check under the porches there.

Not a sign.

He was a dog, for God's sake, Simon told himself. He'd come back. He was a *little* dog, so how far could he go? Reassuring himself, he walked back to the shop where he'd last seen the damn troublemaker and started into the woods.

Now, with his interlude of peace shattered, the play of light and shadow, the sigh of wind, the tangled briars all seemed ominous.

Could a hawk or an owl snag a dog that size? he wondered. Once, he'd thought he spotted a bald eagle. But . . .

Sure, the pup was little, but he was *solid*.

Stopping, he took a breath to reassure himself he wasn't panicked. Not in the least. Pissed off, that's what he was. Seriously pissed off at having to waste the time and energy hunting for a stupid puppy he'd imagined braining with a mallet.

Christ.

He bellowed the dog's name—and finally heard the answering yips. Yips, Simon determined, as the nerves banging in his gut settled down, that didn't sound remotely scared or remorseful but full of wild joy.

"Goddamn it," he muttered but, determined to be cagey, tried for the same happy tone in his call. "Come on, Jaws, you little bastard. Here, boy, you demon from hell."

He quickened his steps toward the sound of puppy pleasure until he heard the rustling in the brush.

The pup emerged, filthy, and manfully dragging what appeared to be the decaying corpse of a very large bird.

And he'd actually worried a very large bird would get the dog? What a joke.

"Jesus Christ, put that thing down. I mean it."

Jaws growled playfully, eyes alight, and dragged his find backward.

"Here! Now! Come!"

Jaws responded by hauling the corpse over, sitting and offering it.

"What the hell am I supposed to do with that?" Judging the timing, Simon grabbed the dog and booted what was left of the bird back into the brush. Jaws wiggled, struggling for freedom.

"This isn't a game of fet— Don't say the *f* word. On the other hand, fuck, fuck, *fuck!*" He held the dog aloft. The stench was unspeakable.

"What did you do, roll in it? For God's sake, why?"

With no other choice, Simon tucked the odorous dog firmly under his arm and, breathing through his teeth, hiked back to the house.

On the way back he considered and dismissed hosing the dog off. No way a hosing would combat the smell—even if he could keep the dog still long enough. He considered a bath, wished he had a galvanized tub—and shackles. An indoor bath gave him visions of a flooded bathroom.

On his porch he managed to take off his boots while Jaws

bathed his face in loving, death-smell kisses. He tossed his wallet on a table when he went inside and straight up to the shower.

When he'd closed them both in, Simon stripped down to boxers, ignoring the dog while Jaws attacked jeans and shirt. Then he turned on the spray.

"Deal with it," Simon suggested when Jaws bashed into the tile, then the glass door in a bid to escape.

Teeth set, Simon picked up the soap.

THEY WERE LATE. Fiona checked the time again, shrugged and continued to fill a pot with pansies and trails of vinca. She'd simply have to train Simon to respect her schedule, but for the moment having the luxury of a bit of gardening satisfied her. Her dogs snoozed nearby, and she had a rocking mix on her iPod.

If her new students didn't show, she'd get the second planter done, then maybe take her boys for a little hide-and-seek in the woods.

The day, sunny and mild, all blue skies and pretty breezes, was meant to be enjoyed.

She studied her work, fluffed petals, then started the second pot.

She spotted the truck.

"That's Simon," she said when her dogs rose. "Simon and Jaws." And went back to her pansies.

She continued to plant as man and dog got out of the truck, as her dogs greeted them—as man waded through the dogs. And took her time placing the next cell pack of pansies, precisely.

When Simon tapped her shoulder, she pulled out her earbuds. "Sorry, did you say something?"

"We're probably late."

"Uh-huh." She patted dirt.

"There were circumstances."

"The world's full of them."

"We had a large share of the world's circumstances, but the biggest involved the dead bird."

"Oh?" Fiona glanced over at the puppy, now engaged in fierce tug-of-war with Bogart. "Did he get a bird?"

"Something else got the bird, days ago from the look—and smell—of it."

"Ah." She nodded and, deciding to take pity, pulled off her gloves. "Did he bring it to you?"

"Eventually. After he rolled in it for a while."

"How'd he handle the bath?"

"We had a shower."

"Really?" She swallowed back the laugh since he didn't look inclined to appreciate it. "How'd that work out?"

"After he stopped trying to butt his way through the shower door and eat the soap, okay. Actually, he liked it. We may have found a shaky foothold of mutual ground."

"It's a start. What did you do with the corpse?"

"The bird?" He stared at her, wondering why the hell she'd care. "I kicked it back in the brush. I had my hands full with the dog."

"You'd better bag it and dispose of it. Otherwise, he's going to find it again first chance he gets."

"Great. Perfect."

"Smells are a dog's crack. He did what instinct told him to do." And the human, she decided, had done just as he should— except call and tell her he'd be late. "Given the circumstances, I'll give you the full session. Did you do your homework?"

"Yeah, yeah. Yes," he corrected when Fiona raised an eyebrow. "He'll sit on command—almost every time. He'll come on command when he damn well feels like it. Since we were here last, he's tried or succeeded in eating a TV remote, a pillow, an entire roll of toilet paper, part of a stair tread, most of a bag of barbecue potato chips, two chairs and a mallet. And before you ask, yes, I corrected and replaced. He doesn't give a damn."

"Learn to puppy-proof," she advised with no particular sympathy. "Jaws!" Fiona clapped her hands to get his attention, held them out in invitation and smiled. "Come. Jaws, come!"

He bounded over to scrabble at her knees. "Good dog!" She pulled a treat out of her pocket. "What a good dog."

"Bullshit."

"There's that positive attitude and reinforcement!"

"You don't live with him," Simon muttered.

"True enough." Deliberately, she set her trowel on the steps. "Sit." Jaws obeyed and accepted another treat, more praise, more rubs.

And she watched his eyes shift over to the trowel.

When she set her hands on her knees, he struck, fast as a whiplash, and with the trowel in his teeth raced away.

"Don't chase him." Fiona grabbed Simon's hand as he turned. "He'll only run and make it a game. Bogart, bring me the rope."

She sat where she was, the rope in her hand, and called Jaws. He raced forward, then away again.

"See, he's trying to bait us into it. We respond, go after him, he's won the round."

"It seems to me if he eats your tool, he's won."

"It's old, but in any case, he doesn't know he's won unless we play. We don't play. Jaws! Come!" She pulled another treat out of her pocket. After a brief debate, the pup loped back to her.

"This is not yours." She pried his mouth open, took the trowel, shook her head. "Not yours. This is yours." And passed him the rope.

She set the trowel down again, and again he lunged for it. This time, Fiona slapped her hand on it, shook her head. "Not yours. This is yours."

She repeated the process, endlessly patient, schooling Simon along the way. "Try not to say no too often. You should reserve it for when you need or want him to stop instantly. When it's important. There, see, he's lost interest in the trowel. We won't play. But we'll play with the rope. Grab the other end, give him a little game of tug."

Simon sat beside her, used the rope to pull the dog in, gave it slack, tugged side to side. "Maybe I'm just not cut out for a dog."

Willing to give some sympathy now, she patted Simon's knee. "This from a man who takes showers with his puppy?"

"It was necessary."

"It was clever, efficient and inventive." And they both smelled of soap and . . . sawdust, she realized. Very nice. "He'll learn. You'll both learn. How about the housebreaking?"

"Actually, that's working."

"Well, there you go. You've both learned how to handle that, and he sits on command."

"And wanders into the forest to roll in dead bird, eats my universal remote."

"Simon, you're such a Pollyanna."

He sent her a narrow stare and only made her laugh. "You're making progress. Work on training him to come, every time you call. Every time. It's essential. We'll work on some leash training, then give him a refresher on coming."

As she rose, she saw the cruiser heading down her lane. "It's a good time to teach him not to run toward a car—and not to jump on a visitor. Keep him controlled, talk to him."

She waved and waited for Davey to pull up and get out of the car. "Hi, Davey."

"Fee. Hi, guys, how's it going?" He bent to rub black, yellow and brown fur. "Sorry, Fee, I didn't know you had a lesson going."

"No problem. This is Simon Doyle and Jaws. Deputy Englewood."

"Right, you bought the Daubs' place a few months back. Nice to meet you." Davey nodded at Simon, then crouched to greet the puppy. "Hey, little fella. I don't want to interrupt," he said as he scratched and rubbed the exuberant Jaws. "I can wait until you're done."

"It's okay. Simon, why don't you get the leash, do a little solo work on heeling? I'll be right there. Is there a problem, Davey?" she murmured when Simon walked to his truck.

"Why don't we take a little walk ourselves?"

"Okay, now you're scaring me. Did something happen? Syl?"

"Syl's fine, far as I know." But Davey put a hand on her shoulder, steered her into a walk toward the side of the house.

"We got some news today, and the sheriff thought, since we go back, I should come talk to you about it."

"About what?"

"A woman went missing mid-January back in California. Sacramento area. Went out for a jog one morning and didn't come back. They found her about a week later in Eldorado National Forest, shallow grave. An anonymous tip gave them the basic direction."

She swallowed the flutter in her throat and said nothing.

"Ten days ago, another woman went out for a morning run in Eureka, California."

"Where did they find her?"

"Trinity National Forest. The first woman, she was nineteen. The second was twenty. College students. Outgoing, athletic, single. Both had part-time jobs. The first worked as a bartender, the second in a bookstore. They both were taken down with a stun gun, then bound with nylon rope, gagged with duct tape. Both were strangled with a red scarf left on the body."

She couldn't feel the flutters now, not when her body had gone numb. "And tied in a bow."

"Yeah, and tied in a bow."

Fiona pressed a hand to her heart, felt it pounding. "Perry's in prison. He's still in prison."

"He's never getting out, Fee. He's locked up, locked down."

"It's a copycat."

"It's more than that." He reached out, gave her shoulders a rub. "It's more than that, Fee. There are details the Perry investigation didn't release, like how Perry took a lock of hair from his victims and wrote a number on the back of their right hand."

Already the numbness was wearing off. She wanted it back, wanted it to block this sickness roiling in her belly. "He told someone, or one of the investigators did—someone in the crime lab or the medical examiner's office."

Davey kept his eyes on hers, his hands on her shoulders. "Has to be. They're going to track that down."

"Don't treat me like an idiot, Davey. Any of dozens of

people could've passed that information on. It's been nearly eight years since . . ."

"I know. I'm sorry, Fee. I want you to know the cops are all over this. We wanted you to be informed, and it's likely the media's going to make the connection pretty quick. They might poke at you about it."

"I can handle the press. Greg's family?"

"They're being notified, too. I know this is hard for you, Fee, but I don't want you to worry. They'll get him. And as bad as it is, this asshole's sticking to Perry's pattern. Young college girls. You're not twenty anymore."

"No." She bore down to keep her voice steady. "But I'm the only one who got away."

SIMON DIDN'T HAVE TO HEAR the conversation to know something was wrong. Bad news or trouble, maybe both. He couldn't see why Fiona would want anyone around—especially when the anyone was the next thing to a stranger.

He considered loading the dog back in the truck and taking off. It would be rude, but he didn't particularly mind rude.

But it also seemed downright cold, and that he did mind.

He'd just wait until the deputy left, let the woman make whatever excuses suited her, then escape. Nobody lost face.

Plus, miracle of miracles, he was actually getting Jaws to heel about thirty percent of the time. Even the pup's cooperation stemming from having the other dogs stroll along, stop on command, didn't negate success.

So he could go home flush from that, get a little more work done, then have a beer.

Take the dead bird out of the equation and it added up to a pretty good day.

When the cruiser headed out, he expected Fiona to wander over, make those excuses, then go handle whatever needed handling.

Instead, she stood where she was for several minutes, just staring out at the road. Then she walked back to the porch steps, sat. And sat.

So he'd make the excuses, Simon decided. Easy enough. Just remembered something I have to do. Dog's coming along, blah, blah, see you.

He crossed toward her, pleased it only took a couple of tugs to have the pup fall in line. And as he approached, he saw she was dead white, and the hands clutched on her knees trembled lightly.

Crap.

With walking casually away no longer an option, he scooped up the puppy before Jaws could try to leap into her lap.

"Bad news," he said.

"What?"

"The deputy brought bad news. Is Sylvia all right?"

"Yes. It's not about Sylvia."

Her dogs, sensing her mood, clustered around her. The big yellow Lab rested his head on her knee.

"Ah . . . we should . . ."

He watched her struggle to pull herself out of whatever hole she'd fallen into.

"We should work on sit and stay."

"Not today."

She looked up at him then, but he couldn't translate what clouded her eyes. Grief? Fear? Shock?

"No," she agreed, "not today. Sorry."

"No problem. I'll see you next time."

"Simon." She drew a breath as he hesitated. "Would you mind . . . Could you stay for a while?"

He wanted to say no—wished he had it in him to say no. Maybe he'd have found it in him if it hadn't been so obvious it was as hard for her to ask as for him to agree.

"All right."

"Why don't you let him run awhile. The big guys'll watch him. Play," she said as Simon unclipped the leash. "Stay close. Close," she repeated, stroking fur. "Watch Jaws, go play."

They whined a little, and each glanced back at her as they started into the yard.

"They know I'm upset. They'd rather stay until I'm not. You'd rather go."

He sat beside her. "Yeah. I'm not much good at this kind of thing."

"Not much good's better than no good."

"Okay. I guess you want to tell me the bad news."

"I guess I do. It'll get around the island anyway."

Still, for a few moments she said nothing at all, then seemed to gather herself.

"Several years ago there was a series of abduction murders. Young women, ranging from eighteen to twenty-three. They were all college students, twelve of them over a three-year period. California, Nevada, Oregon, New Mexico, Washington state were either abduction sites or burial sites—or both."

It rang a bell somewhere, dimly, but he said nothing.

"They were all the same type—not physically, as he crossed races and coloring, but basic body types and all college students, athletic, outdoorsy, outgoing. He'd stalk them for weeks once he'd chosen a target. Sometimes longer. Meticulous, patient, he'd record their routines, habits, wardrobe, friends, family, schedules. He used a tape recorder and kept a notebook. All of them either jogged or hiked or biked routinely. Habitually."

She drew another breath and made him think of someone preparing to execute a surface dive in murky water.

"He preferred women who went out alone, early morning or dusk. He approached from the opposite direction—just another jogger, another hiker. And when he closed in, he used a stun gun to take them down. While they were incapacitated, he carried them to his car. He had the trunk lined with plastic so there'd be no trace on the bodies, and no trace of them in the trunk."

"Thorough," Simon said, thinking out loud.

"Yes. Very." She continued briskly, without inflection, like a woman giving a report she knew by rote. "He bound them with nylon cord, gagged them with duct tape, then gave them a mild sedative to keep them under, keep them quiet. He'd drive to a national park. He'd already have the spot picked out. While the search went on for her, in the area she'd been abducted, he was hours away, forcing this groggy, terrified woman to walk, through the dark, off the trail."

Now her voice hitched, a quick tremble as she linked her fingers together in her lap and stared straight ahead. "He dug the grave first—not too deep. He wanted them to be found. He liked them to watch him dig so he tied them to a tree. They couldn't beg, couldn't even ask him why because he kept them gagged the entire time. He didn't rape them or torture them, physically. Or beat them or mutilate them. He just took out the red scarf and, while they were bound and gagged, unable to defend themselves, strangled them. He tied it in a bow when he was finished, and buried them."

"The Red Scarf Killer. That's what the press called him," Simon commented. "I remember this. They caught him after he shot some cop."

"Greg Norwood. The cop was Greg Norwood, and his dog, his K-9 partner, Kong."

The words throbbed in the air between them like an open wound.

"You knew him."

"Perry laid in wait for them. Greg had a place, a nice little weekend place near Lake Sammamish. He liked to take Kong there, work on his training. Once a month, just the two of them. Boy-bonding, he called it."

She laid her hands on her knees, a casual gesture, but he saw the way her fingers dug in.

"He shot Greg first, and maybe that was his mistake. He put two bullets in Kong, but Kong kept coming. That's what they reconstructed, and that's what Perry said happened, trading confessions, information, details against the threat of the death penalty when he knew he'd lose the trial. Kong tore Perry up pretty good before he died. Perry was strong, and he managed to get back to his car, even drove a few miles before he passed out, wrecked. Anyway, they got him. Greg, he was strong, too. He lived two days. That was in September.

September twelfth. We were going to be married the following June."

Useless words, Simon thought, but they had to be said. "I'm sorry."

"Yeah, me too. He staked Greg out for months, maybe longer. Meticulous, patient. He killed him to pay me back. See, I was supposed to be his number thirteen, but I got away."

She closed her eyes briefly. "I want a drink. Do you want a drink?"

"Yeah. Sure."

When she rose and went in, he debated going with her, and decided maybe she needed a little time to pull it together.

He remembered bits and pieces of the story. Remembered now there'd been a girl who escaped, and who gave the FBI a description of the man who abducted her.

Years ago, he thought now, and tried to think what he'd been doing when the story had been hot.

He just hadn't paid that much attention, he thought now. He'd been, what, about twenty-five? He'd just moved to Seattle and had been trying to build a reputation, make a living. And his father had that cancer scare about that time. That had eclipsed everything else.

She came out with a couple glasses of white wine.

"It's an Aussie chardonnay. All I've got, apparently."

"It's fine." He took the glass, and they sat in silence, watching the heap of dogs who'd decided to take a nap. "Do you want to tell me how you got away?"

"Luck, on the heels of stupidity. I shouldn't have been out alone that morning on that jogging path. I should've known better. My uncle's a cop, and I was already seeing Greg, and they'd both made a point of telling me not to run without a partner. But I couldn't get one who'd keep up with me. Track star," she added with a ghost of a smile.

"You've got the legs for it."

"Yeah. Lucky me. I didn't listen to them. Perry hadn't crossed over to Washington at that point, and there hadn't been an abduction for months. You never think it's going to be you.

You especially never think that when you're twenty. I went out for my run. I liked to go early, then hit the coffee shop. It was a crappy day, gloomy, rainy, but I loved running in the rain. This was early November, the year before Greg died. I had a second, just a second when I saw him. So ordinary-looking, so pleasant, but I had that click. I had a panic button on my key chain. I even reached for it, but it was too late. I felt that shock of pain, then nothing works."

She had to stop a moment, had to breathe. "Nothing works," she repeated. "Pain, shock, then numb, useless. I felt sick when I came to in the trunk. It was dark, and I felt the movement, the sound of the tires on the road. Can't scream, can't kick, can hardly move."

She stopped, breathed it out, took a slow sip of wine. "I cried awhile because he was going to kill me and I couldn't stop him. He was going to kill me because I wanted to take a morning run by myself. I thought about my family, and Greg, my friends, my life. I stopped crying and got mad. I hadn't done anything to deserve this."

She stopped again, drank again while the breeze whispered through the pines. "And I had to pee. That was humiliating, and as stupid as it is, the thought that I'd pee my pants before he killed me just revved me up. So I'm fighting that, sort of squirming around, and I felt the lump in my pocket. I had a hidden pocket in my jogging pants—one of those inside-the-back deals. Greg had given me this little Swiss Army knife." She reached in the pocket of her jeans, pulled it out.

"Tiny little knife, cute little scissors, mini nail file. A girl knife." She closed her hand around it. "It saved my life. He'd taken my keys, the coffee money I had zipped in my jacket pocket, but he hadn't thought of the inner pocket in the pants. Couldn't know it was there, I guess. My hands were tied behind my back. I could just reach it. I think I was most scared then, when I managed to get the knife, when I started to think maybe, maybe there was a way out."

"Can I see it?" When she offered it, Simon opened it, studied the knife in the bright afternoon sun. Half as long as his thumb, he thought. "You cut through the nylon cord with this?"

"Cut, sawed, hacked. It took me forever just to get it open, or it seemed like it, and a lifetime to saw through the rope. I had to cut through the one around my ankles because I couldn't loosen the knot. First I was terrified he'd stop the car before I'd finished, then I was terrified he'd never stop that fucking car. But he did. He did, and he got out whistling a tune. I'll never forget that sound."

He thought of it—a girl, trapped, terrified, very likely bloody where the cords had cut into her. And armed with a knife barely more lethal than a thumbtack.

"I put the duct tape back over my mouth."

She said it so calmly now, so matter-of-factly that he turned his head to stare at her.

"And I wound the rope around my ankles, put my hands behind my back. I closed my eyes. When he opened the trunk, he kept right on whistling.

"He leaned in, tapped my cheek to bring me around. And I stuck that little knife in him. I'd hoped for the eye, but I missed and got him in the face. Still it surprised him, hurt him enough to give me a second. I rammed my fist into his face and swung my legs around and kicked. Not as hard as I wanted because the rope got tangled some, but hard enough to knock him back so I could get out. The shovel was right there, where he'd dropped it when I stabbed him. I grabbed it and I slammed it against his head—a couple of times. I got his keys. I'm still a little blurry on all of it—shock, adrenaline, they said—but I got in the car and floored it."

"You knocked him out and drove away," Simon murmured, stunned and fascinated.

"I didn't know where I was, where I was going, and I'm lucky I didn't kill myself, but I drove like a bat out of hell. There was a lodge, a hotel—I saw the lights. He'd taken me into the Olympic National Forest. They called the rangers, and the rangers called in the FBI and so on and so on. He got away, but I gave them a description. They had the car, his name, his address. Or the one he had on record. And still, he eluded them for nearly a year. Until he shot Greg and Kong, and Kong stopped him. Kong gave his life to stop him."

She took the knife back, slipped it into her pocket.

"You seem like a fairly smart woman," Simon commented after a few moments. "So you know that what you did saved other women. The bastard's put away, right?"

"Multiple and consecutive life terms. They made the deal after I testified, after he realized he'd be convicted for Greg, for me, and he'd face the death penalty."

"Why'd they deal?"

"For confessions on Greg, on me, on the other twelve victims, for the whereabouts of his notebooks, his tapes, for closure for the families of the murdered women. For answers. And the certainty he'd never get out."

She nodded as if to a question in her head. "I always thought it was the right thing to do. It gave me, strangely enough, relief to hear him go through all of it, step by step, and to know he'd pay for it, for all of it, for a very, very long time. I wanted to put it behind me, close the door. My father died just nine weeks later. So suddenly, so unexpectedly, and the bottom dropped out again."

She rubbed her hands over her face. "Horrible times. I came out to stay with Syl for a few weeks, a couple months, I thought, but I realized I didn't want to go back. I needed to start over, and I wanted to start over here. So I did, and most of the time that door stays closed."

"What opened it today?"

"Davey came to tell me someone is using Perry's pattern, including details that weren't released to the public. There've been two so far. In California. It's started again."

Questions circled in his head, but he didn't ask them. She was done, he thought. Purged what she'd needed to purge for now.

"Rough on you. Brings it all back, makes it now instead of then."

Again she closed her eyes, and her whole body seemed to relax. "Yes. Yes, exactly. God, maybe it's stupid, but it really helps to have someone say that. To have someone *get* that. So thanks."

She laid a hand on his knee, a brief connection. "I have to go in, make some calls."

"Okay." He handed her the glass. "Thanks for the drink."

"You earned it."

Simon walked over to pick up the puppy, who immediately started bathing his face as if they'd been parted for a decade.

As he drove away, he glanced back to see Fiona going inside, closely followed by her dogs.

FIVE

Fiona thought about dinner, and had another glass of wine instead. Talking to Greg's parents tore off the scar tissue and opened the wound again. She knew the healthy option was to fix a meal, maybe take a long walk with the dogs. Get out of the house, get out of herself.

Instead she shooed the dogs outside and indulged in a long session of brooding so wide and deep her hackles rose at the interruption of another visitor.

Couldn't people just let her wallow?

The chorus of happy barks translated to a friend. She wasn't surprised to see James and his Koby exchanging greetings with her dogs.

She leaned against the porch post, idly sipping her wine and watching him. In the floodlights she'd flipped on, his hair had a sheen. But then, something about James always did. His skin, an indescribable shade she thought of as caramel dipped in gold dust, was a testament to his widely mixed heritage. His eyes, a bright, shining green, often laughed out of a forest of lashes.

He turned them on Fiona now, with a quick and easy smile as he shook a jumbo take-out bag.

"I brought provisions."

She took another slow sip of wine. "Davey talked to you."

"Seeing as he's married to my sister, he often does."

He walked to her, bringing the scent of food, then just wrapped his free arm around her to bring her close. Swayed.

"I'm okay. I've just been holding the first meeting of my Pity Me Club."

"I want to join. I'll be president."

"I've already elected myself president. But since you brought provisions, you can be the second official member."

"Do we get badges? A secret handshake?" He leaned back to press his lips to her forehead. "Let's go inside and vote on it over burgers."

"I talked to Greg's mother," Fiona told him as she led the way.

"Hard."

"Brutal. So I've been sitting here drinking wine in the dark."

"Fair enough, but I'm calling time's-up on that. Got any Coke?"

"Pepsi. Diet."

"Blech. I'll take it."

As much at home in her place as in his own, he got out plates, set a burger, loaded, on each, then divvied up the mountain of fries from an insulated box. She poured out the drinks after dumping the rest of the wine in her glass down the sink.

"We should've had sex before we got to be friends."

He smiled, sat. "I think we were eleven and twelve when you started coming on island to see your dad, so we were a little young for sex when we got to be friends."

"Still." She plopped down in her chair. "If we'd had sex back then, we could have a revival now. It'd be a good distraction. But now it's too late because I'd feel stupid getting naked with you."

"It's a problem." He took a bite of burger. "We could do it

in the dark, and use assumed names. I'd be Rock Hard and you'd be Lavender Silk."

"Nobody can call out 'Lavender' while in the throes. I'll be Misty Mars. I like the alliteration."

"Fine. So, Misty, you want to eat first or just go jump in the sack?"

"It's hard to resist that kind of romance, but we'll eat." She nibbled on a fry. "I don't want to beat on the drum all night, James, but it's so strange. Just the other day I was telling Syl how I could hardly get Greg's face in my head. How he's faded on me. Do you know?"

"Yeah, I think I do."

"And the minute Davey told me about what's happened, it was there again. I can see him, every detail of his face. He's back. And . . . is it awful?" she managed as tears rose in her throat. "Is it? That I wish he wasn't. A part of me wants him to fade, and I didn't realize that until he came back."

"So what? You should wear black and read depressing poetry for the rest of your life? You grieved, Fee. You broke, and you mourned, and you healed. You started the unit out of love and respect for him." Reaching over, he gave her wrist a squeeze. "And it's a hell of a tribute."

"If you're going to be all rational and sensible, I don't see how you can be a member of the Pity Me Club."

"We can't have a club meeting while there are burgers. That requires really bad wine and stale crackers."

"Damn you, James, you've screwed up a really good wallow." She sighed, ate her burger.

EVEN THE COMFORT of a friend, the familiarity of her dogs and the nighttime routine didn't spare her from the bad dreams. She woke every hour, struggling out of the goop of a nightmare only to sink in again the next time she drifted off.

The dogs, as restless as she, got up to pace or rearrange themselves. At three a.m., Bogart came to the side of the bed to offer her the rope as if a game of tug would set things right.

At four, Fiona gave it up. She let the dogs out, made coffee. She did a hard, sweaty workout then settled down with paperwork.

She balanced her checkbook, drafted upcoming newsletters for her classes and for the Search and Rescue subscribers. While the sky lightened she updated her Web page and spent some time surfing various blogs because she couldn't drum up the enthusiasm to write her own.

By the time her first class began, she'd been up for over four hours and wanted a nap.

She loved her classes, Fiona reminded herself. She loved them for the work itself, the dogs, the social opportunity, the interaction. She loved being outside most of the day.

But right then she wished she'd canceled the other two classes on the schedule. Not to wallow, she told herself, but just for some alone time, just to catch up on sleep, maybe read a book.

Instead, she prepared for round two, took a call from Sylvia—word traveled—and got through it.

By the end of her workday, after she and the dogs had gathered and stowed all the toys and training tools, she realized she didn't want to be alone after all. The house was too quiet, the woods too full of shadows.

She'd go into town, she decided. Do some shopping, maybe drop by and see Sylvia. She could walk on the beach after. Fresh air, exercise, change of scene. She'd keep at it until she was too damn tired for dreams, bad or otherwise.

She decided on Newman for company. As he leaped in the car, she turned to the other dogs.

"You know how it is. Everybody gets a chance for some one-on-one. We'll bring you something. Be good."

When she got in, she gave Newman a sidelong glance. "No smirking," she ordered.

Stress eased as she drove, snaking along while the early evening sun dipped beams into the water. Fatigue lessened as she opened the windows wide and cranked up the radio while the wind tossed her hair.

"Let's sing!"

Always ready to oblige, Newman howled in harmony with Beyoncé.

She intended to drive to Eastsound, stock up on essentials and treat herself to something she absolutely didn't need. But as she wound along between hill and water, by field and forest, she followed impulse and made the turn at the mailbox marked simply DOYLE.

Maybe he needed something from the village. She could be neighborly, save him a trip. It didn't have anything to do with wanting to see where and how he lived. Or hardly anything.

She liked the way the trees screened, and let the sunlight shimmer and shine on rock and tall grass. And she liked the house, she thought, as it came into view. The central double peaks, the tumbling lines that followed the slope of the land.

It could use some paint, she decided. Something fresh and happy for the trim. And some chairs, some colorful pots of flowers on the porch and the sweet little second-story deck. Maybe a bench under the weeping cherry that would burst into bloom in the spring.

She parked beside Simon's truck, noted he'd replaced the headrest he'd patched with duct tape. Then she spotted the outbuilding a few yards from the house, nearly enveloped by the trees.

Long and low, it likely held as many square feet as her house, and offered a generous covered porch on the front. A scatter of tables, chairs and what she took as parts of other pieces of furniture stood or leaned under the shade.

She heard the sound of sawing—at least she thought it was sawing—buzzing under heroically loud rock and roll.

She got out, signaled Newman to join her. He scented the air—new place, new smells—as he fell into step with her.

"Great view, huh?" she murmured, looking out over the sound to the opposing shorelines and the little nubs of green on the water. "And look, he's got a little beach down there, and a pier. He needs a boat, but it's nice. Water, woods, some nice stretches of ground, and not too close to the road. It's a good home for a dog."

She scratched Newman's ears and wandered closer to the outbuilding.

She spotted him through the window—jeans, T-shirt, goggles, tool belt. And noted she'd been right about the saw. It was, she thought, one big, scary mother. He slid wood under its fast, toothy blade. Her stomach tightened a little at the thought of what it could do to fingers, and with that in mind, she moved carefully around to the door, standing out of range until the buzzing paused.

Then she knocked, waved through the glass. When he only stood there, frowning at her, she opened the door. The pup lay on the floor, feet in the air as if he'd been electrocuted.

"Hi!" She had to pitch to just under scream level to beat out the music. "I was on my way to the village and thought . . ."

She trailed off as he pulled out earplugs.

"Oh, well, no wonder it's so loud. Listen—"

She broke off again when he pulled a remote from a pocket of the tool belt, shut down the music. The silence roared like a tsunami—and woke the puppy.

He yawned, stretched, then spotted her. Insane joy leaped into his eyes as he sprang up, did a kind of bouncing dance, then charged her. Fiona crouched, held out a hand, palm facing dog so he bumped into it first.

"Hi, yes, hi, good to see you, too." She rubbed his head, his belly. She pointed a finger at the ground. "Sit!" His butt vibrated a moment, then plopped down. "Aren't you smart, aren't you good?" She grabbed him when he spotted Newman, sitting patiently outside. "Can he go out? I've got Newman, and he'll watch out for him."

Simon simply shrugged.

"Okay. Go play." She laughed when Jaws took a flying leap out the door and belly-flopped into the grass. When she glanced back, Simon remained by the table saw, watching her.

"I've interrupted you."

"Yeah."

Blunt, she thought. Well, she didn't mind blunt. "I'm heading into the village and thought I'd see if you needed anything. Sort of a payback for playing sounding board."

"I'm good."

"Okay, then. We both know the do-you-need-anything's just an excuse, but we can leave it at that. I'll— Oh my God, that's beautiful!"

She headed straight for the cabinet across the shop, skirting benches and tools.

"Don't touch it!" Simon snapped, and stopped her in her tracks. "It's tacky," he added, in an easier tone. "Varnish."

Obediently, she linked her hands behind her back. It was the varnish she smelled, she realized, and sawdust, and freshly sawed wood. The combination merged into a fascinating aroma. "Those are the doors? The carving's just exquisite, and the tones of the wood. Delicious, really." As delicious as the scent that soaked the air. "I want it. I probably can't afford it, but I want it anyway. How much?"

"It doesn't suit you or your place. It *is* elegant, and a little ornate. You're not."

"I can be elegant and ornate."

He shook his head, then walked over to an old, squat refrigerator, took out two Cokes. He tossed her one, which she caught one-handed.

"No, you can't. You want something either simpler, cleaner or going the other direction into fanciful. A little tension with the primarily Mission and Craftsman style you lean toward."

"Is that where I lean?"

"I've been in your house," he reminded her.

She yearned to run a finger over the deep carving— elongated hearts—on the raised panel of the door. "This could be tension."

"No."

Sincerely baffled, she turned to him. "You actually won't sell it to me because I'm not elegant?"

"That's right."

"How do you sell anything?"

"On commission or direct sale. By designing what works with the client." He eyed her while he took a deep drink. "Rough night."

Now she jammed her hands in her pockets. "Thanks for

noticing. Well, since I'm interrupting and I'm not suitable to buy your stupid cabinet, I'll leave you alone with your monster saw."

"I'm taking a break."

She drank, studying him as he studied her. "You know, given my line of work, really crappy manners such as yours don't bother me."

"If you're thinking of training me like my dog, you should know I'm intractable."

She only smiled.

"So, if the need-anything-in-town was an excuse, are you hitting on me?"

She smiled again, wandered. She saw a lot of clamps and chisels, a skinnier saw and a stationary drill thingee that looked as scary as the monster saw.

She saw tools she had no names for and empty coffee cans full of nails and screws and other strange things.

What she didn't see was any semblance of organization.

"Hitting on you? Not yet. And given your behavioral flaws, I'm reconsidering."

"Fair enough, and to be fair back, you're not really my type."

She stopped examining a wonderful wide-armed rocker she coveted to send him a cool stare. "Is that so?"

"Yeah, it's so. Mostly I lean toward the arty, feminine type. Curvy's a bonus."

"Like Sylvia."

"Yeah."

"Or Nina Abbott." She couldn't help the smug smile when annoyance flicked briefly in his eyes.

"Or" was all he said.

"Thank God we got that cleared up before I gave my squishy, susceptible heart into your hands."

"Lucky break. But . . . it's good to mix things up now and then. Try new things."

"Great. I'll let you know when I want to be mixed and tried. Meanwhile, I'll take my inelegant, art-starved, unfeminine, flat-chested self out of your way."

"You're not flat-chested."

The laugh escaped before she knew it was there. "God, you're a weird sucker. I'm going while I still have enough crumbs of ego left to sweep into a pile."

She went to the door, called his dog. When the puppy raced to her, she petted and praised. Then she nudged his butt farther into the room, closed the door with him inside. She flicked one glance at Simon through the glass before striding to her truck, Newman faithfully at her side.

He watched her through the window, the long, athletic stride, the easy grace. She'd looked lost when she came into the shop. Hesitant, uncertain. Tired.

Not anymore, he thought as she hopped into her truck. Now she was brisk, distracted and maybe a little pissed.

Better. Maybe he was one weird sucker, but he'd worry less about her now.

Satisfied, he replaced his earplugs, his goggles, turned on the music. And got back to work.

EYES BRIGHT, SYLVIA leaned on the counter of her pretty little shop while Fiona debated earrings. "He did *not* say that."

"He absolutely said that." Fiona held long pearl drops to one ear, funky, colored glass balls to the other. "I'm not elegant enough for his overrated cabinet. I can be elegant." She turned. "See? Pearls."

"Very pretty. But the fused glass ones are really you."

"Yeah, but I *could* wear the pearls, if I wanted." After setting them back in the display, Fiona wandered over to a tall raku vase.

There was always something new to see in Sylvia's place. A painting, a scarf, a table, a treasure trove of jewelry. She stopped by a bench with high, curved sides and skimmed her fingers over the wood.

"This is beautiful."

"It's one of Simon's."

She resisted giving it a flick with her formerly admiring

fingers. "Figures. Then he said I wasn't his type. As if I'd asked. You are."

"I am?"

"He even used you as an example. Arty and female and built."

"Really?"

"Sure, go ahead and look smug."

Deliberately, obviously, Sylvia fluffed at her hair. "It's hard not to."

"Well, feel free to follow up," Fiona added with a dismissive wave.

"It might be interesting, but I think I'll just stay smug. I'm sure he didn't mean to insult you."

"Oh yes he did."

"Tell you what. I'm closing in ten minutes. We'll go have dinner and trash him. Better, men in general."

"That sounds like fun, but I need to get back. I really just came in to bitch. Jesus, Syl, it's been a crappy couple of days."

Sylvia skirted the counter to give Fiona a bolstering hug. "Why don't I come over and fix you some pasta while you take a nice long bath?"

"Honestly, I think I'm going to open a can of soup, then go to bed. I didn't get much sleep last night."

"I worry about you, Fee." She gave Fiona's tail of hair a little tug. "Why don't you come stay with me until they catch this maniac?"

"You know I'm fine. Me and the boys. Besides, the maniac's not interested in me."

"But—" She broke off when the door opened.

"Hi, Sylvia. Hi, Fiona."

"Jackie, how are you?" Sylvia smiled at the pretty blonde who ran a local B&B.

"I'm just fine. I meant to get in earlier. I know you close in a few minutes."

"Don't worry about that. How's Harry?"

"Tucked up in bed with a cold—which is one of the reasons I ran out. I swear you'd think he had the plague instead of the sniffles. He's driving me crazy. I've been doing a little early spring cleaning between waiting on him hand and foot and listening to him moan. I decided I need to spruce the place up a little, do some redecorating. Mind if I look around, get some ideas?"

"You go right ahead."

"I'd better get going. Nice to see you, Jackie."

"You, too. Oh, Fiona, my boy and his wife just got a puppy. Practice, they say, before they start working on making me a grandmother." She rolled her eyes.

"That's nice. What kind did they get?"

"I don't know. They went to a shelter." She smiled then. "Brad said they'd save a life, then start thinking about starting one."

"That's really nice."

"They named her Sheba—as in Queen of. He said if I ran into you I should tell you they're going to sign up for your puppy classes."

"I'll look forward to it. I'd better go."

"I'll come by tomorrow, give you a hand with your classes," Sylvia told her. "Oreo could use a little refresher course."

"I'll see you then. Bye, Jackie."

As she walked out she heard Jackie exclaim over the bench, "Oh, Sylvia, this is a wonderful piece."

"Isn't it? It's by the new artist I told you about. Simon Doyle."

Fiona grumbled all the way to the truck.

IN HIS CELL in Washington State Penitentiary, George Allen Perry read his Bible. While his crimes had earned him a maximum-security cage for the rest of his life, he was considered a model prisoner.

He joined no gangs, made no complaints. He did the work assigned to him, ate the food served him. He kept himself clean, spoke respectfully to guards. He exercised regularly. He did not smoke or swear or use drugs, and spent most of the endless days reading. Every Sunday he attended services.

Visitors came rarely. He had no wife, no child, no staunch friends outside, or inside, the walls.

His father had long ago deserted him, and his mother, who the psychiatrists agreed was the root of his pathology, feared him.

His sister wrote him once a month, and made the long trek from Emmett, Idaho, once a year, considering it her Christian duty.

She'd given him the Bible.

The first year had been a misery that he'd borne with downcast eyes and a quiet manner that had disguised a raging fear. In the second year he'd lost fear in depression, and by the third he'd accepted that he would never be free.

He would never again be free to choose what to eat, and when to eat it, to rise or repose at his own whim. He would never again walk through a forest or glade or drive a car along a dark road with a secret in the trunk.

He would never again feel the power and the peace of a kill.

But there were other freedoms, and he earned them carefully. Meticulously. He expressed regret for his crimes to his lawyer, to the psychiatrist.

He'd wept, and considered the tears humiliation well spent.

He told his sister he'd been born again. He was allowed private consultation with a minister.

By his fourth year, he was assigned to the prison library, where he worked with quiet efficiency and expressed gratitude for the access to books.

And began his search for a student.

He applied for and was granted permission to take courses, both by visiting instructors and by video feed. It gave him an opportunity to interact with and study his fellow inmates in a new setting.

He found most too crude, too brutal, too lacking in intellect. Or simply too old, too young, too deeply entrenched in the system. He continued to further his education—he found it interesting—and he held to the thinning hope that fate would offer him the spiritual freedom he sought.

In his fifth year in Walla Walla, fate smiled on him. Not in the guise of a fellow inmate, but an instructor.

He knew instantly, just as he'd known the woman he would kill the moment he saw her.

This was his gift.

He began slowly, assessing, evaluating, testing. Patient, always, as he outlined and refined the methods by which he would create his proxy, the one who would walk outside the walls for him, hunt for him and kill for him.

Who would, in time, in good time, correct his single mistake. One that haunted him every night in the dark cage where silence and comfort were strangers.

Who would, in time, kill Fiona Bristow.

That time, Perry thought as he read Revelation, was nearly here.

He glanced up as the guard came to the cell. "Got a visitor."

Perry blinked, carefully marking his place before setting aside the worn Bible. "My sister? I didn't expect her for another six weeks."

"Not your sister. FBI."

"Oh, my goodness." A big man with thinning hair and prison pallor, Perry stood meekly as the door clanged and slid open.

Two guards flanked him, and he knew others would search his cell while he was gone. No matter, none at all. They'd find nothing but his books, some religious tracts, the dry, God-fearing letters from his sister.

He kept his head down, repressed the smile that strained to spread over his face. The FBI would tell him what he already knew. His student had passed the next test.

Yes, Perry thought, there were many kinds of freedom. And at the thought of gaming with the FBI again, he took wing and soared.

SIX

Grateful for the bright, brisk morning and work that demanded her full attention, Fiona studied her advanced special-skills students.

Today was a very big day for dogs and handlers. They'd attempt their first blind search.

"Okay, the victim's in place." She thought of Sylvia, three-quarters of a mile away, sitting cozily under a forked-trunk cedar with a book, a thermos of herbal tea and her radio. "I want you to work as a unit. We're going to use the sector system. You can see I've set up the base." She gestured to a table she'd placed under a pole tarp and the equipment on it. "For today, I'll handle base and stand as operational leader, but by next week I want you to elect your officers."

She gestured to the whiteboard under the tarp. "Okay. The local authorities have notified the operations officer—me, in this case—and asked for assistance in the search and rescue of an adult female hiker who's been lost approximately twenty-four hours. You see on the board temperatures last night dropped to forty-three degrees. She has only a day pack, and little experience. The victim is Sylvia Bristow."

That brought out some grins, as the class knew Sylvia as Fiona's sometime assistant. "She's age-deleted for my own well-being, Caucasian, brown hair, brown eyes, five feet, five inches, and about a hundred and thirty pounds. When last seen she was wearing a red jacket, jeans, a blue baseball-style cap. Now, what do you need to know before being given your sectors?"

She answered with details from the scenario she'd devised. The subject was in good health, had a cell phone but often neglected to charge it, had been expected to hike two to four hours, was not local and had only recently taken up hiking.

She called the unit to the map and the log she'd already begun. Once she'd assigned sectors, she ordered everyone to load on their packs.

"I have items worn recently by the subject. Take a bag, give your dogs the scent. Remember to use the subject's name. Refresh the scent whenever you think your dog may be confused, or if he or she becomes distracted or disinterested. Remember the boundaries of your sector. Use your compass, check in by radio. Trust your dogs. Good luck."

She felt their excitement, and the nerves, as well as a sense of competition. Eventually, if they made it as a unit, the competition would shift into cooperation and trust.

"When you get back, all dogs who didn't find our victim need a short find, to keep up morale. Remember, it's not just your dogs being tested. You're honing your skills, too."

She watched them spread out, separate, and nodded in approval at the way each gave his or her dog the scent, the command.

Her own dogs whined as the others scented the air, began to roam.

"We'll play later," she promised them. "These guys need to do it on their own."

She sat, noted the time, wrote it in the assignment log.

They were a good group, she thought, and should make a solid unit. She'd started with eight, but over the past ten weeks three had dropped out. Not a bad percentage, she mused, and what was left was tight, was dedicated. If they pushed through the next five weeks, they'd be a good asset to the program.

She picked up her radio, checked the frequency, then contacted Sylvia. "They're off and running. Over."

"Well, I hope they don't find me too soon. I'm enjoying my book. Over."

"Don't forget. Sprained ankle, dehydration, mild shock. Over."

"Got it. But until then, I'm going to eat my apple and read. See you when they haul me back. Over and out."

To keep her own dogs occupied, and give them some consolation for not being able to play the find game with the others, Fiona ran them through their paces on the agility training equipment.

It may have looked comical to an outsider—cheerful Labs climbing up and down the ladder of a child's sliding board, or taking that slide on command. But the skill taught and reinforced a search dog's ability to cope with difficult footing. The fact that they enjoyed it, as well as balancing on the teeter-totter, negotiating along narrow planks, maneuvering through the open drums she'd formed into tunnels, added a bonus.

The demands of the search exercise required her to order sit-and-stays while she took radio calls from the unit, answered questions, logged in positions.

At the end of an hour, the dogs settled down with chew treats, and Fiona at her laptop. When her radio crackled, she continued to keyboard one-handed.

"Base, this is Tracie. I have Sylvia. She's conscious and lucid. Her right ankle may be sprained and is causing her some discomfort. She appears to be somewhat dehydrated and shaky, but otherwise uninjured. Over."

"That's good, Tracie. What's your location, and do you require assistance transporting Sylvia to base? Over."

Exercise or not, Fiona logged in the location, the time, the status. She may have smiled when she heard Sylvia playing up her victim role in the background, but she created a professional and complete log.

While they'd debrief as if the search had been real, Fiona felt such moments deserved commemoration. She set trays of brownies on her picnic table, added fruit platters for the more healthy-minded, pitchers of iced tea.

She had dog biscuits and a toy for the dogs—and for Lolo, Tracie's clever German shepherd, a gold star for her tag collar.

As she carried glasses outside, Simon's truck drove over her bridge.

It annoyed her to feel annoyed. She was basically a happy person, Fiona thought. A friendly one. She liked Simon well enough, and his dog quite a bit. But irritation pricked none-theless.

Maybe part of it was because he just looked good—sort of rough and arty at the same time in battered jeans and expen-sive sunglasses—and somehow approachable (a misconcep-tion, in her opinion) with his adorable puppy.

He let the puppy race unleashed to greet her, then bounce like an overwound spring to the other dogs, back to her before he tore off in circles around the yard in a bid to get her dogs to play.

"Having a picnic?" Simon asked.

"Of sorts." She mimicked his oh-so-casual tone. "I have an advanced class on their way in from a practice search. Their first with a person. So we'll have a little celebration."

"With brownies."

"I like brownies."

"Who doesn't?"

Jaws demonstrated his opinion by trying to climb onto the picnic bench to steal a sample. Fiona simply put his front paws back on the ground. "Off!"

"Yeah, good luck with that. He's a freaking acrobat. Yester-day he managed to climb up on a stool and eat my sandwich—he likes pickles, apparently—in the five-point-two seconds my back was turned."

"Consistency." Fiona repeated the "Off!" command the second and third times Jaws attempted the snatch. "And dis-traction."

She walked back a few steps, called him. He ran to her as if they'd just been reunited after a war. He sat when she ordered him to, then preened under her praise and pets. "Positive reinforcement."

She dug a treat out of her pocket. "Good dog. He's coming along."

"Two days ago, he ate my flash drive. Just swallowed it whole like a vitamin pill."

"Uh-oh."

"Yeah, so I rush him to the vet—and she takes a look and decides it's small enough he doesn't need it surgically removed. I'm supposed to . . ." Jaw set, he scowled off into the distance. "I don't want to talk about that part, so we'll just say I eventually got it back."

"This, too, shall pass."

"Yeah, yeah." He picked up a brownie. "It still works. I haven't decided if that's amazing or disgusting." He took a bite. "Good brownie."

"Thanks. They're the only things I can bake with regular success." And since these had been a product of her two a.m. jitters, she'd had two for breakfast.

"What are you doing here, Simon?"

Some of her irritation must have come through as he gave her a long, silent look before answering. "I'm socializing my idiot dog. And you still owe me part of a lesson. Two for one. Three for one adding in the brownies."

"Your dog's handler could use some socialization."

He polished off the brownie, poured himself a glass of iced tea. "I'm probably past the training age."

"Despite the maxim, you actually can teach an old dog new tricks."

"Maybe." After downing the tea, he glanced around. "Shit. Where the hell is he?"

"He went in the tunnel."

"The what?"

She gestured to the line of drums. "Let's see what he does," she suggested, and began to stroll to the far end.

They were here, she thought, with the human helping himself to her celebratory snacks. She might as well work in the lesson.

"If he just comes back out where he went in, let it go for now. But if he goes on through, give him praise, and a treat." She handed Simon one.

"For going through a bunch of fifty-five-gallon drums?"

"Yes." Her tone took on a scolding edge. "It takes curiosity, courage and some agility to not only go in, but go through and come out again."

"And if he doesn't come out at all?"

"I guess you leave him there and go home and watch ESPN."

He studied the drums. "Some people would complain it's sexist to assume I watch ESPN. Maybe I'm a fan of Lifetime."

She gave up. "If he doesn't come out on his own, you call, coax, try to lure. Failing that, you go in after him."

"Great. Well, at least he can't get into trouble in there. So you set up the radio, the computer, all those maps and charts for a make-believe rescue?"

"Eventually it won't be make-believe. How's sit and stay going?"

"Fine, unless he wants to do something else. Consistency," he said before Fiona could. "I got the mantra, boss."

Jaws gave a yip, then zipped out of the drum.

"Hey, he did it. That's pretty good." Simon crouched, and, in Fiona's observation, didn't pet and praise by rote. He enjoyed his dog's success and excitement. When he laughed, gave the pup a good scratch with those long, artistic hands, she began to see why the dog found the man so appealing.

"He's intrepid." She hunkered down to add her approval to Simon's, and realized they both smelled of his wood shop. "If a client's interested in agility training, I'd start a puppy this age off with one drum, so he can see all the way through. Jaws just skipped a few grades on this one."

"Hear that? Intrepid eater of flash drives, wood chips and kosher pickles."

He grinned at Fiona, eye to eye. She saw fascinating flecks of bronze scattered on the tawny gold.

As the look held, one beat, then two, Simon gave a considering *Hmmm*.

"Forget it." She got to her feet. "Let's see his sit and stay. My class should be back any minute."

"You're still bent about the cabinet."

"What cabinet?" she asked with the sweetest of smiles.

"Uh-huh. Okay, sit and stay. Jaws, you're about to lose your head-of-the-class status."

"You know, a little optimism and confidence translate, to dogs and to people. Or maybe you just like anticipating failure."

"I consider it realism." When he ordered the pup to sit, Jaws plopped his butt down cooperatively. "He's got that one, mostly, but now it gets tricky. Stay." He held up a hand. "Stay," he repeated and began to back up.

The dog thumped his tail but stayed seated.

"He's doing well."

"Showing off for teacher. At home, odds are he'd be chasing his tail by now, or trying to chew on my boots while I'm wearing them." He called the dog, rewarded.

"Do it again. Increase the distance."

Simon took Jaws on the second round, stretching the space between them on the "Stay." Then, at Fiona's instructions, a third time until dog and man were a good twenty-five feet apart.

"Don't frown at the dog when he's doing what he's told."

"I'm not frowning."

"Let's call it your default expression. You're confusing him. Call him in."

Jaws responded and took the last couple of feet on his belly before rolling over to expose it.

"You did good, you did fine. Show-off," Simon muttered as he bent down to rub.

"He switched to submissive mode because he wasn't sure what you were after. You asked him for something, he gave it, and you stand there scowling at him. He gets an A." Fiona knelt down to stroke Jaws into delirium. "You get a C minus."

"Hey."

"My class is coming back. Hold him. Give him the stay

command and keep him still for a few seconds. Then you can give him the release, let him go greet."

"How?"

"Sit and stay—holding him as he's going to want to run and see who's coming." As she spoke she checked her watch for the log. "Then give him the go—use simple phrasing, something natural to you. Say hi, go ahead, greet. Whatever. Then let him loose."

She rose, walked away to meet the first of her returning students.

"You wanted me to look bad, didn't you? You think I'm not on to you?" Simon held the puppy in place while rubbing his ears. "Not as dumb as you look, are you? Just wanted to impress the pretty girl. Okay . . . check it out," he said, and let Jaws race over to sniff and dance around the returning students.

By the time he walked over, Fiona was listening to the handlers describe how their dogs had performed, noting down the area covered, the number of alerts.

Simon pulled the leash out of his pocket.

"Why don't you let him hang out, play with the others awhile," Fiona suggested. She glanced up from her log. "You want him to get used to being around people, other dogs, ones he hasn't met before. A little socialization wouldn't hurt you either. Have another brownie. Maybe you can end the day on a higher grade."

"I'll take the brownie, but—" He broke off as Sylvia limped out of the woods, leaning on a makeshift crutch, with a woman supporting her on one side and a man on the other while a pair of dogs pranced ahead.

"She's all right." Fiona laid a hand on his arm to stop him from crossing over to help. "Make-believe, remember? The exercise involved a lost woman with a minor injury. She plays it up."

The class broke into applause. Sylvia took an exaggerated bow, then gestured grandly to the woman and dog beside her.

"That's Tracie and her Lolo. They found Syl in just under seventy-five minutes. Not bad. Not bad at all. Mica's the one helping her out, with his Ringo. His positioning at the successful find was close enough for him to intersect with Tracie and assist in bringing Syl, with her fake sprained ankle, back to base. Besides, he's got a crush on her."

"On Syl? Like brownies, who doesn't?"

"Not on Syl." Though she shook her head, Fiona found herself amused and a little proud at Simon's comment. "On Tracie. They're both from the Bellingham area, like the rest of the unit. Excuse me."

She closed the distance to give Tracie a handshake, then a hug, to fuss over the dogs. To laugh with Sylvia, he noted.

She did have an appealing way, he supposed. If you liked the über-outgoing, the type who tended to touch or embrace in a kind of second nature, and looked good in jeans or work pants, sweatshirts or sweaters.

He couldn't think of a woman who fell into that subset ever attracting him before, not sexually in any case. The fact that she did presented an interesting puzzle.

Maybe it was her eyes. They were so clear, so calm. He suspected they were just one of the reasons animals responded to her. You felt you could trust those eyes.

He watched as she slung her arm around Tracie's shoulders—there was that just-have-to-touch, just-have-to-connect aspect of her—and led the woman over to . . . What would she call it? he wondered. Base? HQ? Anyway, it was a table under a pole tarp.

Debriefing, he assumed, noting down whatever data needed to be noted down. It struck him as a little over the top for an exercise. Then he remembered she'd found a little boy in the very big woods, in a cold rain.

Details mattered. Discipline and efficiency mattered.

In any case, the brownies were excellent, and the interlude gave him a chance to flirt with Sylvia.

"How are you coping after your ordeal?" he asked her.

Sylvia laughed, poked him in the chest. "I love when I get to play the lost woman. I get some exercise—wandering around, then either plopping in my spot or wandering some more. It depends on which victim behavior Fee wants to replicate. It's handy you came by. I was going to call you when I got home today."

"Yeah? To ask me on a date?"

"You're so cute. I sold two of your pieces yesterday. The high-sided bench and the five-drawer chest. I'll take more whenever you can get it to me."

"I finished a couple of things this morning actually. A wine cabinet and a rocker."

"Ah, the famous wine cabinet."

He shrugged, glanced back at Fiona. "It's not her style, that's all."

Sylvia smiled and nibbled on a strawberry. "She has a lot of styles. You should ask her out to dinner."

"Why?"

"Simon, if I thought that was a serious question, I'd be worried about you."

She hooked her arm through his as Fiona addressed her class.

"Everyone did a solid job today, as individuals, as teams and as a unit. Next class we'll be working a different terrain with an unconscious victim. I want you to work your dogs thirty to sixty minutes, mixing in short ten-minute problems. Let's keep using someone your dog is familiar with. After the next class, you can try someone he or she doesn't know. Please don't skimp on your first-aid training, and let's try some of those exercises compass only. Keep your logs up-to-date. Any problems, any questions before next time, shoot me an e-mail or give me a call.

"And please, God, finish off those brownies so I don't."

Sylvia gave Simon a kiss on the cheek. "I've got to run. Check on my shop and my Oreo. You can bring the new pieces in whenever you want. And take my girl out to dinner."

He lingered out of curiosity, and because his dog had finally played himself out and was passed out under the table.

"He's had enough for today," Fiona commented when they were alone. She began to gather dishes.

"Question." He picked up empty glasses and followed her toward the house. "Those people take your class."

"Obviously."

"This was what, like two hours?"

"A little more. This is an advanced stage, and a mock Search and Rescue, so it was set up, search, debrief—add the pat on the back."

"And between that they've got to work with the dogs an hour here, an hour there, study first aid—"

"Yes. One of them's an EMT, and they'll all need to be certified in CPR, and basic field treatments. They'll also have to know how to read a topographical map, have a good working knowledge of climate, wind, foliage, wildlife. Both they and their dogs have to be in good physical shape."

She set the dishes on the counter in the kitchen.

"So when do any of them have time for an actual life?"

She leaned back. "They have lives, jobs, families. They also have dedication. Becoming a Search and Rescue team takes months of hard, focused training. It means sacrifice and it brings enormous satisfaction. I've been working with this unit for weeks," she added. "They have an almost ninety percent success rate on individual problems. Now we're working simultaneously. We'll be repeating this sort of training exercise over and over, in all weather situations."

"Have you ever kicked anybody out?"

"Yes. As a last resort, but yes. Most of the time someone who isn't suited drops out before I have to. Are you interested?"

"I don't think so."

"Well, it might cut into your Lifetime addiction. Still, I wouldn't mind giving Jaws some of the early training. It'll help him be well rounded, if nothing else. Once he heels, sits and stays, masters recall and drop on recall, we can give him a little more."

"More than the obedience deal?" Simon studied her, dubious. "What's it cost?"

She angled her head. "I might be open to the barter system on this one. Say, working on additional training and specialized skills for . . . a wine cabinet."

"It doesn't suit you."

Narrow-eyed, she pushed off the counter. "You know, every time you say that it just makes me want it more. I ought to know what suits me."

"You're just being stubborn."

"I am?" She pointed the index fingers of both hands at him. "You're the hardhead here. What do you care who buys the cabinet? Aren't you building to sell?"

"What do you care if a dog's crap at training? Don't you teach to get paid?"

"It's not the same thing. Plus it's usually the handler that's crap. Case in point, Mr. C Minus."

"I wasn't frowning."

"Hold that. Don't move, don't change expression. I'm going to get a mirror."

He grabbed her arm but didn't quite swallow the laugh. "Cut it out."

"Next class I'll make sure I have a camera. A picture's worth a thousand, after all." She gave him a little shove.

He gave her a little nudge.

And behind him the dog growled low in his throat.

"Stop!" Fiona ordered sharply, and the dog froze. "Newman, friend. Friend. He thought you were hurting me. No, don't back off. Simon," she said to the dogs. "We're playing. Simon's a friend. Put your arms around me."

"What?"

"Oh, for God's sake, don't be so dainty." She put her arms around Simon, hugged, laid her head on his shoulder. "Playing with Simon," Fiona said to the dog, and smiled. She gestured so the dog walked to them, rubbed against Simon's leg. "He wouldn't have bitten you."

"Good to know."

"Unless I told him to." She tipped her head back, smiled again. Then gave Simon another gentle shove. "Push back. It's okay."

"It better be." He nudged her again, and this time the dog used his head to nudge Simon.

"Fun." She wrapped her arms around Simon again, nuzzled. "He reads me," she said. "If I was afraid now, he'd know it. But he sees, hears, senses I'm fine, I'm good with you. That's what I'm trying to get through your head about Jaws and your reactions, what you transmit. Your mood influences his behavior, so—"

She broke off when she looked up again into eyes that were very close, and very focused.

"What mood do you think I'm transmitting now?"

"Funny. It's just an exercise," she began.

"Okay. Let's try advanced class."

He closed his mouth over hers, very firm and just a little rough.

She'd known he'd be just a little rough. Impatient, direct, with no testing moves, no easy flirtation.

She didn't resist. It would be a waste of time, effort and a very hot and healthy kiss. Instead she slid her hands up his back, let herself drop into it, let herself enjoy the warring sensations of the moment.

Soft lips, hard hands, firm body—and just a hint of chocolate on the tongue that tangled with hers.

And when she felt herself dropping close to the point of no return, when climbing back would be painful, she worked her hand between them and pushed against his chest.

He didn't stop. Her heart went from flutter to pound. Intractable, she thought, and wished she didn't find that quality in him quite so exciting.

She pushed again, harder.

He eased back, just a little, so their eyes met again. "Grade that."

"Oh, you definitely aced it. Congratulations. But playtime's over. I have some lesson planning and . . . things to get done. So . . ."

"So, I'll see you."

"Yes. Ah, keep working on the basics. Throw sticks. Lots of sticks."

"Right."

When he walked out, she blew out a breath, looked at Newman. "Wow."

His own fault, Simon thought as he loaded Jaws into the

car. Or hers, he decided. It was really more her fault. Wrapping around him, rubbing in, smiling up.

What the hell was a man supposed to do?

He hadn't expected her to be so receptive. To just give, to just open until that subtle, almost quiet sexy peeled back a corner and showed him all the heat beneath.

Now he wanted it. And her.

He glanced at the dog, currently in bliss with his nose stuck out the two-inch opening of the window.

"I should've just sold her the damn cabinet."

He flipped the radio up to blast, but it didn't swing his mind away from Fiona.

He decided to try his own "exercise," and began to design a wine cabinet suited to her, in his head.

Maybe he'd build it; maybe he wouldn't. But it was a damn sure bet he'd end up going back to peel up another corner.

SEVEN

A trip to the vet invariably included comedy and drama, and required persistence, stamina and a flexible sense of humor. To simplify, Fiona always scheduled her three dogs together at the end of office hours.

The system also gave her and the vet, her friend Mai Funaki, a chance to recover and unwind after the triple deed was done.

At a scant five-two, Mai appeared to be a delicate lotus blossom, a romantic anime character brought to life with ebony hair curved at her gilded cheeks and fringing flirtatiously above exotic onyx eyes. Her voice, a melodious song, calmed both animals and humans in the course of her work.

Her pretty, long-fingered hands soothed and healed. And were as strong as a bricklayer's.

She'd been known to drink a two-hundred-pound man under the table, and could swear the air blue in five languages.

Fiona adored her.

In the exam room of her offices in her home just outside Eastsound, Mai helped Fiona heft seventy-five pounds of trembling Peck onto the table. The dog, who had once courageously negotiated smoldering rubble to locate victims after an earthquake in Oregon, who tirelessly searched for the lost, the fallen and the dead through bitter winds, flooding rain and scorching heat, feared the needle.

"You'd think I hammered spikes into his brain. Come on now, Peck." Mai stroked, even as she checked joints and fur and skin. "Man up."

Peck kept his head turned away, refusing to look at her. Instead he stared accusingly into Fiona's eyes. She swore she could see tears forming.

"I think he was tortured by the Spanish Inquisition in another life."

While Mai examined his ears, Peck visibly shuddered.

"At least he suffers in silence." Mai turned Peck's head toward her. He turned it away again. "I've got this Chihuahua I have to muzzle for any exam. He'd eat my face off if he could."

She took the dog's head firmly to examine his eyes, his teeth.

"Big healthy boy," she crooned. "Big handsome boy."

Peck stared at a spot over her shoulder and shivered.

"Okay," Mai said to Fiona. "You know the drill."

Fiona took Peck's head in her hands. "It's only going to take a second," she told him as Mai moved behind and out of eye line. "We can't have you getting sick, right?"

She talked, rubbed, smiled, as Mai pinched some skin and slid the needle in.

Peck moaned like a dying man.

"There. All done." Mai walked back to Peck's head, held up her hands to show them empty of all tools of torture. Then she laid a treat on the table.

He refused it.

"Could be poisoned," Fiona pointed out. "Anything in this room is suspect." She signaled the dog down, and he couldn't jump off the table fast enough. Then he stood, facing the wall, ignoring both women.

"It's because I cut off his balls. He's never forgiven me."

"No, I really think it all comes down from Newman. He fears, so they all fear. Anyway, two down, one to go."

The women stared at each other. "We should've taken him first. The worst first. But I just couldn't face it."

"I bought a really nice bottle of Pinot."

"Okay. Let's do this thing."

They released Peck into the yard where he could exchange horrors with Bogart and seek sympathy with Mai's one-eyed bulldog, Patch, and her three-legged beagle-hound mix, Chauncy.

Together they approached Fiona's car where Newman lay on the backseat, nose pressed tight in the corner, body limp as overcooked pasta.

"Heads or tails?" Fiona asked.

"You take the head. God help us."

He squirmed, tried to roll into a ball, leaped over the seats, then back again. He slithered like a snake in an attempt to wedge himself under the seat.

Then, unable to escape, went limp again, forcing the two women to carry his dead dog weight into the examining room.

"Fuck *me*, Fee. Couldn't you raise Poms?"

"He could be a face-eating Chihuahua."

"Please tell me you got his weight at home because there's no way we're getting him on the scale."

"Eighty-two."

It took a solid and sweaty thirty minutes as Newman resisted every second.

"You know," Fiona panted, using her own body to hold Newman's down, "this dog would walk through fire for me. Through fire over broken glass while meteors rained out of the sky. But I can't get him to just hold the hell still for a routine exam. And he *knew*. The minute I called them to get in the car, he knew. How many times do I put them in the car for work, for play, for whatever? How does he *know*? I had to get the others in first—they're more easily fooled. Then drag him. It's humiliating," she said to Newman. "For both of us."

"Thank all the gods, we're done."

Mai didn't bother to offer the treat as Newman would very likely spit it in her face. "Cut him loose, and let's open that wine."

Mai's pretty bungalow sat with its back to the sea. Once it had been part of a farm, then the house had morphed into a B&B. When Mai and her husband moved to Orcas, he'd wanted to farm.

Mai moved her Tacoma practice to the island, pleased to work at home, content with the slower lifestyle while her husband raised chickens, goats, berries and field greens.

It took less than four years for the bloom to wear off on the gentleman farmer, whose next brainstorm had been buying a bar and grill in Jamaica.

"Tim's moving to Maine," Mai said as they carried the wine out to the yard. "He's going to be a lobsterman."

"Not kidding?"

"Not. I have to say, he lasted longer than I expected with the bar." Even as they sat, dogs hurried over to vie for attention. Tails wagged, tongues licked. "Sure, *now* we're pals."

Mai passed out the biscuits she'd brought with her.

"They love you—and the treats aren't poison except in the exam room."

"Yeah, all's forgiven. I'm sorry I couldn't run the base for the search on the little boy. I had that emergency surgery, and I just couldn't postpone it."

"It's no problem. That's why we have alternates. They're a nice family. The kid's a champ."

"Yeah?" Mai sighed. "You know, it's probably—certainly—best that Tim and I put off having kids. Can you imagine? But my clock's ticking double time. I know I'm going to end up adopting another dog or cat or other mammal to compensate."

"You could adopt an actual human child. You'd be a great mom."

"I would. But . . . I still have a tiny crack of a sliver of hope that I could start a family with a man, give the kid the full complement of parents. Which means I have to actually date, and have sex. And when I think of men, dating and sex, I remember how horny I am. I'm considering naming my vibrator Stanley."

"Stanley?"

"Stanley is kind, and thinks only of my pleasure. I'm still winning our dry spell contest, I assume. Fourteen months."

"Nine, but I don't think that one time really counts. It was lousy sex."

"Lousy sex is still sex. It may be a crap contest to win, but there are rules. And while there will always be Stanley, I'm seriously considering other options."

"Girls? Club trolling? Personal ads?"

"All weighed and rejected. Don't laugh."

"Okay. What?"

"I've been checking out the Internet dating sites. I even have a profile and application ready to go. I just haven't hit *send*. Yet."

"I'm not laughing, but I'm not convinced. You're gorgeous, smart, funny, interesting, a woman with a wide range of interests. If you're serious about getting back into the dating arena, you need to put yourself out there more."

Nodding, Mai took a long sip of wine, then leaned forward. "Fee, you may not have noticed, but we live on a small island off the coast of Washington state."

"I've heard rumors."

"The population of this small island is also relatively small. The single-male element of that population, considerably smaller. Why else are two gorgeous, smart and sexy women sitting here on a pretty evening drinking wine with dogs?"

"Because we like to?"

"We do. Yes, we do. But we also like the company of men. At least I think we do as it's been some time. And I believe I'm correct in saying we both enjoy good, healthy, safe sex."

"This is correct, which is why I really think that one time shouldn't count in the contest."

"Old business." Mai flicked it away. "I've made a considerable if unscientific study of that single-male element of our island population. For my own purposes, I have to eliminate males under the age of twenty-one and over the age of sixty-five. Both boundaries are a stretch as I'm thirty-four, but beggars, choosers. The pool's shallow, Fee. It's pretty freaking shallow."

"I can't argue with that. But if you add in tourists and seasonals, it's a little deeper."

"I do have some small hope for summer, but meanwhile? I took a hard look at James."

"James? *Our* James."

"Yes, our James. Mutual interests, age appropriate. Low spark, admittedly, but you work with what you've got. The trouble is he's got his eye on Lori, and there's no poaching within the unit. There is one intriguing possibility on island. Single, age appropriate, dog owner, very attractive. Creative type. A little taciturn for my taste, but there's that beggars, choosers again."

"Oh," Fiona said, and took a drink.

"Simon Doyle. Sylvia carries his work. Wood artist, furniture."

"Mmm," Fiona said this time, and took another drink.

Mai's eyes narrowed. "You're looking at him? Damn it, he might be all that's standing between me and HeartLine-dot-com."

"I'm not looking. Not exactly. He's a client. I'm working with his dog."

"Cute dog."

"Very. Hot guy."

"Very. Look, if you're going to call dibs, call it, because I have plans to make. I have a serious need to get laid."

"I'm not calling dibs on a man. Jesus, Mai. He's really not the kind of guy you tend toward."

"Shit," Mai said, and took a slug of wine. "He's alive, single, within the age boundaries and, as far as I know, not a serial killer."

"He kissed me."

"Two scoops of shit. Okay, give me a minute to hate you." Mai drummed her fingers on the table. "All right, hate time's done. Sexy kiss or friendly kiss?"

"It wasn't friendly. He's not especially friendly. I don't think he likes people that much. He stopped by so I could work with Jaws. I was running the mock search with the Bellingham unit. So I invited him to stay, mix, have some brownies. I doubt he said five words to anybody. Except for Syl. He likes Syl."

"Maybe he's shy. Shy can be sweet."

"I don't think so, and sweet's not a word I'd use in the same sentence with Simon. He's an exceptional kisser, and that's a plus."

"Bitch, don't make me hurt you."

Fiona grinned. "And I don't need a relationship, but I do require some basic conversation when I sleep with a guy."

"You had conversation with the one-time guy nine months ago. Look where that got you."

"That's true." Fiona was forced to sigh in remembrance. "But I'm not calling dibs. If the opportunity presents, help yourself."

"No, it's too late. He's out of the running. HeartLine-dot-com, here I come."

"We need to go on vacation."

Mai choked out a laugh. "Yeah, sure."

"No, I mean it. You, me, Syl. A girl trip, a girl thing. A spa," she decided, inspired. "A long girl spa weekend."

"Don't toy with me, Fiona. I'm a woman on the edge."

"Which is why we need a break."

"Question?" Mai held up a finger. "When's the last time you took a vacation—even a long weekend type vacation?"

"A couple years maybe. Okay, probably three. Which just cements the point."

"And with your work, mine, Syl's, the responsibility for the animals, just how do we manage it?"

"We'll figure it out. We know how to plan things, how to organize." Now that the idea popped out, Fiona wanted it like Christmas. "Massages and facials and mud baths, room service and sparkly adult beverages. No work, responsibility or schedules."

"It may be better than sex."

"It's possible. What we'll do is check our schedules and find the best time to clear three days. We can clear three days, Mai. We all have friends who'll take care of our animals for that length of time. How often have we done it for them?"

"Countless times. Where?"

"I don't know. Close so we don't spend too much time on travel. I'll start researching, and I'll get Syl on board. What do you say?"

Mai raised her glass. "I am so in."

Determined to seal the deal, Fiona swung by Sylvia's before heading home.

Pansies spilled out of tubs in front of the tranquil bayside house. Fiona knew the greenhouse would be crowded with flowers and vegetables and herbs her stepmother babied like children, and would soon tranfer to her extensive gardens.

As much at home there as in her own cabin, Fiona opened the bright red door and called out, "Syl?"

"Back here!" Sylvia called out as Oreo raced to say hello. "In the great room."

"I was just at Mai's." Fiona wound her way through the house where Sylvia had lived with Fiona's father throughout their marriage. Like her shop, it was a bright, fascinating, eclectic mix of styles and art and color.

She found Sylvia on her yoga mat mimicking the twisting pose of the instructor on the TV. "Just winding down from the day," Sylvia told her. "Nearly done. Did you bring the boys?"

"They're in the car. I can't stay."

"Oh, why don't you? I'm thinking of making couscous."

"Tempting." Not in the least, Fiona thought. "But I've got a project. Mai's horny and her biological clock's ticking. She's thinking of trying one of those online dating services."

"Really?" Sylvia untwisted, then twisted in the other direction. "Which one?"

"I think she said HeartLine-dot-com."

"They're supposed to be pretty good."

"I don't . . . Have you used that kind of thing?"

"Not yet. Maybe never. But I've looked around." Sylvia lowered to the floor, folded.

"Oh. Huh. Well, anyway, what do you say the three of us take a long weekend and go to a spa?"

"Gosh, let me think." Sylvia unfolded. "It'll take me five minutes to pack."

"Really?"

"I can do it in four if pressed. Where are we going?"

"I don't know yet. It's part of the project. I need to check the schedule, refine it with yours and Mai's and find us a destination."

"I've got that. One of my artists has a connection at a spa. Supposed to be fabulous. It's near Snoqualmie Falls."

"Seriously?"

"Mmm-hmm." Sylvia lay back in corpse. "Tranquillity Spa and Resort. I'll take care of it—but you might want to check out the website to make sure it's what you have in mind."

"Do they have massages, room service and a pool?"

"I can pretty much guarantee that."

"It's perfect." She did a quick dance in place. "God, this is going to be great."

"Can't miss. But what brought this on?"

"I told you. Mai's hormones."

"And?"

Fiona walked to the window to look at the water. "I really haven't been sleeping all that well since Davey told me about the murders. It's just . . . there. On my mind. Keeping busy tamps it down, then when I'm not, it's just there. A break would be good, I think. And a break with two of my favorite women, the best. Plus I'm feeling conflicted about Simon since he kissed me."

"What?" Sylvia's eyes popped open as she sat up. "You tried to sneak that by me. When did he kiss you?"

"The other day, after you and the others left. It was just an impulse of the moment, and the circumstances. And yes, before you ask, it was very, very good."

"I suspected it would be. What happened next?"

"He went home."

"Why?"

"Probably because I told him to."

"Oh, Fee, I worry about you. I do." Shaking her head, Sylvia rose, reached for her bottle of water.

"I wasn't ready for the kiss, much less any follow-through."

Sylvia sighed. "See? No wonder I worry about you. Not being ready is part of the thrill. Or should be. The unexpected and the passionate."

"I don't think unexpected works for me. At least not right now. Who knows, maybe it will after a spa break."

"Clear your schedule and we're gone. I can work mine around yours and Mai's."

"You're the best." Fiona gave her a quick hug. "I'm going to see what classes I can juggle. I'll e-mail you and Mai."

"Wait. I'm going to get you some of this tea. It's all natural, and it should help relax you, help you sleep. I want you to take a long bath, drink some tea, put on some quiet music. And give those meditation exercises I showed you a chance," she added as she got the tin out of a cupboard in the adjoining kitchen.

"Okay. Promise. I'm already relaxed just thinking about the spa." She moved in for another hug. "I love you."

"I love you back."

She should have thought of it before, Fiona realized. An indulgent break with good friends was the perfect prescription for restlessness and stress. Then again she rarely felt the need for a break as she considered her life on the island the best of all possible worlds.

She had independence, reasonable financial security, a home and work she loved, the companionship of her dogs. What else was there?

She remembered the hot, unexpected kiss in her kitchen and Simon's rough, proprietary hands on her.

There was that, she admitted. At least now and again there was that. She was, after all, a healthy woman with normal needs and appetites.

And she could admit she'd considered the possibility of a round or two with Simon—before he'd shut *that* down in no uncertain terms. Before he'd opened it up again. Blew the lid off it again, she corrected.

Which only served to prove any sort of relationship with him promised to be complicated and frustrating and uncertain.

"Probably best to leave it alone," she said to the dogs. "Really, why ask for trouble? We're good, right? We're good just as we are. You and me, boys," she added and had tails thumping.

Her headlights slashed through the dark as she turned onto her drive—and reminded her she'd forgotten to leave the porch light on again. In a few weeks, the sun would stay longer and the air would warm. Long evening walks and playtime in the yard, porch sitting.

The approach had the dogs shifting and tails swishing in excitement. The trauma of the exam room was forgotten in the simple pleasure of coming home.

She parked, got out to open the back. "Make your rounds, boys." She hurried inside to hit the lights before making her own. She checked water bowls and the feeder, got a smile from her new planters.

While the dogs circled outside, stretched their legs, emptied their bladders, she opened the freezer and grabbed the first frozen dinner that came to hand.

While it buzzed up she started checking her phone messages. She'd set up her laptop, she decided, go over the schedule while she ate, find the best hole, check out the website Sylvia had recommended.

"Get the party started," she murmured.

She took notes on her pad, saving or deleting messages as necessary.

"Ms. Bristow, this is Kati Starr. I'm a reporter with *U.S. Report*. I'm writing a story on the recent abduction murders of two women in California that seem to parallel those committed by George Allen Perry. As you were the only known victim to escape Perry, I'd like to speak with you. You can reach me at work, on my cell or via e-mail. My contacts are—"

Fiona hit *delete*. "No way in hell."

No reporters, no interviews, no TV cameras or mikes pushed at her. Not again.

Even as she took a breath the next message came on.

"Ms. Bristow, this is Kati Starr with *U.S. Report* following up on my earlier call. I'm approaching deadline, and it's very important that I speak with you as soon as—"

Fiona hit *delete* again.

"Screw you and your deadline," she murmured.

She let the dogs in, comforted by their presence. Dinner, such as it was, didn't hold much appeal, but she ordered herself to sit down, to eat, to do exactly what she'd planned to do with her evening before the reporter flooded her mind with memories and worries.

She booted up her laptop, poked at chicken potpie. To boost her mood, she checked the resort's website first—and in moments was cruising on anticipatory bliss.

Hot stone massages, paraffin wraps, champagne and caviar facials. She wanted them all. She wanted them now.

She took the virtual tour, purring over the indoor pool, the post-treatment meditation rooms, the shops, the gardens, the lovely appointments in the guest rooms. That included, she thought, a two-story, three-bedroom "villa."

She closed one eye, glanced at the cost. Winced.

But split three ways . . . it would still sting like hellfire.

But it had its own hot tub, and, oh God, fireplaces in the bathrooms.

In. The. Bathrooms.

And the views of the waterfall, the hills, the gardens . . .

Impossible, she reminded herself. Maybe when she won the lottery.

"It's a nice dream," she told the dogs. "So, now we know where. Let's figure out when."

She brought up her class schedule, calculated, tried some juggling, recalculated, shifted.

Once she'd settled on the two best possibilities, she e-mailed Sylvia and Mai.

"We'll make it work," she decided, and shifted over to check her incoming e-mail.

She found one from the reporter.

Ms. Bristow:

I haven't been able to reach you by phone. I found this contact on the website for your canine training service. As I explained, I'm writing a story on the California abduction-murders which echo the Perry homicides. As you were a key witness for the prosecution in the Perry trial that resulted in his conviction, your comments would be very valuable.

I can't write a salient or accurate story on the Perry angle without including your experiences, and the details of the murder of Gregory Norwood, which resulted in Perry's capture. I would prefer to speak with you directly before the story goes to press.

Fiona deleted the e-mail, including the list of contacts. Then simply laid her head down on the table.

She was entitled to say no. Entitled to turn her back on that horrible time. She was entitled to refuse to be fodder for yet another story on death and loss.

Reliving all that wouldn't, couldn't bring Greg back. It wouldn't help those two women or their grieving families.

She'd started her life over, and she was damn well entitled to her privacy.

She pushed herself up, shut down the laptop.

"I'm going to take that long bath, drink that stupid tea. And you know what? We're going to book that damn villa. Life's too damn short."

EIGHT

Though her puppy classes invariably kept Fiona's mood up, tension lingered, an endless echo of memories and loss.

Kati Starr, persistent if nothing else, called shortly after eight a.m.

One glance at the caller ID had Fiona letting the machine take it. She deleted it without listening, but the call itself lodged in the back of her neck like a brick.

She reminded herself her clients deserved her full attention.

Simon was late. Of course. He pulled in while the rest of the class ran through the basics.

"Just pick it up where we are," she said coolly. "If we're not interfering too much with your busy schedule."

She moved away to work with each of her students individually, demonstrating how to discourage the exuberant Great Dane pup, who promised to be massive, from jumping up—and the perky schnauzer to stop crotch sniffing.

When they began to work off leash, she sighed as Jaws raced away to chase a squirrel—and led a stampede.

"Don't chase them!" Fiona pushed a hand through her hair as Jaws did his level best to climb the tree the squirrel skittered up. "Call them back. Use your return command, then order your dog to sit. I want all the dogs back to their handlers and sitting."

What she wanted took time and persistence—and some hands-on.

She reviewed sit and stay, individually and as a group, careful to keep her tone detached whenever she had to address Simon.

With leashes on, she worked on the stop and drop.

The class that usually amused and warmed her had a headache carving dully just above the brick at the base of her neck.

"Keep up the good work." She ordered up a smile. "And remember: positive reinforcement, practice and play."

As always, there were comments, questions, a story or two that had to be shared with her by one of the clients. Fiona listened, answered, stroked and petted. But felt none of her usual pleasure.

When Simon lingered, letting Jaws off leash to run with her dogs, Fiona decided it was fine. She'd deal with him, and eliminate a minor problem on her list.

"You've got a bug up your ass today," he said before she could speak.

"Excuse me?"

"You heard me. And you look like hell."

"You have to stop throwing all these pearls at my feet."

"Did that guy in California kill someone else?"

"I don't know. Why would I know? It has nothing to do with me." She jammed her hands into the pockets of her hooded jacket. "I'm sorry for the women, for their families, but it has nothing to do with me."

"Who's arguing? You weren't listening, not really, when Larry started on about how his supermutt figured out how to open doors or when Diane showed you the picture of her toddler drawing with crayons on the bulldog. I'd say that's your version of having a bitch on. So, what's the deal?"

"Listen, Simon, just because I kissed you, sort of—"

"Sort of?"

She set her teeth. "That doesn't mean I'm obliged to share

the details of my life with you, or explain the reasons for my moods."

"I'm still stuck on 'sort of,' and wondering what would be actually."

"You'll have to keep wondering. We're neighbors and you're currently a client. That's it."

"A definite bitch on. Well, enjoy." He whistled for his dog, which naturally brought the whole pack.

When Simon bent down, ruffled and praised, Fiona sighed again. "He's doing well on the return. He doesn't get stay yet, but he's doing well in most areas."

"He hasn't eaten anything I needed to worry about in the last couple days." He clipped on the leash. "See you."

He got halfway to the car when she called his name.

She hadn't planned to, couldn't think why she had. And yet . . .

"Do you want to take a walk? I need to walk."

"A walk? Where?"

She gestured. "One of the perks of living in the woods is being able to walk in them."

He shrugged, crossed back to her.

"You'd better leash him," she said. "Until you're confident he'll obey the stop command. He might take off after a rabbit or deer and get lost. Come on, boys, take a walk."

Her dogs fell in happily, then ranged ahead. Jaws pulled on the leash.

"Wait," Fiona ordered, sympathizing. The dogs paused, continuing at a slower pace at her signal when Jaws caught up.

"He thinks he's one of the big guys. It's good for him to get out like this, explore new territories, respect the leash, respond to you."

"Is this another lesson?"

"Just making conversation."

"Do you ever talk about anything other than dogs?"

"Yes." Irritated, she hunched her shoulders, lapsed into momentary silence. "I can't think of anything right now. God, I wish spring would hurry up. There, that's other than. I can bitch about the weather. But it's a nice day, so it's hard to. Still,

I wish it would get warmer faster, and I want the sun to stay out till ten. I want to plant a garden and chase the deer and rabbits out of it."

"Why don't you just put up a fence?"

"Then I don't have the entertainment value of chasing the deer and rabbits, do I? They're not afraid of the dogs, which is my own fault because I trained the boys not to chase—oops. Dog talk. I love the way it smells in here."

She took a deep breath of pine, grateful the headache had backed off a bit. "I love the way it looks—the lights, the shadows. I thought I'd be a photographer, because I like light and shadows, and people's faces and the way they move. But I don't take very good, or interesting, pictures. Then I thought I'd be a writer, but I bored myself so I suspect I'd have flopped at that one. Except I like to write—for the blog or the newsletter, or little articles about, you know, the thing I'm not talking about in this conversation. Then I thought I could coach track or be a trainer but . . . I didn't really have a center, I guess. I'm not sure you're required to have a center when you're twenty. Why don't you say something?"

"Mostly because you haven't shut up."

She blew out a breath. "That's true. I'm babbling useless conversation because I don't want to think. And I realize I asked you to come so I wouldn't think or start brooding. I don't have a bitch on. I have a brood on, and it's entirely different."

"Comes off the same to me."

"You're a hardass, Simon. That shouldn't be appealing to me."

They moved through a clearing where the trees soared overhead, beefy giants that sighed like the surf where their tops met sky.

"Why Orcas?" she asked him. "Of all the places to live."

"It's quiet. I like being near the water. Hold this." He shoved the leash into her hand and walked over to a large, twisted stump, heaved half out of the needle-strewn ground.

While she watched, he circled it, crouched, knocked on it.

"Is this your property?"

"Yeah. We haven't walked that far."

"I want this." His eyes, the color of old gold in the luminous streams and dapples of light, shifted briefly to hers. "Can I have this?"

"You want . . . the stump?"

"Yes. I'll pay for it if you want to be greedy."

"How much? I'm going on a spa vacation." She walked closer trying to see what he saw.

"Pee somewhere else." He gave Jaws a nudge as the pup prepared to squat. "Ten bucks."

She *pff*d.

"It's just sitting here. You're not using it, and I'm going to have to yank it out and haul it off. Twenty, but that's it."

"Replace it. Plant a tree in the hole and we're good."

"Done."

"What'll you do with it?"

"Something."

She studied it, circled it as he had, but still only saw the twisted remains of a tree broken off in some long-ago storm. "I wish I could see like that. I wish I could look at a tree stump and see something creative."

He glanced up again. "You looked at that dog and saw something."

She smiled. "I think that was an actual nice thing to say. Now I guess I have to be sorry for being mean to you."

"You have a strange scale, Fiona. 'Sort of' kissed me when you were locked on like a clamp. Being mean when you told me to mind my own business."

"I yelled at you in my head."

"Oh, well, now I'm crushed."

"I can be mean. Harsh and mean, and I can be okay with it. But it has to be justified. You just asked what was wrong. You can come back and get the stump anytime."

"Next couple of days." He straightened, glanced around to orient himself. Then he looked at her. "You might as well spill it."

"Let's keep walking." She held the leash, bringing Jaws to heel, letting him range, bringing him back while they wound through the trees, skirted the curve of a quiet creek.

"This reporter's hounding me," she began. "Calling, e-mailing. I haven't talked to her—just deleted all the messages."

"What does she want?"

"To talk to me about Perry—in connection with the two women in California. She's writing a story on it. That's her job; I get that. But it's not mine to talk to her, to feed that fire. The only victim who escaped—that's how she put it. I'm not a victim, and it just pisses me off to be called one. I had enough of that when it all happened."

"Then keep deleting."

"Sounds simple—and I will—but it's not simple."

The headache was gone, she realized, but the anger and frustration that had caused it remained lodged like splinters.

Small, sharp and nasty.

"When it happened, the prosecution and the cops kept me away from the press as much as possible. They didn't want me giving interviews—and God knows, I didn't want to give them. But a story like that? It's got juice, right? They kept calling, or talking to people who knew me—people who knew people who knew me. Squeezing the juice." She paused, glanced at him again. "I guess you'd understand that, from your relationship with Nina Abbott."

"Relationship's a pretty word for it."

"And now you like quiet islands."

"One doesn't have much of a connection with the other. And this isn't my brood."

None of her business, she thought. Well, he had a point. "All right. After Greg, it started up again. Then the trial. I don't want any part of what's happening now. So I'm angry all over again, and that makes me feel sick inside. Because twelve before me, and Greg after me, died. And I didn't. I barely had a scratch, but they say I'm a victim or they say I'm a heroine. Neither's true."

"No, neither's true. You're a survivor, and that's harder."

She stopped, stared at him. "Why do you get it? That's the mystery."

"It's all over you. It's in your eyes. So calm, so clear. Maybe because they've already seen so much. You've got wounds. You live with them. That shouldn't be appealing to me."

She might have smiled at the way he tossed her own words back at her, but they made her stomach flutter. "What have we got here, Simon?"

"Probably just some heat."

"Probably. I haven't had sex in almost ten months."

"Okay, it's getting hotter."

Now she laughed. "God, you've actually made me feel better. But what I meant was I haven't had sex in ten months, so waiting longer isn't such a big deal. We both live on island— have a connection with Sylvia. I like your dog, and right now I'm part of his team. I think I need to figure out if sleeping with you would just be a nice release, or cause too many complications."

"It wouldn't be nice. Nice is cookies and milk."

"Confident. I do like confidence. Since I'm not going to have sex with you in the woods, especially since we've only got about twenty minutes before the sun sets, I think we're safe. So why don't you give me a little preview of possible coming attractions?"

He reached behind her, wrapped her hair around his fist. "You like living on the edge?"

"No, I really don't. I like stability and order, so this is unusual for me."

He gave her hair a tug, enough to lift her face, to bring his mouth within a breath of hers. "You're looking for nice."

"I'm not really looking at all."

"Me either," he said, and closed the distance.

She'd asked for it, and thought herself prepared. She'd expected the fast strike, that immediate explosion of heat and lust and want that flashed through the brain and body.

Instead, he came in easy, disarming her with a slow kiss, the sort that shimmered through the system just before it fogged the brain. She sighed into it, lifting her arms to link them around his neck as he tempted her to offer more.

As she did, he pulled her deeper, gradually building that

heat they both acknowledged, degree by degree, so when the strike came, she was defenseless.

The world snapped off—the woods, the sky, the deepening shadows. All that was left was the wonder of mouth against mouth, body against body, and the floodwall of need rising in her.

Even as he started to pull back, she dragged him back and dived again, dived deep.

She frayed his control. That combination of yielding and demand tore at his resolve to set both tone and pace. She reached inside him somehow, opening doors he'd determined to keep locked until he was no longer sure who led the way.

And when he intended to step back, regain some distance, she lured him back.

Soft lips, lithe body and a scent that was somehow both earthy and sweet. Like her taste—neither one thing nor the other, and utterly irresistible.

He lost more ground than he gained before the pup began to bark—wild joy—and scrabble at his legs in an attempt to nudge through and join the fun.

This time they stepped back together.

Fiona laid a hand on Jaws's head. "Sit," she ordered. "Good dog."

Not so calm now, Simon thought as he looked at her eyes. Not so clear.

"I can't think of a single sensible thing to say," she told him. She signaled for her dogs, then handed Simon the pup's leash. "We should start back. Um, he's doing better on the leash. This is new territory for him, and there are a lot of fun distractions, but he's responding pretty well."

Back in her safe zone, he thought, with dog talk. Curious how she'd handle it, he simply walked along in silence.

"I'd like to work with him a little on some other skills and behaviors. Maybe an extra half hour in ten- or fifteen-minute sessions a week. A couple of weeks, no charge. Then if you like the way it's going, we can discuss a fee."

"Like a preview of possible coming attractions?"

She slid a glance in Simon's direction, then away again. "You could say that. He learns quickly, and has a good personality for . . . And this is silly. It's cowardly. I wanted to kiss you again to see if the other day was just a fluke, which, obviously, it was not. There's a strong physical attraction, which I haven't felt for anyone in a long time."

"Just under ten months?"

He watched her color come up, but then she smiled. Not sheepish but amused. "Longer actually. To spare us both the embarrassment of details, that particular incident was a failure on several levels. But it does serve as a baseline, and causes me to wonder if the just-under-ten-months factor is part of the reason for the attraction. It also makes me cautious. I'm not shy about sex, but I am wary of repeating what turned out to be a mistake."

"You'd rather be stable and ordered."

She pushed her hands back in her pockets. "I talk too much and you listen too well. That's a dangerous mix."

"For who?"

"For the talker. See, you give the impression you don't pay all that much attention, just aren't interested enough. But you do pay attention. Not big on the interacting, but you take in the details. It's kind of sneaky, really. I like you. Or at least I think I do. I don't know much about you because you don't talk about yourself. I know you have a dog because your mother gave him to you, which tells me you love your mother or fear her wrath. It's probably a combination of both."

They walked in silence for a full thirty seconds.

"Confirm or deny," she insisted. "It can't be a deep, dark secret."

"I love my mother and prefer, when possible, to avoid her wrath."

"There, that wasn't so hard. How about your father?"

"He loves my mother and prefers, when possible, to avoid her wrath."

"You realize, of course, that the less you say the more curious people get about you."

"Fine. That can be good for business."

"So, it's a business. Your work."

"People pay you, the government takes a cut. That's business."

She thought she had a handle on him now, even if it was a slippery one. "But it's not business first or you'd have sold me that cabinet."

He paused while Jaws found a stick and pranced along like a drum major at halftime. "You're not letting that one go."

"It was either a display of artistic temperament or bull-headedness. I suspect, in this case, the former, though I also suspect you're no stranger to the latter. I'd still like to buy it, by the way."

"No. You could use a new rocker for your porch. The one you have is ugly."

"It's not ugly. It's serviceable. And it needs repainting."

"The left arm is warped."

She opened her mouth to deny it, then realized she wasn't sure either way. "Maybe. But to turn this back on you, Mr. Mysteriosa, it only proves you notice detail."

"I notice crappy workmanship and warped wood. I'll trade you a rocker for the lessons, with the caveat you bust that ugly warped chair up for kindling."

"Maybe it has sentimental value."

"Does it?"

"No, I bought it at a yard sale a few years ago, for ten bucks."

"Kindling. And you teach the dog something interesting."

"That's a deal." As they came out of the woods, she looked up at the sky. "It's cooling off. I could probably use the kindling. A nice fire, a glass of wine—of course I won't be able to get the bottle out of a beautiful cabinet, but I'll live. I won't be inviting you in, either."

"Do you think if I wanted to finish up what we started back there I'd wait for an invitation?"

"No," she said after a moment. "I should find that arrogant and off-putting. I have no idea why I don't. Why don't you want to finish up what we started back there?"

He smiled at her. "You'll be thinking about that, won't you? I like your house."

Baffled, she turned to study it as he was. "My house?"

"It's small, a little fanciful and right for the spot. You should think about adding a solarium on the south face. It'd add some interest to the architecture, opening up your kitchen and bringing more light in. Anyway, do yourself a favor and don't check your e-mail or messages. I'll bring the dog and the chair back in a couple days."

She frowned after him as he and the dog walked to the truck. Simon unclipped the leash, boosted Jaws inside, where he sat, proudly holding his stick.

HE HAD PLENTY to keep him busy—his work, his dog, a half-baked idea of planting a garden just to see if he could. Every couple of days, depending on the weather, he'd take a drive with Jaws around the twisting, up-and-down roads of the island.

The routine, or the lack of routine, was exactly what he'd been after without fully realizing he'd been looking.

He enjoyed having his shop only steps away from the house where he could work as early or as late or as long as he pleased. And though it surprised him, he enjoyed having the dog for company, at work, on walks, on drives.

It pleased him to paint a flat-armed rocker a bold blue. Fiona's coloring might be soft, subtle, but her personality was bright and bold. She'd look good in the chair.

She looked good.

He thought he'd haul the chair, and the dog, over to her place that afternoon. Unless he got caught up in work.

Luckily, he thought as he drank his morning coffee on the porch, there was plenty of work to get caught up in. He had the custom breakfront for a Tacoma client, another set of rockers. There was the bed he intended to make for himself, and the cabinet he'd started for Fiona.

Maybe.

He had to get the stump—and should go ahead and deal

with that today. He'd check and see if Gary—fellow obedience school client and local farmer—was still willing to help him out with the chain and the Bobcat.

Whistling for the dog—and ridiculously pleased when Jaws responded by racing happily to him—Simon went back inside. He'd have his second cup of coffee while he checked the stories online in *U.S. Report*, as he'd done the last two days.

He'd begun to think the reporter had given up on the article, stymied by Fiona's lack of cooperation.

But he found it this time, with the bold headline:

ECHOES OF FEAR

Photos of the two women—hardly more than girls, really, he thought—featured prominently in the lead of the story. As far as he could tell the reporter had done her homework there, with details of their lives, the last hours before they vanished and the ensuing search and discovery of their bodies.

He found the photo of Perry chilling. So ordinary—the middle-aged man next door. The history teacher or insurance salesman, the guy who grew tomatoes in the backyard. Anyone.

But it was the photo of Fiona that stopped him cold.

Her face smiled out, as did those of a dozen others, the ones who hadn't escaped. Young, fresh, pretty.

It contrasted sharply with the file shot of her being hustled into the courthouse through the gauntlet of reporters. Her head down, her eyes dull, her face shattered.

The article added the details of her escape, her fiancé's murder, and added briefly that Bristow could not be reached for comment.

"Didn't stop you," he murmured.

Still, people did what they did, he thought. Reporters reported. The smartest thing Fiona could do would be to ignore it.

The urge to call her irked him, actually brought an itch between his shoulder blades. He ordered himself to leave it—and her—alone.

Instead he called Gary and arranged for the stump removal. He gave Jaws ten minutes of fetch—they were both starting to get the hang of it—then went to work.

He focused on the breakfront. He thought it best not to do any further work on the cabinet, not until he could block the image of Fiona, that sick mix of fear and grief on her face, out of his head.

He took a short break in the early afternoon for a walk on the beach, where Jaws managed to find a dead fish.

After the necessary shower—he really had to remember to buy the damn dog a bathtub—Simon decided to load up some of his smaller items for Sylvia. He boxed cutting boards, weed pots, vases, bowls, then loaded them, along with the dog, into the truck.

He'd meet Gary, deal with the stump, and with the stock already loaded, have an excuse not to linger too long with Fiona.

It surprised him, and caused Jaws untold sorrow, when she wasn't there. Nor were the dogs. Maybe she'd taken off for some solitude and distraction.

Jaws perked up when Gary arrived shortly with his chirpy border collie, Butch.

Gary, a cap over his grizzled hair, thick lenses over faded green eyes, watched the pups greet each other. "Coupla pips," he said.

"At least. Fiona's not home, but I told her I'd be by for the stump."

"Got unit practice up in the park. They do a day of it once a month. Keep in tune, you know? Would've headed out at first light, most likely. Well, let's get the Cat off the truck and go get you a stump. What the hell do you want it for?"

"You never know."

"You sure don't," Gary agreed.

They lowered the ramp, and Gary backed the machine down. With the two dogs on board, they puttered their way into the woods.

"I appreciate this, Gary."

"Hell, it's no big thing. Nice day to be out and about."

It was, Simon thought. Warm enough, sunny, with little signs of encroaching spring showing themselves. The dogs panted in desperate joy, and Gary smelled—lightly—of fertilizer.

When they reached the stump, Gary hopped out, circled it, shoved his cap back to scratch his head. "This what you want?"

"Yeah."

"Then we'll get her. I knew a guy once made statues out of burl wood and a chain saw. This isn't any stranger."

They hauled out the chain, discussed strategies, baseball, dogs.

Simon tied the dogs to a tree to keep them out of harm's way while Gary began maneuvering the machine.

It took an hour, and considerable sweat, re-angling, reversing, resetting the chain.

"Easy!" Simon called out, grinning widely. "You've got it now. She's coming."

"Cocksucker put up a fight." Gary set the machine to idle when the stump rolled free. "You got yourself a stump."

Simon ran his gloved hand over the body, along one of the thick roots. "Oh yeah."

"Happiest I've seen you look since I met you. Let's get her in the bucket."

Once they were rolling out of the woods, the bucket full of stump, Gary glanced over. "I want you to let me know what you do with that thing."

"I'm thinking a sink."

Gary snorted. "You're going to make a sink out of a stump?"

"The base of it, yeah. Maybe. If it cleans up like I think it will. I've got this round of burl wood could work as the basin. Add high-end contemporary fixtures, half a million coats of poly. Yeah, maybe."

"That beats a chain saw and burl wood for strange. How much would something like that go for?"

"Depends, but if this works like I see it? I can sell it for about eight."

"Eight hundred dollars for a stump sink?"

"Thousand."

"You're shitting me."

"Upscale Seattle gallery? Might get ten."

"Ten thousand dollars for a sink. Fuck me sideways."

Simon had to grin. "One of a kind. Some people think of it as art."

"Some people have shit for brains. No offense."

"Some people do—no offense taken. I'll let you know when it's finished, whatever it turns out to be. You can take a look for yourself."

"I'm doing that. Wait until I tell Sue," he said, speaking of his wife. "She won't believe it."

NINE

By the time he and Gary hauled the stump home and unloaded it, Simon considered skipping the trip to town and just staying put to play with his new toy. He'd already drafted half a dozen design possibilities in his head.

But the stock sat in his truck, packed and ready. If he didn't go now, he'd have to go later, so he gave Jaws the thrill of another ride with the window half down, the dog's snout pressed through the opening, and his ears flapping in the breeze.

"Why do you do that?" Simon wondered. When Jaws banged his tail against the seat in answer, Simon stuck his head out his own window. "Huh. Feels pretty good, actually. Next time you drive and I'll catch the breeze."

He tapped his fingers on the wheel in time with the radio while he refined and discarded more designs on the sketch pad in his head. The physical labor combined with the creative possibilities, the dog's sheer and simple pleasure combined in a near perfect mix that had him grinning his way into the village. He'd finish his errand, go home, study his material, measure, then take a walk on the beach to let the ideas stew. Top it off with some design work over a beer, maybe a pizza, and it was a damn good day.

And that, he thought, was the answer to Fiona's question. Why Orcas?

Water drew him—kicky surf on beaches, wide river, busy creeks, quiet inlets. That yen had pulled him from Spokane to Seattle. That, he mused, and the city itself—its style, its openness to art. The nightlife, the movement, he supposed, had appealed at that stage of his life.

As Nina had, for a while.

He'd had good years there. Interesting, creative, successful years. But . . .

Too many people, too much movement and not enough space.

He liked the idea of an island. Self-contained, just a little apart and surrounded by water. Those wicked, twisting roads offered countless views of blue and green and the pretty boats that plied it, the green-knuckled clumps of rough land that seemed to float on it.

If he wanted more he could drive into a village, have a meal, watch the tourists. If he wanted solitude, he could stay home—his island on the island. Which, he admitted, was his usual choice.

And which, he thought with a glance toward Jaws, was why his mother had pushed a dog on him.

Watching those ears flap and the tail thump, he acknowledged his mother was right. Again.

He pulled in the back of Sylvia's shop and raised the windows, leaving a three-inch crack. "You stay here. Don't eat anything." At the last minute he remembered *distraction*, reached over and took a chew toy from the glove box.

"Play with this," he ordered.

When he carted in the first load, he caught the scent of home cooking—a little spicy—and spotted a Crock-Pot on the shipping counter.

He poked his head into the shop. Sylvia, pretty and bright in one of her colorful skirts, chatted up a customer while her clerk rang up sales for another.

Business was good, he thought. Another plus for the day.

He gave her a quick wave, started to back out.

"Simon! This is perfect timing. This is Simon Doyle," she told the customer. "Simon, Susan's over from Bainbridge Island. She's interested in your wine cabinet."

Sylvia gave him a blinding smile and a subtle "Come over here" signal.

This was the part he hated. But trapped, he stepped over.

"I was just telling Susan how lucky we are you moved to Orcas and let us display your work. Susan came over for the day with her sister. Also lucky for us."

"It's nice to meet you." Susan offered a hand sporting a perfect French manicure and a canary diamond. "It's beautiful work."

"Thanks." He rubbed his hand on his jeans. "Sorry. I've been working. I'm just dropping off some new pieces."

"Anything as impressive as this?"

"Smaller pieces, actually."

The sister wandered over, holding an earring up to each ear. "Susan, which pair?"

Susan angled her head, tipped it side to side. "Both. Dee, this is the man who made the bowl I'm buying for Cherry's birthday, and this cabinet I can't seem to walk away from. Simon Doyle."

"I love the bowl." Dee gave Simon's hand a hard, fast shake. "But she saw it first. Sylvia said you might be persuaded to make another."

"Simon's just brought some new pieces in."

"Really?" Dee glanced from Sylvia back to Simon. "Any bowls?"

"A couple," he began.

"Why don't I go unpack so you can take a look," Sylvia suggested.

"That'd be great. First pick," Dee said, giving her sister a little poke.

"There's more in the truck. I'll go—"

"No, no, I'll take care of it." Sylvia patted Simon's arm, then gave it a warning squeeze. "Why don't you tell Susan more about the cabinet? It's our current showpiece," she added, then glided off before Simon could find an escape hatch.

He hated the selling part, the feeling of being on display as much as the work.

"I love the tones of the wood." Susan traced a hand down the grain. "And then the detail. It's elegant without being ornate and showy."

"It suits you."

Her face lit up. "That's a clever thing to say."

"I'd tell you if it didn't. You like the understated and the unique. You don't mind if it's impractical, but you're happier if it serves a purpose."

"God, you nailed her. Psychic woodworker," Dee said with a laugh. "You'd better buy it, Susan. It's karma."

"Maybe it is." Susan opened the doors again, slid open one of the drawers. "Smooth as silk. I appreciate good work."

"Me too." He noted that Sylvia had stocked it with some excellent wineglasses and a couple bottles of good wine.

"How long have you been working with wood?"

"According to my mother, since I was two."

"Time well spent. Sylvia said you moved to the island. From where?"

He felt his skin begin to itch. "Spokane via Seattle."

"Doyle," Dee murmured. "I think I read something about you and your work some time ago, in the art section."

"Maybe."

Susan tilted her head again, as she had when judging her sister's earring choices. "Not much on self-promotion, are you?"

"The work should speak for itself."

"I absolutely agree with that, and in this case, it does. I'm buying it."

"Ladies," Sylvia called from the doorway. "Why don't you come into the stockroom. Dee, I think we have your bowl. Simon, I brought the puppy in. I hope you don't mind. I know this is taking a little longer than you planned, and he was so happy to see me."

"A puppy."

"Careful," Dee said as her sister bolted for the stockroom. "She'll want to buy him, too. She's wild about dogs."

It took another thirty minutes, with Sylvia cagily blocking his escape and Jaws being stroked and cuddled into delirium. He loaded boxes and bags into their car and decided the entire event had been more exhausting than pulling a stump.

Sylvia dragged him back into the stockroom and into a circling dance while Jaws barked and leaped. "Simon! Those two women didn't just make our day, they made our week! And they'll be back, oh yes, they'll be back. Every time Susan looks at her wine cabinet, or the vase, or Dee uses the bowl, they'll think of the shop, and of you. And they'll be back."

"Go, team."

"Simon, we sold pieces as we unpacked them. And the cabinet? I honestly thought we'd have it on display until well into the tourist season. You have to make me another!" She plopped down on the little sofa where she'd served her two customers lemon water.

"Then I'd better get to work."

"Be excited. You just made an excellent amount of money. *Ch-ching*. And we sold pieces that those two ladies will enjoy. Really enjoy. My day needed a lift, and this really did it."

She bent down to pet Jaws. "I'm worried about Fee. There was an article on Perry and the recent murders in *U.S. Report* this morning. I went by to see her, but she was already gone. Her unit works today."

"I heard."

"I talked to Laine, her mother. We both decided not to call her while she's out practicing."

"You talk to her mother?"

"Laine and I have a good relationship. We both love Fee. I know she'll have heard about the article by now, and I know it'll upset her. You could do me a big favor."

He felt his skin start to itch again. "What kind of favor?"

"I made her minestrone." She gestured to the Crock-Pot. "And a round of rosemary bread. She should be getting home soon, if she's not home already. Would you take it by?"

"Why? You should take it by."

"I would. I planned to, but it occurs to me it'd be good to have someone else around, someone closer to her own age. And this one." She stroked Jaws again. "It's hard to be blue around this guy."

She tipped up her face, and even knowing she was using her eyes deliberately, he couldn't fight it.

"Would you mind, Simon? I get so emotional when I think of what she went through. I might make it worse. I'd really feel better if I knew she had a good meal, maybe a little company."

HOW WAS IT, Simon wondered, that some women could talk you into doing the opposite of what you wanted to do?

His mother had the same talent. He'd watched her, listened, attempted to evade, maneuver, outfox—and she could, without fail, nudge him in the opposing direction.

Sylvia was cut from the same cloth, and now he had a Crock-Pot and a loaf of bread, an assignment—and that contemplative walk on the beach was over before it had begun.

Was he supposed to let Fiona cry on his shoulder now? He hated being the shoulder. He never knew what to say or do.

Pat, pat, there, there. What the fuck?

Plus, if she had any sense—and he thought she did—she'd want solitude, not company.

"If people let other people alone," he told Jaws, "people would be better off. It's always people that screw things up for people anyway."

He'd just give her the food and take off. Better all around. Here you go, *bon appétit*. Then, at least, he'd have his studying, measuring time, his design time over pizza and a beer.

Maybe she wasn't back yet. Better. He could just leave the pot and loaf on the porch and be done with it.

The minute he turned into her drive, Jaws perked up. The pup danced on the seat, planted his paws on the dash. The fact that he could without doing a header to the floor caused Simon to realize the dog had grown considerably in the last couple weeks.

He probably needed a new collar.

Reaching over, he slid his finger between the collar and the fur. "Shit. Why don't you tell me these things?"

As he drove over the bridge, the pup's tail slashed—door, seat, door, seat—in a jubilant rhythm.

"Glad somebody's happy," Simon muttered.

The truck sat in the drive; the dogs raced in the yard.

"We're not staying," he warned Jaws. "In and out."

He let the dog out first and considered that what with stump hauling with Gary and Butch, a visit to town, the adoration of women and now the unscheduled playdate with pals, this had turned into the canine version of a day at Disney World for Jaws.

He retrieved the pot and the foil-wrapped bread.

Fiona stood in the doorway now, leaning casually on the jamb. And to Simon's puzzled surprise, she was smiling.

"Hi, neighbor."

"I had to go in to Sylvia's. She asked me to drop this off."

She straightened to take the lid off the pot and sniff. "Mmm, minestrone. I'm very fond. Bring it on back."

She moved aside to let him pass and left the door open as she often did.

The fire crackled, the whiff of soup spiced the air, and she smelled like the woods.

"I heard you got your stump."

"Is it out on the newswire?"

"Grapevine's faster. I ran into Gary and Sue on my way home. They were heading to their son's for dinner. Just set it on the counter, thanks. I was going to have a beer, but Syl's minestrone requires a good red. Unless you'd rather beer."

The plan to get in and out shifted, weighed by curiosity. The grapevine *was* fast, he thought. She had to know about the article. "The red's good."

She crossed to a long, narrow cupboard—she really could use a wine cabinet—to select a bottle. "So, a sink?"

"What?"

"The stump." She opened a drawer, pulled out a corkscrew without any rooting around. "Gary said you're going to make a sink. A stump sink. It's going to be the talk of the island."

"Because not that much goes on here. I'll get your tree planted in a couple days."

"Works for me."

He studied her face while she pulled the cork, saw no signs of distress, shed tears, anger. Maybe the grapevine had broken down after all.

She poured the wine, plugged in the cord on the pot. "Let's give it a few minutes," she said, and tapped her glass to his. "So, a solarium."

"A what?"

"You said I should think about a solarium, south side. Open the kitchen. How would it work?"

"Ah . . . that wall." He gestured with his glass. "Load-bearing so you'd need support. Maybe a couple of beams, columns—keep it open but give it a sense of entry. Wall out, beams up. Take it out ten, twelve feet. Maybe pitch the roof. Skylights. A good, generous window would give you a view into the woods. Maybe wide-planked floors. You'd have room for a table if you wanted an alternate to eating in the kitchen."

"You make it sound simple."

"It'd be some work."

"Maybe I'll start saving my pennies." She took a sip of wine, then set the glass down to get a jar of olives out of the refrigerator. "You know about the article."

"Apparently you do."

She transferred olives from bottle to a shallow dish. "James read it before we met up this morning—and passed the word to the rest of the unit. They were all so worried about bringing it up, not bringing it up, nobody could concentrate. So they finally told me and we got started on our work."

"Did you read it?"

"No. This is my version of an appetizer, by the way." She shoved the olives toward him. "No, I didn't read it, and I won't. No point. There's nothing I can do to change what happened before, and nothing I can do to change what's happening now. I knew it was coming, now it has. Tomorrow it'll be yesterday."

"That's one way to look at it."

"Syl sent my favorite soup. She thought I'd be upset."

"I guess."

Fiona picked up her wine again, pointed at him with her free hand. "You know very well, as she'd have told you—and maneuvered you into coming by so I wouldn't be alone."

The dogs rushed in then, a happy pack of fur. "You're not alone anyway."

"True enough." She gave everyone a rub. "You figured I'd be upset—and probably couldn't outmaneuver Syl."

"Does anybody?"

"Not really. I am upset—but in a controllable way. I've already had two brooding days this month, so I'm not allowed another one."

He found himself unwillingly fascinated. "There's a limit?"

"For me there is. And now I have soup and . . ." She peeled back the foil. "Mmmm, rosemary bread. This is exceptional. I have a stepmother who'd take the time to make it for me, a neighbor who'd bring it by even though he'd rather not, and my dogs. I'm not allowed to brood. So we'll have dinner and conversation. But I'm not going to sleep with you after."

"Cocktease."

She nearly choked on the wine. "You did not just say that."

"Say what?"

She threw back her head and laughed. "See? This is better than brooding. Let's eat."

She ladled out bowls of soup, put the bread on a board and poured some sort of dipping sauce into a dish.

"The candles," she said as she lit them, "aren't for seduction. They just make the food taste better."

"I thought they were to make me look prettier."

"But you're so beautiful already." She smiled, spooned up soup. "To Syl."

"Okay." He sampled. "Wait." Sampled again. "This is really good. Like dinner-in-Tuscany good."

"She'd love to hear that. Mostly, I think Sylvia's developed too close an attachment to tofu and strange grains of rice. But when she does minestrone, she's a genius. Try the bread."

He broke off a hunk, dipped. "She called your mother."

"Oh." Distress came into those clear blue eyes. "I should've thought of that. I'll call them both later and let them know I'm all right."

"You're right about the bread, too. My mother bakes bread. Baking's kind of a hobby for her."

"I can bake. You know you buy that cookie dough in rolls, slice it, stick it in the oven?"

"My specialty's frozen pizza."

"Another fine skill."

He went back to his soup. "Everyone I know who's divorced hates all parties involved. Or at least coldly disdains."

"My father was a very good man. My mother's a lovely woman. At some point they just stopped being happy together. I know there were fights, and anger, probably some blame tossed around, but for the most part they handled it as well as it can be handled. It still hurt unbelievably, for a while. But then, it didn't, because he was a very good man, and she's a lovely woman, and they were happy again. And, oddly, came to like each other again. Then Dad met Syl, and they were . . . well, they were just beautiful together. She and my mother took the time, made the effort to get to know each other, because of me. And they just hit it off. They really like each other. My mother sends Syl flowers every year on the anniversary of my father's death. Sunflowers, because they were my father's favorite. Okay." She pressed her hands to her eyes briefly. "Enough of that. It gets me weepy.

"Tell me what you did today besides hauling a stump out of the woods."

Before he could speak, the dogs wandered back in. Jaws scented the air and bulleted for the table. He plopped his paws on Fiona's leg and whined.

"Off." She snapped her fingers, pointed to the ground. He sat, but the tail swished and the eyes shone with anticipation. She shifted her gaze to Simon.

"You feed him from the table."

"Maybe. He keeps at me until—"

He broke off when she huffed out a breath. She rose, walked to the pantry. She got out small chew bones. One for Jaws, and one each for the three dogs who looked at the pup with pity.

"These are yours." She laid the bones across the room. "Go ahead. Distract," she said to Simon. "Replace, discipline. As long as you give in and feed him from the table—and people food isn't good for his diet—he'll keep begging. And you're teaching him to be a nuisance by rewarding bad behavior."

"Yes, Mom."

"Keep it up, you'll raise a counter-grazer. I've had more than one student who's chowed down on the Thanksgiving turkey, the dinner party rack of lamb or the Christmas ham because they weren't taught proper manners. One stole a neighbor's steaks right off the grill."

"Was that a fetch/retrieve? Because that could be a good skill."

She shook her spoon at him. "Mark my words. Anyway, other than the stump?"

"Nothing much. I had some work, and I took some pieces into Syl's, which is why I'm eating soup." It wasn't a chore after all, he realized, this dinner conversation with candlelight and dogs gnawing on rawhide. "She's buzzed because a couple of women were in there when I came in, and they walked out loaded down. She's shipping the wine cabinet because it was too big for their car."

"The wine cabinet." Her spoon stopped halfway to her mouth. "You sold my wine cabinet."

"That's one way to look at it."

She sulked a moment, then shrugged. "Well, hell. Congratulations."

"It suited her." He shrugged back when Fiona's eyes narrowed. "Susan from Bainbridge Island. Canary diamond, good leather jacket, stylish boots. Subtle but expensive Susan from Bainbridge Island."

"What am I? Obvious and cheap?"

"If you were cheap we'd be having sex now, soup later."

"That's supposed to be funny. It is, but only a little."

"What do you do when you're out with your unit like today? Don't you just know all the stuff anyway?"

"It's essential to practice, individually and as a team. We work a different problem, over different terrain, at least once a month. Then we can go over any mistakes, any flaws or any room to improve. We worked a cadaver find today."

Simon frowned at his soup. "Nice."

"Happy to change the subject if you're sensitive."

"Where'd you get the cadaver? Corpses Are Us?"

"They were out. We use cadaver material—bone, hair, body fluid—in a container. Mai, as base operations, plants it earlier. Then we set up, just as we would for a real search, assign sectors and so on."

He tried to think if he'd ever had a more unusual conversation over minestrone. Absolutely not.

"How does the dog know it's supposed to find a dead person instead of a live one?"

"That's a good question. Different command. For mine, I use 'find' for a live search and 'search' for cadaver work."

"That's it?"

"There's more, but most of it deals with the cross-training, the early work, the advanced work."

"Jaws might be good at it. He found a dead fish today. No problem."

"Actually, he could be. He can be taught to differentiate between the scent of a dead fish, or animal, and human remains."

"And not to roll in it when he finds it?"

"Definitely."

"Might be worth it just for that." He glanced over to see Jaws bellying toward the table. Fiona simply turned, pointed. Jaws slunk back to the other dogs.

"He responds well, see? Not only to you but to another handler. That's another essential skill."

"I think he responds better to you, and I'm not sure that's all that helpful."

She nudged her bowl aside. "Maybe not, but this has been.

I wouldn't have brooded because it's against the rules, but I'd have come close on my own."

He studied her while the candlelight flickered. "You don't look like hell tonight."

"Oh my goodness." She fluttered a hand at her heart. "Am I blushing?"

"I figured you would," he added, unperturbed. "A full day out on maneuvers, or whatever they are."

"Unit training."

"Sure, and the fallout from the article. But you look good."

"Wow, from not looking like hell to looking good in one leap. What could be next?"

"Your smile. I also figure you have to know it's your best feature—the most appealing, the sexiest thing about you. That's why you use it so often."

"Really?"

"See, like right now."

Still smiling, she rested her chin on her fist. "I'm still not sleeping with you tonight. This wasn't a date. I may want you to take me on a date before we sleep together. I haven't decided."

"You haven't decided."

"That's right. It's one of the privileges of the female to decide these things. I don't make the rules. So I'm not going to sleep with you yet."

"Maybe I don't want to sleep with you."

"Because I'm not your type," she said with a nod. "But I've already seduced you with my smile, and softened you up with Sylvia's soup. I could lay you like linoleum."

"That's insulting. And provocative."

"But I won't because I like you."

"You don't really like me that much."

She laughed. "I actually do, and I'm not altogether settled tonight, so it wouldn't be what it should be. But I'll take this."

She rose to walk around the table. And slid into his lap. She grazed her teeth over his bottom lip, then soothed it with her tongue before sinking them both into the kiss.

Comfort and fire, she thought, promise and threat. The

hard body and thick, soft hair, the rough stubble and smooth lips.

She sighed into it, retreated, then locked her eyes on his.

"A little more," she murmured, and took his mouth again.

This time his hands slid up her sides, skimmed her breasts. Possessed. Small and firm, with her heart thudding under his palms.

"Fiona."

She broke the kiss to lay her cheek to his. "You could convince me; we both know it. Please don't. It's so unfair, but please don't."

Some women, he thought, had the power to turn a man in the opposite direction from what he wanted. It seemed his fate to run up against them. And, damn it, to care.

"I need to go."

"Yeah." She drew back again, this time cupping his face in her hands. "You do. But thanks, because when I'm restless tonight it won't be over some damned article in the paper."

"Just call me Samaritan."

For a moment, she rested her brow to his. "I'll give you a container of soup. And a bigger collar for Jaws. He's outgrown that one."

He didn't argue as she gave him time to settle.

And still, all the way home while the pup snored in the seat beside him, he could taste her, smell her.

He glanced at the dog. "This is your fault," he muttered. "I wouldn't be in this situation except for you."

As he turned into his own drive, he reminded himself to go buy a damn tree and plant it.

A deal was a deal.

TEN

She got through it, got past it. Work and routine pushed her hour to hour. She channeled excess nerves into workouts, shedding tension with sweat until an article rehashing her ordeal, her loss no longer mattered.

Her classes, her blog, the daily care and interactions with her dogs filled her days. And since a casual dinner over soup and bread, she had the idea of a relationship—however far it went—with Simon to entertain her mind.

She enjoyed him, quite a bit. Maybe, she considered, because he wasn't as protective and easy as her circle of friends or the two women who made up her family. He was a little hard, a lot blunt and, she thought, a great deal more complicated than most people she knew.

In many ways, since Greg's murder, the island had become her sanctuary, her safe place where no one looked at her with pity, or particular interest, and where she'd been able to restart her life.

Not on bare ground, she thought. She was who she was, at the core. But like an island, she'd broken off from the mainland and allowed herself to change direction, to grow, even to re-form.

Not so many years before, she'd imagined herself raising a family—three-kid plan—in a pretty suburb. She'd have learned to cook good, interesting meals and would love her part-time job (to be determined). There would have been dogs in the house and a swing set in the yard, dance lessons and soccer games.

She'd have been a steady and supportive cop's wife, a devoted mother and a contented woman.

She'd have been good at it, Fiona thought as she sat on the porch taking in the quiet morning. Maybe she'd been young to have been planning marriage and family, but it had all unfolded so seamlessly.

Until.

Until there was nothing left of that pretty picture but shattered glass and a broken frame.

But.

But now she was good at this. Content and fulfilled. And she understood she'd come to this place, to this life, to these skills because all those lovely, sweet plans had shattered.

The core might be the same, but everything around it had changed. And she was, because of or despite that, a happy, successful woman.

Bogart came over to bump his head under her arm. Automatically, she shifted, draped her arm over him to rub his side.

"I don't think everything happens for a reason. That's just the way we cope with the worst that happens to us. But I can be glad I'm here."

And not feel disloyal, she thought, to Greg, to all those pretty plans and the girl who made them.

"New day, Bogart. I wonder what it'll bring."

As if in answer, he came to alert. And she saw Simon's truck rolling down her drive.

"Could be interesting," she murmured as the other dogs raced over to join her and sit, tails drumming.

She smiled at Jaws's happy face peering out from the

windshield on the passenger's side, and Simon's unreadable one behind the wheel.

She rose and, when the truck stopped, gave her dogs the release signal. "A little early for class," she called when Simon stepped out, and Jaws leaped into the reunion with his buddies.

"I've got your damn tree."

"And so cheerful, too." She wandered over as he waded through the dogs.

"Give me the coffee." He didn't wait for the offer but took her mug, downed the rest of the contents.

"Well, help yourself."

"I ran out."

Because he looked surly, unshaven and sexy, she fluttered her lashes at him. "And still, here you are bright and early with a tree, just for me."

"I'm here bright and fucking early because that dog chewed open five pounds of dog food somewhere before dawn, then opted to puke it up, bag and all, on my bed. While I was in it."

"Awww."

Simon scowled as the concern and attention went straight to the dog. "I'm the injured party."

Ignoring him, Fiona rubbed the puppy, checked his eyes, his nose, his belly. "Poor baby. You're okay now. That's all right."

"I had to throw out the sheets."

From her crouch, Fiona rolled her eyes. "No, you clean off the puke, then you wash the sheets."

"Not those sheets. He heaved like a drunk frat boy."

"And whose fault is that?"

"I didn't eat the damn kibble."

"No, but you didn't have it stowed where he couldn't get to it, or better yet in a lidded container. Plus, he's probably not ready to have free rein in the house. You should put up a baby gate."

His scowl only deepened. "I'm not putting up a baby gate."

"Then don't complain when he gets into something he shouldn't while you're sleeping or otherwise occupied."

"If I'm getting a lecture, I want more coffee."

"In the kitchen." Once he'd stomped out of earshot, she let the wheezing laugh escape. "He's mad at you, isn't he? Yes, he's very mad. He'll get over it. Anyway"—she gave Jaws a kiss on his cool, wet nose—"it was his own fault."

Rising, she walked to the back of the truck to get a look at her tree.

She stood there, grinning still, when Simon strode out with his own mug of coffee.

"You got me a dogwood."

"It seemed appropriate when I bought it yesterday. But that was before this morning when I was reminded dogs are a pain in the ass."

"First, it's a beautiful tree. Thank you. Second, any and everything that depends on us can be pains in the ass. He booted on your bed because when he felt sick and scared he wanted you. And third"—she laid her hands on his shoulders, touched her mouth to his—"good morning."

"Not yet."

She smiled, kissed him again.

"Marginally better."

"Well, let's plant a tree and see what that does for you. Let's put it over there. No . . ." She changed direction. "There."

"I thought you wanted it back in the woods, where the stump was."

"Yes, but it's so pretty, and back there hardly anyone will see it but me. Oh, there, back there, just on this side of the bridge. Maybe I should get another one for the other side. You know, so they'd flank the bridge."

"You're on your own there." But he shrugged, opened the truck door.

"I'll go with you, give you a hand." So saying, she hopped nimbly in the back of the truck and sat on the bag of peat moss.

He shook his head but maneuvered the truck around, eased to the bridge and parked again. When he got out to lower the tailgate, she slung the bag of peat moss over her shoulder.

"I'll get that."

"Got it," she said, and jumped down.

He watched as she carted it over to the spot she wanted, set it down. When she came back, he took her arm. "Flex," he ordered.

Amused, she obeyed, saw his eyes register surprise when he tested her biceps. "What do you do, bench-press your dogs?"

"Among other things. Plus, I just have excellent protoplasm."

"I'll say." He climbed up to pull the tree to the tailgate. "Get the tools, Muscle Girl. There should be an extra pair of work gloves in the glove box."

The dogs sniffed around but soon lost interest. He said nothing when she hauled over the bag of soil he'd bought to mix with the peat, still nothing when she walked back to the house trailing the dogs.

But he stopped digging to watch her walk back carrying two pails like some lean-muscled milkmaid.

"My hose won't reach this far," she told him—and he was gratified she was at least a little winded. "If it needs more water, I can get it from the stream."

She set the buckets down. The dogs immediately began to lap at the water.

"I don't know why I never thought to plant something pretty here before. I'll see it whenever I come home, go out, from the porch, when I'm training. Them," she corrected, "if I put one on the other side of the drive. Want me to dig awhile?"

It was probably stupid to take that as a challenge to his manhood, but he couldn't help it. "I've got it."

"Well, let me know." She walked off to play with the dogs.

He'd never considered tough especially sexy, but despite the willowy frame, the soft coloring, the apparently bottomless patience, the woman had an underlayment of steel. Most of the women he'd been involved with hadn't lifted anything more challenging than an apple martini—and maybe a five-pound free weight at a fancy health club. But this one? She shouldered a sack of dirt like a seasoned laborer.

And damn if it wasn't sexy. And it made him wonder just what that body would look like, feel like, when he got her naked. Maybe he needed to push a little harder on that goal, he thought, and put his back into the digging.

She came back when he cut open the bags of soil and peat to mix into the hole.

"Hold off on that a second, and I'll do it. But I want to show you something first." She stepped beside Simon, then signaled Jaws—hand command only. He trotted right over and, when she pointed, sat. "Good dog, good." She slipped him one of the treats she never seemed to be without. "Stay. Go on and get down to his level," she told Simon.

"Do you want this tree planted or not?"

"It'll only take a second. Stay," she repeated firmly when Jaws bunched for a leap as Simon hunkered down. "Stay. He's getting it, and we'll work on the sit and stay with distance. But I thought you'd like this. Hold out your hand, say, 'Shake.'"

Simon slid a cynical glance up at her. "No way."

"Just give it a try."

"Right." He held out a hand. "Shake."

Jaws lifted a paw, plopped it into Simon's palm. "Son of a bitch." He laughed, and the dog forgot himself in pride and pleasure to rear up and lap at Simon's face. "That's pretty good. That's pretty damn good, you dumbass."

Fiona smiled down as man and dog congratulated each other.

"Do it again," Simon demanded. "Sit. Okay, shake. Nice." He stroked the pup's ears, looked up at Fiona. "How'd you teach him that so fast?"

God, they looked adorable together, she realized. The tawny-eyed man with his morning stubble, the young dog who was growing into his feet.

"He wants to learn, to please. He has a strong drive." She passed treats into Simon's free hand. "Reward him. He'll be happy with your approval and affection, but the food reward's extra incentive."

She picked up the shovel, began to toss dirt, then peat, then dirt into the hole.

"That's enough. We need to set the root-ball."

"I don't know much about planting trees." She swiped the

back of the work glove over her brow. "In fact, this is my first. Do you?"

"I've plugged in a few."

"I thought you lived in the city before Orcas."

"I didn't grow up in the city. My family's in construction."

"Okay, but doesn't that mean planting buildings?"

His lips quirked. "You could say. But my dad's policy was to buy a tree or a shrub for any new house he built. So I plugged in a few."

"That's nice. Your dad's policy, that's nice."

"Yeah. Nice gesture, and good business."

He hefted the dogwood, lowered the root-ball into the hole. "That's about right." Crouching, he opened the burlap around the root-ball to expose it.

Together they dumped in topsoil and peat, mixed it.

"Shouldn't we cover it more?" she asked when Simon stopped.

"No, just to the height of the root-ball." He lifted a bucket. "You want to deep-water, and do that about once a week unless we get a good rain."

It had been fun, she thought, planting a tree with him in the cool morning air. "Once a week, check."

"I didn't get mulch. Figured it was going in the woods and I could just use pine needles. You'll want to mulch it."

"Okay." She stepped back. "I've got a dogwood tree. Thank you, Simon."

"We had a deal."

"And you could've picked up a pine and stuck it in the hole from the stump. This is lovely."

She turned to kiss him, a friendly gesture, but he moved in and made it more.

"We've got some time before school starts," he told her.

"Hmm, that's true." She tipped up her wrist to check the time. "Not a lot. We'd have to be pretty quick and pretty motivated."

"You're the former track star. You be quick. I'll be motivated."

He smelled of the soap from his shower twined with a touch

of healthy sweat from the effort of digging. He looked rough, and ready. And the long, hard kiss beside the sweet young tree had stirred her to aching.

Why wait? she asked herself. Why pretend?

"It might be a good way to celebrate a tree planting. Why don't we—"

She broke off as she heard tires on gravel. "Apparently someone else is early," she began, then saw the patrol car. "Oh God." Reaching down, she groped for Simon's hand.

Davey pulled up behind the truck, got out. "Nice-looking tree," he said, and took off his sunglasses and hooked them in his shirt pocket. He gave Simon a nod as he walked toward them. "Simon."

"Deputy."

Davey reached out to run a hand down Fiona's arm. "Fee, I'm sorry to have to tell you, but they found another one."

The breath she'd held came out with a jump. "When?"

"Yesterday. In Klamath National Forest, near the Oregon border," he said before she asked. "She'd been missing a couple days. A college student, Redding, California. So he moved west and a little south for the abduction, then drove over a hundred miles to . . . bury her. The details are the same as the others."

"Two days," she murmured.

"They've got a couple of feds going in to push on Perry, to see if they can pull anything out of him, if there's anything to pull."

"He's not waiting as long between," she said. "He's not as patient." She shuddered once. "And he's heading north."

"He's targeting the same victim type," he reminded her, then set his teeth. "But goddamn it, Fee, after that newspaper thing, I've got some concerns."

"He knows where to find me if he wants me." Panic wanted to beat its wings in her throat. And panic, she reminded herself, solved nothing. Nothing.

And still those wings fluttered.

"If he wants to finish Perry's work, a kind of homage, he

can find me. I'm not stupid, Davey. It's something I considered when I knew there was going to be an article."

"You could move in with Sylvia or Mai for a while. Hell, Fee, you can stay with Rachel and me."

"I know, but the fact is I'm as safe here as anywhere. Safer, maybe, with the dogs." Her sanctuary. She had to believe it or the panic would win. "Nobody can get near the house without me knowing."

Davey glanced toward Simon. "I'd feel better if you had more than the dogs."

"I've got a gun, and you know I can use it. I can't uproot my life on the possibility he may decide to come here in a week, a month, six months." She dragged a hand through her hair, ordering herself to stay sensible. "He's not as patient as Perry," she repeated, "and he's following someone else's pattern. They'll catch him. I have to believe they'll catch him. Until they do, I'm not helpless."

"One of us is going to check in with you every day. We take care of our own, even when they aren't helpless."

"That works for me."

Simon held his silence until he and Fiona were alone. "Why don't you go visit your mother for a while?"

"Because I have to work. And I do have to work," she added. "I have a mortgage, a car payment, bills. I've had to juggle like a circus clown to manage the time and money for a long weekend off." She picked up the shovel to put it in the back of the truck. "And what happens if he doesn't go after some other poor girl for weeks? Do I just put everything on hold because of a maybe? I won't be stupid and I won't be careless." Because it made her feel strong and capable, she hauled up the sagging bag of peat. "But I will not let this ruin my life. Not again. And I won't be taken. Not again. Not ever again."

"You leave your door unlocked. Half the time you leave it open."

"Yes, that's true. And if someone they didn't know tried to get within twenty feet of the house, or me, the dogs would stop them. But you can believe I'll be locking up at night now, and my nine millimeter's going in the drawer next to my bed."

It took him a minute. "You have a nine millimeter?"

"That's right." She tossed the bag of topsoil after the bag of peat. "Greg taught me how to shoot, how to respect a weapon. And after . . . after I started going to the range regularly until I was proficient. I'm probably a little rusty, but I'll fix that. I'll fix it." The words came out too fast, too fast, and she fought to slow them. "I'll take care of myself. I need my life. I need my home and my work, my routine."

She pressed the heel of her hand to her forehead. "I need it."

"Okay. Okay." He glanced toward the dogs. They looked like happy, friendly, lick-your-face-off types. But he remembered the low growl from Newman when he'd tussled a little with Fiona in the kitchen. "Why don't you cancel your classes for the day?"

"No, no. Some of them are already on the ferry, or heading in. Besides, routine. It keeps me centered."

"Is that what does it?"

"Apparently. The tree's still pretty," she said, calmer again. "It's still a nice morning, and I still have work to do. It helps."

"Then I'd better move my truck." He opened the door. "Teach him something else." He lifted his chin at Jaws. "Like how to get me a beer out of the fridge."

"Not altogether impossible. But we'd better nail down the basics first."

ROUTINE DID HELP, and part of that routine was people, and their dogs. She listened, as always, to clients relating progress, or the lack of it. She listened to problems, and arranged her lesson for the day around them.

She used the first few minutes for walk, heel, sit to get both handlers and pups settled in.

"Some of us are having problems with jumping, so we're going to take that discipline first today. Puppies jump on us because it's fun and because they want our attention, and

they're so cute we give in to them, even encourage it, rewarding bad manners—and behavior that won't be so cute in bigger
dogs as they grow. Annie, why don't you tell us what happened
the other day."

Annie from San Juan Island gave her collie mix an apolo-
getic glance. "My niece came to visit with her little boy. He's
three. Casey was so happy to see them, she ran over and jumped
on Rory. She knocked him down and he hit his head. He wasn't
really hurt, but he could've been, and it scared him. She didn't
mean it."

"Of course not. Casey's a friendly, happy dog. Energetic.
I imagine most of us have had something like this happen. Or
at least scratched legs, dirtied pants, shredded hose."

"Bruno's always tearing up my panty hose." Jake, all 220
pounds of him, got a laugh at the remark.

"We'll fix that for you, Jake. Like everything else, it takes
consistency, firmness and understanding. Do not reward your
dog when it jumps. No attention, no smiles, no petting. I find
the best command is generally 'Off.' Using the 'Down' command can confuse them, as we want to use this to get them to
lie down. I'm going to use Casey to demonstrate. Go ahead
and take her off the leash, Annie."

She called the dog, who raced over and, as Fiona expected,
rose up on her hind legs to jump. Fiona stepped forward, coun-
tering the balance. "Off!" Casey's feet hit the ground. "Good
dog. Good girl." Fiona offered a treat and a rub.

"Obviously it's going to take more than once, but the dog
will learn. The instinct is to step back when a dog jumps, to
take their weight. But by stepping forward, the dog can't get
its balance. You use the step and the command—both firm—
and when your dog has all four feet on the ground again—not
before—you offer praise and reward."

She demonstrated again. "You and everyone in your family have to get on board with this. The discipline can't come
from just you. Don't let your kids encourage jumping because
it's fun for them, too. Call her back, Annie, and repeat what I
just did if she jumps. Step forward, say 'Off!' Then reward."

Fiona nodded in satisfaction as the routine played out.

"Okay, let's spread out so everyone can work on this. We move on to how to teach your dog not to jump on others next."

She walked around, offered advice, encouragement. People needed praise and reward, too, she knew, so she doled them out.

She ended the class with a second round of sit and stay.

"Good job, everybody. I've got a tip for you this week since spring's coming: some of you might be planning a garden or have one already started. I just blogged about this, so you can refer to that if and when you need a reminder. You'll be unhappy if your dog digs up your petunias or tomatoes. Dogs dig for several reasons. Sometimes it's just because they like it. Sometimes because they're bored. Regular play, exercise and attention can discourage digging, but not always. You're not always going to be right on hand when that digging urge strikes. So, fill the holes."

She got a moan out of several students.

"Yeah, it's an irritating cycle initially. But a lot of young dogs will get discouraged when the hole they've dug keeps getting filled. What's the point? Also offer alternatives to digging. Playtime, a walk, a chew toy. Distract. But because some will just, well, dig in, I advise you to put a few additives in the dirt you replace. Chili pepper's a good deterrent, and so is dog poop. Seriously. Sometimes a dog digs to find a cool spot. If you have enough room you might designate some shady spot in the yard for him to dig and clear and hang out in when it's hot.

"Last, those of you who have no plans to breed your dog and haven't already made arrangements for spaying or neutering, it's time."

She didn't lecture on the subject. Yet.

As her students began heading out, she strolled over to Simon. "I saw your face."

"That's because it's right here, on the front of my head."

"The look on your face when I mentioned neutering." She gave him a poke. "He'll still be a guy. Balls don't make the man."

"Easy for you to say, sister."

"And what are you going to say the first time he catches a whiff of some sexy bitch in heat and runs off to bang her?"

"Score?"

She poked him again. "And following those instincts, he could get hit by a car on the road, get lost. Now, do you really want to add to the stray and/or unwanted dog population? The number of dogs put to sleep every year just so yours keeps his balls and scores?"

"He's more into dead fish than sex."

"For now. Responsibly neutering him will help his behavior. Odds are he'll be somewhat calmer."

"Most eunuchs are."

"You force me to give you literature." She picked up the ball Peck dropped at her feet, winged it. Then watched the car cruise down her drive. "They timed it."

"Who?"

"I expect Davey let some people know about what happened. That's Meg and Chuck Greene, from my unit. First class is over, and I don't have another today until this afternoon. So here they are to see if I need company."

She seemed touched rather than annoyed, and Simon took it as his cue to go. "I've got to take off."

"Oh, don't be rude. Wait two minutes so I can introduce you. You didn't bring Quirk and Xena," Fiona called out.

"We're having a people day," Meg called back.

They got out of opposite sides of the car, met in front of the hood and joined hands before they crossed over. Stopping, Simon noted, to greet the dogs.

"Who's this handsome boy!"

Simon watched as Meg, a breezy-looking woman he pegged as late forties, stepped into Jaws's excited leap.

It worked, he had to admit. They'd have to practice.

"That's Jaws. Meg and Chuck Greene, this is Simon Doyle, Jaws's human."

"Simon!" Meg stuck out a hand, then grasped Simon's in both of hers. "I bought a set of your stacked tables from Sylvia. I love them. I've been hoping to run into you."

"Meg and Chuck live over in Deer Harbor. Chuck's a retired

cop, and Meg's one of our lawyers. Simon was here when Davey came by," Fiona added. "And I'm fine."

"We needed to check the cabin," Meg told her. "We've got somebody coming in over the weekend."

"Uh-huh." She didn't buy that for a minute. "Meg and Chuck have a pretty cabin in Moran State Park they rent out."

"Since we were so close, we just came by to see if we could talk you into meeting us for lunch. We thought we'd grab an early one at the Rosario."

"Meg."

"And we're entitled to look after you."

"Thanks, but I'm going to stick close to home today. You can pass that on to the next shift."

"Where's your cell phone?" Chuck asked her.

"Inside."

"I want you to start carrying it with you." The tap he gave her nose spoke of affection, and authority. "I don't think you've got a thing to worry about, but use that common sense you've got so much of. Carry your phone."

"All right."

"Are you spending any nights here?" Chuck asked Simon.

"Chuck!"

"I'm not talking to you," he said to Fiona.

"Not yet."

"Wouldn't hurt. You do custom work, don't you?"

"Are you talking about sex or wood?"

There was a beat of silence before Chuck roared out his big laugh, then slapped Simon on the back. "Maybe we'll talk sex over a beer sometime. On the wood, Meg's been after a new china cabinet. Can't find anything that suits her. This one's too big, that one's too small, the other one's not the right wood. If she could tell you what the hell it is she wants and you make it, I'd stop hearing about it."

"We can talk about that. You'd want to show me the space."

"If you've got time this afternoon, after three." Chuck reached in his wallet and pulled out a business card. "Home address is on there."

"Okay. More like four."

"That'll work. Well, come on, Meg, let's get this party started. You?" He pointed at Fiona, then kissed her cheek. "Put your phone in your pocket."

"Yes, sir, Sergeant Greene."

"You take care, Fee. We'll see you this afternoon, Simon."

They walked back to their car as they'd walked from it. Hand in hand.

"They've been married over thirty years, and they still hold hands," Fiona murmured. "He was a cop for twenty-five, down in San Francisco." She waved as they drove out. "They moved here about ten years ago, and he runs a tackle shop. He loves to fish. She does real estate and some family law."

"Did they get married when she was twelve?"

"Oh, boy, she'd love that. She's in her late fifties, he had his sixty-third birthday in January. And yeah, they both look easily ten years younger. I think it's love and happiness. Or just lucky genes."

She picked up the ball one of the dogs had dropped hopefully at her feet, threw it again. "I'm telling you because I always want to know about people, so I tend to give backgrounds, but also because it might help you with the design." She tilted her head. "Since you're so strict about it. Anyway, Chuck figures everybody can find every place on the island. I can give you directions."

"I'll find it."

"All right. I've got to go clean my house, do some laundry and other exciting domestic chores before my afternoon session."

"I'll see you later, then."

He called the dog, headed for his truck.

He didn't kiss her good-bye, Fiona thought, and sighed a little, thinking of the Greenes holding hands.

He boosted the dog in, hesitated, then shut the truck door and strode back to her. He gripped her shoulders, drew her up and into a kiss that was hard and brief and satisfyingly hot.

"Put your phone in your pocket."

When he went back to the truck, drove off without another word, she smiled after him.

PART TWO

The great pleasure of a dog is that you may make a fool of yourself with him and not only will he not scold you, but he will make a fool of himself too.

SAMUEL BUTLER

ELEVEN

Two days later, Fiona started her day with a call on a missing elderly man who'd wandered out of his daughter's home on San Juan Island.

She alerted her unit, checked her pack, added the necessary maps and, choosing Newman, was on her way to Deer Harbor and Chuck's boat. With Chuck at the helm she briefed the unit while they carved through the passage.

"The subject is Walter Deets, eighty-four. He has early-onset Alzheimer's and lives with his daughter and her family on Trout Lake. They don't know what time he left the house. The last time anyone saw him was before he went to bed at about ten last night."

"There's a lot of wooded area around the lake," James put in.

"Do we have any information on what he's wearing?" Lori rubbed Pip's head. "It's pretty chilly out."

"Not yet. I'll talk to the family when we get there. Mai, you'll be working with Sheriff Tyson."

"Yeah. We've worked with him before. Is this the first time he's wandered off?"

"Don't know yet. We'll get all that. The search began just after six, and the family notified the authorities by six-thirty. So they've been searching for about ninety minutes."

Mai nodded. "Tyson doesn't waste time. I remember from before."

"They've got a couple of volunteers picking us up, driving us to the location."

By the time they got to the lake, the sun had burned away the mist. Tyson, brisk and efficient, greeted them.

"Thanks for the quick response. Dr. Funaki, right? You're base?"

"Yes."

"Sal, show Dr. Funaki where she can set up. The son-in-law and his boy are out on the search. I've got the daughter inside. He got dressed—brown pants, blue shirt, red cotton jacket, navy Adidas sneakers, size ten. She says he's wandered once or twice, but hasn't gone far. He gets confused."

"Is he on any meds?" Fiona asked him.

"I had her make a list for you. Physically, he's in good shape. He's a nice guy, used to be sharp as a tack. Taught my father in high school. History. He's five-ten, about a hundred and sixty-five pounds, full head of white hair, blue eyes."

He led her inside a spacious, open-floor-plan house with killer views of the lake.

"Mary Ann, this is Fiona Bristow. She's with Canine Search and Rescue."

"Ben—Sheriff Tyson—said you'd need some things of Dad's—for the dogs to smell. I got his socks, and his pajamas from last night."

"That's good. How was he feeling when he went to bed last night?"

"Fine. Really fine." Her hand fluttered to her throat and away again. Fiona could hear barely controlled tears in her voice. "He'd had a good day. I just don't know when he left. He forgets, and gets confused sometimes. I don't know how long he's been gone. He likes to take walks. Keep fit, he says. He and my mother walked miles every day before she died last year."

"Where did they like to walk?"

"Around the lake, some light hiking in the woods. Sometimes they'd walk over to see us. This was their house, and after Mom died and when Dad started having trouble, we moved here. It's bigger than our house, and he loves it so much. We didn't want him to have to leave his home."

"Where was your house?"

"Oh, it's about three miles from here."

"Could he have gotten confused? Tried to walk there to find you?"

"I don't know." She pressed her knuckles to her lips. "We've lived here for nearly a year now."

"We checked Mary Ann's old place," Tyson added.

"Maybe he and your mother had a favorite spot, or route."

"They had so many. Even five years ago he'd have been able to find his way through the woods around here in the dark, blindfolded." Her eyes teared up. "He taught Jarret—our son—how to hike and camp and fish. He'd declare Hook and Line Day—hook school and drop a line so he and Jarret could— Oh God, wait."

She dashed away.

"How's his hearing?" Fiona asked Tyson.

"He wears a hearing aid—and no, he didn't take it. He's got his glasses, but—"

He broke off when Mary Ann rushed back. "His fishing gear. He took his fishing gear, even his old fishing hat. I didn't think— I don't know why I didn't think of it before."

ARMED WITH DATA, Fiona worked with her unit on strategy.

"He had three favorite fishing spots." She marked the map Mai had posted. "But he also tended to try others, depending on his mood. He's both physically fit and physically active. So while his mental condition may bring on confusion, turning him around, disorienting him, he could overdo it. He takes meds for high blood pressure and, according to the daughter, tends to get emotional and upset when he can't remember things, and he's starting to have some trouble with his balance. He needs a hearing aid and isn't wearing it."

The problem, as Fiona saw it, as she assigned sectors, was that Walter might not, as small kids and the elderly tended to, take the paths of least resistance. He'd tax himself, she thought, facing steep climbs rather than easy slopes.

He'd probably had a purpose and a destination when he started, she thought as she gave Newman the scent. But along the way, it was very likely he'd become confused.

How much worse to be lost, to look around and see nothing familiar, when you once knew every tree, every path, every turn?

Newman was eager and scented along a drainage. The air would rise upslope, and the chimney effect, the rise of the tree lines, would disperse the scent in several directions. When they moved into an area of heavy brush she looked for signs— a bit of torn clothing in the briars, bent or broken branches.

Newman alerted, then chose a path that challenged the quadriceps. When it leveled, she stopped to give her partner water and drink some herself.

She checked her map, her compass.

Could he have detoured, backtracked or looped away from the fishing spot, angled toward his daughter's old house? Going for his grandson after all? The Hook and Line Day?

Pausing, she tried to see the trees, the rocks, the sky, the paths as Walter would see them.

For him, she imagined, getting lost here would be like getting lost in his own home. Frightening, frustrating.

He might become angry and push himself, or scared, only more confused and wander in aimless circles.

She gave Newman the scent again. "This is Walt. Find Walt."

She followed the dog as he clambered over a pile of rocks. Veering toward Chuck's sector, she noted, and called her position in.

When they headed downhill, Newman alerted, strongly, then pushed his body through brush.

She pulled out her tape to mark the alert. "What've you got?" She used her flashlight, switching it on to chase away those green shadows.

She saw the disturbed ground first, the depressions, and

got a picture in her mind of the old man taking a spill, catching himself by the heels of his hands, his knees.

Briars pulling and tearing, she thought. And, playing the light, she saw a few strands of red cotton snagged on thorns.

"Good boy. Good boy, Newman. Base, this is Fee. I'm about fifty yards from my west boundary. We've got some red threads on briars and what looks like signs of a fall. Over."

"Base, this is Chuck. We just found his hat. Fee, Quirk's alerting in your direction. We're moving east. My boy's got something. I'm going to— Hold on! I see him! He's down. Ground falls off here. We're going down to him. He's not moving. Over."

"I'm heading your way, Chuck. We'll assist. Over. Newman! Find Walt. Find!"

She ignored the radio chatter as they continued west, until Chuck reported again.

"We've got him. He's unconscious. Pulse is thready. He's got a head wound, a lot of scratches—face, hands. He's got a gash on his leg, too. We're going to need some assistance getting him out. Over."

"Copy that," Mai said. "Help's on the way."

TIRED, BUT FORTIFIED with the hot dog she'd grabbed in Deer Harbor, Fiona turned toward home. They'd done their job, she thought, and well. Now she had to hope Walter's physical stamina would hold the line against his injuries.

"We did what we could, right?" She reached over and gave Newman a pat. "It's all you can do. You need a bath after all that . . ."

She trailed off, stopped the car. A second dogwood stood pretty as a picture across from the first. And both, she noted, were tidily mulched.

"Uh-oh," she said as her heart sighed. "Direct hit."

Peck and Bogart, thrilled to see her, raced to her car, back to the house as if to say, *Come on! Come on home!*

Instead, she followed impulse, got out and opened the back. "Let's go for a ride."

They didn't have to be asked twice. While her dogs greeted one another, and the stay-at-homes explored all the fascinating scents Newman brought back from the search, she turned her car around.

ON THE PORCH of his shop, Simon sanded a table. The warm day, the sweet air had tempted him outside. With the care and precision of a surgeon, he smoothed the sleek walnut legs. He'd leave this one natural, he decided, and play up that beautiful grain with clear varnish. If somebody wanted uniform, they'd have to buy something else.

"Don't even think about it," he ordered as Jaws tried to belly up for the sandblock Simon used for larger areas. "Not now," he said when the dog bumped his arm with his nose. "Later."

Jaws scrambled off the porch to choose a stick from the piles of other sticks, balls, chew toys and assorted rocks he'd dumped together in the past ninety minutes.

Simon stopped long enough to shake his head. "When I'm finished."

The dog wagged his tail, danced in place with the stick clamped in his jaw.

"That's not going to work."

Jaws sat, lifted a paw, tilted his head.

"Still not going to work," Simon muttered, but he felt himself weakening.

Maybe he could take a break, throw the damn stick. The problem was, if he threw it once, the dog would want him to throw it half a million times. But it was kind of cool he'd actually figured out that if he brought it back and dropped it, he got to chase it again.

"Okay, okay, but I'm only giving you ten minutes, then— Hey!"

Annoyed, after he'd decided to play, he watched Jaws race away. Seconds later, Fiona's car made the curve toward the house.

When she got out, Simon cursed under his breath as Jaws bunched to jump. Hadn't they been working on that for two damn days? She countered, had him sit, then accepted the stick he offered, hurled it like a javelin.

When she opened the back of her car, it became dog mania.

Simon went back to sanding. If nothing else, maybe she'd keep his dog out of his hair until he finished the job. By the time she'd made it to the porch, Jaws had mined his pile for three more sticks.

"Treasure trove," she said.

"He's been trying to con me by dumping stuff there."

She bent down, chose a bright yellow tennis ball, then threw it high and long.

More mania.

"You brought me another tree."

"Since you decided to plant the first one where you did, it skewed the balance. It bothered me."

"And you mulched them."

"No point in going to the trouble to plant something if you don't do it right."

"Thank you, Simon," she said primly.

He spared her a glance, noted her eyes laughed. "You're welcome, Fiona."

"I'd have given you a hand if I'd been home."

"You were out early."

She waited, but he didn't ask. "We had a Search and Rescue on San Juan."

He paused, gave her his attention. "How'd it go?"

"We found him. An elderly man, with early-onset Alzheimer's. He'd wandered out, took his fishing gear. It looks like he got confused, maybe had a little visit to the past in his head and just headed out to one of his fishing holes. More confusion and, from the tracking, he got turned around and tried to hike to his daughter's old house to get his grandson. They live with him now. He did a lot of circling, backtracking, walked miles, we think. Wore himself out, then he took a bad fall."

"How bad?"

"Gashed his head and leg, concussion, hairline fracture on his left ankle and a bunch of bruises, lacerations, dehydration, shock."

"Is he going to make it?"

"He's got a strong constitution, so they're hopeful, but boy, he took a beating. So, you're glad you found him, satisfied the unit did the job and concerned you might've been too late anyway." She picked up another stick. "That looks like it's going to be a nice table. Why don't I thank you for the tree by playing with your dog while you finish?"

He passed the sandblock from hand to hand as he studied her. "Did you come over to play with my dog?"

"I came over to thank you, and since Syl took my morning classes and I don't have my last class of the day until five-thirty, I decided to thank you now, in person."

"What time is it?"

She arched her eyebrows, glanced at her watch. "Three-fifteen."

"That'll work." He tossed the sandpaper down, then stepped off the porch to take her arm and pull her toward the house.

"Are we going somewhere?"

"You know damn well."

"Some might attempt at least a little warming up before—"

He swung her around, crushed his mouth to hers while his hands streaked down to mold her ass.

"You're right, that'll work. I want to say I'm not normally this easy, but—"

"Don't care." This time his hands streaked under her jacket, her shirt, up her bare back.

"Me either. Outside."

"I'm not doing this outside with all these dogs around."

"No." She choked out a laugh, struggled to stay on her feet as they groped each other. "I'm telling the dogs to stay outside."

"Good thinking." He dragged her onto the back deck, through the door.

He yanked off her jacket, shoved her against the wall. As desperation spiked, she dragged at his shirt.

"Wait."

"No."

"No, I mean—I know you're happy to see me, but I really think that's an actual hammer pressing into my . . . Oh God."

He pulled back, glanced down. "Shit. Sorry." And unstrapped his tool belt, dumped it on the floor.

"Just let me—" She shoved his unbuttoned work shirt aside, then pulled up the T-shirt he wore beneath. "Oh, *mmm,*" she said as she pushed her hands up his chest. "Too long," she managed when his mouth clamped on the side of her neck. "Need to hurry."

"Okay." With that he tore her shirt open, popping buttons into the air.

She should've been shocked, possibly annoyed—it had been a decent shirt—but the sound of ripping cloth followed by the rough hands on her breasts shot her within a hairbreadth of the edge.

She shuddered, grinding against him, urgent sounds humming in her throat as she fumbled with his zipper. He tugged hers down, one quick, impatient motion, then slid his hand in, down, over. He watched her face, watched those calm eyes glaze like blue glass as she erupted against him. Then he took her mouth again and drove her until she went limp.

"No, you don't," he murmured when she started to slide down the wall.

The simplest solution was to toss her over his shoulder and find the handiest flat surface. He dumped her on the dining room table, shoved debris aside. Whatever crashed and shattered could be replaced.

Because he wanted her naked, he pulled off her boots. "Your belt, undo it."

"What? Oh." Like a shock victim, she stared at the ceiling while she unhooked her belt. "Am I on the table?"

He pulled her pants down her legs by the hems.

"Am I naked on the table?"

"Not quite yet."

But close enough. He wanted his hands on every inch that was, every inch that wasn't. He dealt with his own boots, pants, then climbed on to straddle her.

"Handy," he decided when he noted the front hook of her bra. He flipped it, then simply lowered to devour.

"Oh. God." She arched, her hands fisting on the table before she dug her fingers into his back. "Thank God. Don't stop. Just don't stop."

He used his teeth, and she thought she'd go mad. Too much, too much, this tidal wave of needs and pleasures and demands. And yet her body consumed them, starved for more.

She heard cloth ripping again and realized he'd torn her panties away.

She was being ravished, she thought as she gasped for air—and the little kernel of shock only added to the wild thrill.

She tried to say his name, to slow things down—just enough to breathe—or to give back. But he shoved her knees back and drove into her. Hard as steel, fast as lightning. And she could only cry out and ride the storm.

She closed around him when she came, squeezing like a fist. The sensation only whipped him on. He'd wanted her, and that want had sharpened over the last days. But now, with that long, tight body quaking under his, those surprising and sexy muscles taut under his hands, that want turned its keen edge inside him.

He took until she went lax, then took more until that edge sliced through him and emptied him out.

She heard music. Angels singing? she thought, dizzy. It seemed odd for angels to sing after table sex. She managed to swallow on a throat wildly dry.

"Music," she murmured.

"My phone. In my pants. Don't care."

"Oh. Not angels."

"No. Def Leppard."

"Okay." She managed to find the energy to lift her hand, stroke it down his back. "Once again, I have to say thank you, Simon."

"No problem."

She let out a rusty laugh. "That's good because I don't think I did much of the work."

"Am I complaining?"

She smiled, closed her eyes and kept stroking his back. "Where are we, exactly?"

"It's the dining-room-slash-downstairs-office area. For now."

"So we had sex on your dining-room-slash . . . workstation."

"Yeah."

"Did you make the table?"

"Yeah."

"It's very smooth." A giggle tickled her throat, then escaped. "And remarkably sturdy."

"I do good work." He lifted his head then, looked down at her. And smiled. "It's cherry with a birch inlay. Pedestal style. I was going to sell it, but now—maybe not."

"If you change your mind, I'd like first bid."

"Maybe. Obviously it suits you."

She touched a hand to his cheek. "Can I get some water? I feel like I climbed Mount Constitution without a bottle."

"Sure."

She lifted her eyebrows when he rolled off the table and strode, naked, out of the room. She was pretty comfortable with her own body, but she couldn't see herself walking around her house naked.

Still, he looked damn good doing it.

She sat up, took a breath, started to stretch with a huge smile on her face. Then stopped in shock. They'd just had crazed sex on the dining room table, in front of open, uncurtained windows. She could see the dogs romping, his drive, her own car.

Anyone could've driven up, hiked up from the beach, out of the woods.

When he walked back in with a bottle of water, already uncapped and half empty, she pointed. "Windows."

"Yeah. Table, windows, ceiling, floor. Here." He passed her the bottle. "I started it, you can finish it off."

"But windows. Daylight, open."

"It's a little late to get shy now."

"I didn't realize." She took a long drink, then another. "It's probably for the best. But next time—if you're interested in next times."

"I'm not done with you yet."

"That's a very Simon way to put it." She took another, slower drink. "Next time I think we should try for a little more privacy."

"You were in a hurry."

"I have no argument."

He smiled at her again. "You make a hell of a centerpiece. All I need is a picture of you, sitting there in the middle of the table, your hair catching just the right amount of sun, all messy around your face, and those long legs drawn up right below those very pretty breasts. I could get a freaking fortune for that table."

"No dice."

"I'll give you thirty percent."

She laughed, but wasn't entirely sure he was joking. "And still no. I wish I didn't have to, but I need to get dressed and go."

He took her hand, turned her wrist to check the time. "We've still got an hour."

"During which I have to get home, clean up. Dogs are . . . very sensitive to scent."

"Got it. They'll smell the sex."

"In indelicate terms, yes. So I need a shower. I also need a shirt. You ripped mine."

"You were—"

"In a hurry." She laughed and, despite the uncurtained windows, was tempted to leap up and do a happy dance on the table. "But I still need to borrow a shirt."

"Okay."

When he walked out naked again, she shook her head. After sliding off the table, she pulled on her pants, her bra.

Just as casually, he walked in and tossed her the shirt she'd recently yanked off him.

"Thanks."

He tugged his work pants on while she pulled on her boots. Though she felt a little dreamy, she matched his easy tone when she stepped over, touched his face again.

"Next time, maybe we'll have dinner first." She kissed him lightly. "Thanks for the tree, and the use of the table."

She walked out, called up her dogs and gave Jaws a body-scrub good-bye. It pleased her to see Simon standing out on the deck, shirtless, his hands in the pockets of his yet to be buttoned jeans, watching her as she drove away.

TWELVE

Francis X. Eckle completed the last of his daily One Hundred. A hundred push-ups, a hundred crunches, a hundred squats. He performed these, as always, in the privacy of his motel room.

He showered, using his own unscented shower gel rather than the stingy sliver of motel soap. He shaved, using a compact electric razor that he cleaned meticulously every morning. He brushed his teeth with one of the travel brushes in his kit, which he then marked with an X for future disposal.

He never left anything personal in the motel waste can.

He dressed in baggy sweatshorts and an oversized white T-shirt, nondescript running shoes. Under the T-shirt he wore a security belt holding cash and his current ID. Just in case.

He studied himself in the mirror.

The clothes and the bulk of the belt disguised the body he'd sculpted to mean and muscular perfection, and gave the illusion of an ordinary man, a bit thick in the middle, about his ordinary morning. He studied his face—brown eyes, long, bladed nose, thin, firm mouth, smooth cheeks—until he was satisfied with its pleasant, even forgettable expression.

He kept his brown hair close-cropped. He wanted to shave it for ease and cleanliness, but though a shaved head had become fairly common, his mentor insisted it drew more attention than ordinary brown hair.

This morning, as every morning over the past weeks, he considered ignoring that directive and doing what suited him.

This morning, as every morning, he resisted. But it was becoming harder as he felt his own power grow, as he embraced his new self, to follow the lesson plan.

"For now," he murmured. "But not for much longer."

Over his head, he fit a dark blue cap with no logo.

There was nothing about him to draw the eye, to earn a glance by a casual observer.

He never stayed in the same hotel or motel more than three nights—two was better. He sought out one with a gym at least every other stop, but otherwise looked for the lower-end type of establishment where service—and the attendant attention—was all but nonexistent.

He'd lived frugally all of his life, dutifully pinching pennies. Before he'd begun this journey he'd gradually sold everything he owned of value.

He could afford a great many cheap motel rooms before the journey's end.

He slipped his key card into his pocket and took one of the bottles of water from the case he'd brought in himself. Before leaving the room, he switched on the camera hidden in his travel alarm by his bedside, then plugged in the earbuds for his iPod.

The first would assure him housekeeping didn't poke through his things; the second would discourage conversation.

He needed the gym, needed the weights and machines, and the mental and physical release they provided. Since he'd converted, the days without them left him tense and angry and nervous, clouded his mind. He'd have preferred to work out in solitude, but traveling required adjustments.

So with his pleasant expression in place he walked outside and across to the tiny lobby and the tiny health club.

A man walked with obvious reluctance on one of the two treadmills, and a middle-aged woman rode a recumbent bike while reading a novel with a bright cover. He timed his gym visit carefully—don't be the first or the only.

He chose the other treadmill, selected a program, then switched off the iPod to watch the news on the TV bracketed in the corner.

There would be a story, he thought.

But as the newscasters reported on world events, he started his run and let his mind focus on the latest correspondence from his mentor. He'd memorized every line before destroying it, as he had all the others.

Dear friend, I hope you're well. I'm pleased with your progress to date, but want to advise you not to push yourself too fast, too soon. Remember to enjoy your travels and your accomplishments, and know you continue to have my support and my gratitude as you prepare to correct my foolish and disappointing mistake.

School your body, your mind, your spirit. Maintain your discipline. You are the power, you are the control. Use both wisely and you will amass more fame, more fear, more success than any who have come before you.

I look forward to hearing from you, and know that I am with you, in every step of your journey.

Your Guide

Fate had taken him to that prison, Eckle thought, where George Allen Perry had unlocked the cell he'd been trapped in all of his life. He'd toddled like a child with those first steps of freedom, then had walked, then had run. Now, now he craved the heady taste of that freedom like breath. Craved it until he'd begun to twitch at the rules, the regulations, the absolutes Perry asked of him.

He was no longer the soft, awkward boy desperate for approval and hounded by bullies. No longer the child passed from hand to hand because of a selfish whore of a mother.

No longer the pimply, overweight teen ignored or laughed at by girls.

All of his life he'd lived inside that cage of pretense. Stay quiet, tolerate, obey the rules, study and take whatever was left when the stronger, the more attractive, the more aggressive took theirs.

How many times had he seethed in silence when passed over for a promotion, a prize, a girl? How many times had he, alone, in the dark, plotted and imagined revenge against co-workers, students, neighbors, even strangers on the street?

He'd begun these travels, as Perry had explained to him, before they'd met—but he'd carried the cage with him. He'd worked to discipline his body, pushing through pain and frustration and deprivation. He'd sought and found a rigid internal control, and still had failed in so many ways. Because he'd still been locked in that cage. Unable to perform with women when, at last, one deigned to sleep with him. Forced to humiliate himself with whores—like his mother.

No longer. Perry's creed preached that the act of sexual intercourse diminished a man's power, gave that power to the woman—who would always, *always* use it against him. Release could be gained in other, more potent ways. Ways only a relative few dared practice. With that release power and pleasure rose.

Now that the cage was open, he'd discovered in himself both an aptitude and an appetite for that release, and the power that charged through it.

But with the power came responsibility—and that, he could admit, he found difficult to navigate. The more he gained, the more he wanted. Perry was right, of course. He needed to maintain his discipline, to enjoy the journey and not rush it.

And yet . . .

As he pushed up the speed and resistance on the treadmill, Francis promised himself and his absent mentor he would refrain from seeking his next partner for at least two weeks.

Instead he would travel a bit more—meandering. He would allow his power to recharge, feed his mind with books.

He wouldn't head north, not yet.

And while he recharged and fed, he'd monitor Perry's disappointing mistake through her blog, her website. When it was time, he would correct that mistake—the only payment Perry asked of him, the price for tearing down the cage.

He looked forward, like a child to a parent's applause, to Perry's approval when he took, strangled and buried Fiona Bristow.

Bringing her image into his mind pushed him through the next mile while sweat ran down his face, his body. His reward came when the newscaster reported on the discovery of a young woman's body in Klamath National Forest.

For the first time that morning, Eckle smiled.

ON SUNDAY, Mai and her dogs came for a visit. Saturday night's rain left the air cool and fresh as sorbet and teased out a haze of green on the young dogwoods flanking the bridge. In the field the grasses sparkled with wet while the creek bubbled busily and the dogs romped like kids in a playground.

On the scale of lazy Sunday mornings, Fiona rated this one a solid ten. With Mai, she relaxed on the porch with the mochaccinos and cranberry muffins the vet had bought in the village.

"It's like a reward."

"Hmm?" Slumped down, eyes half open behind the amber shades of her sunglasses, Mai broke off another piece of her muffin.

"Mornings like this, they're like a reward for the rest of the week. All the get-up, get-going, get-it-done mornings. This is the carrot on the stick, the brass ring, the prize at the bottom of the cereal box."

"In my next life I'd like to come back as a dog because, really, in the great scheme? Every morning is the prize at the bottom of the cereal box for a dog."

"They don't get mochaccinos on the porch."

"True, but toilet water would taste just as wonderful."

Fiona studied her coffee, considered. "What kind of dog?"

"I think a Great Pyrenees, for the size, the majesty. I think I deserve it after being short in this life."

"It's a nice choice."

"Well, I've given it some thought." Mai yawned, stretched.

"Sheriff Tyson called me this morning to let me know they upgraded Walter's condition to stable. He's going to be in the hospital for another few days, but if he stays level, they'll let him go home. The daughter and her family are making arrangements for a visiting nurse."

"That's good news. Do you want me to pass it along?"

"I let Chuck know, so I figure he'll take care of that. Since I was heading over, I thought I'd just tell you in person. By the way, I really like your trees."

"Aren't they great?" Just looking at them made Fiona smile. "I don't know why I didn't think of it before. Now I'm thinking maybe I should plant something splashy at the far end of the drive. Like an entryway. It'd be a kind of landmark for new clients, too. Turn at the drive with the . . . whatever I decide on."

Mai tipped down her glasses to peer at Fiona over the tops. "Moving out of the low-key stage? And I worried you'd put a gate up."

Sipping her coffee, Fiona watched the dogs troop around the yard in what she thought of as The Peeing Contest. "Because of Vickie Scala?" she said, referring to the latest victim. "A gate wouldn't do me much good if . . . and it's a big if."

But like Mai and her next life as a dog, she'd given it some thought.

"It makes me sick to think about those girls, and their families. And there's nothing I can do, Mai. Nothing at all."

Mai reached over, squeezed Fiona's hand. "I shouldn't have said anything."

"No, it's okay. It's on my mind. How could it not be? And I'm scared. You're probably the only one I can say that to, just flat-out." Fiona held on to Mai's hand a moment, steadied by the contact. "I'm scared because if. I'm scared because there's nothing I can do. I'm scared because it took them years to catch Perry, and I don't know how I'll cope if the pattern repeats. If I said that to Syl or my mother, they'd turn themselves inside out with worry."

"Okay." Tone brisk, Mai shifted to face Fiona. "I think you'd be stupid not to be scared, and why the hell would you be stupid? I think if it wasn't on your mind, you'd be hiding in denial, and what good would that do? And I think if you didn't feel sick and sorry about those girls, you'd be heartless, and how could you be?"

"And there," Fiona said on a wave of relief, "is why I could say it to you."

"Now, on the other end of the scale, on the solid reasons not to freak—scared, yes, freaked, no—you have the dogs, and you have people who're going to be checking on you with such annoying regularity you'll be tempted to tell them to butt the fuck out. Oh, and don't bother to tell me to butt the fuck out," she added. "I'll just kick your ass. Short, yes, but mighty."

"Yes, you are. I also know we're sitting here drinking mochaccinos and watching our dogs play because you're checking on me. And I appreciate it."

"You're welcome. I want you to plant your splashy whatever at the end of your drive, Fee, if it makes you happy. But I want you to be careful, too."

"Part of me wonders if I've ever really stopped being careful since the day Perry grabbed me."

"What do you mean?"

"I stopped running, and God, Mai, I used to love it. Now I use a treadmill, and it's not the same rush. But I settle because I feel safer. I haven't gone anywhere alone in years."

"That's not . . ." Mai paused. "Really?"

"Really. You know, it didn't occur to me until this started that I never go anywhere without at least one of the dogs—and part of the reason is what happened to me. I wait for movies to come out on DVD or cable instead of going to the movies because I don't want to leave one of the dogs in the car that long—and more, I only take all three of them, leaving the house unguarded, when it's for training or when I'm taking them into your office."

"There's nothing wrong with that."

"No, and I'm okay with it—I just didn't realize the underlying reason for it. Or didn't admit it. I leave my door open a lot. I rarely lock it—until recently—because the dogs give me the sense of security I need. I haven't actively thought about all that happened, not really, in the last year or two, but I've protected myself, or at least my sense of security, all this time."

"Proving you have a smart unconscious."

"I like to think so. My conscious is also doing some target practice. I haven't done any shooting in a couple years either. So . . ." She shook it all off. "I'm doing whatever I can, which includes not obsessing about it. Let's talk about the spa."

Enough, Mai decided. She hadn't come to drag Fiona into the stress but to help ease it. "We could, and we should, but first I could tell you about my date for drinks this evening."

"You have a date?" This time Fiona lowered her sunglasses. "With who?"

"With Robert. He's a psychologist, with his own practice in Seattle. Forty-one, divorced, with a nine-year-old daughter. He shares custody. He has a three-year-old Portuguese water dog named Cisco. He likes jazz, skiing and travel."

"You used HeartLine-dot-com."

"I did, and I'm taking the ferry over and meeting him for drinks."

"You don't like jazz, or skiing."

"No, but I like dogs, I like to travel when I can, and I like kids, so it balances out." Stretching out her legs, Mai studied the toes of her shoes. "I like ski lodges, with roaring fires and Irish coffee, so that's half a point. Besides, I have a date, which means I'm going to put on a nice outfit, fuss with my makeup and go have a conversation with someone I haven't met. And if there's no zing, I get on the ferry, come home and try again."

"I'd be nervous. Are you nervous?"

"A little, but it's a good nervous. I want a relationship, Fee, I really do. It's not just the dry spell, because, hello, Stanley. I want someone I care enough about to want to spend time with, be with, fall in love with. I want a family."

"I hope he's wonderful. I hope Robert the psychologist is freaking amazing. I hope there's zing and common ground and palpitations and laughs. I really do."

"Thanks. The best part is, I'm doing something for myself. Taking a chance, which I haven't done, not really, since the divorce. Even if there's zing, I'm going to take it slow. I want to get a feel for how this whole thing works before I jump into the pool."

Feeling the vibes of Mai's good nerves and anticipation, Fiona sat silently a minute. "Well, speaking of zing, I guess I have to tell you I've lost the contest."

"The— You had sex?" Mai scooted around in her chair, whipped off her sunglasses. "You had sex and didn't tell me?"

"It was only a couple of days ago."

"You had sex a couple of days ago and didn't immediately call me? Who— Well, shit, why would I even ask? It has to be Simon Doyle."

"It could've been a new client I was suddenly hot for."

"No, it was Simon—who actually is a new client you're hot for. Details. The nitty and the gritty."

"He gave me the trees."

"Oh." Mai sighed, turned to look at them. "Oh," she sighed again.

"I know. The first one was part of a deal, a trade for this stump he wanted."

"The stump sink. I heard about it."

"I said maybe I should get another, and he got it, planted it—when we were out on the search. I came home, and there it was—planted, mulched, watered. I got the other dogs and went over to thank him. And I guess I thanked him by having sex with him on his dining room table."

"Sweet magnetic Jesus on the dashboard. On the table?"

"It just sort of happened."

"How does it happen that trees lead to table sex?"

"One minute we're outside talking, then he's pulling me to the house. Then we're all over each other and pulling and dragging each other toward the front door."

"This is the flaw in the Stanley system—the lack of pulling and dragging. Then what?"

"And when we got there, I'm up against the wall, actually telling him to hurry. So he dumped me on the table, shoved things off and wow. Wow."

"A moment to recover, please." Sitting back, Mai waved a hand in front of her face. "Obviously this wasn't crappy sex."

"I almost hate to say it because it might make it more than it might be, but it was, it really was the best sex of my life. And I loved Greg, Mai, but this? It was outrageously stupendous sex."

"Are you going to see him again that way?"

"Definitely." Fiona laid a hand on her heart, did a pat-pat. "Plus or moreover or first and foremost, I like him. I like the way he is, the way he looks, the way he is with his dog. And you know, I like that I'm not his type—at least according to him—but he wants me. It makes me feel . . . powerful, I guess."

"That much like could get serious."

"It could. I guess, like you, I'm doing something for my-self, and taking a chance."

"Okay. Here's to us." Mai lifted what was left of her coffee. "Adventurous women."

"It feels good, doesn't it?"

"Seeing as you had sex on the dining room table, it prob-ably feels better to you. But yeah, it feels good."

They both glanced over as the dogs sounded the alert.

"Well, well, lookie here," Mai murmured as Simon drove over the bridge. "Is your table cleared off?"

"Ssh!" Fiona strangled a laugh. "Either way," she mut-tered, "I've got the first of my Sunday sessions in about twenty minutes."

"Just enough time to—"

"Cut it out." She watched Simon get out and Jaws leap after him. Jaws raced for her dogs, then stopped to sniff and wag at and around Mai's. "No aggression," she commented, "no shyness. He's a damn happy dog."

Simon walked over, held out a collar. "The one I borrowed before. Dr. Funaki."

"Mai. Nice to see you, Simon, and with such good timing as I have to go. But first. Jaws, come here. Here, Jaws."

The pup reacted with joy, bulleting over and onto the porch. Mai held her hand out, palm first, as he bunched to leap. He shivered, so obviously dying for just one jump, but stayed down.

"What a good dog." She stroked, rubbed, smiled up at

Simon. "He reacts well to a group, is cheerfully friendly, and he's learning his manners. You've got a winner here."

"He's stealing my shoes."

"The chewing stage can be a problem."

"No, he's not chewing them—anymore. He just steals them and hides them. I found my boot in the bathtub this morning."

"He's found a new game." Mai ruffled his ears while the other dogs came up to bump and squeeze in for attention. "Your shoes carry your scent, obviously. He's attracted to and comforted by your scent. And he's playing with you. Aren't you clever?" She gave Jaws a kiss on the nose, then rose. "It's time to think about neutering."

"What are you two, a tag team?"

"Read the literature I gave you. We'll talk soon," she said to Fiona. "Oh, cleavage or legs?"

"Legs, save the girls for round two."

"That's what I thought. Bye, Simon. Come on, babies! Let's go for a ride."

"You won't ask," Fiona said as she waved Mai and her dogs off, "so I'll just tell you. She has a date—a first date—and was asking which asset to highlight."

"Okay."

"Men don't have to worry about that particular area of dating ritual."

"Sure we do. If it's cleavage we still have to look you in the face and pretend not to notice."

"You've got a point." Since he stood on the steps, she laid her hands on his shoulders, leaned in for an easy kiss. "So, I've got a class in a few minutes. Did you time this visit to check up on me?"

"I returned the collar."

"So you did. If you want you can stay for the class. It might be good for Jaws to interact with another set of dogs. It's a small group, and we're going to work on some basic search skills. I'd like to see how he does."

"We've got nothing else going on. Teach him something else."

"Now?"

"I need a distraction. I've been thinking about getting you naked since I got you naked. So teach him something else."

She slid her hands up, brushed them over his cheeks. "You know, that's oddly romantic."

"Romance? I'll pick a couple wildflowers next time I think about getting you naked. And this isn't distracting me, so . . . where the hell is he?"

Simon scanned the porch, turned. "Oh, shit."

Fiona grabbed his arm as he braced to run.

"No, wait. He's fine." She studied Jaws as he climbed up the ladder of the sliding board after Bogart. "He wants to play with the big guys. If you run or call out, you'll break his focus and balance."

Jaws climbed to the top, tail waving like a flag, but unlike Bogart, who pranced his way down the short slide, he slipped at the top, belly-flopped, then did a slow header into the soft ground below.

"Not bad," Fiona declared as Simon snorted out a laugh. "Get your treats." She walked over, calling out praise and approval in a cheerful voice. "Let's try it again, want to try it again? Climb," she said, adding a hand signal. "He does well on the ladder," she said as Simon joined her, "and that's generally the most difficult. It's open and it's vertical. He's agile, and he's watched the other dogs do it. He's figured out how to go up. So . . . there we are, good boy."

She took a treat from Simon, rewarded the dog when he reached the top. "You just need to give him a little help figuring out how to walk down, keep his footing. Walk. That's it. Good balance. Good, good job." She rewarded him again at the bottom. "You do it with him so . . . What?" she demanded when she looked up to find him staring at her.

"You're not beautiful."

"There you go again, Mr. Romance."

"You're not, but you grab hold. I haven't figured out why."

"Let me know when you do. Take him up and down."

"And I'm doing this because?"

"He's learning how to navigate unstable footing. It gives him confidence, enhances his agility. And he likes it."

She stepped back, watched the two of them play the game a few times. Not beautiful, she thought. The observation, and the fact that he just *said* it, should've been a flick to the ego—even though it was perfectly true. So why had it amused her, at least for the few seconds between that and his next comment?

You grab hold. That made her heart flutter.

The man incited the oddest reactions in her.

"I want him," Fiona said when Jaws all but swaggered down the slide.

"You've got your pronouns confused. Me. You want me."

"I admire your ego, but I meant him."

"Well, you can't have him. I'm getting used to him, and besides, my mother would be seriously pissed if I gave him away."

"I want him for the program. I want to train him for S-and-R."

Simon shook his head. "I've read your website, your blog. When you say train him, you mean us. Those crazy pronouns again."

"You read my blog?"

He shrugged. "I've skimmed it."

She smiled. "But you have no interest in S-and-R?"

"You have to drop everything when a call comes in, right?"

"That's pretty much right."

"I don't want to drop everything, or whatever."

"That's fair enough." She took a little band out of her pocket, bound her hair back with a couple of quick twists. "I could train him as an alternate. Just him. He responds to me, obviously. And any S-and-R dog needs to respond to other handlers. There are times one of our dogs is unable—sick, maybe, injured."

"You have three."

"Yes, because, well, I want three, and yes, because if someone else's dog is unable, one of mine can go as backup. I've been doing this for years now, Simon, and your dog would be good. He'd be very good. I'm not giving you the pitch to join the unit, just to train your dog. On my own time. If nothing else, you'll end up with a dog with superior skills and training."

"How much time?"

"Ideally, I'd like to work with him a little every day, but at least five days a week. I can do it at your place and stay out of your way while you're working. Some of what I teach him you'll want to follow up on."

"Maybe. We can see how it goes." Simon glanced over to where Jaws was engaged in one of his favorite activities: chasing his own tail. "It's your time."

"Yeah, it is. Clients coming," she announced. "You can sit this one out if you want. I can work with him solo."

"I'm here anyway."

IT WAS INTERESTING, Simon decided, and semi-distracting. Fiona called it The Runaway Game, and it involved a lot of running—dogs and people—in the field across her bridge. The class worked in pairs, or with Fiona as a partner—one dog at a time.

"I don't get the point," he said when Jaws was up. "He's going to see where I'm going. He'd have to be an idiot not to find me."

"It teaches him to find you on command, and to use his scenting skill—that's why we're running against the wind, so our scent goes toward the dog. Anyway, he's going to find me. You need to get him excited."

He looked down at the dog, whose tail chopped the air like a Ginsu knife. "He gets excited if somebody glances in his direction."

"Which is to his advantage. Talk to him, be excited. Tell him to watch me when I run away. Watch Fee! Then the minute I drop down behind the bush, tell him to find and release him. Keep telling him to find me. If he gets confused, give him a chance to catch my scent. If it doesn't work the first time, I'll call him, give him an audio clue. You need to hold him, keep him with you while I get his attention, and run. Ready?"

He finger-combed his breeze-ruffled hair out of his face. "It's not brain surgery."

She gave Jaws a rub, let him lick and sniff at her before she straightened. "Hey, Jaws! Hey." She clapped her hands. "I'm going to run. Watch me, Jaws, watch me run. Tell him to watch me. Use my name."

She took off at a dash.

She hadn't exaggerated, Simon noted. She was *fast*.

And he'd been wrong. When she moved, she was beautiful.

"Watch Fee. Where the hell's she going, huh? Watch her. Jesus, she's like an antelope. Watch Fee."

She dropped down, out of sight, behind a bush.

"Find her! Go find Fee."

The pup tore across the field, expressing his excitement with a couple happy barks. Not as fast as the woman, Simon thought, but . . . Then he felt a quick surge of surprise and pride as Jaws homed straight in.

A couple of the other dogs had needed the hider to call out, and one had required the visual clue of the hider waving a hand beside the bush.

But not Jaws.

Across the field he could hear Fiona laughing and praising even as his temporary classmates applauded.

Not half bad, Simon thought. Not bad at all.

She ran back with the dog happily chasing her.

"We do it again, right away. Praise first, reward, then we go again."

"HE ACED IT," Simon murmured when the class was over. "Three times in a row, different hiding spots."

"He's got the knack. You can work with him at home, with objects. Use something he likes, that he knows the name of— or work to teach him the name. Show it to him, then make him sit/stay and go hide it. Easy places at first. Go back, tell him to find. If he can't find it, guide him to it. You want success."

"Maybe I should tell him to find my tennis shoe. I don't know where the hell he put it." He looked at her, a long, thorough look that had her raising her eyebrows. "You run like the fucking wind, Fiona."

"You should've seen me run the four-hundred-meter hurdles in college. I was amazing."

"Probably because you have legs up to your ears. Did you wear one of those skinny little uniforms—aerodynamic?"

"I did. Very flattering."

"I bet. How long before the next class?"

"Forty-five minutes."

"Long enough." He began to back her toward the house.

She kept her eyes on his, and he saw the laugh in them, a sparkle on the serene blue. "No 'Would you like to?' or 'I can't resist you'?"

"No." He clamped her waist, lifted her up the porch steps.

"If I said I'm not in the mood?"

"I'd be disappointed, and you'd be lying."

"You're right about the lying. So . . ." She pulled the door open, tugged him inside.

But when she backed toward the steps, he shifted directions.

"Couch is closer."

It was also softer than the dining room table, at least until they rolled off and hit the floor. And it was, Fiona thought when she lay beside him trying to regain her breath and the path to coherent thought, every bit as exciting.

"Eventually we might make it to a bed."

He trailed, very lightly, a fingertip over her breast. "Cancel the class and we'll go up now."

"It's a shame I'm a responsible woman—and one who barely has time to take a shower."

"Oh yeah, the obligatory shower. I could use one."

"Doubling up would only lead to shower sex."

"Damn straight."

"Which, while fun, I have no time for. Besides, you and Jaws can't do the next class. It risks overtraining. But you could—" She broke off when the dogs announced visitors. "Oh hell, oh shit!" Scrambling, she grabbed her shirt, her pants, bundled them in front of her as she hunched toward the window.

"It's James, and oh God, Lori. It's James and Lori and I'm naked in the living room on a Sunday afternoon." She glanced back. "And you're naked on the floor."

She looked so sexily flustered, a little wild in the eye and pink from her toes to her hairline.

Delicious, he thought. He could've lapped her up like ice cream. "I like it here."

"No! No! Get up!" She waved her hands, dropped her shirt, grabbed it again. "Up, get something on. Go . . . go tell them I'll be out in five minutes."

"Because you're taking an after-sex shower?"

"Just . . . get your pants on!" Still hunched, she sprinted for the stairs.

Grinning—she looked even more interesting running naked—he tugged on his pants, tossed on his shirt and, grabbing his socks and boots, strolled out onto the porch.

James and Lori stopped greeting the dogs. James's eyes narrowed. Lori flushed.

"She'll be out in a couple minutes." Simon sat to put on his socks and boots. Jaws instantly made a lunge for a boot. Simon swung it out of reach, said, "Cut it out."

"Nice-looking dog. How's his training coming?"

"It's coming. We just took in a class."

James's eyes stayed narrowed. "Is that what you just did?"

Simon laced up his boot, smiled coolly. "Among other things. Is that a problem for you?"

Lori patted frantically at James's arm. "We just dropped by to see if Fiona wanted to grab some dinner after her classes. You could join us."

"Thanks, but I've got to get on. See you around." He walked to his truck. Jaws danced in place, obviously torn, then ran after Simon, leaped into the cab of the truck.

"I don't know about this," James muttered.

"It's not our business—exactly."

"It's the middle of the afternoon, practically. It's daylight."

"Prude." Lori elbowed him and laughed.

"I'm not a prude, but—"

"People make love in the daylight, James. Plus I like knowing he's around, spending time with her. Didn't you say we should come by just to check on her?"

"Yeah, but we're her friends."

"I think Fee and Simon are pretty friendly. Just a wild guess. I'm sorry if you're jealous, but—"

"I'm not." Genuinely surprised, he stopped scowling after Simon and turned to her.

"I know you and Fee are close," Lori began, lowering her lashes.

"Wow. No. Not that way."

The lashes lifted again. "At all?"

"At all, as in never. Jeez, do people actually think . . . ?"

"Oh, I don't know about people. I guess I just thought you were, or had been or maybe hoped to." She managed an embarrassed laugh. "I'll shut up now."

"Listen, Fee and I are . . . we're like family. I don't think about her that way. I don't think that way." He paused until she looked at him, looked in his eyes. "About Fee."

"Maybe you think that way about somebody else?"

"All the time."

"Oh." She laughed again. "Thank God."

He started to touch her; she started to let him. And Fiona rushed out of the house.

"Hey! Hi. It's my day for pals. Did Simon leave?"

James let out a long breath. "Yeah, he said he had to go."

"Sorry," Lori put in. "Lousy timing."

"Actually, it could've been worse. Or much more embarrassing for all. Let's just close the door on all that. So." She offered a big, bright smile. "What are you two up to?"

THIRTEEN

O rganic milk." Fiona unloaded the items she'd picked up for Sylvia. "Free-range eggs, goat cheese, lentils, brown rice and one shiny eggplant. Mmm, yummy."

"I shudder to think what you've got in the car."

"Besides Bogart? You're better off not knowing."

"Fat, salt, starch and sugar."

"Maybe, but also a couple of very pretty apples. And look what I got for you," she said to Oreo, "because you're so cute."

She pulled out a squeaky toy, gave it a squeeze and sent the little dog into a quiver of delight. "Sylvia," she said when she offered the toy, and Oreo pranced off with it. "I'm having an affair." With a laugh she turned two quick circles. "I'm closing in on thirty, and I've never been able to say that before. I'm having a hot, steamy, crazy affair."

With the one shiny eggplant in her hand, Sylvia smiled. "It's certainly giving you a relaxed, happy glow."

"Is it?" Fiona laid her hands on her own cheeks. "Well, I am relaxed and happy. You know it was never an affair with Greg. It was friendship and a crush and a relationship one after another, or altogether. But a slow build. And this? This has been *pow!* Explosive."

She leaned on the kitchen counter, grinned. "I'm having scorching, no-strings sex, and it's fabulous."

"Do you want to keep it that way?" Sylvia gave Fiona's hair, loose today, swinging, a quick stroke. "The no strings?"

"I'm not thinking about that yet." Fiona lifted her shoulders, let them fall in a kind of internal hug. "I like this phase of not thinking about it."

"Exciting. A little dangerous. Unpredictable."

"Yes! And that's all so unlike me. No plans, no checklist."

"And all glow."

"If it keeps up, I may turn radioactive." Charged, she broke a sprig of glossy green grapes from the bunch in the bowl on the counter and began popping them into her mouth. "I've been training Jaws one-on-one. Over a week now, which means either I go over there or Simon brings the dog to me. And we don't always . . . There isn't always time, but there's always heat."

"Don't you ever go out? I mean, wouldn't you like to go have dinner or catch a movie?"

"I don't know. That all seems . . ." She whisked a hand through the air. "Outside right now. Maybe we will, or maybe it'll burn off. But right now, I feel so *involved*, so excited, so—cliché time—alive. I'm a walking buzz. Did you ever have one? A hot, steamy affair?"

"Yes, I did." After tucking the eggs away, Sylvia closed the refrigerator. "With your father."

Fiona patted a hand to her throat as a grape threatened to lodge. "Seriously?"

"I think we both decided it was just sex, just a fast, exciting ride—during that no-thinking phase."

"Hold on a minute, because I want to hear this but I don't want to get a picture in my head. That's too weird. Okay, okay." She squeezed her eyes shut, nodded. "No video. You and Dad."

Sylvia licked her fingertip, made a hissing sound. "Scorching. I was managing Island Arts in those days. I have many, *many* fond memories of the stockroom."

"I must say . . . wow. Dad in the stockroom."

"Exciting, a little dangerous, unpredictable."

"Like you," Fiona murmured. "Not so much like him—or my perception of him."

"We were like teenagers." She sighed, smiled. "God, he made me feel that way. Of course, I was much too unconventional to consider marriage, so I imagined we'd just continue as we were, until we stopped. And then, I don't know, Fee, how or when or why, not specifically, but then I couldn't imagine my life without him. Thank God he felt the same."

"He was so nervous the first time he took me to meet you. I know I was young, but I knew he loved you because he was so nervous."

"He loved us both. We were lucky. Still, when he asked me to marry him, I thought, Oh no, absolutely not. Marriage? Just a piece of paper, just an empty ritual. I thought absolutely not, but I said yes—and stunned myself. My heart," she murmured, laying her hand over it. "My heart wouldn't say no."

Fiona ran those words through her mind on the drive home. *My heart wouldn't say no.*

She thought it lovely, and at the same time felt relief that, at the moment, her heart kept silent. A speaking heart could break—she knew that very well. As long as hers remained content, she'd stay relaxed and happy.

Spring was beginning to show her face as field and hill and forest steeped in green, sprinkled by the bold yellow of wild buttercups, like grains of shaken sunlight. Maybe there was a dusting of snow high up on Mount Constitution, but the contrast of white peaks against soft blue only made the shy blooms of the early white fawn lilies more charming, the three-note call of the sparrow more poignant.

Right at the moment, she felt like the island—coming alive, blooming, busy with the business of being.

Classes and clients and work on her blog packed her days, while her unit and training added the spice of satisfaction. Her own three dogs gave her love, entertainment, security. Her very hot neighbor kept her excited and aware—*and* had a dog she believed she could mold into a solid, even superior, Search and Rescue dog.

The police didn't have any news—not that they were sharing, in any case—on the three murdered women, but . . . There'd been no more abductions reported in two weeks.

As she rounded a curve she caught sight of the iridescent blur of a hummingbird zipping along a clump of red-flowering currant.

If that couldn't be taken as a good omen, she mused, what could?

"No bad news, Bogart, just the—what is that song?—the birds and the bees and the flowers and the trees. Hell, that's going to stick in my head."

He thumped his glossy black tail, so she sang it again. "I don't know the rest—before my time, you know. Anyway, errands are done, we're nearly home. And you know what? Maybe I'll give Jaws's daddy a call, see if he wants to come over for dinner. I could cook. Something. It might be time we had ourselves a date—and a sleepover. What do you say? Do you want Jaws to come over and play? Let's get the mail first."

She turned into the drive, parked and walked over to the box on the side of the road. She tossed the mail into one of the grocery bags. "We'd better get this stuff put away so I can see if I actually have anything to make for dinner—the sort you make when somebody comes over."

As she carried bags inside she wished she'd had the idea earlier. Then she could've picked up something, put together an actual adult menu.

"I could go back," she mused, stowing frozen dinners, cans. "Pick up a couple of steaks. You know what?" She tossed the mail on the table, put away the cloth bags Sylvia had given her for grocery runs. "I could just call the pizza place and sweet-talk them into a delivery."

Considering the options, she picked up the mail. "Bill, bill, oh, and, surprise, bill." She lifted the padded mailing bag.

"Not a bill. Hey, guys, maybe this is some pictures from one of our graduates."

Her former clients often sent her photos and updates. Pleased to have something that wasn't a bill, she zipped open the bag.

The gauzy red scarf fell onto the table.

She stumbled back, revulsion and panic rising in her throat like burning reflux. For a moment the room spun around her, gray at the edges so the snake coil of the scarf boiled red. Pain crashed into her chest, blocking her breath until the gray swam with white dots. She groped behind her, clamped one white-knuckled hand on the counter as her legs liquefied.

Don't faint, don't faint, don't faint.

Bearing down, she sucked in air, hissed it out, and forced her quivering legs to move. Even as she reached for the phone, the dogs milling around her in concern went on alert.

"Stay with me. Stay with me." She gasped it out as hammers of panic slammed against her ribs. She swore she heard the strike of them cracking her bones like glass.

Fiona grabbed the phone with one hand, a carving knife with the other.

"Damn it, Fiona, you left the door open again."

Simon strode in, annoyance in every line. Faced with a woman, pale as wax, holding a very large knife and guarded by three dogs who all growled a low warning, he stopped short.

"You want to tell them to stand down?" he asked. Coolly, calmly.

"Relax. Relax, boys. Friend. Simon's a friend. Say hi to Simon."

Jaws galloped in with a rope, ready to play. Simon walked to the back door, opened it. "Everybody out."

"Go on out. Go outside. Go play."

Still watching her, Simon closed the door behind the rush of bodies.

"Put down the knife."

She managed another breath. "I can't. I can't seem to let go of it."

"Look at me," he ordered. "Look at me." His eyes on hers,

Simon put a hand on her wrist and used the other to release the vise of her fingers on the handle of the knife. He shot it back into the slot on the cutting board.

"What happened?"

She lifted a hand, pointed at the table. Saying nothing, he walked to the table, stared down at the scarf, the open bag.

"Finish calling the cops," he told her, then turned when she didn't speak, didn't move. He took the phone.

"Speed dial one. Sheriff's office. Sorry. I need to just . . ." She slid down, sat on the floor and dropped her head between her knees.

His voice was a vague buzz under the thunder of her heart in her ears. She hadn't fainted, she reminded herself. She'd armed herself. She'd been ready.

But now, now all she wanted to do was come apart.

"Here. Drink." Simon took her hand, wrapped it around a glass of water. "Drink it, Fiona." Crouching, he guided the glass to her lips, watching her steadily.

"Your hands are hot."

"No, yours are cold. Drink the water."

"Can't swallow."

"Yes you can. Drink the water." He nudged it on her, sip by slow sip. "Davey's on his way."

"Okay."

"Tell me."

"I saw a hummingbird. I saw a hummingbird, and I stopped to get the mail. It was in the mail. I picked up the mail, brought it in with the groceries. I thought it might be pictures of one of my dogs—students. I get them sometimes. But . . ."

He rose, took the bag by the corner with two fingers, flipped it over. "It's postmarked Lakeview, Oregon. There's no return address."

"I didn't look. I just opened it—right before you came in. Right before."

"I couldn't have walked in and scared you if you hadn't left your door open."

"You're right." The knot at the base of her throat wouldn't loosen. The water wouldn't wash it away, so she focused on

Simon's face, the rich tea color of his eyes. "That was careless. Comes from being relaxed and happy. Stupid." She pushed to her feet, set the glass on the counter. "But I had the dogs. I had a weapon. If it hadn't been you, if it had been . . ."

"He'd have a hard time getting by the dogs. Odds are he wouldn't. But if he did, goddamn, if, Fiona, he'd have taken that knife away from you in two seconds."

Her chin came up; so did her color. "You think so?"

"Look, you're strong, and you're fast. But grabbing a weapon you have to use close in, and can be used against you, isn't a smart alternative to running."

Her movements jerky, she yanked open a drawer, pulled out a spatula. The knot dissolved, with anger and insult in its place. "Take it away from me."

"For Christ's sake."

"Pretend it's a knife. Prove your point, goddamn it."

"Fine." He shifted, feinted with his right hand, then reached for her arm with his left.

Fiona changed her leg base, grabbed his reaching arm and used his momentum to drag him by. He had to slap a hand against the wall or run face-first into it.

"Now I've just stabbed you in the back with the knife—or if I'd been feeling less murderous, I'd have kicked you in the back of the knees and taken you down. I'm not helpless. I'm *not* a victim."

He turned toward her. Fury shone on her face now, infinitely preferable to fear.

"Nice move."

"That's right." She nodded sharply. "That's goddamn right. Do you want to see another? Maybe the one where I kick your balls up against the back of your teeth, then beat you into a coma when you're on the ground writhing in pain."

"We can skip that one."

"Being scared doesn't make me weak. Being scared means I'll do anything and everything I have to do to defend myself." She heaved the spatula into the sink. "Couldn't you show some compassion, some understanding instead of jumping down my throat?"

"You're not sitting on the floor shaking anymore. And I'm feeling less inclined to punch my fist through the wall."

"And that's your method?"

"I haven't been in a situation like this before but apparently, yes, that's my method." He took the spatula out of the sink, shoved it back in the drawer. "But if you want the strong male to blubbering female, we can go with that."

"Blub— *God!* You piss me off. Which is," she said after a righteous breath, "exactly the goal. Well, bull's-eye for you."

"It makes me crazy."

She pushed her hands over her face, back into her hair. "What?"

"Seeing you like that. Have you ever seen yourself when you're seriously scared, seriously sad? You lose every drop of color in your face. I've never seen anybody still breathing get that white. And it makes me crazy."

She dropped her hands again. "You're damn good at leashing the crazy."

"Yeah, I am. We can talk about that some other time. Don't think—" He broke off, shoved his own hands in his pockets. "Don't think you don't matter. You do. I just haven't— Now, see?" he said with raw frustration. "The minute I stop pissing you off you start crying."

"I'm not crying." She blinked desperately at the tears welling in her eyes. "And what's wrong with crying? I'm entitled. I'm entitled to a jag of major proportions, so be a man, damn it, grow a pair and suck it up."

"Crap." He yanked her against him, chained his arms around her.

She felt the sob flood her throat. Then he eased her back, skimmed his fingers down her cheek, laid his lips on her brow.

The tenderness shocked her eyes dry, killed the sob before it released. Instead she let out a long, shuddering sigh and leaned on him.

"I don't know how to take care of people," he muttered. "I'm barely able to take care of a damn dog."

You're wrong about that, she thought. So wrong about that.

"You're doing okay," she managed. "I'm okay." Still she jolted when the dogs barked the alert. "That'll be Davey."

"I'll go let him in." He stroked his hand down her hair once, twice. "Sit down or something."

Sit down or something, Fiona thought as Simon walked out. Then she took his advice and made herself sit at the kitchen table.

Simon walked out onto the porch. "She's inside, back in the kitchen."

"What—"

"She'll fill you in. I need about twenty minutes, and I need to know you'll be here that long."

"All right."

Simon headed to his truck, ordered Jaws to stay, then drove away.

Calmer, Fiona thought, she was much calmer when Davey came in. "I haven't touched it since I opened it," she began. "I don't guess that's going to matter." She looked over his shoulder, frowned. "Where's Simon?"

"He had something to do."

"He— Oh." The pressure on her chest returned, just for a moment. "Fine. It was in the mail. It's got an Oregon postmark."

He sat first, took her hands. Just took her hands.

"Oh God, Davey. I'm scared senseless."

"We're going to look out for you, Fee. If you want it, we'll have somebody parked outside the house twenty-four hours a day until they catch this bastard."

"I don't think I'm ready for that. Yet. It could come to it."

"Have you gotten any unusual calls, any hang-ups? Anything troubling on your website or blog?"

"No. This is the first thing. And I know it might not be from him. It's probably not. It's from some vicious person who read that damn article, got my address. That's just as likely."

"Maybe it is." He released her hands, took out two evidence bags. "I'm going to take these in. We'll do what we can. There's a federal task force on this now, and we'll probably need to turn these over to them. Fee, it's likely they're going to send someone out to talk to you."

"I'm okay with that." Wouldn't be the first time, she thought bitterly. "I'm good with that."

"We'll be reaching out to the police in Lakeview. I know this is hard for you, but maybe it's a break. We might get prints or DNA off the stamp. Something from the handwriting, or we'll trace the scarf."

Investigations, routines, procedures. How was it all happening again?

"What about Perry? He might have paid somebody to send it to me."

"I'm going to see what I can find out, but I have to think they've talked to Perry. They'd monitor his contacts, his visitors, his mail. We're not really in the loop, Fee, but after this the sheriff's going to push that. Maybe this was just some asshole's idea of a nasty joke, but everybody's going to take it seriously. I can bunk on the couch."

He would, she thought, for as long as she needed. "You've got a family. I have the dogs."

He leaned back. "Do you have anything cold to drink?"

She cocked her head. "Because you're thirsty, or because you don't want to leave me alone?"

He gave her a hard stare. "You can't spare a cold drink for a hardworking civil servant?"

She got up, opened the fridge. "You're lucky I just hit the market. I have Coke, OJ, bottled water and V8 Splash. Beer, too, but as you're a hardworking civil servant on duty—"

"I'll take the Coke."

"Ice and lemon?"

"Just hand over the can, Fee. Why don't we take it out on the porch, take advantage of the weather?"

She got out a second can. "I'm all right on my own, Davey. I'm scared," she added as they walked toward the front door, "but I feel safer and more secure in my own place than I would anywhere else. I'm carrying my cell phone in my pocket. I've done some practicing with my gun—and believe I'll do more before dark. And you'll be happy to know that when Simon walked in while I was having my freak-out, the dogs warned him back until I released them."

"All good, Fee. I'd just be happier if you had somebody staying with you. Why don't you call James?"

The fact that she considered doing just that told her she was shakier than she'd realized. "I don't know. Maybe—"

The dogs alerted when they reached the door. Davey nudged her to the side, opened it himself. And nodded when Simon drove back up. "I guess I'll get going."

She'd been tag-teamed, she realized.

"What about the cold drink and taking advantage of the weather?"

"I'm taking the drink with me." He gave her arm a reassuring squeeze before walking out to meet Simon.

Fiona waited where she stood while the two of them had a brief conversation. Davey got in his car, and Simon slung a small knapsack over his shoulder.

"I thought you went home."

"I did. I had to take care of a couple things and get some stuff. I need some of my stuff since I'm staying over tonight."

"You're staying over tonight?"

"Yeah." He took the can of Coke from her, downed some. "If you've got a problem with that, too damn bad."

Her insides softened as another woman's might if a man read her a love sonnet. "I guess you'll expect sex and a hot meal?"

"Yeah, but you can pick the order." He handed her back the Coke.

"I'm a lousy cook."

"Luckily you're good in bed—or wherever." He shrugged. "Don't you have any frozen pizza?"

Still scared, she realized, but she didn't feel like crying anymore, didn't have to fight off trembling anymore.

"I do, but I also have a menu from Mama Mia's. They'll deliver for me."

"That works." He started to move by her, into the house, but she turned, stepped into his arms, held hard.

"Simon." She murmured it as she relaxed against him. "I have no idea why, but you're exactly what I need right now."

"I don't know why either." He tossed the duffel through the open door, then stroked a hand down her back. "You're really not my type."

"That's because I defy typing."

He studied her face when she laughed and leaned back. "Yes, you do."

"Let's take a walk before we order dinner. I need to shake off the last of the jitters."

"Then I want a beer."

"You know what, so do I. Two walking beers coming up."

LATER, THEY SAT on the sofa with a second beer, the fire chasing the evening chill, with a pepperoni pizza in the delivery box between them. Fiona crossed her ankles on the coffee table.

"You know, I keep telling myself I'm going to start eating like an adult."

"We are eating like adults." Simon blocked Jaws's attempt to scoot under his legs for a stab at the pie. "Get lost," he told the dog. "Kids have to eat when and what they're told," he continued. "We get to eat when and what we want. Because we're adults."

"That's true. Plus, I love pizza." She bit into her slice. "There's no food to match it. Still, I was actually thinking before . . . before you came by that I'd ask you over to dinner."

"Then how come I paid for the pizza?"

"You got out your wallet; I let you. I was going to ask you over to dinner that I cooked."

"You're a lousy cook."

She jabbed him with her elbow. "I was going to make an attempt. Besides, I can grill. In fact, I'm superior on the grill. A couple of good steaks, Idahos wrapped in foil—some vegetable kabobs as a nod to a balanced meal. That's where I rule."

"You cook like a guy." He picked up a second slice. "I admire that."

"I guess I owe you a steak dinner, since you paid for the pizza, and you're keeping me company tonight. Tell me about leashing the crazy."

"It's not that interesting. Why don't you have a TV down here?"

"Because I never watch TV down here. I like to watch it in bed, all sprawled out or nested in. The living room's for company and conversation."

"The bedroom's for sleeping and sex."

"Until recently sex wasn't that much of a factor, and watching TV in bed helps me fall asleep." She licked sauce off her thumb. "I know when you're changing the subject, and it won't work. I'm interested."

"I've got an ugly temper. I learned how to keep it under control. That's it."

"Define ugly temper."

He took a pull on his beer. "Fine. When I was a kid and something, someone pissed me off, tried to push me around, I'd go off. Fighting was my answer, the bloodier the better."

"You liked to brawl."

"I liked to kick ass," he corrected. "There's a difference. Brawl? There's something good-natured about that word. I wasn't good-natured about it. I didn't pick fights, I didn't bully other kids, I didn't look for trouble. But I could find a reason to swing, I could find trouble, no problem. Then the switch would go off."

He turned the beer around, idly read the label. "Seeing red? That can be literal. And I'd wade in, and when I waded in, it was to do damage."

She could imagine him wading in—his build, those big, hard hands, the hard line of heat she caught in his eye now and then. "Did you ever hurt anyone seriously?"

"I could have. Probably would have eventually. I got hauled down to the office in school more times than I can count."

"I never did. Not bragging," she added when he turned his

head to eye her. "I sort of wish I hadn't been such a good girl all the damn time."

"You were one of those."

"Sadly, yes. Keep going. Bad boys are so much more interesting than good girls."

"Depends on the girl, and what it takes to bring out the bad." He reached over, released the top two buttons of her shirt until her bra peeked out. "There you go. Pizza slut. Anyway," he continued when she laughed, "I got in some trouble, but I never started the fight—and there were always people around to back me up on that. My parents tried different things to channel it. Sports, lectures, even counseling. The thing was, I got decent grades, didn't smart-mouth teachers."

"What changed?"

"Junior year in high school. I had a rep—and there are always going to be the type who need to challenge the rep. New guy comes along—tough guy. He goes after me; I take him down."

"Just like that?"

"No. It was vicious, on both sides. We hurt each other. I hurt him more. A couple weeks later, he and two of his buddies jumped me. I was with a girl, making out in the park. Two of them held me while he took his shots. She's screaming for them to stop, screaming for help, and he's laughing and beating me until I don't even feel it anymore. At some point I blacked out."

"Oh my God, Simon."

"When I came to, they had her on the ground, holding her down. She's crying, begging. I don't know if they'd have raped her. I don't know if they'd have gone that far. But they didn't get the chance. I went crazy, and I don't remember any of it. I don't remember getting up off the ground and going after them. I beat two of them unconscious. The third ran off. I don't remember any of it," he repeated, as if it still troubled him. "But I remember coming out of it, out of that red zone, and hearing the girl—a girl I was half in love with—crying and screaming and begging me to stop. I remember the look on her face when I pulled in enough to see her. I'd scared her as much as the ones who jumped me and nearly raped her."

Then she was a wimp, in Fiona's opinion. Instead of scream-ing and crying, she should've run for help. "How badly were you hurt?"

"Enough for a couple days in the hospital. Two of the three who came at me spent longer. I woke up in the hospital—a world of hurt. I saw my parents sitting together across the room. My mother was crying. You had to practically cut her arm off with a hatchet to make my mother cry, but tears were just running down her face."

That, Fiona saw clearly, troubled him more than the mem-ory lapse. That had been the mark that had turned his path. His mother's tears.

"And I thought, That's enough. It's enough. I leashed the crazy."

"Just like that?"

"No. But eventually. Once you learn how to walk away the first time, or realize the one baiting you is an idiot, it gets easier."

So, she thought, that's where the control had its roots. "What about the girl?"

"I never made it past second base with her after all. She broke it off," he added when Fiona said nothing. "I couldn't blame her."

"I can. She should've found a big stick and helped you instead of crying. She should've grabbed some rocks and started throwing them. She should've kissed your goddamn feet for saving her from being mauled and raped."

He smiled. "She wasn't the type."

"You have faulty taste in types."

"Maybe. Up till now, anyway."

She smiled, leaned over the take-out box to kiss him—and flipped open another button on her shirt. "Since I'm tonight's pizza slut, I say we take the rest of this upstairs, where it'll be handy if we want some after."

"I'm a fan of cold pizza."

"I've never understood people who aren't." She rose, held out a hand for his.

FOURTEEN

Simon woke with the sun in his eyes. At home he slept in a cave, shuttering the bedroom windows so he could wake up, get up, whenever the hell he wanted. He considered it, like eating whatever and whenever, a perk of adulthood aided by being self-employed.

Of course, the dog had changed that, demanding to be let out at questionable hours by jumping on the bed, or licking any body part that might hang over the bed. Or his newest, and fairly creepy, method: standing beside the bed and staring at the human.

Still, they'd worked out a routine where he let the dog out, stumbled back into bed and caught some more sleep until Jaws wanted in again.

So where the hell was the dog? And more important, where the hell was Fiona?

Deciding they were undoubtedly together, Simon grabbed a pillow and put it over his face to block the light so he could sleep.

No good, he realized in seconds.

The pillow smelled of her, and her scent drove him crazy.

He indulged himself for a moment, just breathing her in while a picture of her formed in his mind. The soft coloring, the sharp features, the long, strong body. The dash of freckles and clear, calm eyes.

He'd thought if he figured out what there was about her he found so damn compelling, he'd get past it, or around it.

But now that he had, at least partially, he found himself only more tangled up. Her strength—mind and body—her resilience, her humor and what seemed an almost bottomless well of patience combined with an innate kindness and an easy, almost careless self-confidence.

He found the mix fascinating.

He shoved the pillow aside and lay there squinting at the light.

Her bedroom, he thought, showed a strong, imaginative use of color. The walls glowed a coppery hue in the sunlight and formed a good backdrop for some decent local art—probably picked up at Syl's. She'd indulged herself with a big iron bed with hints of dark bronze along with that copper, and high, knobbed posts.

No fuss, he thought. Even the obligatory female bottles and bowls on the dresser had a sense of organization, while the trio of dog beds across the room spoke of her passion and profession.

Attractive lamps, simple in style, an oversized chair draped with a beautifully made throw—likely Syl's again. A low cabinet holding books—and he'd bet they were shelved alphabetically—photos, trinkets.

No clothes tossed around, no shoes left on the floor, no pocket stuff scattered on the dresser.

How did anyone live like that?

In fact, he noted, the clothes he'd peeled, tugged and yanked off her the night before were nowhere to be seen, and the clothes she'd peeled, tugged and yanked off him sat neatly folded on the chest under the window.

And since he was lying there thinking about how she decorated and organized her bedroom, he obviously wasn't getting any more sleep.

He used her shower, found it stingy on the pressure and the hot water. Her bathroom, he thought, needed some serious updating. The old fixtures should be replaced, the tile work redone, and the basic layout wasted space.

Despite what he considered a poor design, it was tidy, organized, scrupulously clean.

He dropped his towel on the floor, went out into the bedroom to dress. Walked back into the bath, picked up the towel and slung it over the shower rail.

He dressed, thinking about coffee, then started out of the room. Walked back, snarling a little, and picked up the pillow he'd shoved off his face and onto the floor. Tossed it back onto the bed. Muttered, but pushed his neatly folded clothes into his duffel. Satisfied, he started out again.

"Goddamn it." Since he couldn't shrug off the guilt line between his shoulder blades, he backtracked again, yanked the sheets into some semblance of order, then flipped the bold blue comforter up and over—and considered the bed made.

Feeling put-upon, he trudged downstairs and decided there better damn sight be coffee.

It waited for him, hot, fragrant and seductive. Next to a woman, he thought as he sloshed some into a mug, coffee was the best thing a man could consume in the morning.

He drank, topped off the mug, then went to find the woman and his dog.

They were in the sunny side yard fooling around on what he thought of as the playground equipment while the other three dogs sprawled on the grass. He leaned against the porch post, drinking his coffee, watching the woman—her stone gray hoodie zipped against the early morning chill while she walked his dog up a teeter-totter.

It tilted down at his weight when he passed the center, but rather than jump off, as Simon expected, he walked straight down.

"Good!"

Jaws got a treat, a pat before she directed him to the tunnel.

"Go through." She moved down the outside as he—

probably, Simon thought—wound through the inside. He wiggled out the far side.

After his reward, she turned to a platform. Simon watched his dog leap on command, preen at the praise, then trot down the ramp on the other side and straight to the ladder of the slide.

"Hup!"

Without hesitation he climbed up, navigated the slide down.

Amazed, Simon started over as Fiona turned Jaws to a lower platform. At her command, he jumped over it and, at the next, scrambled up a pile of logs.

"Call the circus," Simon said. At his voice, Jaws broke ranks and charged over.

"Morning." Fiona gave her dogs the release signal.

"Yeah." She'd done something to her hair, he noticed. Some kind of braiding deal at the sides that merged into one at the back.

Where the hell did she find time to do that stuff?

"What are you doing up and out this early and playing recess?"

"I have morning classes, including a one-on-one with a behavioral problem."

She stepped in to him the way she did, kissed him the way she did—light and easy. He liked light and easy well enough, but . . . He pulled her back in for stronger.

"Off." She held a hand down to Jaws as he jumped, skimmed the other through Simon's hair. "Your hair's still wet. So you found the shower and the coffee."

"Yeah." She smelled like spring, he thought, with just a hint of heat. "I'd rather have found you in bed, but I settled."

"The dogs needed to go out, and since we were up and out, I thought I'd work with Jaws. That was his third round with the obstacle course this morning. He thinks it's great fun, and he's picked up several skills. If you want to leave him here today, he can hang with the boys, and I'll work with him some between classes."

"Ah . . ."

"Or if you want him with you, you can just drop by later and we'll work in a session."

Stupid, Simon thought, that he'd gotten so used to the dog he'd hesitate over the offer of a day without the responsibility of him.

"Keep him if you want. Any special time I should come back for him?"

"Anytime. Play your cards right and you could get that steak dinner out of it since I know you'll be back. If I'd known you were coming by yesterday . . . Why did you come by yesterday?"

"Maybe I wanted sex."

"Mission accomplished."

He grinned at her, ran a finger over one of those fancy braids. "The sex and pizza were a bonus. I had a reason, but I lost it with everything."

"There was a lot of everything. I'm glad you were here, whatever the reason."

"It's in the truck. I'll get it. Here." He pushed the empty mug into her hand.

"What's in the truck?"

"The reason." Jaws grabbed a stick and bounded along with him. "We're not going for a ride yet." To keep his legs from being bashed and poked, he took the stick. "Give." Then tossed it.

The entire pack of dogs gave merry chase.

Simon lowered the tailgate, climbed in and tossed aside a tarp. He muscled the chair out of the truck.

"Oh my God, is that *mine*? Is that my chair?" Fiona scrambled over as he hauled it to the porch.

She lit up, he thought, as if he'd given her diamonds. "It's mine. I'm not sitting on that piece of crap when I'm over here."

"It's beautiful. Look at the color! It's, what, Caribbean Vacation, maybe? It's fun!"

"It works with the house, the trim." Though he shrugged,

her reaction brought him ridiculous pleasure. "It won't look half bad around you."

"It's so smooth." She ran a hand along the side arm. The minute he set it on the porch she plopped into it. "Oh, and it's comfortable." Laughing, she rocked. "An easy ride. So, does it suit me?"

"Yeah, it suits you." He picked up the old chair.

"What are you going to do with— Oh, Simon!" She winced when he snapped one of the rungs—which also gave him ridiculous pleasure. "Someone could use it."

"It's crap."

"Yes, but, I should at least recycle so—"

He broke off another rung. "There. Recycled crap into kindling. Or"—he tossed it, and sent the dogs into another mad dash—"dog toy."

He needed to go, he thought. If he was up this early, he ought to be working.

"When's your first class?"

"The one-on-one's first. They ought to be here in about a half hour."

"I'm going to get more coffee. Is there anything around here that resembles breakfast food?"

"Simon, you don't have to stay. I'm going to be alone here sometimes."

"I make you a chair and you can't spare a bowl of cereal?"

She rose, laid her hands on his cheeks. "I have Froot Loops."

"That's not a cereal. Frosted Flakes is a cereal."

"Out of stock. I do have Eggos."

"Now you're talking."

IT TOOK A few days, but in the middle of her last afternoon class, Fiona spotted the mid-level American-made car easing down her drive—and thought, The feds.

"Keep working on bringing your dogs to heel. Astrid, you're hesitating and tensing up. You have to show Roofus you're pack leader."

She stepped away from the class, turned to walk to the car. Her own tension eased when she saw the driver get out.

He wore a dark suit over a stocky build, and the flecks of gray in his hair had multiplied since the last time she'd seen him.

"Special Agent Tawney." Fiona held out both hands. "I'm so glad it's you."

"Sorry it has to be anybody, but it's good to see you. My partner, Special Agent Erin Mantz."

The woman wore a suit as well, trim over a compact build. Her hair fell in a sleek blond tail, leaving her strong, serious face unframed.

"Ms. Bristow."

"If you could wait? I have about another fifteen minutes to go. And, no offense, but I'd rather not announce to my clients that the FBI's on the premises."

"No problem," Tawney told her. "We'll have a seat on the porch, watch the show."

"I'll wrap it up as soon as I can."

Mantz stood where she was for a moment. "She looked pretty happy to see you. Not our usual reception."

"I was with her after she escaped from Perry. She felt comfortable with me, so I was on her during the trial."

Mantz studied the terrain, the house, the setup from behind dark glasses. "And here you are again."

"Yeah, here I am again. Perry's in this, Erin, there's not a doubt in my mind. And if there's one person in this world he hasn't forgotten, it's Fiona Bristow."

Mantz watched, cool-eyed, as Fiona supervised owners and dogs. "Is that what you're going to tell her?"

"Let's hope I don't have to."

He walked to the porch and, a gentleman to the core, sat on the toy chest to leave the rocker for his partner.

"She's pretty isolated out here," Mantz began, then reared back, hands out, when Bogart bopped up to say hello. "Stay back. Go away."

Tawney patted his knee, inviting Bogart over. "Good dog. What's the problem, Erin?"

"I don't like dogs."

They'd only been partners a few months and were still learning each other's quirks and rhythms. "What's not to like?"

"Dog breath, shedding, big, sharp teeth." Bogart's tail whapped her legs as Tawney rubbed him. Mantz got to her feet, moved out of range.

Peck sauntered up, glanced at Mantz, got the message. He bumped his nose on Tawney's knee.

"These must be her dogs. You read her file, didn't you?" he asked Mantz. "They're S-and-R dogs. She has three. Trains them, too. She started her own unit out here."

"You sound like a proud daddy."

He glanced up, cocking his eyebrows at the edge of sarcasm. "I find her a tough, admirable young woman, one who helped us put a monster in a cell by standing up in court, hanging in, even after her fiancé was murdered."

"Sorry. Sorry. The dogs make me nervous, and being nervous makes me bitchy. I read Greg Norwood's file, too. He was a good cop. Came off solid. A little old for her, don't you think?"

"I'd say that was up to them."

"Proud and protective daddy."

"Is that you being nervous and bitchy?"

"Just me observing. Jesus, here comes another one."

She moved over another foot as Newman trotted onto the porch.

By the time Fiona finished class, her three dogs were sprawled happily at Tawney's feet, and his partner stood rigidly at the far end of the porch.

"Sorry to keep you waiting. Did you make friends with the boys?"

"I did. Agent Mantz doesn't like dogs."

"Oh, sorry. I'd have kept them off the porch. Why don't we go inside? They'll stay out. Stay out," she repeated, and opened the front door.

"You're not fenced," Mantz observed. "Aren't you worried they'll run off?"

"They're trained not to go past certain boundaries with-

out me. Please, sit down. Why don't I make some coffee?
I'm nervous," she said before Tawney could respond. "Even
though it's you, even though I was expecting someone and
I'm glad it's you. I'll make some coffee and settle down."

"Coffee'd be good."

"Is it still coffee regular?"

He smiled. "It still is."

"Agent Mantz?"

"Same for me, thanks."

"I'll just be a minute."

"Nice place," Mantz commented when she was alone with
her partner. "Tidy. Quiet, if you like quiet. I'd go nuts."

"Deb and I talk about getting a quiet place in the country
when we retire."

Mantz glanced back at him. They hadn't been partners
long, but she knew enough. "You'd go nuts."

"Yeah. She thinks we could take up birding."

"Does that mean watching them or shooting them?"

"Watching them. Jesus, Erin, why would I go out and
shoot birds?"

"Why would you watch them?"

He sat a moment. "Damned if I know."

When Fiona came back, she carried three mugs on a tray.
"I've got these cookies Sylvia baked, which means they're
disguised health food, so I can't promise anything."

"How is Sylvia?" Tawney asked.

"She's great. Her shop's doing really well, and it keeps
her busy. She helps me out here, taking classes if I get called
out on a search. She's huge into organic gardening, heads up
a monthly book club, and she's making noises about starting
yoga classes—teaching them, I mean. I'm rambling. Still
nervous."

"You have a nice place here. You're happy?"

"Yes. I needed to move, the change, and it turned out to be
the best thing I could've done for myself. I love my work, and
I'm good at it. At first, I think it was just escape, immerse
myself in something so I'd have a reason to get up in the

morning. Then I realized it wasn't escape, it was finding my place, my purpose."

"You're not as easily accessible here, for your business, as you would've been in Seattle."

"No. I started out slow, and small. The Internet and word of mouth helped me grow, and starting the unit, building a reputation. I'm still pretty small, but it's the right fit for me. And that was all a way to ease me into saying I live in a fairly remote location and spend a lot of time either alone or with people I don't really know—at least not initially."

"Do you do any sort of screening before you take on a client?" Mantz asked.

"No. A good chunk of my business comes from referrals. Friends, family, coworkers recommending me. I do offer personal behavior training, but that's a really small percentage of my business. Most are classes, ranging from about five dogs to a max of twelve per class."

"How about anyone who's signed up for your class who gave you trouble? Wasn't satisfied with the results."

"It happens sometimes. I usually offer them their money back, because it's better business. A pissed-off client's going to trash you to friends, family, coworkers, and that could cost me more than a refund."

"What do you do when a client hits on you? You're a young, attractive woman," Mantz continued. "It's a pretty sure bet it's happened."

She hated it, hated the intrusion into every corner of her private life. All the questions they asked of victims and suspects. She was neither, Fiona reminded herself.

She was something else entirely.

"If a client's single and I'm interested, I'd consider seeing him outside class." She spoke briskly, almost carelessly. "It doesn't happen often. If he's not single, or I'm just not interested, there are ways to discourage and deny without causing friction."

Fiona picked up a cookie, then just turned it in her fingers. "Honestly, I can't imagine anyone I've discouraged or who hasn't been satisfied with my work mailing me a red scarf. It's cruel."

"Someone you broke off a relationship with?" Mantz continued. "Angry exes can be cruel."

"I don't have any angry exes. That's not being naive. After I lost Greg, and then my father, I wasn't interested in dating or relationships. It must've been close to two years before I so much as had dinner with somebody who wasn't a close friend. I haven't had a serious relationship in a very long time, until recently."

"You're involved with someone now?"

"I'm seeing someone, yes."

"For how long?"

Resentment tightened her belly. "Altogether, a couple months. He lives here, on the island. I'm working with his dog. He's not connected to this."

"We'll need his name, Fiona, just so we can eliminate him."

Fiona looked at Tawney, sighed. "Simon Doyle. He's a wood artist. He made the rocker on the porch."

"Nice chair."

"The scarf was mailed from Oregon. Simon hasn't been off the island. Agent Tawney, we all know there are two possibilities. The first is somebody following the news reports of the murders, somebody who read the article that brought me into it, sent me that scarf as a sick joke or for some prurient thrill. If that's the case, it's unlikely you'll ever find out who it was. The second is whoever's following Perry's pattern sent it to me as a warning, a tease. If that's the case, I have to hope you find out who he is and stop him, really soon. Because if you don't, at some point he's going to come at me and try to correct Perry's mistake."

"You hung tough through everything that happened before. You're going to need to hang tough again. The scarf mailed to you is the same as those used on the three victims. The same manufacturer, the same style, even the same dye lot."

"So." Her skin went cold, numbed under a sheath of ice. "That's probably not a coincidence."

"We've traced the outlets, and we know this specific scarf, this dye lot, was shipped to those outlets at the end of October of last year for distribution in the Walla Walla area."

"Near the prison," she murmured. "Near Perry. Why would he buy them there if he didn't live or work or have business there? A prison guard." She fought to keep her voice steady. "An inmate who was released or, or a family member. Or—"

"Fiona, believe me, trust me, we're covering all possibilities. Agent Mantz and I have interviewed Perry. He claims he doesn't know anything about these murders—how could he?"

"He's lying."

"Yes, he is, but we haven't been able to shake him. Not yet. We've had his cell searched, multiple times, all of his correspondence is being analyzed. We've interviewed prison officials and inmates he interacts with. We're watching his sister and are in the process of identifying, locating and contacting anyone—former inmates, prison personnel, outside contractors and instructors—he may have had contact with since he went in."

"A long time." She set the cookie aside. She'd never be able to swallow it now. "Do you think he's directing this, or at least lit the fuse?"

"At this point, we have no proof—"

"I'm not asking for proof." She paused to smooth the sharp edge out of her tone. "I'm asking what you think. I trust what you think."

"If he isn't directing it or hasn't incited it, he'd be furious. He'd control the anger, but I'd have seen it."

She nodded. Yes, he'd have seen it. They knew Perry, she and Tawney. They knew him all too well.

"This was his power, his accomplishment," Tawney continued. "Having someone else pick up that power, claim new accomplishments while he's locked up? Insulting, demeaning. But selecting or approving the person to continue for him, he'd find pride and pleasure in that. And that's what I saw when we talked to him. Under the control, the feigned ignorance, he was proud."

"Yes." She nodded, then got to her feet to walk to the window, to comfort herself watching her dogs roam the front yard, the field. "That's what I think, too. I've studied him, too. I needed to. I needed to know the man who wanted to kill me, who killed the man I loved because he failed with me. I read the books, watched the TV specials, dissected all the articles. Then I put them away, put them aside because I needed to stop.

"He never has," she said, turning back. "Not really, has he? He's just bided his time. But why didn't he send this proxy for me first, before I could prepare?"

She shook her head, waved away the question as the answer was right there. "Because I'm the big prize—I'm the main event, the reason. And you need to build up to that. The others? They're opening acts."

"That's a hard way to put it," Mantz commented.

"It's a hard way to think of it, but that's how he sees it. It's a kind of rematch, isn't it? Last time, I won. Now he's going to fix that. Maybe by remote, maybe by proxy, but it'll clear his record. And the opening acts give him his sick satisfaction with the bonus of making the big prize sweat. He wants my fear. It's part of his method and a large part of his reward."

"We can take you in, put you in a safe house, offer you protection."

"I did that before," Fiona reminded Tawney, "and he just waited me out. Waited me out, then killed Greg. I can't put my life on hold again, I can't give him that. He's already taken so much."

"We have more leads this time," Mantz told her. "He's not as careful, not as smart as Perry. Sending you the scarf was stupid. It's taunting. Buying them in multiples, from one area, another mistake. We'll find him."

"I believe you will, and I hope it's soon, before someone else dies. But I can't hide until you do. That's not being brave so much as realistic. And I have the advantage here. He has to come to me. He has to come onto the island."

"Your local police department can't monitor everyone who gets off the ferry."

"No, but if he does manage to get this far, he's not going to come up against a twenty-year-old girl."

"At the very least you should take more precautions," Mantz advised. "You should have better locks installed. You should think about an alarm system."

"I have three of them. I'm not being glib," she added. "The dogs are always with me, and between the police and my friends, I'm being checked on several times a day. Simon's staying here at night. I'm actually going away next week for a couple of days with a friend and my stepmother. I have a friend staying here with his dog to watch mine and the house."

"You mentioned that on your blog."

She smiled at Tawney. "You read my blog."

"I keep up with you, Fiona. You said you were taking a quick mental health trip with girlfriends, and intended to relax and pamper yourself."

"Spa," Mantz said.

"Yeah."

"You didn't say where you were going, specifically."

"No, because everyone and anyone can read a blog. I'll talk about it after, if it seems interesting. But most of what I write about is dog related. I'm not careless, Agent Tawney."

"No, you're not. Still, I'd like the information—where you'll be, the exact dates, how you'll get there."

"Okay."

When his phone signaled, he held up a finger. "Why don't you give them to Agent Mantz," he suggested, and walked out onto the porch to take the call.

"We're driving up to Snoqualmie Falls next Tuesday," Fiona told her. "Tranquillity Spa and Resort. We're coming back Friday."

"Nice."

"Yeah, it will be. It's our version of a long weekend, as actual weekends are busiest for all of us. I'm going with Sylvia and a friend. Mai Funaki, our vet."

Mantz noted down the information, then glanced over as Tawney stepped back in.

"We need to go."

Fiona got to her feet even as Mantz did. "They found another."

"No. A twenty-one-year-old woman's been reported missing. She left her off-campus housing at about six this morning,
on foot, on her way to the university's fitness center. She never
got there."

"Where?" Fiona demanded. "Where was she taken?"

"Medford, Oregon."

"Just a little closer," she murmured. "I hope she's strong. I
hope she finds a way."

"I'm going to stay in touch, Fiona." Tawney pulled out a
card. "You can reach me anytime. My home number's on the
back for you."

"Thanks."

She walked out with them, stood with her arms folded over
her chest against her thudding heart and the dogs sitting at her
feet as they drove away. "Good luck," she murmured.

Then she went inside to get her gun.

FIFTEEN

Simon carved the scrolled detail into the header for the custom china cabinet while The Fray blasted out of the radio. Meg Greene, a woman who knew exactly what she wanted—except when she changed her mind—had asked to adjust the design four times before he hit the mark for her.

To ensure she didn't adjust it again, he'd put aside other work to focus on the cabinet. It was a big, beautiful bastard, Simon thought, and would be the showpiece of Meg's dining room. Another few days, and he'd be done with it, and between the staining and varnishing, he could get serious about the sink base. Maybe work in a few pieces for Syl and have them done when she got back from the spa deal.

If he delivered the stock while she was gone, she couldn't drag him into talking with her customers. That added motivation.

Starting the day earlier meant he got a jump on things, which almost offset quitting at specific times each day instead of going until he'd had enough.

Stopping, even though he might be on a solid roll, went

against the grain, but knowing Fiona would be alone if he didn't would only screw with his concentration anyway.

But the arrangement had benefits—and not just the sex.

He liked hearing her talk, and listening to the stories she told him about her day. He didn't know why she relaxed him, but she did. Most of the time.

Then there was the dog. He still chased his tail like a maniac, and stole footwear—and the occasional tool if he could get to it. But he was so damn happy, and a hell of a lot smarter than Simon had given him credit for. He'd gotten used to having the dog curled up under the workbench snoozing or running around outside. And the sucker could field a ball like Derek Jeter.

Simon stood back, studied the work.

Somehow he'd gotten himself a dog and a woman, neither of which he'd particularly wanted. And now he couldn't imagine his days, or his nights, without them.

He'd gotten more done than he'd expected, and glanced at the clock he'd hung on the wall. Funny, it felt like more than a couple hours since he'd started back up after the grab-a-sandwich, throw-the-ball break he'd taken.

Frowning, he pulled out his phone, read the time on the display and swore.

"Damn it. Why didn't you remind me to change the batteries in that thing?" he demanded as Jaws trotted through the open shop door.

Jaws only wagged his tail and dropped the stick he'd brought in.

"I don't have time for that. Let's move."

He tried to time his trip to Fiona's so he arrived long enough after her final class to avoid the inevitable stragglers. Otherwise, she'd start introducing him to people, and there had to be conversations. But he aimed for timing it so she wasn't alone more than fifteen or twenty minutes.

It was, for him, a delicate balance.

Now, he was nearly two hours behind.

Why hadn't she called? Wouldn't any normal woman call

to say, Hey, you're late, what's going on? Not that they had a formal sort of arrangement. He said see you later every day, left, then he came back.

Nice and easy, no big deal.

"Women are supposed to call," he told Jaws as they got in the truck. "And nag and bug you. It's the way of the world. But not her. There's never any Are you going to be here for dinner? or Can you pick up some milk? or Are you ever going to take out that trash?"

He shook his head. "Maybe she's lulling me into complacency, stringing me along until I'm . . . more hooked than I already am. Except she's not, which is one of the reasons I'm hooked, and I'm already taking out the trash because it's just what you do."

The dog wasn't listening, Simon noted, because he had his head out the window. So he might as well save his breath.

No reason to feel guilty because he was a couple hours later than usual, he told himself. He had his work; she had hers. Besides, he thought as he turned into her drive, if she'd called, he wouldn't be later than usual.

Maybe she hadn't been able to call. His stomach knotted. If something had happened to her . . .

He heard the gunshots as he drove across the bridge where dogwoods bloomed snowy white.

He floored it, then fishtailed to a stop even as Fiona's dogs charged around the side of the house. Gunshots ripped through the fear that buzzed in his head as he leaped out of the truck. He left the door swinging open as he ran toward them. When they stopped abruptly, he heard his own heart roaring in his ears.

He pulled in the breath to shout her name, and saw her.

Not lying on the ground bleeding, but standing, coolly, competently shoving another clip into the gun she held.

"Jesus Christ." The anger flew through him, stampeding out the fear. Even as she started to turn, he grabbed her arm, spun her around. "What the hell are you doing?"

"Careful. It's loaded." She lowered the gun, pointing it toward the ground.

"I know it's loaded. I heard you blasting away like Annie fucking Oakley. You scared the hell out of me."

"Let go. Earplugs," she said. "I can barely hear you." When he released her arm, she pulled them out. "I told you I had a gun, and I told you I'd be practicing. There's no point getting pissed off that I am."

"I'm pissed off about the five years you shaved off my life. I had plans for them."

"Look, I'm sorry. I didn't think to send out a notification I'd be getting in some target practice." Her movements as testy as her tone, she shoved the gun into the holster on her belt, then stalked over to set up a variety of cans and plastic water bottles she'd obviously killed before his arrival.

"We can argue about that, seeing as you knew I'd be coming by and might have a strong reaction to gunfire."

"I don't know anything. You just show up."

"If you have a problem with that you should've said so."

"I don't." She pushed her hands through her hair. "I don't," she repeated. "Go ahead and take the dogs inside if you want. I won't be much longer."

"What crawled up your ass? I know your face, so don't tell me about not getting pissed when you're already there."

"It's got nothing to do with you. You should take Jaws inside. My dogs are used to the sound of gunshots. He's not."

"Then we'll see how he deals."

"Fine."

She took out the gun, shifted into the stance he'd seen cops use on TV and in movies. As she fired away, Jaws moved closer to his side, leaning against him, but cocked his head and watched—as Simon did—the cans and bottles fly.

"Nice shooting, Tex."

She didn't smile, but walked over to set up fresh targets. Behind her a few big-leaf maples, boughs heavy with clusters of blossoms, shimmered in the sunlight.

It made, to his mind, an odd contrast of violence and peace.

"Do you want to shoot?"

"What for?"

"Have you ever shot a gun?"

"Why would I?"

"There are a lot of reasons. Hunting, sport, curiosity, defense."

"I don't hunt. My idea of sport is more in line with baseball or boxing. I've never been especially curious, and I'd rather use my fists. Let me see it."

She put the safety on, unloaded it, then offered it to him.

"Not as heavy as I figured."

"It's a Beretta. It's a fairly light and very lethal semiautomatic. It'll fire fifteen rounds."

"Okay, show me."

She loaded it, unloaded it again, showed him the safety. "It's double-action, so it'll fire whether the hammer's cocked or not. The recoil's pretty minor, but it's got a little kick. You want to stand with your feet about shoulder-distance apart. Distribute your weight. Both arms out, elbows locked, with your left hand cupped under your gun hand for stability. You lean your upper body toward the target."

It was an instructor's voice, he realized, but not *her* instructor's voice. That was bright and charming and enthusiastic. This instructor was flat and cool.

"And you remember all that when bullets fly?"

"Maybe not, and maybe one-handed or a different stance would suit the situation better, but this is the best, I think, for target shooting. And like with anything, practice enough and it becomes instinctual. Tuck your head down to line up the sight with the target. Try the two-liter bottle."

He fired. Missed.

"A little more square, and with your feet pointed at the target. Aim a little lower on the bottle."

This time he caught a piece of it.

"Okay, I wounded the empty Diet Pepsi. Do I get praise and reward?"

She did smile, a little this time, but there wasn't any light in it. "You learn fast, and I have beer. Try it a couple more times."

He thought he got the hang of it, and confirmed the hang of it didn't particularly appeal to him.

"It's loud." He put the safety on, unloaded it as she'd shown him. "And now you have a bunch of dead recyclables in your yard. I don't think shooting cans and bottles comes close to shooting flesh and blood. Could you actually aim this at a person and pull the trigger?"

"Yes. I was stun-gunned, drugged, tied up, gagged, locked in the trunk of a car by a man who wanted to kill me just for the pleasure it gave him." Those calm blue eyes fired like her pistol. "If I'd had a gun, I'd have used it then. If anyone tries to do that to me again, I'd use it now, without a second's hesitation."

A part of him regretted she'd given him exactly the answer he'd needed to hear. He handed the Beretta back to her. "Let's hope you never have to find out if you're right."

Fiona holstered the gun, then picked up a bag and began to gather up the spent cartridges. "I'd rather not have to prove it. But I feel better."

"That's something then."

"I'm sorry I scared you. I didn't think about you driving up and hearing gunshots." She leaned down, gave Jaws a body scrub. "You handled that, didn't you? Big noises don't scare you. Search and Rescue dogs need to tolerate loud noises without spooking. I'll get you that beer after I pick up the targets."

Odd, he thought, he'd learned her moods. Odd, and a little uncomfortable. "Got any wine?"

"Sure."

"I'll get the bodies. You can pour out some wine, and maybe use your sexy voice to score us a delivery. I feel like spaghetti."

"I don't have a sexy voice."

"Sure you do." He took the bag, walked across her makeshift range.

By the time he'd finished, she was sitting on the back deck, two glasses of red on the little table.

"It'll be about forty-five minutes. They're backed up some."

"I can wait." He sat, picked up his wine. "I guess you could use a couple decent chairs back here, too."

"I'm sorry. I need a minute." She wrapped her arms around the nearest dog, pressed her face into fur and wept.

Simon rose, went inside and brought out a short trail of paper towels.

"I was okay when I was doing something." She kept her arms around Peck. "I shouldn't have stopped."

"Tell me where you put the gun and I'll get it so you can shoot more soup cans."

She shook her head and, on a long breath, lifted it. "No, I think I'm done. God, I hate that. Thanks," she murmured when he pressed the paper towels into her hand.

"That makes two of us. So what set you off?"

"The FBI was here. Special Agent Don Tawney—he's the one from the Perry investigation. He really helped me through all of that, so it was easier going through all this again with him. He has a new partner. She's striking—sort of like the TV version of FBI. She doesn't like dogs." She bent down to kiss Peck between the ears. "Doesn't know what she's missing. Anyway."

She picked up the wine, sipped slowly. "It stirs up the ghosts, but I was ready for that. They traced the scarf, the one he sent me. It's a match for the ones used on the three victims. The same make, dye lot. He bought a dozen of them from the same store, near the prison. Near where Perry is. So that squashes even the faint hope that somebody sent it to me as a sick joke."

Fury burned a low fire in his gut. "What are they doing about it?"

"Following up, looking into, pursuing avenues. What they always do. They're monitoring Perry, his contacts, his correspondence, on the theory that he and this one know each other. They'll probably contact you because I told them you were staying here at night."

She folded her legs up, drawing in. "It occurs to me that I'm a lot of work to be involved with right now. It's not usually true—I don't think. I'm not high maintenance because I know how to maintain myself, and I prefer it. But right now . . . So if you want to call a time-out, I get it."

"No you don't."

"I do." She turned her head to meet his eyes straight on,

and now, he thought, there was the faintest light in them. "I'd think you were a cold, selfish bastard coward, but I'd get it."

"I'm a cold, selfish bastard, but I'm not a coward."

"You're none of those things. Well, maybe a little bit of a bastard, but it's part of your charm. Simon, another woman's missing. She fits the pattern, the type."

"Where?"

"South-central Oregon, just north of the California border. I know what she's going through now, how afraid she is, how confused, how there's this part of her that won't—can't—believe it's happening to her. And I know that if she doesn't find a way, if there isn't some intersection with fate, they'll find her body in a matter of days, in a shallow grave with a red scarf around her neck and a number on her hand."

She needed to see something else, he thought. Control meant channeling the emotion into logic. "Why did Perry pick athletic coeds?"

"What?"

"You've thought about it, the FBI, the shrinks, they'd have a lot to say on it."

"Yes. His mother was the type. She was an athlete, a runner. Apparently, she just missed being chosen for the Olympics when she was in college. She got pregnant, and instead of pursuing her interests or career, she ended up a very bitter, dissatisfied mother of two, married to a forcefully religious man. She left them, the husband, the kids—just took off one day."

"Went missing."

"You could say—except she's alive and well. The FBI tracked her down once they'd identified Perry. She lives—or lived—outside of Chicago. Teaches PE in a private girls' school."

"Why the red scarf?"

"Perry gave her one for Christmas when he was seven. She left them a couple months later."

"So, he was killing his mother."

"He was killing the girl his mother was before she got pregnant, before she married the man who—according to his mother and those who knew them—abused her. He was killing the girl she talked about all the time, the happy college student who'd had her whole life in front of her before she made that mistake, before she was saddled with a child. That's what the shrinks said."

"What do you say?"

"I say all that's just a bullshit excuse to cause pain and fear. Just like whoever's killing now uses Perry as a bullshit excuse."

"You stand there because of what he did to you. Motivation matters."

She set down her glass. "You really think—"

"If you shut it down a minute, I'll tell you what I think. Motivation matters," he said again, "because why you do something connects to how you do it, who you do it to, or for. And maybe what you see at the end of it—if you're looking that far."

"I don't care why he killed all those women, and Greg, why he tried to kill me. I don't care."

"You should. You know what motivates them." He gestured to the dog. "Play, praise, reward—and pleasing the ones who dole all that out. Knowing it, connecting to it, and them, makes you good at what you do."

"I don't see what—"

"Not done. He was good at what he did. It was doing something he wasn't as good at— When he deviated from his skill area, he got caught."

"He murdered Greg and Kong in cold blood." She shoved out of the chair. "You call that a deviation?"

He shrugged and went back to his wine.

"I don't know what you're getting at."

"Because you'd rather be pissed."

"Of course I'd rather be pissed. I'm human. I have feelings. I loved him. Haven't you ever loved anyone?"

"Not that way."

"Nina Abbott?"

"Jesus, no."

There was just enough shocked derision in his tone to carry the truth. "It didn't seem that far-out a question."

"Look, she's gorgeous, talented, sexy, smart."

"Bitch."

Pleased, he let out a short laugh. "You asked. I liked her, except when she was batshit crazy—which, looking back, was pretty damn regular. It was steam and smoke, then it was just drama. She liked the drama. No, she fucking loved the drama. I didn't. That's it."

"I guess I assumed there was more than—"

"There wasn't. And it's not about me anyway."

"So you just expect me to be logical and objective about Greg, about Perry, about this. I should be analytical when—"

"Be whatever the hell you want, but if you don't *think*, if you don't step outside and look at the whole, you can shoot that gun as much as you like and it's not going to help. For fuck's sake, Fiona, are you going to pack it twenty-four/ seven? Are you going to strap it on while you're running your classes, or driving to the village for a quart of milk? Is that how you're going to live?"

"If I have to. You're mad," she realized. "It's hard to tell with you because you don't always show it. You've been mad since you got here, but you've only let it sneak out a couple times."

"We're both better off that way."

"Yeah, because otherwise you're Simon Kick-Ass. You come here every night. There's probably some mad in that, too."

Considering, she picked up her wine again, walked to the post to lean back, study him as she drank. "You've got to stop what you're doing, toss some things in a bag, drive over here. You don't leave anything, except what you forget. Because you're messy. It's another thing you have to do every day."

She'd managed to turn it around so it was about him after all, he realized. The woman had skills. "I don't have to do anything."

"That's true." She nodded, drank again. "Yeah, that's true. You get a meal and sex out of it, but that's not why you do it. Not altogether anyway. It has to irritate you, to some extent. I haven't given you enough credit for that."

"I don't do it for credit either."

"No, you don't work on the point system. You don't care about things like that. You do what you want, and if an obligation sneaks in—a dog, a woman—you figure out how to handle it and continue to do what you want. Problems are meant to be solved. Measure, cut, fit the pieces together until it works the way you want it to work."

She lifted her glass, sipped again. "How's that for looking at motivation?"

"Not bad, if this was about me."

"Part of it is, for me. See, it was okay when this was an affair. This you and me. I never had one before, not really, so it was all new and shiny, sexy and easy. Really attractive guy who gives me the tingles. Enough in common and enough not to make it interesting. I like the way he is, and maybe partly because he's so different from my usual. I think it's the same with him about me. But that changes without me realizing it—or at least without me admitting it. Affair becomes relationship."

She sipped again, let out a little sigh. "That's what we have here, Simon. We're in a relationship whether either of us wanted it or were ready for it. And as stupid as it is, as useless and wrong as it is, part of me feels disloyal to Greg. So I'd rather be pissed. I'd rather not admit I'm not having an affair with you, a no-problem, casual little fling I can walk away from anytime."

She watched the dogs scramble off the porch like runners at the starting gun, then bound around the side of the house.

"I guess you're going to have to remeasure and refit. That's dinner. We should eat inside. It's cooling off."

She walked into the house, leaving him wondering how the hell the conversation had flipped on him.

IN THE KITCHEN, Fiona gave the pasta a quick buzz in the microwave. By the time Simon came in, she'd dumped the spaghetti in a bowl, set the garlic bread on a small plate and brought the wine to the table.

When she turned with dinner plates in her hands, he took her by the shoulders. "I've got some say in what this is."

"Okay. What is it?"

"I'll let you know when I figure it out."

She waited. Waited another moment. "Are you figuring it out now?"

"No."

"Then we should eat before I have to heat it up again."

"I'm not competing with a ghost."

"No. No, believe me, Simon, I know it's not fair. He was my first, in every way." She set the plates down, crossed over to get the flatware, napkins. "And the way I lost him left scars. There hasn't been anyone since who was important enough to make me take a good look at those scars. I didn't know that's what I'd have to do when I started falling for you. I think I'm in love with you. It's not like it was with Greg, so it's confusing, but I think that's what it is, going on with me. And that's a dilemma for both of us."

She topped off both glasses of wine. "So I'd appreciate it if you'd let me know when you figure it out on your end."

"That's it?" he demanded. "Oops, we're in a relationship, and by the way, I think I'm in love with you. Let me know what you think?"

She sat, tipped her face up to look at him. "That pretty much sums it up. Love's always been a positive in my life." She scooped some spaghetti onto his plate. "It adds and enhances and opens all sorts of possibilities. But I'm not stupid, and I know that if you can't or don't feel it for me, it'll be painful. That's a dilemma. I also know you can't force love, or demand it. And I've already dealt with the worst. If you can't or don't love me, it'll hurt. But I'll get through it. Besides, maybe I'm wrong."

She took a portion of pasta. "I was wrong about being in love with Josh Clatterson."

"Who the hell is Josh Clatterson?"

"Sprinter." She wound pasta around her fork. "I pined for him for nearly two years—tenth and eleventh grade, and the summer between. But it turned out it wasn't love. I just liked the way he looked when he ran the twenty-yard dash. So maybe I just like the way you look, Simon, and how you smell of sawdust half the time."

"You haven't seen me run the twenty-yard dash."

"True. I might be sunk if I ever do." When he finally sat down, she smiled. "I'm going to try to be logical and objective."

"It seems to me you're doing a damn good job at it already."

"About you and me? I guess it's a defense mechanism."

He frowned, ate. "It doesn't work as a defense once you tell me it's a defense."

"That's a good point. Well, too late. I meant logical and so forth about Perry and what's going on now. You were right about that, about the importance of understanding motivation. He didn't try to kill me just because. I represented something, just like the others had. And failing with me, he needed to inflict punishment? Do you think punishment?"

"It's a good enough word for it."

"It had to be more severe than the others. Death ends— though I imagine if he hadn't been caught he'd have come for me again. Because he'd have needed to end it—to tie off that thread. How am I doing?"

"Keep going."

"He understood it's hard to live when you know, when you understand someone you love is dead because you lived. He knew that, understood that, and used that to make me suffer for . . . breaking his streak, spoiling his record. What then?" she asked when Simon shook his head.

"For leaving him."

She sat back. "For leaving him," she repeated. "I got away. I ran away. I didn't stay where he put me, or . . . accept the gift. The scarf. All right, say that's true, what does it tell me?"

"He's never forgotten you. You left him, and even though he managed to scar you, he was the one who was punished. He can't get to you, can't close that circle, tie off the thread. Not with his own hands. He needs someone to do it for him. A stand-in. A proxy. How does he find one?"

"Someone he knows, another inmate."

"Why would he use someone who's already failed?"

Her heart knocked at the base of her throat. "He wouldn't. He waits. He's good at waiting. So he'd wait, wouldn't he, until he found someone he believed smart enough, good enough. The women he's killed—this proxy—it's a kind of building-up. I understand that. They're a horrible kind of practice."

"And they're bragging. 'You locked me up, but you didn't stop me.'"

"You're scaring me."

"Good." For an instant those tawny eyes went fierce. "Be scared, and think. What motivates the proxy?"

"How can I know?"

"Jesus, Fee, you're smarter than that. Why does anyone follow someone else's path?"

"Admiration."

"Yeah. And you train someone to do what you want, how you want, when you want?"

"Praise and reward. That means contact, but they've searched Perry's cell, they're monitoring his visitors—and his sister's the only one who goes to see him."

"And nobody ever smuggles anything into prison? Or out? Did Perry ever send a scarf before he abducted a woman?"

"No."

"So this guy's deviated. Sometimes you follow another person's path because you want to impress them, or outdo them. It has to be someone he met, more than once. Someone he was able to evaluate, and trust, and speak to privately. A lawyer, a shrink, a counselor, a guard. Somebody in mainte-nance or prison administration. Somebody Perry looked at, listened to, watched, studied and saw something in. Someone that reminded him of himself."

"Okay. Someone young enough to be maneuvered and trained, mature enough to be trusted. Smart enough not to simply follow instructions, but to adjust to each particular situation. He'd have to be able to travel with nobody questioning him about where he'd been, what he'd done. So, single, someone who lives alone. Like Perry did. The FBI must already have a profile."

"He'd have to have some physical stamina, some strength," Simon continued. "His own car—probably something nondescript. He'd need enough money to carry him along. Food, gas, hotels."

"And some knowledge of the areas where he abducts them, and where he takes them. Maps, time to scope it all out. But under it, doesn't there have to be more? The reason why. Admiring Perry? Nobody could unless they were like him. What made this person like that?"

"It'll be a woman, or women. He's not killing Perry's mother. My guess would be she's his proxy."

IT MADE SENSE, though she didn't know what good it did her. Maybe the fact that it made sense was enough. She had a theory about what she was facing—or who.

She supposed it helped that Simon pushed her to think. No promises that nothing would happen to her, to protect her from all harm. She wouldn't have believed those claims, she thought as she tried to soak out the tension with a hot bath. Maybe she'd have been comforted by them, but she wouldn't have believed them.

He didn't make promises—not Simon. In fact, he was very careful not to, she decided. All those casual *see you later*s rather than just saying he'd be back. Then again, a man who didn't make promises didn't break them.

Greg had made promises, and kept them when he could. It occurred to her now that she'd never worried about Greg or wondered or doubted. He'd been her sweetheart before the abduction, and he'd been her rock after.

And he was gone. It was time, maybe long past time, to fully accept that.

Wrapped in a towel, she stepped into the bedroom as Simon came in from the hall.

"The dogs wanted out," he told her. He crossed over,

flicked his fingers over the hair she'd bundled on top of her head. "That's a new look for you."

"I didn't want it to get wet." She reached up to pull out pins, but he brushed her hand aside.

"I'll do it. Did you finish your brood?"

She smiled a little. "It was only a partial brood."

"You had a rough day." He pulled a pin out.

"It's done now."

"Not quite." He drew out another pin. "Scent's the thing, right? How you find someone. I've got yours inside me. I could find you whether I wanted to or not. Whether you wanted me to or not."

"I'm not lost."

"I still found you." He took out another pin, and her hair tumbled after it. "What is it about the way a woman's hair falls?" He speared his hands through it, locked his eyes on hers. "What is it about you?"

Before she could answer, his mouth was on hers, but softly, testing and easy. She eased into him as she had the bath, with every muscle sighing its pleasure.

For a moment, just a moment, he simply held her, with his hand stroking down her hair, her back. It undid her, the offer of comfort she hadn't asked for, the gift of affection she hadn't expected.

He slipped the towel off, let it fall, and even then just held her.

"What is it about you?" he repeated. "How does touching you calm me down and excite me at the same time? What is it you want from me? You never ask. Sometimes I wonder, is this a trick?" His eyes on hers, he backed her slowly toward the bed. "Just a way to pull me in? But it's not. You're not built that way."

"Why would I want anything I had to trick out of you?"

"You don't." He lifted her, held, then laid her on the bed. "So you pull me in. And I end up being the one who's lost."

She framed his face with her hands. "I'll find you."

He wasn't used to tenderness, to feeling it spread inside him. Or this need to give her what she never asked of him. It was easier to let the storm come, let it ride over both of them. But for tonight, he'd embrace the calm and try to soothe the fears he understood hid behind those lake-blue eyes.

Relax. Let go. As if she'd heard his thoughts, she sank into the kiss that offered quiet and warmth. Slow and easy, his mouth tasted hers, changing angles, gently deepening in a seduction that shimmered sweet.

She'd been wrong, she realized. She was lost. Floating, untethered, in an unfamiliar space where sensation layered gauzily over sensation to blur the mind and enchant the body.

She surrendered to it, to him, yielding absolutely as his lips gently conquered hers, as his hands trailed over her—tender touches soothing a troubled soul.

The softly lit bedroom transformed. A magic glade steeped in green shadows silvered at the edges with moonlight, with the air thick and still and sweet. She didn't know her way, and was content to wander, to linger, to be guided.

His mouth grazed down her throat, over her shoulders until her skin tingled from the quiet onslaught. He tasted her breasts, patiently sampling until on a groan she arched and offered.

He feasted, but delicately.

Hands and mouth skimmed down in whispering trails, inciting sighs and shivers that rolled into a slow rise, a gilded peak, a breathy fall.

He was with her in the magic, steeped in her, in the rich glow of the moment, in the slow glide of movements. Seduced as he seduced, enraptured by the sound of his name murmured from her lips, the slide of her hands, the taste of her skin.

She welcomed him, warm and wet, took him in—into her body, into her arms. The need stayed slow and sweet, tender as an open heart even as it climbed.

And when he fell, he fell into her eyes.

SIXTEEN

In the shabby excuse for a rented cabin squatting in the magnificence of the Cascade Mountains, Francis Eckle read Perry's letter. They had, many months before, determined the route, the timing, the towns, colleges, burial sites.

Or Perry had, he thought.

The preplanning made it a simple matter to obtain a mail drop for the letters Perry smuggled out of prison. The answers returned by a similar method—mailed to Perry's minister, who believed in his repentance.

In the beginning, he'd been thrilled by the correspondence, the exchange of details and ideas. Perry's understanding, guidance and approval meant so much.

Someone, finally someone who *saw* him.

Someone who didn't require the mask, the pretense, but instead recognized the chains required to keep them in place. Someone, at last someone who helped him gather the courage to break those chains and release what he was.

A man, a friend, a partner who offered to share the power that came from throwing off the shackles of rules and behavior and embracing the predator.

The teacher had become a willing student, eager to learn,

to explore all the knowledge and experiences he'd so long denied himself. But now he believed the time had come for commencement.

Time to move beyond the boundaries and the tenets he'd been so meticulously taught.

They were rules, after all, and rules no longer applied.

He studied the two fingers of whiskey in his glass. Perry had decreed there could be no drugs, no alcohol, no tobacco during the journey. The body and mind remained pure.

But Perry was in prison, he thought, and sipped with the pleasure of rebellion. The journey no longer belonged to him.

It was time to make his own mark—or the next mark, as he'd detoured from the plan already by sending the Bristow bitch a little present.

He wished he could have seen her face when she opened the mailer. He wished he could have smelled her fear.

But that would come, soon enough.

He'd detoured as well by renting the cabin—an expense dearer than a dingy motel room, but he felt it earned the cost with its privacy.

He needed privacy for the next detour from his mentor's carefully drawn route.

Perry had given him a new life, a new freedom, and he would honor that by finishing what his mentor hadn't and killing Fiona. But there was much to be done in the meantime, and it was time to test himself.

To celebrate himself.

He took another sip of whiskey. He'd save the rest until after. He moved quietly through the room into the bathroom where he removed his clothes, admired his body. He'd removed all the hair from it the night before, and enjoyed the smooth, sleek skin, the muscles he'd rigorously toned. Perry was right about strength and discipline.

He stroked himself, pleased anticipation hardened him, before sliding on a condom. He didn't plan to rape—but plans could change. But in any case, protection was key, he thought as he drew on leather gloves.

Time to let himself go. To explore new ground.

He stepped into the bedroom, switched on a low light and studied the pretty girl tied to the bed. He wished he could rip off the duct tape over her mouth, hear her screams, her pleas, her gasps of pain. But sounds carried so he'd have to content himself with imagining them.

In any case, her eyes begged him. Her eyes screamed. He'd let the drug wear off so she'd be aware, so she'd struggle—so her fear would perfume the air.

He smiled, pleased to see she'd abraded her wrists and ankles fighting the cords. The plastic under her crackled as she cringed and writhed.

"I haven't introduced myself," he said. "My name is Francis Xavier Eckle. For years I taught useless cunts like you who forgot me five minutes after walking out of my class. No one saw me because I hid myself. But as you see"—he spread his arms as tears spilled out of her eyes—"I stopped hiding. Do you see me? Nod your head like a good girl."

When she nodded, he stepped to the side of the bed. "I'm going to hurt you." He felt the heat spread in his belly as she struggled, as her wild pleas piped against the tape. "You want to know why? Why me? you're thinking. Why not you? What makes you so special? Nothing."

He got on the bed, straddled her—considered the rape dispassionately as she tried to kick, to turn. And rejected it, at least for the moment.

"But you're going to be special. I'm going to make you famous. You'll be on TV, in the newspapers, all over the Internet. You can thank me later."

Balling his gloved hands, he used his fists.

FIONA HESITATED AND BACKTRACKED. Her bag was packed and in the car. She'd made arrangements for everything. She'd left lists—long lists, she admitted—carefully detailed. She'd devised Plan Bs for a number of items—Plan Cs for a few.

Still, she went over everything in her head, again, looking

for anything she'd left out, miscalculated, needed to cover more fully.

"Go away," Simon ordered.

"I've still got a few minutes. I think maybe I should—"

"Get the hell out of here." To solve the matter, he took her arm and steered her through the house.

"If one of the dogs gets sick or injured—"

"I have the name and number of the vet who's covering for Mai. I have your number—hotel, cell, Mai's cell, Sylvia's cell. So does James. We have everything. In triplicate. Between us I think we can handle anything short of nuclear holocaust or alien invasion."

"I know, but—"

"Shut up. Go away. If I'm hauling four dogs home with me this morning, I need to get started."

"I really appreciate it, Simon. I know it's a lot. James will pick my guys up—"

"After work. It's on the list, with the time, his cell phone, his house phone. I think all that's missing is what he'll be wearing. Beat it. I'm finally going to have three days without having to listen to you."

"You'll miss me."

"No I won't."

She laughed, then she crouched down to pet the dogs, to hug them. "You'll miss me, won't you, boys? Poor things having to spend the day with King Cranky. It's okay. James will save you later. Be good. Be good boys."

She straightened. "Okay, I'm going."

"Thank Christ."

"And thank you for letting them hang out with Jaws during the day." She gave him a quick buss on the cheek, opened the car door.

He spun her around, yanked her into a long, hard kiss. "Maybe I'll miss you a little, if a stray thought of you happens to cross my mind." He brushed her hair behind her ears. "Have a good time." Then he grabbed her hand. "Really. Have a good time."

"I will. We will." She got in the car, then leaned her head out the window. "Don't forget to—"

He used the palm of his hand to push her head back in.

"Okay. Okay. Bye."

He watched her go with the dogs plopped down beside him. "All right, guys, it's man-time. Scratch your balls if you've got them."

He walked back to the house, did a quick walk-through check. "It never smells like dog in here," he muttered. "How does she pull that off?"

He locked up, strode to the truck. "Everybody in. Going for a ride."

They scrambled up, except for Newman, jockeying for the passenger side or the narrow bench seat behind it.

"Come on. Gotta go," Simon ordered as the dog sat and studied him. "She'll be back in a couple days." He patted the seat. "Up, come on, Newman. Don't you trust me?"

The dog seemed to consider the question, then apparently took Simon at his word and jumped in.

He had a stray thought of her—maybe a couple of them— as he worked through the morning. He ate lunch with his feet dangling off the porch of the shop, tossing bits of salami (Fiona wouldn't approve) to the dogs and watching them field. He took another twenty minutes, tossing sticks and balls on the beach, laughing his ass off when every one of them bounded into the water.

He went back to work, radio blasting and four wet dogs snoring their way dry in the sunlight.

He didn't hear them bark, not with AC/DC screaming, but looked over as a shadow crossed his doorway.

He set his tool aside and picked up the remote to cut the music when Davey stepped in.

"Got yourself a gang of dogs out there."

"Fiona's away for a couple days."

"Yeah, I know. Girl trip with Syl and Mai. I thought I'd run by her place a couple times a day, just to check. Listen . . . What is that?"

Simon ran a hand down the side of the stump. He'd

stripped off the bark, done the first of some rough sanding. It stood, roots up.

"It's a sink base."

"It looks like a naked, upside-down tree stump."

"It does now."

"I gotta tell you, Simon, that's pretty fucking weird."

"Maybe."

Davey wandered the shop. "You've got a lot going on in here," he commented, winding around chairs, tables, the frame of a breakfront, doors and drawers glued and sporting clamps. "I saw the built-ins you did for the Munsons. They're nice. Real nice. Hey. This is a beauty here."

Like Davey, Simon studied the wine cabinet he'd designed for Fiona. "It's not finished. You didn't come by to critique my work."

"No." Face grim now, Davey shoved his hands in his pockets. "Shit."

"They found her. The girl who got taken last week."

"Yeah. Early this morning. Crater Lake National Park. He kept her longer than the others, so the feds thought maybe she got away, or it wasn't the same guy. Maybe it wasn't. Maybe. Jesus, Simon, he beat the hell out of her before he killed her. Perry never messed them up that way. The other three we know of weren't beaten. But everything else matches. The scarf, the position of the body. She had the number four written on her hand."

Because he wanted to pummel something, Simon walked over, opened his shop fridge. He took out two Cokes. Tossed one to Davey.

"He's finding his own way. It's what you do. You learn, you emulate, then you create your own style. He's experimenting."

"Jesus, Simon." Davey rubbed the cold can over his face before popping the top. "I wish I didn't think you were right on that. I wish I didn't think the same thing."

"Why are you telling me about this?"

"I want your take. Do we contact Fee, let her know?"

"No. She needs a couple days away from this."

"I'm with you on that, too, but it's going to be all over the news."

"Call Syl. Tell her, and tell her to . . . shit, make a girl pact—no news, TV, papers, Internet. Nothing to . . . you know, disturb the nirvana or estrogen field or whatever the hell. Syl will know how to handle it."

"Yeah, she will. That's good. That girl, Simon, she was barely twenty. Her dad was killed in an accident about two years ago. She was an only child. Her mother lost her husband and now her only child. It makes me sick."

He shook it off, gulped down Coke. "I guess you'll be talking to Fee every night."

He hadn't planned to. It seemed so . . . high school. "Yeah. I'll be talking to her. She's fine there."

But he knew as he went back to work, he'd worry until she was back home again.

FIONA ALL BUT floated back to her villa, gliding on bliss and massaged feet. She stepped inside where the scent of flowers and the subtle strains of New Age music embraced her. She drifted through the living area with its sink-into-me furniture and glossy wood, then straight out to the pretty flower-decked terrace where Sylvia basked in dappled sunlight.

"I'm in love." Sighing dreamily, Fiona dropped down onto a chaise. "I'm in love with a woman named Carol who's stolen my heart with her magic hands."

"You look relaxed."

"Relaxed? I'm a noodle. The happiest noodle in the Pacific Northwest. How about you?"

"I've been detoxed, scrubbed, rubbed, polished. My biggest decision is what to have for dinner tonight. I'm considering living here for the rest of my days."

"Want a roommate? God, Syl, why haven't we ever done this before?"

Sylvia, her masses of hair messily pinned on her head, her rose-shaded glasses covering her eyes, set aside the fashion magazine open on her lap. "We fell into the busy-women-with-no-time-to-indulge-themselves trap. We've broken out of the cage now. And I have a decree."

"At your command."

"During our much-deserved indulgence, we'll read only entertaining fiction and/or glossy magazines."

She tapped the cover of the one she'd set on the table.

"We will watch only light, frothy, fun movies—if we so desire movies—on TV. We will banish all thoughts of work, worry and responsibility from our minds. Our only concerns, our only decisions during this time out of time will be room service versus restaurant, and the color of polish we want during our pedicure."

"I'm behind that. I'm so behind that I'm inside it. Mai's not back yet?"

"We crossed paths of bliss in the relaxation room. She said she was going to take a swim."

"If I'd tried that, I'd have sunk like a stone and drowned." Fiona started to stretch, then decided it took too much energy. "Carol balanced my chi, or maybe she aligned my chakras. I don't know how, but having my chi balanced or chakras aligned results in something beyond ecstasy."

Mai glided out wearing one of the spa's cushy robes, slid into a chair. "Ladies. Is this a dream?" she wondered. "Is this all just a dream?"

"It's our reality, for three glorious days." Sylvia rose, wandered inside.

"I had the Mind, Body, Spirit Renewal. I've been renewed." Mai tipped her face up, closed her eyes. "I want to be renewed every day for the rest of my life."

"Syl and I are going to live here, and I'm going to marry Carol."

"Good. I'll be your permanent houseguest. Who's Carol?"

"Carol used her magic hands on my chi or chakras—possibly both—and I have to have her for my own, for always."

"Richie renewed me. I could marry Richie, then I could turn my back on the downward spiral of online dating."

"I thought you liked the dentist."

"Periodontist. I did, enough for a second date where he spent over an hour talking about his ex-wife. She was a bitch, never got off his back, spent too much money, scalped him in the divorce, et cetera, et cetera. Sam the periodontist goes down the tubes with Robert the psychologist, Michael the insurance exec and Cedric the lawyer/unpublished novelist."

"You're better off with Richie."

"Don't I know it."

They both glanced at the doorway, and Fiona's eyes popped wide as Sylvia came out carrying a silver tray.

"Champagne? Is that champagne?"

"Champagne *and* chocolate strawberries. I decided when three busy women and great, good friends finally indulge themselves it needs to be celebrated."

"We're going to have champagne on the terrace of our suite at the spa!" Fiona clasped her hands together. "It is a dream."

"Do we deserve it?"

"Damn right." Mai applauded when Sylvia popped the cork.

Once Sylvia poured the glasses, Mai raised hers. "To us," she said, "and nobody else."

With a laugh, Fiona clinked. "That absolutely works for me." She took the first sip. "Oh, oh, yeah. Syl, this was inspired. It's like the glitter on top of the shine."

"We need to make a pact. We do this every spring. Come here, get renewed, balanced, drink champagne and be girls." Mai held up her glass again.

"I'm in." Fiona tapped glasses, grinned while Sylvia did the same. "I don't even know what time it is. I can't think of the last time I didn't know, or had to think about, my schedule. I actually had one outlined for here. What time to get up to hit the gym, what classes to take, how long I'd have to take a swim or use the steam room before a treatment."

She mimed tearing a page from a book and tossing it away. "There's no room for organized Fee here. Spa Fee does what she likes when she likes."

"I bet Spa Fee's up before seven and trotting down to the gym."

"That may be." Fiona nodded at Mai. "But Spa Fee won't be on a schedule. And it's all because of the amazing Carol. Five minutes on the table and I stopped wondering how the dogs were doing with Simon, how Simon was doing with the dogs, how the rest of the unit would handle it if they got a call while we are here. What the police are . . . No," she decided. "I'm not even mentioning that one. Everything just blurred into a quiet ecstasy, which I'm going to perpetuate now by having more champagne."

They all had more.

"How's the dating going, Mai?" Sylvia asked.

"I was telling Fee about the thumbs-down on the periodontist. Ex-wife-obsessed," she explained.

"Never good."

"First guy," Mai continued, ticking off on her fingers, "obviously going off prepared remarks, and when I finally got him off-script, he was not only dull but so narrow-minded I'd be surprised if any new thought could squeeze in for consideration. Guy two, slick, self-absorbed and hoping for a quick bang. Guy next? A strange and unappealing combination of guys one and two. I'm going to give it one more shot, but I think this experiment has failed."

"It's too bad. Not even a potential casual dinner companion?" Sylvia asked.

"Not for me. I tell you, the most interesting conversations I had with the male of the species in the past couple of weeks have been with Tyson."

"Sheriff Tyson?" Fiona broke in. "From San Juan?"

"Yeah. He's looking into getting a dog, a rescue. He called me for some advice and input."

"Really?" Fiona picked up a strawberry, studied it. "And there aren't any vets on San Juan Island?"

"Sure, but I've got rescue dogs." She shrugged. "It helps to talk to somebody who's had the experience."

"You said conversations," Sylvia pointed out. "Plural."

"Yeah, we've talked a few times. He was thinking a Lab or Lab mix because he likes Fee's dogs. But then he thought, maybe just hit the shelter and see how it went, or go online and check out what's available and who needs a home. It's sweet," she added. "He's putting a lot of time and thought into it."

"And checking in with you." Fiona exchanged a glance with Sylvia.

"That's right. I'm going to go with him to check out the shelter once we get back from Spa Bliss."

"He asked you to go with him to the animal shelter?"

"A little professional and moral support," she began, then goggled at Fiona. "Come on! It's not like he asked me out for a moonlight cruise. It's not like that."

"A man, a single man, calls you multiple times to talk to you about one of your pet interests—pun intended," Fiona added, "progresses to having you go out with him. But it's not like that?" Fiona gestured to Sylvia. "Opinion, please."

"It's absolutely and completely like that."

"But—"

"Your radar's skewed," Sylvia continued. "You've been focused on meeting strangers, looking for a spark and common interests so you missed the approach of a man you already know."

"No, I . . . God, wait a minute." She closed her eyes, held up her finger as she reviewed conversations, tones. "Holy shit. You're right. It never blipped on my screen. Hmmm."

"Hmmm, good or hmmm uh-oh?" Fiona asked.

"I think . . . good. He's interesting, funny when he's not being official, steady and a little shy. And nice-looking. And a little bit sneaky, which I like. Luring me into a date. I'm . . . flattered," she realized. "Jesus, I'm seriously flattered. God. I've been renewed and I have a guy who interests me and vice versa. This is an excellent day."

"Then . . ." Sylvia topped off all three glasses. "It's a good thing I got a second bottle in the fridge."

"You are so wise," Mai told her. "Who's for ordering dinner in here later, sitting around in our pajamas, getting lit on champagne and finishing it off with some ridiculously high-caloric dessert?"

They all raised their hands.

"I'm in love with Simon," Fiona blurted out, then shook her head. "Wow, I really stepped on your Sheriff Tyson news. We can get back to this."

"Are you kidding? Are you fucking *kidding*?" Mai demanded. "Tyson—why do I refer to him by his last name?—Ben and the possibilities of dating him can wait. In love, like the *big* one, or in love like oh, this is so much fun and makes me feel good, and he's really sexy."

"The big one, with a lot of the other, which is why I thought it was all the other, but it's not. All, or only. Why can't I have an affair like a normal person? Now I've complicated it."

"Life's complicated, or what's the point?" Sylvia beamed even as her eyes filled. "I think this is wonderful."

"I don't know if it's wonderful or not, but it is. He's so not what I imagined for myself."

"You stopped imagining for yourself," Sylvia pointed out.

"Maybe I did. But if I had imagined, I don't think it would've been Simon Doyle—not for the big one."

Mai propped her elbow on the table, gestured with her glass. "Why are you in love with him? What are the qualifications?"

"I don't know. He's solitary and I'm not, he tends to be cranky and I don't. He's messy and blunt, doesn't quibble about being rude, and only ekes out information about himself when you pump or when he's in the mood."

"This is music to my ears," Sylvia murmured.

"Why, O Wise One?" Mai demanded.

"Because he's not some perfect fantasy. He's flawed and you understand that. It means you've fallen for who he is, not who you want him to be."

"I like who he is. And on the other side of it, he makes me laugh, and he's kind. The fact that he's reluctant about it only gives the kindness more impact. He can't be bothered to say what he doesn't mean, and that makes him honest."

"Does he love you?"

Fiona let her shoulders lift and fall at Mai's question. "I don't know, but I know if he ever says he does, he'll mean it. For now, it's fine the way it is. I need time to get used to the way I feel—and to be sure he's not with me or getting involved with me because, well, I'm in trouble, aren't I?"

"I bet he wasn't thinking, Hey, this woman's in trouble, when you had sex on the dining room table."

She nodded at Mai. "Excellent point. And one worthy of more champagne. I'm going to get the second bottle."

Mai waited until Fiona went back inside. "We're right, aren't we, not telling her about the murder?"

"Yes. She needs this. Apparently we all do, but she needs it most of all. She'll have to deal with it soon enough."

"I think he loves her, by the way."

Sylvia smiled. "Why?"

"Because he told Davey to call you, not Fee, to suggest not telling her. We love her, and that's why we're not telling her— and I think we'd have decided not to whatever Davey said. But Simon had the same instinct. That's a loving instinct, that's what I think."

"I think so, too."

"It might not be the big one, but—"

"It's enough for now, and what she needs. Honestly, Mai, I think they need each other, and they're both going to be better and stronger together. At least that's what I want."

Mai glanced at the doorway, lowered her voice. "I told the concierge not to leave a paper at our door in the mornings. Just in case."

"Good thinking."

They heard the pop of a cork and Fiona's shouted *"Woo-hoo!"*

"Put it out of your mind," Sylvia murmured, "so we can keep it out of hers."

SEVENTEEN

Given what she did for a living, and the gardening she'd be working on throughout the season, Fiona knew manicures were a waste of time and money.

But this was Indulgence Central.

Their last day, too, she reminded herself. She might as well make the most of it—and go home with pretty fingers and toes even if she'd mangle them within twenty-four hours in reality.

Besides, it felt good.

She admired the breezy, beachy pink on her short but currently well-shaped nails as she slid her feet into the warm, churning water at the base of the pedicure chair. A chair, she thought, that offered a slice of heaven as it vibrated up and down her back.

Cindy, who'd given her the pretty nails, brought her a cup of water with thin lemon slices floating in it. "Comfortable?"

"I passed comfortable and am on my way to euphoria."

"That's what we like to hear. Do you want the same polish on your toes?"

"You know, let's go crazy on the toes. The Purple Passion."

"Fun!" She lifted Fiona's feet out, patted them dry, then brushed on a warm green clay. "We're going to let this mask set for just a few minutes, so you just relax. Can I get you anything?"

"I've got it all."

Snuggling into her chair, Fiona opened her book and let herself fall into a romantic comedy that was as much fun as her choice of toenail polish.

"Good book?" Cindy asked when she came back to sit and rinse off the clay.

"It is. Exactly perfect for my mood. I feel happy, relaxed and pretty."

"I love to read. I like crazy horror and gruesome murder mysteries. I don't know why they relax me, but they do."

"Maybe because when you're reading the book, you know you're safe, so it's fun to be scared."

"Yeah." Cindy began to smooth Fiona's heel with a pumice stone. "I hate listening to the news because, well, it's real, and so much of it's just awful. Accidents, natural disasters, crime."

"Or politics."

"Worse yet." Cindy laughed. "But when you're reading about bad things happening in a book you can hope the good guys are going to win. I like when they do. Save the girl—or the guy—or the human race. Catch the killer and make him pay. It doesn't always happen for real. I'm scared they're never going to catch that maniac who's killing those women. Four now. Oh! Did I hurt you?"

"No." Fiona willed herself to relax her foot again. "No, you didn't hurt me. Four?"

"They found her a couple of days ago. Maybe you didn't hear. In the Cascades, in Oregon. I know it's miles and miles away, but it really scares me. If I have late appointments, my husband comes by to pick me up. I guess it's silly because I'm not a college girl, but it just spooks me."

"I don't think it's silly." Fiona sipped the lemon water to ease her dry throat. "What does your husband do?" she asked to change the subject so Cindy could chatter, and she could think.

A couple of days. Sylvia's decree—no papers, no TV.

She'd known, which meant Mai knew, too. And they'd kept it from her. To give her some peace of mind, she thought. A little slice of oblivion before reality grabbed her by the throat again.

So, she'd do the same for them, she decided. She'd maintain the pretense for this last day. If death haunted her, she could, for now, keep the ghosts to herself.

IT WASN'T LIKE HIM, Simon thought as he frowned at the flowers on Fiona's kitchen table. He didn't buy flowers.

Well, for his mother every now and again, sure. He wasn't a philistine. But he didn't buy flowers for women on impulse, or for no good reason.

Coming home after a couple days—okay, four days— away wasn't a good reason.

He didn't know why the hell he'd bought them, or why the hell he'd missed her so much. He'd gotten a lot of work accomplished without her taking up his space and time, hadn't he? And he'd drafted out more designs because he'd had more time alone, working and living on his own schedule.

His and the dogs', anyway.

He liked a quiet house. He *preferred* a quiet house—one without the annoying obligation of having to remember to pick up his socks or hang up wet towels, or stick dishes in the dishwasher unless he damn well felt like it.

Which, like most normal members of his species, meant when there were no more clean socks, towels or dishes.

Not that she asked him to pick up his socks or hang up his wet towels or stick his dishes in the dishwasher. That was her brilliance. She said nothing, so he felt obligated.

He was being trained, he realized. No doubt about it. She was training him as subtly and consistently and effortlessly as she did the dogs.

To please her. Not to disappoint her. To develop habits and routines.

It had to stop.

He should throw the stupid flowers out before she got home.

When the hell was she getting home?

He looked at the stove clock again, then walked outside so he'd stop looking at the clock.

He didn't wear a watch for the very specific reason he didn't want to be bound up in time.

He should've stayed home working until she called—or didn't call. Instead he'd stopped, went into town to buy some supplies—and the christing flowers—and didn't forget the couple bottles of the red wine she preferred, then came here to check the house.

To make sure, he was forced to admit, that James had picked up his socks and so on. Which, of course, proved unnecessary.

James was either as insanely tidy as Fiona, or well trained.

He hoped it was the latter, at least.

To get his mind off the time, he grabbed a load of tennis balls and thrilled the dogs by throwing them. And when his arm went to rubber decided she needed one of those ball shooters they used for tennis practice.

He changed it up, giving the dogs the stay command, then walking out of sight to hide the balls in various places. He went back around, sat on the porch steps.

"Find the balls!" he ordered.

He had to admit, the stampede and search had its entertainment value, and passed the time he wasn't paying any attention to.

He ended up with a pile of dog-slobbered balls at his feet, then repeated the routine. But this time he ducked inside for a beer.

The pile of balls waited, but the dogs had gone into their sentries-on-alert stance, facing the bridge.

About damn time, he thought, then deliberately leaned against the post. Just out having a beer with the dogs, he decided. It wasn't like he was waiting for her, watching for her.

But it wasn't her car that bumped across the bridge.

He straightened from the post, but waited for the man and woman who got out of the car to come to him.

"Special Agents Tawney and Mantz. We're here to speak with Ms. Bristow."

Simon glanced at the IDs. "She's not here." The dogs, he noted, were looking to him for direction. "Relax," he told them.

"We were told she was coming back today. Do you know when she's expected?"

Simon looked back at Tawney. "No."

"And you are?"

Simon shifted his gaze to the woman. "Simon Doyle."

"The boyfriend."

"Is that an official FBI term?" It stuck in his craw. "I'm helping look out for the dogs while she's gone."

"I thought she had three dogs."

"The one sniffing your shoes is mine."

"Then would you mind telling him to stop it?"

"Jaws. Back off. Fiona told me you were the agent in the Perry case," he said to Tawney. "I'll tell her you came by."

"You don't have any questions, Mr. Doyle?" Mantz wondered.

"You wouldn't answer them, so I'm saving us all time. You want to talk to Fiona. I'll tell her, and if she wants to talk to you, she'll get in touch."

"Is there any reason you're so anxious for us to leave?"

"Anxious isn't the word I'd use, but yeah. Unless you're here to tell Fiona you caught the bastard who picked up where Perry left off, I don't want you to be the first thing she sees when she gets home."

"Why don't we go inside?" Mantz suggested.

"Do you think I've got her tied up or held against her will in there? Jesus, do you see her car? Do you see her dogs?" He jerked a thumb to where Jaws was currently humping a disinterested and patient Newman while Bogart and Peck played tug with one of the ropes. "Don't they teach basic observational skills in the FBI? And no, I'm not letting you in her house when she's not here."

"Are you looking out for her, Mr. Doyle?"

"What do you think?" he said to Tawney.

"I think you have no criminal record," Tawney said easily, "you've never been married, have no children and make a good living, enough to own your own home—which you purchased about six months ago. The bureau also teaches basic data-gathering skills. I know Fiona trusts you, and so do her dogs. If I find out that trust is misplaced, you'll find out what else the bureau teaches."

"Fair enough." He hesitated, then went with instinct. "She doesn't know about the last murder. The friends with her kept her away from the paper and the TV the last few days. She needed a break. I don't want her coming back and ramming face-first into it. So I want you to go."

"That's fair enough, too. Tell her to contact me." With his partner, he walked back to the car. "We haven't caught the bastard yet. But we will."

"Hurry up," Simon muttered as they drove away.

He waited nearly an hour more, relieved now as every passing minute decreased the chance of her passing the agents on the road home. He gave some thought to putting a meal together, then spooked himself at the image of welcoming her home with a dinner *and* flowers.

It was just too much.

The bark of the dogs sent him back outside moments before she drove over the bridge. Thank God, he mused, now he could stop *thinking* so much.

He strolled casually down the porch steps, then the damnedest thing happened. The goddamnedest thing.

When she stepped out of the car, when he saw her standing in the fading sunlight, the fragile blooms of the dogwoods behind her, his heart actually leaped.

He'd always considered that sheer bull—just an overworked phrase in poetry or romance novels. But he felt it—that surge of pleasure and emotion and recognition inside his chest.

He had to restrain himself from rushing her, as the dogs did, bumping one another in their joyful hurry for strokes and kisses.

"Hi, guys, hi! I missed you, too. Every one of you. Were you good? I bet you were." She accepted desperately loving licks while she rubbed wiggling, furry bodies. "Look what I've got."

She reached inside the car for four huge rawhide bones. "One for everybody. Sit. Now sit. There we go. Everybody gets one."

"Where's mine?" Simon demanded.

She smiled, and the quieting sun flared off her sunglasses. As she walked to him, she opened her arms and just took him in.

"I was hoping you'd be here." He felt her breath—the deep in, the deep out. "You made me another chair," she murmured.

"That's for me. You're not the only one who likes to sit. Not everything's all about you."

She laughed, hugged tighter. "Maybe not, but you're just what I need."

He eased back until he found her mouth with his—and found it was just what he needed.

"My turn." He shifted to knee and nudge the dogs back, and caught it. Just an instant as the change of angle let him see through the tinted lenses and into her eyes.

He slipped them off her face. "I should've known women couldn't keep it shut down."

"You're wrong—and sexist. They didn't tell me, and I returned the favor by not letting them know I heard." Her eyes changed again. "Did you tell them not to say anything to me? To make sure I didn't read about it in the paper, catch it on the news?"

"So what?"

She nodded, laid her hands on his cheeks, kissed him lightly. "So thanks."

"That's just like you, slipping around the normal reaction of being pissed and telling me I didn't have the right to butt in and decide for you." He opened the back of her car for her suitcase. "It's how you get around people."

"Is it?"

"Oh yeah. What's this other stuff?"

"I bought some things. Here, I'll—"

"I've got it." He hauled out two shopping bags. "Why do women always come back with more than they left with? And it's not sexist if it's true."

"Because we embrace and enjoy life. Keep it up and you won't get your present."

She led the way in, and he dumped all the bags by the base of her steps. "I'll take them up later. How did you find out?"

She took off her shoes, pointed at her toes.

"Your purple toenails told you?"

"The technician who gave me the pedicure. She was just making conversation."

Damn it. He hadn't considered basic gossip.

"So that's what you people talk about during those rituals? Murder and dead bodies?"

"Let's put it in the category of current events. And let's go back, get some wine. I'd really like a glass of wine."

She saw the flowers when she stepped into the kitchen. The way she stopped cold and stared told him she was just as surprised he'd bought her flowers as he'd been.

"You made me another chair and you brought me flowers."

"I told you, the chair's mine. The flowers just happened to be there so I picked them up."

"Simon." She turned, wrapped herself around him.

Feelings winged into him, slapped against one another. "Don't make a big deal out of it."

"Sorry, but you'll have to tough it out. It's been a really long time since a man brought me flowers. I forgot what it's like. I'll be right back."

The dogs followed her out—afraid, he assumed, she'd leave again. He got out a bottle of wine, pulled the cork. She came back with a small box as he poured her a glass.

"From me and the dogs. Consider it a thank-you for helping out with them."

"Thanks." It had weight for a small box, and, curious, he opened it. He found a slender doorknocker. The copper would verdigris over time, he thought, and add to its appeal. Raised letters ran down its length, and the knocker itself formed a Celtic knot.

"It's Irish. I figured Doyle, there has to be Irish in there. *Fáilte* means—"

"Welcome. Doyle, remember?"

"Right. I thought if you put it on the door, sometimes it might even be true. The welcome, that is."

He glanced up to see her smiling. "It might. Either way it's nice."

"And you could get one made—I bet Syl could find a metal artist to do it—to put up when you're not in the mood for company. It could say 'Go away' in Gaelic."

"That's a pretty good idea. Actually, I know how to say 'Fuck off' in Irish, and that might be more interesting."

"Oh, Simon. I missed you."

She was laughing when she said it, and as she reached for her wine, he laid a hand on her arm.

"I missed you, Fiona. Damn it."

"Oh, thank God." She put her arms around him again, laid her head on his shoulder. "That makes it more balanced, like the two chairs on the porch, right?"

"I guess it does."

"I have to get this out, and I don't mean to put pressure on you. But when I dropped Mai and Sylvia off, after I did, all I could think about was that poor girl and what she went through in the last hours of her life. And when I pulled up here, home, and saw you, I was so relieved, so relieved, Simon, that I didn't have to have all that in my head and be alone with it. I was so glad to see you on the porch, waiting for me."

He started to say he hadn't been waiting. Knee-jerk, he realized. But he had been waiting, and it felt good knowing she'd wanted him to be.

"You got back later than I figured, so I— Crap."

"Last-minute shopping blitz, then the traffic—"

"No, not that." He'd remembered the FBI and decided he should get it all over with at once. "The feds were here—

Tawney and his partner. I don't think they had anything new, but—"

"A follow-up." She backed up, picked up her wine. "I told him before I left that I'd be home sometime today. I'm not going to get back to him tonight. I'll do it tomorrow."

"Good."

"But I need you to tell me what you know about it. There wasn't a way for me to find out any of the details, and I want to know."

"Okay. Sit down. I was thinking about putting something to eat together. I'll tell you while I do."

"I have frozen dinners in the freezer."

He sneered. "I'm not eating those girl diet deals. And before you say 'sexist,' look me in the eye and tell me those Lean Cuisine numbers aren't marketed to women."

"Maybe they are, mostly, but that doesn't mean they're not good, or that guys who eat them grow breasts."

"I'm not taking any chances. You'll eat what I give you."

Amused, as he'd meant her to be, she sat. "What are you going to give me?"

"I'm working on it." He opened her fridge, scanned, poked into compartments. "Deputy Davey came by to tell me the day you left," he began.

As he spoke, he tossed some frozen shoestring fries onto a cookie sheet, stuck them in the oven. Bacon went into the microwave. He found a tomato James must have left behind and sliced it thin.

"She was beaten? But—"

"Yeah. It sounds like he's trying to find his style."

"That's horrible," Fiona murmured. "And it feels true. Was she . . . she was beaten and trapped and strangled. And still rape puts a clutch in the throat."

"No, she wasn't raped. At least that wasn't part of what Davey told me, or in any of the news reports." He glanced over, scanned her face. "Are you sure you want this now?"

"Yes. I need to know what might be coming."

Simon kept his back to her, ordered himself calm as he layered cheese, bacon, tomatoes between slices of bread. "He deviated with the beating, and with keeping her longer. Otherwise, it sounds as if he followed pattern."

"Who was she? You know," Fiona said quietly. "You'd have made it a point to know."

When Simon slid the sandwiches onto the frying pan, the butter he'd spread on the outside sizzled. "She was a student. She wanted to pursue a career in physical education and nutrition. She taught yoga classes and did some personal training work. She was twenty, outgoing and athletic, according to the reports. She was an only child. Her mother's a widow."

"God. God." She covered her face with her hands for a moment, then scrubbed hard and dropped them. "It can always get worse."

"She fits the body type. Tall, slender, long legs, toned." He flipped the sandwiches. "If there's any more, the press doesn't have it."

"Did he mark her?"

"Roman numeral four. You're wondering what number he plans to put on you. I want you to hear me, Fiona, and to understand I don't say what I don't mean."

"I already understand that."

She waited, watched as he slid the sandwiches onto plates. Shook the fries from the pan beside them. He pulled out a jar of pickles, tossed a couple onto each plate and considered it done.

He put a plate in front of her. "He won't mark you. He won't be able to give you a number any more than Perry could. If the cops don't stop him first, then we'll stop him. And that's it."

She said nothing for a moment, but rose to get a knife, to retrieve the wine. She topped off the glasses, then cut her sandwich into two neat triangles before offering the knife.

"No, thanks."

She picked up her wine, sipped, set it down. "All right," she said, meeting his eyes. "All right."

She lifted half of her sandwich, took a bite. And smiled. "It's good."

"A Doyle staple."

She took another bite and brushed his leg under the table with her sexy purple toes. "It's good to be home. You know, one of the things I have in those shopping bags is this incredible honey almond scrub they use at the spa. After dinner, and after I give the dogs some more play and attention, we could take a shower. I'll exfoliate you."

"Is that code?"

She laughed. "You'll have to find out."

"Do you know why I don't cut my sandwiches into triangles?"

"Why?"

"For the same reason I don't want to smell like honey and almonds."

She gave him a wicked look as she picked up a french fry. "Or eat Lean Cuisine. I bet I could change your mind on the scrub. Tell you what. I'll just do your back. Your big, strong, manly back, and we'll see how it goes from there. They also had this shop that sold very interesting lingerie. I bought a little something. A very, very little something, which I'd be inclined to model for you, if you try the scrub."

"How little?"

"Minuscule."

"Just the back."

She smiled and nibbled on a fry. "To start."

She played with the dogs for an hour, endlessly tossing balls, letting them chase her through the obstacle course, then taking turns playing tug with each of them until he wondered that her arms didn't pop out of their sockets.

But he could see, even when he left the games and sat on the porch to watch, she used the activities, the dogs, the connections to focus. To block out what they'd spoken of before dinner.

She'd deal, he thought, because that's what she did. For now, she channeled her energy, and whatever nerves brewed under it, into the dogs and somehow transformed it into joy.

"Now I need that shower." She swiped at her damp face with the backs of her hands.

"You wore them out."

"Part of the plan." She held out a hand. "I never asked what you were up to while I was gone."

"Work. And after work, James and I took in some strip clubs."

"Uh-huh."

"We took the dogs," he said as they walked upstairs.

"Naturally."

"Newman's a mean drunk."

"It's a problem." In the bedroom she dug the box of scrub out of the shopping bag, opened it for the jar.

"Actually, if you want some speculation and gossip, I don't think we're the only ones who'll have exfoliated in the shower recently."

"Sorry, what?"

"I came by to pick up the dogs one morning because I needed some supplies and figured I'd save James the trip. Lori's car was in the drive."

"Really? Well, well. She might've stopped by early, like you did. I hope not, but—"

"He came out when I started rounding up the dogs. He blushed."

"Aw." She crooned it, then laughed. "That's so sweet." After she set the jar down on the bathroom counter, she pulled the band from her hair—shook out all that rose gold.

He went rock hard.

"Strip it off," she ordered. "Let's see if I can make you blush."

"I don't blush, and I'm not sweet."

"We'll see." She tugged off her shirt, but flicked his hand away when he reached out. "Uh-uh. A deal's a deal. Let's get wet."

Maybe it was another way of focusing, channeling, blocking out. But who was he to complain? Naked, he stepped under the spray. "Your bathroom needs to be updated and redesigned."

"I'll take that under advisement." She made a circle with

her finger, so he turned around and gave her his back. "It feels a little rough," she told him as she scooped the scrub out of the jar. "But in a good way."

She began to rub it over his back in slow, steady circles. "The texture, the flesh-to-flesh contact, the aroma—all add to the experience. Your skin wakes up and feels more— Uh-uh," she said again, when he reached back. "I do the touching till we're done. Hands on the wall, Doyle."

"Did you get naked in the shower at the spa for this?"

"No. I'm adjusting it for home use. You smell wonderful already, and mmmm, smooth." She leaned in, let her breasts ride over his back before using more scrub farther down. "Is this all right?" she asked as she circled those firm hands over his ass.

"Yeah."

"Why don't you close your eyes, relax? I'll just keep going until you tell me to stop."

Those hands ran down his legs, the rough texture tingling over his skin to be sluiced away by the spray, then explored by her lips, her tongue.

Need banged in his blood until his hands on the wall were fists. Rich scent curled in the steam, became erotic until even drawing a breath aroused to aching.

"Fiona."

"Just a little more," she murmured. "I haven't even started on the front yet. You'll be . . . unbalanced. Turn around, Simon."

She knelt in front of him, water gleaming off her skin, sleeking her hair back. "I'll just start down here, and work my way up."

"I want you. You couldn't need for me to want you more than this."

"You'll have me, as much as you want. But let's see if you can hold out till I finish. Let me finish, and you can do whatever you want with me."

"Jesus Christ, Fiona. You drive me insane."

"I want to. That's what I want tonight. But not yet."

He reached down for her hands, let out a strained laugh. "Don't even think about putting that stuff on my—"

"That's not what I'm going to put there." She skimmed her tongue over him until he bit back a moan. "Can you hold out?" she murmured, torturing him with her mouth as her hands worked up his legs, over his belly. "Can you hold out until you're inside me? Hot and hard inside me. That's what I want when I'm done. I want you to take me and use me until I can't stand it, then I want you to take me and use me more. I won't tell you to stop. I won't tell you to stop until you're done."

She took him to the edge, then those tormenting lips slicked over his belly, up his chest, while her hands circled, circled.

"The water's going cold," she murmured against his mouth. "We should—"

He put her back to the wet wall. "You'll have to take it, and me."

"Deal's a deal." Her breath caught and shuddered out when he slid his hand between her legs.

"Wider."

She gripped his shoulders, shuddered once as his eyes burned into hers. As he drove into her, they burned still. He took her, ruthlessly, so that her cries echoed with the slap of wet flesh, the sizzle of cold water. When her head fell on his shoulder, he continued to thrust while his hands made rough use of her body.

His own release ripped through him and left him raw.

He managed to shut off the water and pull her out. When she staggered, he half carried her to the bed. They dropped onto it wet and breathless.

"What do you—" She broke off, let out a whistling breath, cleared her throat. "What do you say about honey almond now?"

"I'll be buying a case of it."

She laughed, then her eyes popped open as he straddled her. His eyes, still hot, met hers as his thumbs flicked over her nipples. "I'm not done yet."

"But—"

"I'm not done." Leaning over her, he took her hands,

lifted them, clamped them around the iron rungs. "Leave them there. You're going to need something to hold on to."

"Simon."

"What I want, as much as I want," he reminded her, and slid down, lifted her hips. "Until I'm finished."

The breath trembled between her lips now, but she nodded. "Yes."

EIGHTEEN

As a sop to healthier eating, Fiona tossed some strawberries onto her Froot Loops. She ate them leaning against the kitchen counter, watching Simon drink coffee while leaning against the one across from her.

"You're stalling," she decided. "Stretching out another cup of coffee so you're here until people start coming in for the first class."

He reached into the cereal box she'd yet to put away, took a handful. "So?"

"I appreciate it, Simon, nearly as much as I appreciate being sexed into a coma last night. But it's not necessary."

"I'm drinking this coffee until I finish." He experimented by dunking a Froot Loop into the coffee. Sampled.

Not half bad.

"I'm staying until I leave," he continued. "If you have something you have to do, go do it, but I'm not leaving you alone. Deal with it."

She scooped up more cereal, munched it while she studied him. "You know, somebody else might've said, 'Fee, I'm concerned about you, and I don't want to take any chances with your safety so I'm going to be here for you.'"

He dunked a couple more. "Somebody else isn't here."

"That's very true, and maybe there's something perverse in me that prefers your method." He might've been dunking colorful rounds of cereal into his coffee like tiny doughnuts, but he looked scruffy and irritable. God, why did she love that? "What are we going to do about this, Simon?"

"I'm going to drink my coffee."

"And, using the coffee as a metaphor, are you going to keep drinking it until they catch the person who's killing those women, and may want to add me to his scorecard?"

"Yes."

She nodded, ate more cereal. "Then stop hauling that stupid duffel over here every night. I'll give you room in the closet, clean out a drawer. If you're sleeping here, it's ridiculous not to leave some of your things here. You deal with it."

"I'm not living here."

"Understood." He'd inconvenience himself for her, but he'd be careful not to step over the next line. "You're just hanging out here, and drinking coffee with coffee-soaked Froot Loops—"

"It's pretty good."

"I'll put it on the menu. And sleeping here after making crazed love with me in the shower."

"That was your idea."

She laughed. "And a damn good one. Restrictions that apply are acknowledged. Leave your damn toothbrush in the bathroom, Simon, you idiot. Put your underwear in a drawer and hang up a couple of shirts in the closet."

"I've already got a shirt in the closet. You washed it because I left it on the floor."

"That's right. And if you leave clothes on the floor, they're going to get washed and put away whether you like it or not. If I can agree to you drinking coffee, you can agree not to haul that duffel back and forth like a security blanket."

When his eyes narrowed, she narrowed hers back at him. And smiled. "What? Did that hit the mark?"

"Are you looking for a fight?"

"Let's say I'm looking for your famous balance. I give, you give." She tapped her chest, pointed at him, then wiggled a hand between them. "And it levels out in the middle. Think about it. I've got to get ready for class," she added, and strolled away.

Twenty minutes later as her first class of the day started their socialization exercises, she watched Simon walk to his truck. He called his dog—and shot Fiona a look from behind his sunglasses.

He drove away—without the duffel.

She considered it a small, personal victory.

MIDWAY THROUGH THE DAY, she'd logged "visits" from Meg and Chuck, Sylvia and Lori, topped off by her daily check from Davey.

Apparently no one was going to leave her alone. As much as she appreciated the concern, it occurred to her just why she'd chosen a place several miles outside the village. As much as she loved company, she needed those small pockets of solitude.

"Davey, I've got a call in to Agent Tawney—who's probably going to make yet another trip out here. I've got my phone in my pocket, as promised, and barely thirty minutes between classes. Less when one of the clients is an islander because they stall until whoever's next on the Watch Out for Fee list shows up. I'm not getting any of my office work done."

"So go do it."

"Do you really think this guy's going to drive up here in the middle of the day to attempt an abduction between my Basic Obedience class and my Advanced Skill Set?"

"Probably not." He took a swig from the Coke she'd provided. "But if he does, he's not going to find you alone."

She cast her eyes up to the puffy clouds dotting the sky. "Maybe I should start serving refreshments."

"Cookies would be good. You can't go wrong with cookies."

She punched him lightly on the shoulder. "Look, here comes one of the next class. Go protect and serve someone else."

He waited until the car came close enough for him to see the driver was female. "I'll see you tomorrow. Don't forget the cookies."

Davey gave a nod to the other driver as he got into his cruiser and she parked.

She climbed out, a tall, pretty brunette with a swingy wedge of chin-length hair and what Fiona thought of as city boots. Stylish and thin-heeled under trim gray pants.

"Fiona Bristow?"

"That's right."

"Oh, what great dogs! Can I pet them?"

"Sure." Fiona signaled, so her dogs stepped up to the woman and sat politely.

"They're so sweet." She shoved her enormous shoulder bag behind her back and crouched down. "The pictures on your website are good, but they're even better in person."

And where's your dog? Fiona wondered. But it wouldn't be the first time a potential client came out to scope her and her setup before signing up.

"Did you come to monitor a class? I have one starting in about ten minutes."

"I'd love to." She angled her face up, all fresh style and perky smile. "I was hoping I'd hit between classes so I'd have a few minutes to talk to you. I checked the schedule on your website and tried to time it. But you know how the ferries are."

"Yes, I do. You're interested in enrolling your dog?"

"I would be, but I don't have one yet. I'd love a big dog, like one of yours, or maybe a golden retriever, but I'm in an apartment. It doesn't seem fair to coop one up that way. But once I get a place with a yard . . ."

She rose, offered a smile and her hand. "I'm Kati Starr. I work for—"

"*U.S. Report,*" Fiona finished, in a tone that went cool. "You're wasting your time here."

"I just need a few minutes. I'm doing a follow-up, actually a series of stories on RSK Two, and—"

"Is that what you're calling him?" It revolted her on every level. "Red Scarf Killer Two—like a movie sequel?"

Starr traded in her smile for a tough-eyed stare. "We're taking it very seriously. This man has already killed four women in two states. Brutally, Ms. Bristow, and with his latest victim, Annette Kellworth, that brutality escalated. I hope *you're* taking it seriously."

"Your hopes aren't my problem. My feelings aren't your business."

"You have to understand your feelings are relevant," Starr insisted. "He's reprising the Perry murders, and as the only woman known to have escaped Perry, you must have some thoughts and feelings on what's happening now. Insight into the victims, into Perry and RSK Two. Will you confirm the FBI has interviewed you regarding these latest homicides?"

"I'm not going to comment. I already made that clear to you."

"I understand you may have felt reluctant initially, Fiona, but surely now that the death total is up to four, and these abductions and murders are heading north, from California to Oregon, you must want to be heard. You must have something to say—to the families of the victims, to the public, even to the killer. I only want to give you a platform."

"What you want are headlines."

"Headlines draw attention. Attention needs to be paid. The facts need to get out. The victims need to be heard, and you're the only one who can speak."

She might have believed that, Fiona considered, or at least part of it. But reality dictated that the attention focused on the killer with the catchy nickname.

"I have nothing to say to you, except you're trespassing on private property."

"Fiona." All calm and reason, Starr pushed on. "We're women. This man is targeting women. Young, attractive women with their lives ahead of them. You know what it is to be that target, what it's like to be a victim of that kind of random violence. All I'm trying to do is get the story out, get the information out so maybe his next target is more aware, and maybe she'll keep having her life ahead of her instead of ending up in a shallow grave. Something you know, can say, may be what helps her live."

"Maybe you mean that. You're only trying to help. Or maybe what you want is another front-page story with your byline. Maybe it's a little of both."

She didn't know; she couldn't allow herself to care.

"But here's what I do know. You're giving him what he wants. Attention. You published my name, where I live, what I do. And that helps no one except the man who's emulating Perry. I want you off my property, and I want you to stay off my property. I don't want to call the deputy who was just here to escort you off, but I will."

"Why was the deputy just here? Are you under police protection? Do the investigators have any reason to believe you may be a target?"

So much for facts and the public right to know, Fiona thought. What this one wanted, at the base of it, was dish.

"Ms. Starr, I'm telling you to get off my property, and that's all I'm going to tell you."

"I'm going to write the story with or without your cooperation. There's interest in a book deal. I'm willing to compensate you for interviews. Exclusive interviews."

"That makes it easier," Fiona said, and pulled her phone out of her pocket. "You've got ten seconds to get in your car and get off my property. I will press charges. Believe it."

"Your choice." Starr opened her car door. All pretense of the perky dog lover was stripped away. "The pattern says he's chosen his next victim, or he's preparing to. Scoping out the area for the right target. Ask yourself how you're going to feel when he racks up number five. You can reach me through the paper when you change your mind."

Hold your breath, Fiona thought. Please.

SHE PUT IT out of her mind. Her work, her life were more important than a persistent reporter hoping, Fiona imagined, to springboard a book deal off tragedy.

She had her dogs to care for, her little garden to tend to and a relationship to explore.

Simon's toothbrush took up residence in her bathroom. His socks scattered messily in one of her drawers.

They weren't living together, she reminded herself, but he was the first man since Greg who slept consistently in her bed, whose things mixed with hers under the same roof.

He was the first man she wanted with her in the night when ghosts haunted her sleep.

HE WAS THERE, and she was grateful for it, when Tawney and his partner returned.

"You should go on to work," she told Simon when she recognized the car. "I think I'll be safe in the hands of the feds."

"I'll stick around."

"All right. Why don't you let them in? I'll make some more coffee."

"You let them in. I'll make the coffee."

She opened the door, holding it open to the morning air. It looked like rain heading in, she noted. That would save her from watering her pots and garden beds—and add a realistic element to the training classes she had on tap for the afternoon.

Dogs and handlers couldn't pick just sunny days for a search.

"Good morning," she called out. "You're getting an early start. Simon's making some fresh coffee."

"I could use some," Tawney told her. "Why don't we go back, sit in the kitchen?"

"Sure." Remembering Mantz's aversion, she gestured the dogs out. "Go play," she told them. "I'm sorry I missed you the other day," she added, leading the way back. "We'd planned to be back earlier, but we dragged our feet. If you want a place to go and unwind, it's the spot for it. Simon, you've met Agents Tawney and Mantz."

"Yeah."

"Have a seat. I'll get the coffee."

Simon left her to the pouring and doctoring. "Anything new?"

"We're pursuing the avenues," Mantz told him. "All of them."

"You didn't have to make another trip out here to tell her that."

"Simon."

"How are you, Fee?" Tawney asked her.

"I'm all right. I'm reminded daily how many people I know on the island, as somebody drops by to see me—read: check in on me—several times a day. It reassures, even as it makes me itchy."

"We can still offer you a safe house. Or we can work putting an agent here, with you."

"Would it be you?"

He smiled a little. "Not this time."

She took a moment just to look out the window. Her pretty yard, she thought, with its tender spring gardens just starting to pop with color and shape. And all that bumping up against the tower of trees that climbed up the slopes and walked down again, offering countless paths to stroll, lovely surprises of wild lupine and dreamy blue cannas.

Always so quiet and restful to her, so *hers* season by season.

The island, she thought, was her safe house. Emotionally, yes, but she absolutely believed in every practical sense as well.

"I think, realistically, I'm covered. The island itself makes me less accessible, and I'm—literally—never alone."

Even as she spoke, she watched her dogs wander by. On patrol, she mused.

"He broke pattern with Annette Kellworth. It's possible he's not interested in me anymore, not interested in mirroring Perry."

"His violence is increasing," Mantz stated. "Perry duplicated himself, obsessively repeating the same details with each murder. The UNSUB isn't as controlled or disciplined.

He wants to flaunt his power. Sending you the scarf, increasing the time he holds his victims, and now the added physical violence. But he continues to use Perry's methods, to select the same type of victim, to abduct and to kill and dispose in the same way."

"He's adapting his work, finding his own style. Sorry," Simon added when he realized he'd spoken out loud.

"No, you're not wrong. Kellworth may have been an aberration," Tawney continued. "Something she said or did, something that happened that pushed him to the increased violence. Or he may be looking to come into his own."

"I'm not his."

"You're still the one who got away," Mantz pointed out. "And if you're going to talk to the press, it keeps you front and center, and makes you more of a challenge."

Annoyed, Fiona turned from the window. "I'm not talking to the press."

Mantz reached into her briefcase. "This morning's edition." She laid the paper on the table. "And the article's been picked up by a number of online venues and cable news crawls."

TRAIL OF THE RED SCARF

"I can't stop this. All I can do is not give interviews, refuse to cooperate."

"You're quoted. And your picture runs inside."

"But—"

"'Surrounded by her three dogs,'" Mantz read, "'outside her tiny woodland home on scenic and remote Orcas Island where purple pansies tumble out of white pots and bright blue chairs sit on the front porch, Fiona Bristow presents a cool and competent demeanor. A tall, attractive redhead, slender in jeans and a stone-gray jacket, she seems to approach the subject of murder with the same practical, down-to-earth manner that has made her and her canine training school fixtures on the island.

"'She was twenty, the same age as Annette Kellworth, when she was abducted by Perry. Like Perry's other twelve female victims, Bristow was incapacitated by a stun gun, drugged, bound, gagged and locked in the trunk of his car. There, she was held for more than eighteen hours. But unlike the others, Bristow managed to escape. In the dark, while Perry drove the night roads, Bristow sawed through the rope binding her with a penknife given to her by her fiancé, Officer Gregory Norwood. Bristow fought off Perry, disabling him, and used his own car to reach safety and alert authorities.

"'Nearly a year later, still at large, Perry shot and killed Norwood and his K-9 partner, Kong, who lived long enough to attack and wound Perry. Perry was subsequently arrested when he lost control of his car in his attempt to escape. Despite her ordeal, and her loss, Bristow testified against Perry, and that testimony played a major role in his conviction.

"'Now, at twenty-nine, Bristow shows no visible scars from that experience. She remains single, living alone in her secluded home where she owns and operates her training school for dogs, and devotes much of her time to the Canine Search and Rescue unit she formed on Orcas.

"'The day is sunny and warm. The dogwood trees flanking the narrow bridge over the creek that bubbles across the property are in bloom, and the native red currant flames in the quiet morning. In the deep green woods where shafts of light shimmer through the towering firs, birds twitter. But a uniformed deputy drives his cruiser down her narrow drive. There can be little doubt Fiona Bristow remembers the dark, and the fear.

"'She would have been XIII.

"'She speaks of the "movie sequel" title this mimic of George Allen Perry has been given, and the headlines his brutality has generated. It's attention this man known as RSKII seeks, she believes. While she, the lone survivor of the one who came before him, wants only the peace and the privacy of the life she has now. A life forever changed.'"

"I didn't give her an interview." Fiona shoved the paper aside. "I didn't talk to her about all of this."

"But you did talk to her," Mantz persisted.

"She showed up." Struggling with rage, Fiona barely resisted ripping the paper to shreds. "I assumed she was here to ask about a class—and she let me assume that. She talked about the dogs, then she introduced herself. The minute she did I told her to go. No comment, go away. She persisted. I did say he wanted attention. I was angry. Look what they're calling him, RSK Two, so it gives him flash and mystery and importance. I said he wanted attention, and she was giving it to him. I shouldn't have said it." She looked at Tawney now. "I know better."

"She pushed. You pushed back."

"And got just enough to run with it. I ordered her off the property. I even threatened to call Davey—Deputy Englewood—back. He'd just left because we both thought she'd come for class. She was here five minutes. Five goddamn minutes."

"When?" Simon demanded, and a quick chill skipped up her spine at the tone.

"A couple of days ago. I put it away. I made her go, and I thought, I honestly thought I hadn't given her anything—so I put it aside."

She let out a breath. "She's made him see me here, with my dogs and my trees. The quiet life of a survivor. And she's made him see me there, in the trunk of that car, tied up in the dark—another victim, who just got lucky. The one line, the one about attention. The way she's written it, that's me speaking to him, dismissing him. It's the sort of thing he might fixate on. I understand that."

She glanced at the paper again, at the photo of her standing in front of her house, her hand on Newman's head, Peck and Bogart beside her. "She must have taken this from her car. You'd think I posed for it."

"You shouldn't have any trouble getting a restraining order," Tawney told her.

Discouraged, Fiona pressed her fingers to her eyes. "She'll eat that up. I wouldn't bet against her adding column inches on me to that article, my pansies, my chairs—painting a damn picture—*because* I wouldn't play ball. She'll only be more determined to write about me if I make her an issue. Maybe I played it wrong. Maybe I should've given her the interview the first time around. Something dull and restrained, then she'd have lost interest in me."

"You don't get it." Simon shook his head. He had his hands in his pockets, but Fiona knew there was nothing casual about it. "Talk to her, don't, it doesn't matter. You're alive. You're always going to be part of it. You survived, but it's more than that. You weren't rescued, the cavalry didn't come charging up. You fought and escaped from a man who'd killed twelve other women, and who had eluded authorities for more than two years. As long as this bastard's strangling women with red scarves, you're news."

He looked back at Mantz. "So don't look down your dismissive FBI nose at her over this. Until you catch the fucker, they'll use her for print, for ratings, to keep it churned up between murders. And you fucking well know it."

"Maybe you think we're just sitting on our hands," Mantz began.

"Erin." Tawney waved his partner off. "You're right," he told Simon. "About the media. Still, Fee, it's better for you to stick with the straight 'No comment.' And you're right," he said to Fiona, "that this kind of press will very likely pump up his interest in you. You need to continue all the precautions you're taking. And I'm going to ask you not to take on any new clients."

"God. Look, I'm not trying to be difficult or stupid, but I have to make a living. I have—"

"What else?" Simon interrupted.

Fiona rounded on him. "Listen—"

"Shut up. What else?" he repeated.

"Okay. I want you to contact me every day," Tawney went on. "I want you to keep a record of anything unusual. A wrong number, a hang-up, any questionable e-mails or correspondence. I want the name and contact for anyone who inquires about your classes, your schedule."

"Meanwhile, what are you doing?"

Tawney glanced at Fiona's flushed and furious face before answering Simon. "All we can. We're interviewing and reinterviewing friends, family, coworkers, neighbors, instructors, classmates of all the victims. He spent time observing them, he has to have transportation. He's not invisible. Someone saw him, and we'll find them. We're doing background checks and interviewing anyone associated with the prison who had, or may have had, contact with Perry over the last eighteen months. We have a team working the tip line twenty-four hours a day. Forensic experts are sifting through the dirt from every gravesite, looking for any trace evidence—a hair, a fiber."

He paused. "We've interviewed Perry, and will do so again. Because he knows. I know him, Fee, and I know he wasn't pleased when I told him about the scarf that was sent to you. Not in his plans, not his style. Even less pleased when I let it slip, we'll say, that Annette Kellworth had been beaten and her face, in particular, severely damaged. He'll turn on this guy, he'll turn because I'll make him feel betrayed and disrespected. And that—you know—he won't tolerate."

"I appreciate you keeping me informed, coming here and making sure I understand the status and the situation." She held temper under clipped words and a brisk tone. "I have a class starting very soon. I have to get ready."

"All right." Tawney laid a hand over hers in a gesture as fatherly as it was official. "I want that call, Fee, every day."

"Yes. Could you leave that?" she asked Mantz when the agent started to refold the paper. "It'll help remind me not to give even an inch."

"No problem." Mantz rose. "There'll be others now that this story hit. I'd start screening all my calls, and you'd be smart to post some 'No Trespassing' signs around your property. You can tell your clients you've had some trouble with hikers cutting through, and you're concerned for your dogs," she added before Fiona could speak.

"Yes. Yes, that's a good idea. I'll take care of it."

She walked them out, then waited for Simon to join her on the porch. "You want to give me grief for not mentioning the reporter. That's fine, but you have to get in line. I'm first."

"You already gave yourself grief on that."

"No. I mean I have a few things to say to you, and I'm in

a bind. You're pissed at me, and pretty seriously, but you still stood up for me with Agent Mantz. I'd say the standing up wasn't necessary, but that's ungracious. Besides, standing up for someone isn't ever necessary—it's just what you do for someone you care about, or when somebody needs it. So I'm grateful for that, and I appreciate that. And at the same time I'm so angry with you for just taking over the way you did. For pushing my opinion and wants aside, and making it clear you'd see to it I'd do what I was told."

"I'm clear on it, so I figured you and the feds should be."

She swung around. "Don't think for one minute you can—"

"You'd better shut it down, Fiona." His eyes flared hot, singed gold. "You'd better shut it down fast." He took a step toward her. Nearby, Peck let out a quiet warning. Simon responded by jerking his head, aiming a hard look, pointing a finger for silence.

The dog sat instantly but kept watchful.

"You want to go off on me, then *you* get in line. You can go on your I-can-take-care-of-myself routine all you want. I don't give a rat's rabid ass because you're not doing it yourself this time, so just swallow that one down. You can tell me I'm stupid for not leaving my damn toothbrush in the bathroom, and I've got to give that to you. I'm telling you, you're brain-dead if you think you can decide all the rest on your own. That's not how it works."

"I never said—"

"Shut up. This bullshit about not telling me some reporter came by to hassle you because you put it aside? Don't pull that on me again. You don't put things aside, not like this."

"I didn't—"

"I'm not fucking done. You don't run this show. I don't know how you worked it before with your cop, but this is now. You're dealing with me now. You'd better think about that, and if you can't deal with it, you let me know. We'll leave it that we just fuck when we're both in the mood, and move on."

She felt her face go cold and stiff as the blood drained. "That's harsh, Simon."

"Damn right, it is. You've got clients coming, and I've got work to do." He strode away as a couple of cars drove across her bridge.

Jaws, obviously tuned in to his master's mood, leaped quickly into the truck.

"I didn't get my turn," Fiona muttered, then tried some deep breathing to center herself before greeting her clients.

NINETEEN

Fiona deliberately scheduled a solo behavioral correction as her last client of the day. She often thought of those sessions as attitude adjustments—and not just for the dog.

The fluffy orange Pom, Chloe—all four pounds of her—ruled over her owners, reportedly wreaked havoc in her neighborhood, yipping, snarling and lunging hysterically at other dogs, cats, birds, kids, and occasionally tried to take a Pom-sized chunk out of whatever crossed her path when she wasn't in the mood for it.

Struggling to crochet—her newest hobby—Sylvia sat on the porch with a pitcher of fresh lemonade and butter cookies while Fiona listened to the client repeat the gist of their phone consult.

"My husband and I had to cancel our vacation this winter." Lissy Childs stroked the ball of fur in her arms while that ball eyed Fiona suspiciously. "We couldn't get anyone to take her for the week—or house-sit, if she was in it. She's so sweet, really, and so adorable, but, well, she is incorrigible."

Lissy made kissy noises, and Chloe responded by shivering all over and lapping at Lissy's face.

Chloe, Fiona noted, wore a silver collar studded with multicolored rhinestones—at least she hoped they were just rhinestones—and pink booties, open at the toe to show off matching pink toenails.

Both she and her human smelled of Vera Wang's Princess.

"She's a year?"

"Yes, she just had her very first birthday, didn't you, baby doll?"

"Do you remember when she started showing unsociable behavior?"

"Well." Lissy cuddled Chloe. The eye-popping square-cut diamond on her hand flared like fired ice, and Chloe made a point of showing Fiona her sharp, scissorlike teeth. "She's really never liked other dogs, or cats. She thinks she's a person, 'cause she's my baby."

"She sleeps in your bed, doesn't she?"

"Well . . . yes. She has a sweet bed of her own, but she likes to use it as a toy box. She just loves squeaky toys."

"How many does she have?"

"Oh . . . well." Lissy had the grace to look sheepish as she flipped back her long blond mane. "I buy them for her all the time. I just can't resist. And little outfits. She loves to dress up. I know I spoil her. Harry does, too. We just can't resist. And really, she is a sweetheart. She's just a little jealous and excitable."

"Why don't you put her down?"

"She doesn't like me to put her down outside. Especially when . . ." She glanced over her shoulder where Oreo and Fiona's dogs sprawled. "When other d-o-g-s are around."

"Lissy, you're paying me to help Chloe become a happier, better-adjusted dog. What you're telling me, and what I'm seeing, is that Chloe's not only pack leader, she's a four-pound dictator. Everything you've told me indicates she has a classic case of Small Dog Syndrome."

"Oh, my goodness! Does she need medication?"

"She needs you to stop allowing her to lead, fostering the idea that because she's little she's permitted to engage in bad behavior you wouldn't permit in a larger dog."

"Well, but, she *is* little."

"Size doesn't change the behavior, or the reason a dog displays it." Owners, Fiona thought, were all too often the biggest obstacle. "Listen, you can't take her for a walk without stress, or have people over to your house. You told me you and Harry love to entertain, but haven't been able to have a dinner party in months."

"It's just that the last time we tried, it was so stressful with Chloe so upset that we had to put her in the bedroom."

"Where she destroyed your new duvet, among other things."

"It was awful."

"You can't leave her to have an evening away without her having a tantrum, so you and your husband have stopped going out to dinner, to parties, to the theater. You said she bit your mother."

"Yes, it was just a nip really. She—"

"Lissy, let me ask you something. I bet you've been on planes, or in the shops, a restaurant where a child's been running wild, disturbing everyone, kicking the seat, arguing with his parents, creating a nuisance, whining, complaining and so on."

"God, yes." She rolled her eyes as she spoke. "It's so annoying. I don't understand why . . . Oh." Cluing in, Lissy blew out a breath. "I'm not being a responsible mommy."

"Exactly." Or close enough. "Put her down."

The minute Chloe's pink booties hit the ground, she leaped onto her hind legs, yipping, scrabbling at Lissy's lovely linen pants.

"Come on now, baby, don't—"

"No," Fiona said. "Don't give her that kind of attention when she's misbehaving. You need to dominate. Show her who's in charge."

"Stop that right now, Chloe, or no yummies on the way home."

"Not like that. First, stop thinking, But she's so little and cute. Stop thinking about her size and think of her as a misbehaving dog. Here." Fiona took the leash.

"Step away," she told Lissy, and positioned herself between them. Chloe yipped and snarled, attempted a quick lunge and nip.

"Stop!" Voice firm, Fiona kept eye contact and shot a finger toward the dog. Chloe made grumbling sounds, but subsided.

"She's sulking," Lissy said with indulgence.

"If she was a Lab or a German shepherd sitting there growling, would it be cute?"

Lissy cleared her throat. "No. You're right."

"Spoiling her isn't making her happy. It's making her a bully, and bullies aren't happy."

She began to walk the dog. Chloe struggled, trying to turn back to Lissy. Fiona simply shortened the leash, forcing Chloe to fall in line. "Once she understands there's no reward, no affection shown for bad behavior, and that you're in charge, she'll stop. And be happier."

"I don't want her to be a bully or unhappy. Honestly, that's why I'm here. I'm just terrible at discipline."

"Then get better," Fiona said flatly. "She depends on you. When she's already excited and heading out of control, speak to her firmly, correct her quickly, don't placate her in that high baby-talk voice. That only increases her level of stress. She wants you to take control, and you'll all be happier once you do."

For the next ten minutes, Fiona worked with the dog, correcting and rewarding.

"She listens to you."

"Because she understands I'm in charge, and she respects that. Her behavior problems are a result of how she's been treated by the people around her, how she's come to believe she *should* be treated and now demands to be treated."

"Spoiled."

"It's not the squeaky toys, the yummies, the outfits. Why not indulge yourselves there if it makes all of you happy? It goes back to allowing, even encouraging, unacceptable behavior and giving her the controls. She goes on the attack with big dogs, right?"

"All the time. And it was funny at first. You just had to

laugh. Now it's gotten a little scary every time we take her for a walk."

"She does it because you've made her pack leader. She has to defend that position every time she comes in contact with another dog, human, animal. It stresses her out."

"Is that why she goes on those barking jags? Because she's stressed?"

"That, and because she's telling you what to do. People think of Poms as yappy dogs because their owners often allow them to become yappy dogs."

Not yapping now, Fiona thought as she stopped and Chloe sat and watched her with those almond-shaped eyes. "She's relaxed now. I want you to do the same thing with her. Walk her back and forth. Stay in control."

Fiona led Chloe to Lissy, and the dog rose up to paw the air, to scrabble at Lissy's legs.

"Lissy," Fiona said firmly.

"Okay. Chloe, stop."

"Mean it!" Fiona ordered.

"Chloe, stop!"

Chloe sat, tipped her head from side to side as if evaluating.

"Now walk her. Insist that she heel. She's not walking you."

Fiona stepped back to watch. She was, she knew, training the human every bit as much as—possibly more than—the dog. Progress, and a satisfied client, would depend on the human's willingness to adhere to the training at home.

"She's listening!"

"You're doing great." And both of you are relaxed, Fiona thought. "I'm going to walk toward you. If she exhibits unacceptable behavior, I want you to correct. And don't tense up. You're walking your cute little dog. Your cute, polite, happy little dog."

At Fiona's approach, Chloe barked and pulled on the leash. Fiona wasn't sure who was more surprised, Pom or master, when Lissy hissed out a no-nonsense *Stop* and brought Chloe to heel.

"Excellent. Again."

She repeated, repeated until at her approach, Chloe simply continued to walk politely at Lissy's heel.

"Well done. Syl, would you mind? Syl's going to walk by now. Syl, stop and chat, okay?"

"Sure." Sylvia strolled up, crossed paths. "Nice to see you."

"Okay. Gosh." Lissy stopped, blinking when the pretty little Pom did the same without snarling or yipping. "Look what she did."

"Isn't that great? What a pretty dog." Sylvia bent over to stroke Chloe's fluffy head. "What a well-behaved dog. Good girl, Chloe."

"We're going to add Newman in," Fiona announced.

"Oh my God."

"Lissy, don't tense up. Stay relaxed. Newman won't react to her until I allow it. You're in charge. She depends on you. Correct firmly, quickly and as necessary."

With Newman by her side, Fiona walked across Chloe's eye line. The Pom went ballistic.

"Correct," Fiona ordered. "Firmly, Lissy," she added when her flustered client faltered. "No, don't pick her up. Like this. Chloe, stop! Stop!" Fiona repeated, making eye contact, pointing sharply.

Chloe subsided with a few grumbles.

"Newman's no threat. Obviously," Fiona added as the Lab sat placidly. "You need to keep relaxed and remain in charge— and be firm when she's exhibiting unsocial behavior."

"He's so much bigger. She's scared."

"Yes, she's scared and she's stressed—and so are you. You have to relax, let her relax. She'll see there's nothing to be afraid of." At Fiona's hand signal, Newman lay down, sighed a little.

"You said there was a park near you, and several people take their dogs there."

"Yes. I stopped taking Chloe because she'd just get upset."

"It'd be nice to be able to take her, so she could have play-mates, make friends."

"Nobody likes her," Lissy whispered. "It hurts her feelings."

"Nobody likes a bully, Lissy. But people, especially dog people, generally enjoy a well-behaved dog. And one as pretty and smart as Chloe could make a lot of friends. You'd like that for her?"

"I really would."

"When's the last time you took her to the park?"

"Oh gosh, it's been three or four months. There was this little incident. Really she barely broke the skin—*barely*—but Harry and I felt it best not to take her back."

"I think you can give it another try."

"Really? But—"

"Take a look." Fiona held a finger up first. "Don't overreact. Stay calm—keep your voice calm."

Lissy glanced down, then pressed her free hand to her mouth as she watched Chloe sniff curiously at Newman.

"She's checking him out," Fiona said. "Her tail's wagging, her ears are up. She's not afraid. She's interested. Stay calm," she added, then signaled Newman.

When he stood, Chloe retreated, then froze as he lowered his head to sniff her in turn. Her tail wagged again.

"He gave her a kiss!"

"Newman likes pretty girls."

"She's making a friend." Lissy's eyes filled. "It's silly. I know it's silly to get so emotional."

"No it's not. Not a bit. You love her."

"She's never had a friend. It's my fault."

Mostly, Fiona thought, but things were never quite that simple. "Lissy, you brought her here because you love her and you want her to be happy. She has a friend now. How about we let her make a few more?"

"Are you sure?"

"Trust me."

Lissy reached out, a bit dramatically, to clutch Fiona's hand. "I really, really do."

"Correct if necessary. Otherwise, just relax and let her deal."

Fiona called the dogs off the porch, one at a time, to give

Chloe a chance to acclimate. There were a few corrections, some retreat and advance, but before long they had what Fiona thought of as a sniff-and-wag party going on.

"I've never seen her like this. She's not scared or being mean or trying to claw up my leg so I'll pick her up."

"Let's give her a reward. Let her off the leash so she can run around with the boys and Oreo."

Lissy bit her lip but obeyed.

"Go play," Fiona ordered.

As the others ran off, bumping bodies, Chloe stood, shivering.

"She's—"

"Wait," Fiona interrupted. "Give her some time."

Bogart raced back, gave Chloe a few swipes with his tongue. This time when he ran toward the pack, Chloe raced after him on her little designer booties.

"She's playing." Lissy murmured it as Chloe leaped to latch onto the frayed end of the mangled rope Bogart snagged. "She's really playing with friends."

Fiona draped an arm around Lissy's shoulders. "Let's sit on the porch and have some lemonade. You can watch her from there."

"I—I should've brought my camera. I never thought . . ."

"Tell you what. Sit with Sylvia. I'll go get mine and take some shots. I'll e-mail them to you."

"I'm going to cry."

"You go right ahead." Patting Lissy's shoulder, Fiona led her to the porch.

LATER, SYLVIA ROCKED and sipped and watched Lissy drive away with Chloe. "That must be very satisfying."

"And a little exhausting."

"Well, you did give her two solid hours."

"She—they—needed it. I think they'll be all right. Lissy has to keep it up—and bring Harry on board. But I think she will. Our guys helped, a lot." She lifted her foot and gave Peck's rump a rub.

"Now that we've solved Chloe's problem, what about yours?"

"I think that's going to take more than a firm hand and some dog treats."

"How mad is he?"

"Pretty mad."

"How mad are you?"

"Undecided."

Now that the dog party had ended, a trio of jewel-winged hummingbirds dashed and darted along the flowering red currant that Starr had written about in the cursed article.

The blur of color should have charmed her, but it only served to remind Fiona of the harshness of the morning.

"I'm trying to stay calm, to be sensible—because otherwise I think, I really think I'd run screaming and never stop. And Simon's angry I don't run screaming. At least I think that's part of it, and I'm not all 'Oh, you're so big and strong, please take care of me.' Or something."

Sylvia continued to rock, to sip. "It's a wonder to me, it really is, Fee, how someone as insightful and sensitive as you can't seem to understand how painfully hard this is on the rest of us."

"Oh, Syl. I do! Of course I do. I wish—"

"No, honey, you don't. Your solution is to block us out of some of the details, and your own fears. To make the decisions, on your own, about what to do and how to do it. And since I can't completely disagree with that, I'm in a quandary."

Guilt mingled with frustration, and irritation wrapped them with a frayed bow. "I don't block you out."

"Not often. You are a sensible woman, and you're justifiably proud of your ability to take care of yourself and deal with your own problems. I'm proud of you. But I worry that your need to do that will box you into believing you *have* to do that, always. You have an easier time giving help than asking for it."

"Maybe I do. Maybe. But honestly, Syl, I didn't think telling Simon or you, or anyone, about that damn reporter was an issue. Was a thing. It happened, I dealt with it. Telling you wouldn't have stopped her from writing the article."

"No, but telling us would have prepared us for it."

"All right." Tired, next to defeated, Fiona pressed her fingers to her eyes. "All right."

"I don't want to upset you. God knows I don't want to add to your stress. I'd just like you to think about . . . to consider that it's time to really let those who care about you step in."

"Okay, tell me what you think I should do."

"I'll tell you what I wish you could do. I wish you could pack up and go to Fiji until they catch this maniac. And I know you can't. Not just because it's not in your makeup, but because you have your home, your business, your bills, your life to deal with."

"Yes, I do. It's maddening, Syl, because I feel like people don't really understand that. If I crawled in some cave, I could lose my business, my home, not to mention my self-confidence. I worked hard to build all of those."

"In my opinion, honey, people do understand that, but they wish you could dig into that cave. I think you're doing what you can, what you have to do—except asking and allowing others to genuinely help. It's more than having James watch your house and dogs while you take a little trip, or letting Simon share your bed at night. It's opening up to someone, Fiona, fully. It's trusting enough to do that."

"God." Fiona huffed out a breath. "I've practically thrown myself at Simon's feet."

Sylvia smiled a little. "Have you?"

"I told him I thought I was falling in love with him. I didn't get *quid pro quo* out of that."

"Is that what you were after?"

"No." Irritated with herself and everything else, she shoved to her feet. "No. But he's not exactly the sort who tells you what's on his mind—unless he's mad. And even then . . ."

"I'm not talking about him, or to him. If I were, I'd probably have quite a bit to say. But this is you, Fiona. It's you I'm worried about, worried for. It's you I want happy and safe."

"I'm not going to take any chances. I promise you. And I won't make a mistake like I did with the reporter again." She turned back, lifted her hand, palm out. "Solemn oath."

"I'm going to hold you to it. Now, tell me what you want from Simon. With Simon."

"I honestly don't know."

"Don't know, or haven't let yourself dig down and think about?"

"Both. If things were just normal—if all of this wasn't hovering around the edges of my life—maybe I would dig down. Or maybe there wouldn't be anything to dig for in the first place."

"Because what's hovering is why you and Simon are where you are now?"

"It's certainly influenced it. The timing, the intensity."

"I'm full of opinions today," Sylvia decided. "So here's one more. I think you're giving a murderer too much credit, and yourself and Simon not enough. The fact is, Fee, things are what they are, and you and Simon are where you are. That's something to be dealt with."

She lifted her brows when the dogs went on alert. "And I bet that's what you have to deal with coming over your bridge. I'm going to go so you can." Sylvia rose, gathered Fiona in a fierce hug. "I love you, so much."

"I love you. I don't know what I'd do without you."

"Then don't try. And think of this," she murmured. "He left mad, but he came back."

She kissed Fiona's cheek, then picked up her enormous straw bag. She called Oreo as she strolled toward Simon's truck. Fiona couldn't hear what Sylvia said to him, but noticed he glanced toward the porch as her stepmother spoke.

Then shrugged.

Typical.

She stood her ground, though she wasn't quite sure where the ground lay, as Sylvia drove away. "If you're here due to obligation, I'll relieve you of it. I can ask James to stay here tonight, or go bunk at Mai's."

"Obligation for what?"

"Because I'm in trouble, which I freely admit. I know you're mad, and I'm telling you you're not obliged. I won't stay here alone."

He said nothing for a moment. "I want a beer." He walked up the steps and into the house.

"Well, for—" She strode in after him. "Is that how you solve problems? Is that your method?"

"It depends on the problem. I want a beer," he repeated, and pulled one out of the fridge, opened it. "I have a beer. Problem solved."

"I'm not talking about the damn beer."

"Okay." He moved past her and out to the back porch.

She caught the screen on the back swing, slammed it behind her. "Don't just walk away from me."

"If you're going to bitch, I'm going to sit down and drink my beer."

"If I'm going to— You left here this morning pissed off and bossy. Interrupting me every five seconds. Telling *me* to shut up."

"I'm about to repeat that."

"What gives you the right to tell me what to do, what to think, what to say?"

"Not a thing." He tipped the beer in her direction. "And right back at you, Fiona."

"I'm not telling you what to do. I'm giving you a choice, and I'm telling you I won't tolerate this kind of behavior."

His gaze fired to hers, molten gold sheathed in ice. "I'm not one of your dogs. You won't train me."

Her jaw dropped in sincere shock. "I'm not trying to train you. For God's sake."

"Yeah, you are. Second nature for you, I guess. Too bad, because I'd say it's a pretty sure bet I have a lot of behaviors you'd like to change. That's on you. If you'd rather James stay here tonight, give him a call. I'll take off when he gets here."

"I don't know why we're fighting." She pushed her hands through her hair, leaned back on the rail. "I don't even know.

I don't know why I'm suddenly considered someone who's closed in or blocked off or too stubborn or stupid to ask for help. I'm not. I'm not any of that."

He took a long pull as he studied her. "You got yourself out of the trunk."

"What?"

"You got yourself out. Nobody helped you. There wasn't anybody to help you. Live or die, it was up to you. It must've been a hell of a thing. I can't imagine it. I've tried. I can't. Do you want to stay in the trunk?"

Tears stung behind her eyes, infuriatingly. "What the hell are you talking about?"

"You can keep getting out on your own. My money's on you there. Or you can let somebody give you a hand with it, and get it through your head that it doesn't make you incapable, and it sure as hell doesn't make you weak. You're the strongest woman I know, and I've known some strong women. So figure it out, and let me know."

She turned away, pressing a hand to her chest as it ached. "I got myself into the trunk, too."

"That's bullshit."

"How do you know? You weren't there. I was stupid and careless, and I let him take me."

"Jesus Christ. He killed twelve women before you. Do you think they were all stupid, careless? That they *let* him take them?"

"I—no. Yes." She turned back. "Maybe. I don't know. But I know I made a mistake that day. Just a little one, just a few seconds, and it changed everything. Everything."

"You lived. Greg Norwood died."

"I know that it wasn't my fault. I had therapy. I know Perry's responsible. I *know*."

"Knowing isn't always believing."

"I believe it. Most of the time. I don't dwell on it. I don't pull the chains of that with me."

"Maybe you didn't, but they're rattling now."

She hated, *hated* that he was right. "I built a life here, and I'm happy. There wouldn't be this . . . I wouldn't have this if it wasn't happening again. How can it be happening again?" she demanded. "How in God's name can this happen again?"

She drew a shuddering breath. "Do you need me to say I'm scared? I told you I was. I am. I'm terrified. Is that what you want me to say?"

"No. And if I get the chance, he'll pay for making you say it, for making you feel it."

He watched as she swiped a single tear from her cheek. He'd pay for that, too, Simon thought. For that one drop of grief.

And that one drop doused the last sparks of the anger he'd hauled around with him all day.

"I don't know what I'm after with you, Fee, exactly. I can't figure it out. But I know I want you to trust me. I need you to trust me to help you out of that fucking trunk. To trust me enough for that. Then we'll see what happens next."

"That scares me almost as much."

"Yeah, I get that." He lifted the beer again to drink, eyeing her over it. "I'd say you're in a spot."

She let out an unsteady laugh. "I guess I am. I haven't had a serious relationship since Greg. A couple of short-lived pretenses. I can stand here now and look back and see very clearly they weren't fair to anyone involved. I wasn't dishonest, and the other party wasn't after any more than it was. But still, not fair. I didn't intend to have a serious relationship with you. I wanted the company, some conversation, the sex. I liked the idea of having an affair. Look at me, all grown up. Maybe that wasn't fair."

"I didn't have a problem with it."

She smiled. "Maybe not, but here we are, Simon, and it's pretty clear we're both after a little more than we bargained for. You want trust. I want what I guess is the next level of commitment. I think we're scaring each other."

He stood up. "I can take it. Can you?"

"I want to try."

He reached out, tucked her hair behind her ear. "Let's see how we do."

She moved in, sighed as she locked her arms around him. "Okay. This is already better."

"Let's try something different." He stroked a hand down her hair. "Let's go out to dinner."

"Out?"

"I'll take you out to dinner. You could wear a dress."

"I could."

"You have them. I've seen them in your closet."

She tilted her head back. "I'd like to put on a dress and go out to dinner."

"Good. Don't take all night. I'm hungry."

"Fifteen minutes." Rising on her toes, she brushed his lips with hers. "This is better."

Even as she walked inside, the phone rang.

"Business line. One minute. Fiona Bristow." Immediately she reached for the pad, the pen. "Yes, Sergeant Kasper. How long?" She wrote quickly, nodded as questions she didn't have to ask were answered. "I'll contact the rest of the unit immediately. Yes, five handlers, five dogs. Mai Funaki will run our base, as before. We'll meet you there. You still have my cell number? Yes, that's it. We'll leave within the hour. No problem."

She hung up. "I'm sorry. We've got two missing hikers in the Olympic National Forest. I've got to call the others. I've got to go."

"Okay. I'll go with you."

"You don't have any experience," she began even as she speed-dialed Mai. "Mai, we're on." She relayed the information quickly. "Phone tree," she said to Simon as she clicked off and began to move. "Mai makes the next call."

"I'm going with you. One, because you're not going alone. Once you start the search it's just you and the dog, right?"

"Yes, but—"

"And two, if you're going to train my dog to do what you're about to do, I want a better sense of it. I'm going."

"We won't get there before dark. If they haven't found them by then, we're going to start the search at night, and very likely spend the night in very rough conditions."

"What, am I a pussy?"

"Hardly." She opened her mouth to push back again, then

realized what she was doing. "Okay. I've got a spare pack. I have a list of everything you need to take. Most should be in there already. You take the list, make sure it's complete. And I'll need you to call Syl and ask her to keep an eye on the dogs we don't take."

She pulled out her spare pack, tossed it to him. "When we get there, I'm alpha dog. You have to deal with that."

"Your show, your rules. Where's the list?"

TWENTY

A unit was precisely what they were, Simon observed. During the trip, the six members spoke in shorthand, acronyms and the code tight friends or longtime coworkers often fell into.

He did what came naturally to him. He sat back and observed.

The change in James and Lori's relationship was new enough they exchanged quick, secret glances—while the others shot them amused looks. He heard Chuck and Meg Greene discussing weekend plans—yard work topped the list—with the ease of well-marrieds.

Fiona checked in with the cop named Kasper regularly for status, adjusted ETA and other relevant details.

The small surprise, at least it struck him that way, was the addition of another cop—Sheriff Tyson, from San Juan Island.

Something going on between him and the sexy vet, Simon concluded. Something newer than James and Lori and not quite defined.

The evening air whipped by in quick wet bites as Chuck piloted the boat across the chopping, white-tipped waters of the strait. The dogs seemed to enjoy it, sitting or sprawling, eyes glowing.

If not for the fact that two people were lost, possibly injured, out in the dark, it might've been a pleasant evening ride.

He ate one of the sandwiches Meg had provided and let his mind drift.

If they took murder out of the equation, would he be here now, eating ham and cheese with spicy mustard on a kaiser roll on a crowded boat that smelled of water and dog?

He wasn't sure.

Then he glanced toward Fiona. She sat, body swaying with the bump of the waves, her cell phone at her ear, the notebook she scrawled on—make that wrote on; Fiona didn't scrawl, he mused—on her lap, wind whipping the hasty braid she'd tied. That deceptively slender body tucked into rough pants, light jacket, scarred boots.

Yeah, he'd be here. Damn it.

Not his type. He could tell himself that a thousand times and it didn't change a thing. She'd gotten under his skin, into his blood. Gotten somewhere.

He was half dazzled, half irritated by her—a strange and dangerous combination. He kept waiting for it to pass.

No luck there.

Maybe, once things were settled, he'd take a break. Go visit his family for a week. In his experience absence didn't make the heart grow fonder, it generally blurred the edges of the fondness. While it was true nothing had blurred during her short trip away, this could be different. He'd be the one to go.

Mai dropped down beside him. "Are you ready for this?"

"I guess I'll find out."

"My first search? I was scared to death, and so excited. The training, the mock-up, the maneuvers? All essential, but the real thing is . . . well, the real thing. People are depending on you. Real people, with feelings and families and fears. When Fee first talked to me about the unit, I thought sure, that's something I could do. I had no idea how much it takes. Not just time, but physically, emotionally."

"You still do it."

"Once you're in, you're in. I can't imagine not doing it."

"You run the base."

"That's right. Coordinate the dogs and handlers, keep the logs, maintain contact, liaise with the other search teams, the cops or rangers. I don't have a search dog since I end up adopting special-needs types, but I can work with one if they need me. Fee thinks your Jaws is hardwired for this kind of work."

"So she says." He offered her a dip into his bag of chips. "He picks up on the training—at least it looks like it to me. Mostly I think he'd turn himself inside out if he thought it would make her happy."

"Dogs have that reaction to Fee. She's got a gift."

She shifted a little so their knees bumped and her back was to Fiona. "How's she doing, Simon? I try not to bring it up often. I know how she likes to keep things in their proper box."

It was a perfect description, he thought. Dead-on perfect. "She's scared. That only makes her more determined to handle it."

"I sleep better knowing you're with her."

Sylvia had said the same, Simon recalled. But with a warning tone. *Don't let me down.*

Once they arrived at the mainland, a group of volunteers helped them transfer into trucks for the drive to base. Things moved fast, he noted, with a kind of hard-edged efficiency. Proper boxes again, he supposed. Everyone had a purpose, and everyone knew what it was.

Fiona wedged between him and some guy named Bob and continued to work in her notebook as they sped or bumped along.

"What are you doing?"

"Checklist, working out preliminary sections going on the data I have now. It was a long trip, and it's dark—but we've got good moonlight. Possibility of thunderstorms before morning, but it's clear now so we'll do what we can. How's your boy, Bob?"

"Heading off to college come fall. Don't know how that happened. He and my wife are helping out with chow."

"It'll be nice to see them. Bob and his family run a local lodge. They're regulars when we have a search. Sergeant Kasper said the missing hikers are staying at your place."

"That's right." Bob, with his windburned, square-jawed face, gripped the wheel with big-knuckled hands and navigated the switchbacks like a commuter on the freeway. "Them and another couple, traveling together. They headed out at first light, took a box lunch. The one couple, they came back just before dinnertime. They said how they separated on the trail, took different directions. They expected their friends to be back before them."

"They don't answer their cell phones."

"Nope. Sometimes the service gets spotty, but they've been trying since around five, five-thirty."

"I have the formal search starting about seven."

"That's right."

"In good shape, are they?"

"Seem to be fit enough. Early thirties. Woman wore new boots, fancy pack. Came in from New York. Plan to stay two weeks, do some fishing, hiking, sightseeing, use the spa."

"Mmm-hmm."

Simon spotted the lodge—a sprawling two stories lit now like the Fourth of July. Someone had put up a large tarp so it served as a makeshift chow hall, he supposed, with a long table loaded with food, coffee urns, cases of bottled water.

"Thanks for the lift, Bob. I'm looking forward to some of Jill's coffee." She got out behind Simon. "Could you help with the dogs? They'll need to be watered. I need to coordinate with Sergeant Kasper while Mai sets up base."

"No problem."

She crossed to a uniformed cop with a generous belly and a weathered, bulldog face. They shook hands, and when Mai joined them, he shook hers before gesturing. Mai walked briskly into the lodge.

Fiona got herself a cup of coffee while she and Kasper talked.

"Mai says this is your first." Tyson held out a hand to Simon. "Ben Tyson."

"Yeah. I guess it's not yours, Sheriff."

"Keep it at Ben. Not the first, but I'm usually on that end." He jutted his chin toward Fiona and Kasper as he and Simon herded the dogs toward a huge galvanized tub of water.

"Okay. What are they doing?"

"Well, the sergeant's updating her, giving her whatever he's got. How many they've got out, what areas they've covered, time lines, PLS—the point last seen. Fee, she's good about making sure they have the right maps, but he'll fill her in on the topography. Roads, hills, water, barriers, drainage, trail markers. All that's going to help her strategize the unit's search pattern. Mai says they were hiking with friends, so Fee'll talk to them, too, before she briefs the unit."

"That's a lot of time talking."

"It might seem that way. If you rush it, brush by getting all the data, you may miss something. Better to take the time now. And it gives her time to get her feet under her, gauge the air."

"The air?"

Ben smiled. "That's where it goes by me, to tell you the truth. Air pockets and scent cones and whatever the hell. I've worked a few searches with Fee and the unit. Seems to me she's got a nose like one of the dogs." Ben reached down, gave Bogart a scrub between the ears.

For the next twenty minutes, Simon wandered, drank truly exceptional coffee, watched volunteers and uniforms come back to refuel, debrief.

"We're set up in the lobby," James told him. "If you want in on the briefing."

"All right."

"Done much hiking?"

"Some," Simon answered as they walked inside.

"At night?"

"Not really."

James grinned. "You're about to get a workout, and an education."

Simon thought of the lobby as rustic gloss. It worked. Lots

of leather chairs, heavy oak tables stained dark, iron lamps and rough pottery. Fiona stood at a table that held a boxy radio, a laptop, maps. Behind her hung a large topographical map of the area, while Mai worked on a whiteboard.

"We're looking for Ella and Kevin White, Caucasian, twenty-eight and thirty, respectively. Ella is five-five, a hundred and twenty-five, brown hair, brown eyes. She was wearing Levi's, a red shirt over a white tank, and a navy hoodie. Kevin's five-ten, a hundred and seventy. Levi's, brown shirt over white, brown jacket. They're both wearing hiking boots, the friends think Rockports, sizes seven and ten and a half."

She flipped over a page in a notebook, but Simon sensed she didn't need it. She remembered. "They left this location at just after seven a.m. with another couple, Rachel and Tod Chapel. They headed south, along the river."

She stepped back to the map, used a laser pointer. "They kept to posted trails, stopped several times and took an hour's break about eleven-thirty—here, as the witnesses best remember—to eat the boxed lunch the lodge provided. That's when they separated. Ella and Kevin opted to continue south. The other couple headed east. They planned to meet back here around four, maybe four-thirty, for drinks. When they didn't return by five, and neither answered their cell phone, there was some concern. They continued to try their cells and combed the immediate area until shortly before six, when Bob alerted the authorities. Formal search commenced at six fifty-five."

"If they kept south, they'd head into the Bighorn Wilderness Area," James pointed out.

"That's right."

"There's some rough going in there."

"And Ella is an inexperienced hiker."

She moved on, pointing out the areas the search had covered, laying out the sectors for each team, using, Simon noted, natural barriers and landmarks as borders.

"Additional data. The witnesses say Kevin's an overachiever. He's competitive. Both he and Tod wore pedometers and had a bet going. Whoever clocked the most miles won, and the loser bought drinks and dinner tonight. He likes to win. He'd have pushed it.

"I know it's late, but we've got the weather and the moon in our favor. It's a go for a sector search. As OL, I'll go in, inspect the PLS. I think it's good data, but a spot on a map can't replace eyeballing it."

She checked her watch. "They've been out about fourteen hours, had their last real meal nine hours ago. They've got water and some power bars, some trail mix, but the water situation was geared toward a late-afternoon return. Let's have a radio check, then I'll pass out the scent bags outside."

Once they were outside, Fiona hitched on her pack. "Are you sure about this?" she asked Simon.

He scanned the dense, primal dark of the surrounding forest. "I'm sure you're not going in there alone."

"I don't mind the company, but it's a stretch to think a crazed killer heard about a couple of missing hikers, and our unit's call-in, managed to get here and is now lying in wait."

"Do you want to argue about it, or do you want to find these people?"

"Oh, I can do both." She gave Bogart the scent. "That's Ella. That's Ella. And Kevin. Here's Kevin. Let's go find them! Let's find Ella and Kevin."

"Why are you doing that now? I thought you were going to the PLS?"

"Good—and yeah, we are. He needs to start the game now, get revved. Maybe they got lost or turned around on the way back. Maybe one or both of them got hurt and just can't make it back in the dark."

"And sniffing socks is going to do the trick."

She smiled, using her flashlight to add more illumination to the trail. "You like cornflakes, right?"

"Yeah."

"I hope this doesn't put you off them. We shed cornflake-shaped skin cells. Dead cells, called rafts, constantly shed and carry a scent unique to the person who sheds them. They're carried off by the air, by wind currents downwind in a scent cone. The scent cone's narrow, and it's concentrated at the source."

"The person."

"Exactly. It widens with distance, and Bogart can and will find that scent. The problems with following it to the source can be too much wind, too much humidity, looping, pooling, a chimney effect—various ways wind and air work depending on the climate conditions and the terrain. That's my job— judging that, outlining the search plan, helping the dog stay on scent."

"Complicated. Tricky."

"It can be. You get a hot day, no air movement, heavy brush? The scent's not going to disperse out, and that's going to limit the range. I'd have to adjust the search sweeps. A stream, a drainage, those can funnel scents, so the OL, then the handlers, may have to adjust for that."

So it was science, he concluded, as much as training, as much as instinct. "How do you know the dog's working it and not just out for a stroll?"

The reflectors on her jacket, and the ones she'd slapped on his, glowed eerie green in the moonlight. The beam she carried swept over trail and brush and odd clumps of wildflowers.

"He knows his job. He knows the game. See, he's moving pretty briskly, but he checks behind, to make sure we're in sight. He scents the air, moves on. He's a good dog."

Reaching out, she took Simon's hand, gave it a squeeze. "Not exactly dinner out."

"We're out. The sandwich was pretty good. What are you looking for?"

"Signs." She continued to sweep her light. "Tracks, broken brush, candy wrappers, anything. I don't have Bogart's nose, so I have to rely on my eyes."

"Like Gollum."

"Yes, my precious—but I think that was a lot of nose work, too. God, it's beautiful, isn't it? One of my favorite places in the world. And now, with the moon filtering through the canopy, all the shadows and sparkles, it's just amazing." Her light skimmed over gilded mushrooms, exotic jack-in-the-pulpit. "One of these days I'm going to find time to take a course in botany so I know more of what I'm looking at."

"Because you've got nothing but time on your hands."

"You can always squeeze out a little more for something you really want. Sylvia's taking up crocheting."

He paused, couldn't find the connection. "Okay."

"I'm just saying you can always make time for something if you want it. I know the basics on flora and fauna—and I know what not to touch or eat when I'm out on a search like this. Or if I don't know, I don't touch it or eat it."

"Explain why we're hauling crappy hiking food in the packs."

"You won't care if it's crappy when you're hungry."

Each time Bogart alerted, she stopped, marked the spot with tape. Everything they knew said the lost hikers had passed this way hours before, but the dog followed the trail.

Knew his job, Simon concluded, just as Fiona claimed.

"We found a hiker a couple years ago, not all that far from here," she told him. "Dead summer, steaming. He'd been wandering around for two days. Dehydrated, infected blisters, and he had poison ivy in places you really, really don't want poison ivy."

They walked, endlessly it seemed to Simon, lit by moonlight, along the trail with her scanning light. She'd stop, call out, listen, use her radio to check with her unit. Then move on after the dog. Tireless, he noted. Both of them. And there was no doubt the pair of them took the work seriously, and enjoyed every minute.

She pointed out things she knew. The busy life of a nurse log, the strange and fascinating pattern of lichen.

When Bogart stopped to drink, she refreshed the scent for him while owls and night birds filled the air with calls.

Bogart alerted, and began busily sniffing air and ground.

"This is it, where they stopped for lunch. Where they separated. Lots of tracks." She crouched down. "They were respectful, I'll give them that. No litter."

The dog wandered off to relieve himself, and, deciding it was a fine idea, Simon moved deeper into the trees to do the same while Fiona cupped her hands around her mouth and called.

"We made good time," she said when Simon came back. "It's not quite midnight. We can take a break here, start again at first light."

"Is that what you'd do if I wasn't here?"

"I'd probably give it a little longer."

"Then let's go."

"Short break first." She sat on the ground, dug a bag of trail mix and a pouch of kibble out of her bag. "It's important to keep the energy up, and stay hydrated. Otherwise, they'll be sending someone out for us."

She handed Simon the trail mix, then fed the dog.

"Have you ever not found who you were looking for?"

"Yeah. It's horrible to go back empty. The worst. Worse than finding them too late is not finding them at all."

She dipped her hand into the bag. "These two, they're young and strong. I'm guessing they—or he—misjudged their endurance, got disoriented. Probably a combination. The phones are a concern."

"Dead battery. Or they can't get a signal. Dropped them. Lost them."

"Any or all," she agreed. "There's wildlife, but it's unlikely they ran into something that wouldn't walk away. The thing is, a twisted ankle out here knocks you back, especially if you're inexperienced."

In the dark, he thought, probably disoriented, certainly tired, possibly injured. "It took them, what, four hours to get here?"

"Yeah, but they were meandering, stopping, taking photos. Kevin wants to pick up the pace, win the bet when they head south. He probably only planned to go another hour, maybe two—which is too damn much in one day when your hiking's mostly done on Fifth Avenue. But then they could shortcut it back—at least in his head—and get back to the lodge by cocktail time."

"Is that how you see it?"

"From what I got from his friends. He's a good guy, a bit of a know-it-all, but funny. He likes a challenge, and he can't resist a dare. She likes trying new things, seeing new places. It's chilly." Fiona drank from her water bottle while she searched the shadows and moonlight. "But they have jackets. They're probably exhausted, scared, pissed off."

She smiled at him. "Do you think you can handle another hour?"

"Kevin's not the only one who's competitive." He rose, held out a hand for hers.

"I'm glad you came." She rose up, moved into him. "But I still want that dinner out when we get back."

They stretched the hour to ninety minutes, zigzagging on the trails as the dog followed the scent. Fiona's calls went unanswered, and clouds drifted over the moon.

"The wind's changing. Damn it." She tipped her face up, and he'd have sworn she scented the air like her dog. "We're going to get that storm. We'd better pitch the tent."

"Just like that?"

"We can't do any more tonight. Bogart's tired. We're losing the light, and the scent." She pulled out her radio. "So we'll take a couple hours, get some rest, stay dry." She looked at him then, holding the radio. "It's not worth going back to base, getting drenched, exhausted, then heading out again at dawn. A bed and a hot shower's a cheap trade for warm, dry and rested out here."

"You're the alpha."

She cocked her head. "And you're saying that because you agree with me?"

"It helps that I agree with you."

She called their status and location in to base, coordinated or took updates on the other searchers. No chatter, Simon noted. Straight business.

After she shed her pack and began setting up the tent, he found himself again in the position of taking direction. He didn't have a clue, he was forced to admit. The last time he camped out in a tent he was probably twelve—and the deal she called a hyper-light didn't work anything like the ancient pup tent he'd used.

"It'll be cramped, but we'll be dry. You first," she told him. "You're going to have to sort of angle yourself, given your height. Bogart and I will maneuver ourselves in after you."

Light it might've been, but cramped was a kind word for it. By the time he had the dog curled at the small of his back and Fiona shoehorned beside him, there wasn't an inch to spare.

"I think your dog has his nose in my ass."

"Good thing you're wearing pants." Fiona shifted a little. "You can scooch over toward me a little more."

Scooch, he thought, but realized he was too tired to think of a sarcastic comment. So he scooched, muttered and found if he got his arm under her—which he'd probably have to amputate in the morning—he gained a fraction of space.

Thunder belched violently seconds before the skies opened. The rain sounded like a monsoon.

"This would be romantic," Fiona decided, "if we had a bigger tent, were doing this for fun, and there was a nice bottle of wine involved."

"The dog's snoring."

"Yes, he is, and he will. He worked hard tonight." She only had to turn her head a fraction to kiss him. "So did you."

"You're shaking. Are you cold?"

"No. I'm fine."

"You're shaking," he repeated.

"I just need to settle down. I have a problem with closed-in or tight spaces."

"You . . ." It struck him immediately, and he cursed himself for an idiot. She'd been bound, gagged and locked in the trunk of a car, heading for death. "Jesus, Fiona."

"No, don't." She grabbed on to him when he started to move. "Just stay right here. I'm closing my eyes, and it'll pass."

He felt it now, the way her heart beat against him, as violently as the rain. "We should've gone back for the night."

"No, it wastes time and energy. Plus I'm too tired for a full-blown panic attack."

What the hell did she call the shivering and heart-banging? He drew her closer, wrapping his other arm around her to stroke a hand up and down her back. "Is that better or worse?"

"It's better. It's nice. I just need a minute to adjust."

Lightning slashed wildly, illuminating the tent. He saw her cheeks were pale, her eyes closed. "So, is Tyson banging the vet?"

"I don't think it's progressed to banging, Mr. Romance. I think they're just starting to get to know each other on a personal level."

"Banging's personal, if you do it right."

"I'm sure she'll let me know if banging becomes part of the arrangement."

"Because you've told her we're banging."

"I suspect she could've come to that conclusion all on her own, but yes, of course I told her. And in specific and minute detail. She wishes you'd banged her first."

"Huh. An opportunity lost." Her heartbeat was slowing, just a bit. "I could backtrack and make it up to her."

"Too late. She'd never have sex with you now. We have codes and standards. You're no longer on the menu when it comes to any of my friends or relations."

"That doesn't seem fair when you consider you're friends with everybody on the island."

"That may be, but rules are rules." She tipped her face again, touched her lips to his. "Thanks for taking my mind off my neurosis."

"You don't have any neuroses, which is annoying. You have quirks, which make up for it a little. But you're mostly irritatingly stable and normal. You're still not my type."

"But you're still going to bang me."

"At every opportunity."

She laughed, and he felt her fully relax against him. "You're rude, socially stunted and cynical. But I intend to be available for said banging whenever possible. I'm not sure what that makes us, but it seems to be working."

"You're who I want to be with."

He wasn't sure why he'd said it—maybe the forced intimacy of the tent, the rain beating its fists down on it, his concern for her even as her trembling ceased. Whatever the reason, he thought, it was truth.

"That's the best thing you've ever said to me," she murmured. "Even more, given the current circumstances."

"We're warm and we're dry," he pointed out. "And they're not," he added, echoing her thoughts.

"No, they're not. It's going to be a terrible night for them."

This time he turned his head and brushed his lips over her hair. "Then we'd better find them in the morning."

PART THREE

Is thy servant a dog, that he should do this great thing?

THE BIBLE

TWENTY-ONE

She woke in solid dark, unable to move or see or speak. Her head throbbed like an open wound, while nausea churned choppy waves in her belly. Disoriented, terrified, she struggled, but her arms remained pinned behind her back; her legs felt paralyzed.

She could do no more than worm, buck and struggle to breathe.

Her eyes, wide and wild, wheeled in her head. She heard the hum, steady, forceful, and thought—fresh panic—she was in the cave of some wild animal.

No, no. An engine. A car. She was in a car. In the trunk of a car. The man. The man on the jogging path.

She could see it all so clearly, the bold morning sun, the dreamy blue sky like a canvas against the rich hues of fall. That hint of autumn spice on the air like a flavor on her tongue.

Her muscles had warmed. She'd felt so loose, so limber. So powerful. She'd loved that feeling, the heady rush of being alone in a world of color and spice. Just her and the morning and the freedom to run.

Then the man, jogging toward her. No big deal. They'd pass, he'd be gone, and the world would be hers again.

But . . . did he stumble, did he fall, did she stop for a second to help? She couldn't remember, not exactly. All blurred now.

But she could see his face. The smile, the eyes—something in those eyes—an instant before the pain.

Pain. Like being struck by lightning.

It spun in her head as the rhythm beneath her changed and the floor vibrated under her. Rough road, she thought in some dizzy corner of her brain.

She thought of her uncle's warnings, and Greg's. Don't run alone. Keep the panic button handy. Stay alert.

So easily dismissed. What could happen to her? Why would anything happen?

But it had. It had. She'd been taken.

All those girls—the girls she'd seen in the paper. The dead girls she'd felt sorry for—until she'd forgotten them and gone on with her life.

Was she going to be one of them, one of the dead girls in the paper, on the news reports?

But why? Why?

She wept and struggled and screamed. But the sounds drowned against the tape over her mouth, and the movements only cut the bands into her skin until she smelled her own blood and sweat.

Until she smelled her own death.

SHE WOKE IN THE DARK. Trapped. The scream burned up her throat only to be bitten back when she felt the weight of Simon's arm tossed over her, when she heard the steady breathing—his, the dog's.

But the panic was spiders skittering inside her chest, under her skin.

So the scream stayed in her head, piercing.

Get out! Get out! Get out!

She shoved herself toward the flap, fought it open and crawled out where the cool, damp air slapped at her face.

"Hold on. Hey. Hold on."

When Simon gripped her shoulders she pushed at him. "Don't. Don't. Just need to breathe." Hyperventilating—she knew it but couldn't stop it. A boulder pressed on her chest, and her head began to swim in long, sick waves. "Can't breathe."

"Yes you can." He tightened his grip, yanked her up to her knees and gave her a quick, shocking shake. "Breathe. Look at me, Fiona. Right here. Breathe! Now!"

She sucked in air on a short, shaky gasp.

"Let it out. Do what I tell you. Let it out, take it in. Slow it down. Slow it the hell down."

She stared at him, wondered at him. Who the hell did he think he was? She shoved at his chest, met an unmoving wall even as he shook her again.

And she breathed.

"Keep going. Bogart, sit. Just sit. In and out. Look at me. In and out. Better, that's better. Keep it up."

He let her go. Focused on inhaling, exhaling, she sank back to sit on her heels as Bogart nudged his nose against her arm. "It's okay. I'm okay."

"Drink. Slow." Simon cupped her hands around a water bottle. "Slow."

"I know. I've got it. I'm okay." She blew out a long breath first, then sipped carefully. "Thanks, sorry, whatever altogether. Wow." She sipped again. "I guess I wasn't too tired for that panic attack after all. I had a flashback. It's been . . . God, a really long time since I had one, but I guess the circumstances were pretty fertile ground."

Breathing steadier, she draped her arm around Bogart's neck. "You were mean," she said to Simon. "And exactly what I needed to snap me out before I passed out. You could give lessons."

"You scared the *fuck* out of me. Goddamn it."

Before she could speak he held up a hand to stop her, then

spun away to pace over the soggy ground. "Goddamn it. I'm not any good at this kind of thing."

"Beg to differ."

He whirled back. "I like you better tough."

"Me too. Panic attacks and hyperventilating to the edge of unconsciousness are embarrassing moments."

"It's not a damn joke."

"No, it's reality. My reality." She swiped her arm over her clammy face. "Fortunately, it's not something I have to deal with regularly anymore."

"Don't," he said when she started to rise. "You're white as a sheet. If you try standing by yourself, you'll fall on your face."

He moved to her, took her hands to help her up. "You're not supposed to be pale and fragile," he said quietly. "You're bright and bold and strong." He pulled her close. "And this makes me want to kill him."

"It's probably wrong, but God, I appreciate that. Still, Perry's worse off than dead."

"That's a matter of opinion. But maybe beating him half to death would be more satisfying."

His heart, she realized, beat harder and faster than her own. And that, she realized, was another kind of comfort.

"Well, if you want violence, I broke his nose kicking him in the face when he opened the trunk."

"Let me focus on that a minute. It's good. Not complete, but not bad."

She eased back. "Are we okay?"

He stroked her cheek, his eyes intense on hers. "Are you?"

"Yes. But I'm glad it's nearly dawn, because I'm not going back in that tent. If you could get my pack, I've got some bouillon cubes we can heat up."

"Bouillon at dawn?"

"Breakfast of champions, especially when you add a power bar." Better, she thought, so much better to focus on what came next than what had happened before. "Once we eat and break camp, I'll call in to base for the status, and a weather report."

"Fine. Fiona? On the off chance I ever do this with you again, we're getting a bigger tent."

"Bet your ass."

The bouillon was bland, but it was warm. As far as her nutrition bars, or whatever the hell you called them, Simon vowed if he ever came out again, he'd bring Snickers.

She broke camp as she did everything else, he noted. In an organized and precise fashion. Everything had to be put away exactly where it had come from.

"Okay, the forecast is good," she announced. "Sunny, low seventies for a high—and we won't reach that until this afternoon—light winds from the south. We're moving into the northern section of the wilderness area. It's not too rough. We'll have some hills, slopes, some rocky ground. The understory may get thick in places, especially off the marked trails. I'm guessing after the hike they'd already put in, they wouldn't choose the more mountainous terrain, or have kept going southeast into the higher elevations and rougher ground."

"I can't figure out why the hell they'd have come as far as this."

"Again, I'm guessing, but he's competitive, he's pushing. Even if he was a little turned around, he probably wouldn't admit it at first. And that type wouldn't take the easier ground—wouldn't necessarily head downhill instead of uphill."

"Because he's got something to prove."

"More or less. I asked the woman they're traveling with if he was the type who'd stop and ask directions—and she laughed. Nervous laugh, but a laugh. He'd drive to hell before he'd ask for directions. So you figure by the time he, or they, realized they were seriously screwed, it was just too late."

"A lot of space out here to get lost in." Which would he have done, he wondered, uphill or down, call for help or push on?

He wasn't altogether sure, and hoped he wouldn't ever have to find out.

"And if you're not familiar with it, one fir or hemlock looks like the other hundreds. Anyway, we're expanding the search area." She glanced up. "Do you want me to show you on the map?"

"Do you plan on ditching me in the wilderness?"

"Only if you piss me off."

"I'll take my chances."

"Then we saddle up." She shrugged on her pack, gave Bogart the scent and juiced him up for the game.

Watery sunlight sparkled on mists and filtered through to shine on leaves that shed their rainwater from the night's storm. Simon couldn't say what Bogart smelled, but for him, it was clean and damp and green.

The ground roughened and rose, and still wildflowers, tiny stars of color, carved their way through cracks to bask or ranged themselves along skinny streams like waders about to dip their toes.

A downed tree, hollowed out by weather, tooth and claw, had him crossing over.

"Do you see something?"

"A bench," he muttered. "Curve the seat, just like that. Back and arms, all out of one log. Carve a mushroom motif maybe on the base."

He surfaced to see both her and Bogart waiting for him. "Sorry."

"Bogart needed water anyway." She offered the bottle to Simon. "I could use a bench."

"Not that one. Too solid, too hefty for you. It wouldn't—"

"Suit me. Got it." Shaking her head, she checked in with base.

Despite the strengthening sun, Fiona continued to use her flashlight, running the beam over brush and trail as the dog trotted along.

"He's picked it up. The rest did him good."

"Isn't the world basically a banquet of smells for a dog? How come he doesn't get distracted? Hey, a rabbit! Or whatever. Jaws'll chase a blowing leaf."

"It's training, practice, repetition. But basically, that's not the game. The game's to find the source of the scent I gave him."

"The game's moving off the trail," Simon pointed out.

"Yeah." She followed the dog, climbing the rough slope, maneuvering through brush. "They made a mistake here. Bogart may not get distracted, but people do. They left the marked trail, maybe they saw some deer or a marmot, or wanted to take a photo. Maybe they decided they'd try for a shortcut. There's a reason the trails are marked, but people veer off anyway."

"If the dog's right, so were you. Competitive Kevin would go up instead of down."

Bogart slowed down for the humans as they negotiated the climb. "Maybe they figured they'd get a cool view if they went up this way. But . . . Wait. Bogart! Hold!"

She turned her light on a berry bush. "He caught his jacket," she murmured, and gestured to a tiny triangle of brown cloth. "Good dog. Good job, Bogart. Flag the find, will you?" she asked Simon. "I'm going to call this in to base."

She'd shown him how to mark the finds early on the search when they'd come across tracks or other signs. Once he'd tied the flag, he gave Bogart water, took some for himself while she shouted for Kevin and Ella.

"Nothing yet. But this understory sucks up the sound. It's warming up, and the wind's still light, still good for us. He wants to go. He's got a good scent. Let's find Kevin and Ella. Go find!"

"What's the longest you've ever been on a search?"

"Four days. It was brutal. Nineteen-year-old boy, pissed off at his family, walked away from their campsite after they'd bedded down for the night. Got lost, wandered in circles and took a bad fall. High summer—heat, bugs, humidity. Meg and Xena found him. Unconscious, dehydrated, concussed. He's lucky he made it."

Bogart zigzagged now, moving east, then west, turning back to the north.

"He's confused."

"No," Fiona corrected, watching Bogart's body language. "They were."

Ten minutes later Simon spotted the cell phone—or what was left of it—in a huddle of rock. "There."

He quickened his pace to reach Bogart, who stood at alert.

"Good eye," Fiona said. "It's cracked." She crouched to

pull it out. "Broken. Look here. Bandage wrappers on the ground, and this looks like blood—the rain didn't wash it all off in here."

"So one of them fell? Hit the rock, phone dropped, hit the rock?"

"Maybe. Only a couple bandages, so that's a plus." She nodded as he took out a flag without her asking. Once again, she cupped her hands and shouted. "Damn it. Damn it. How much farther would they go after this? I'll call it in."

"And eat something." He dug into her pack himself. "Hey, you've got Milky Ways."

"That's right. Quick energy."

"And I ate that crap bar. Sit down for five minutes. Eat. Drink."

"We're close. I know it. He knows it."

"Five minutes."

She nodded and, sitting on the rocks, ate a candy bar while she talked to Mai.

"We're realigning the search. We've hit two finds, and Lori hit one that indicates this direction. Air search will sweep this way. It's a red phone, and I'm betting hers. Mai's going to check on that, but I don't see Kevin with a bright red phone."

"So that's probably her blood."

"Probably. He's nuts about her, according to the friends. Just nuts about her. She's hurt, he'd panic a little. Or maybe a lot, considering. You panic, you make it worse most of the time."

"He could've called for help from right here."

Fiona pulled out her cell. "Nope. Dead zone. That's why they call it the wilderness. He probably tried to find a signal, ended up more lost, more off any kind of trail."

They headed out again. Bogart was deep into the "game," Simon concluded, trotting ahead, sending what could only be impatient looks over his shoulder as if to say, *Hurry the hell up!*

"Lost," Fiona said half to herself. "Scared now—not an adventure anymore. One of them injured, even if it's minor. Tired. New boots."

"New boots?"

"Ella. New boots. She's bound to have blisters by now. The instinct would be to take easier ground whenever they can. Downhill, or level ground, and they'd probably stop often to rest if she's hurting. The storm last night. They're wet, cold, hungry. They— Hear that?"

"Hear what?"

She held up a finger, concentrated. "The river. You can just hear the river."

"Now that you mention it."

"When you're lost, scared, people often try to find high ground—to see more, to be seen. That might not be an option with an injury. Another instinct is to head for water. It's a landmark, a trail, a comfort."

"What happened to the deal about staying in one place and somebody'll find you?"

"Nobody listens to that."

"Apparently not. He's got something." Simon gestured to Bogart. "Look up. There's a sock on that branch."

"Once again, good eye. It's a little late, but far from never. He's started marking a trail. Good dog, Bogart. Find! Come on, let's find Ella and Kevin!"

When they found a second sock in roughly a quarter mile, Fiona nodded. "Definitely the river, and he's thinking again. He could use his phone here, see?" She showed Simon the service on hers. "So something's up with that. But he's trying to take easy ground, and he's moving toward the river."

"More blood, more bandage wrappers," Simon pointed out.

"Dry. After the storm. These are from this morning."

She lifted her voice to encourage the dog and, once again, to shout. This time, Simon heard it, a faint call in return.

Bogart gave a happy bark, then broke into a lope.

He felt it, a rise of excitement, a fresh spurt of energy as he quickened his pace to match Fiona's and the dog's.

In moments he saw a man, muddied, bedraggled, hobbling up a small rise.

"Thank God. Thank God. My wife—she's hurt. We're lost. She's hurt."

"It's okay." Even as she hurried toward him, Fiona pulled out her water bottle. "We're Canine Search and Rescue. You're not lost anymore. Drink some water. It's okay."

"My wife. Ella—"

"It's okay. Bogart. Good dog. Good dog! Find Ella. Find. He'll go to her, stay with her. Are you hurt, Kevin?"

"No. I don't know." His hand trembled on the water bottle. "No. She fell. Her leg's cut, and her knee's bad. She's got awful blisters, and I think a fever. Please."

"We're going to take care of it."

"I've got him." Simon put an arm around Kevin, took his weight. "Go."

"It's my fault," Kevin began as Fiona rushed after the dog. "It's—"

"Don't worry about that now. How far is she?"

"Just down there, by the water. I tried to move more into the open after last night. There was a storm."

"Yeah."

"We tried to stay covered. Jesus God. Where are we? Where the hell are we?"

Simon wasn't entirely sure himself, but he saw Fiona and Bogart sitting beside a woman. "You're found, Kevin. That's what counts."

He passed out candy bars, heated bouillon while Fiona checked and rebandaged the wound, elevated Ella's swollen knee, treated the very nasty blisters on both her feet and Kevin's.

"I'm such an idiot," Kevin murmured.

"Yes, you are." Huddled in a blanket, Ella managed a small smile. "He forgets to charge his phone battery. I'm so caught up in taking snapshots I talk him off the trail. Then *he's* all, hey let's try this way. Then I don't look where I'm going and fall. We're both idiots, and I'm burning those hiking boots the first chance I get."

"Here." Simon pressed the cup of bouillon on her. "Not as much fun as the Milky Way, but it should help."

"It's delicious," Ella said after a small sip. "I thought we were going to die last night in that storm. I really did. When we were still alive this morning, I knew we'd make it. I knew somebody would find us." When she turned to lay a hand on Bogart, the shine in her eyes shimmered with tears and relief. "He's the most beautiful dog in the world."

Bogart wagged his tail in agreement, then laid his head on Ella's thigh.

"They're sending an off-road." Fiona hooked her radio back on her belt. "We can get you out in that. Your friends say you won the bet hands down, and they're adding a magnum of champagne to drinks and dinner."

Kevin dropped his head on his wife's shoulder. As his shoulders shook, Bogart licked his hand in comfort.

"SHE'S NOT EVEN PISSED at him," Simon observed as they bumped and rocked in a second off-road.

"Survival tops pissed off. They shared an intense, scary experience—and probably went off on each other a number of times during it. That's done. They're alive, and riding on euphoria. How about you?"

"Me? I had a hell of a time. It's not what I expected," he added after a moment.

"Oh?"

"I guess I thought you went out and tromped around, followed the dog, drank cowboy coffee and ate trail mix."

"That's not far off."

"Yeah, it is. You've got one purpose out there, just like the dog. Find what's lost, and find them as quickly as possible. You follow the dog, sure, but you handle the dog, and yourself while playing detective and psychologist and tracker."

"Hmm."

"All while being a team player—not just with the dog, but with the rest of the unit, the other searchers, the cops or whoever's in authority. And when you find them, you're paramedic, priest, best friend, mom and commander."

"We wear many hats. Want to try some on?"

He shook his head. "You've already got my dog. He could do this. I get that now. Thank Christ," he added when he saw the lodge through the trees. "I want a hot shower, a hot meal, a couple vats of coffee. Does that come with the package?"

"It will here."

Chaos came first. Relief, tears, hugs, even as actual paramedics took over. Somebody slapped his back and shoved hot coffee into his hands. Nothing had ever tasted better.

"Good work." Chuck tossed him a doughnut every bit as good as the coffee. "Helluva job. There's a room for you inside if you want a hot shower."

"Only as much as I want my next breath."

"With you there.. Ugly night, huh? But a damn good morning."

He glanced over, as Chuck did, toward Ella and Kevin as the medics loaded Ella's stretcher into an ambulance. "How's she doing?"

"Knee's banged up good, and she'll need a few stitches. But they're both better than they ought to be. They'll fix her up. I guarantee this is a vacation they won't forget."

"Me either."

"Nothing like a find," Chuck said, and did another quick fist pump. "Well, go get that shower. Jill made up her spaghetti and meatballs, and you haven't lived till you've eaten her meatballs. We'll debrief over lunch."

When he went inside, some motherly woman hugged him before pressing a room key in his hand. He turned toward the stairs, ran into Lori, got caught in another hug. Before he could get to the second floor, he had his hand shaken twice, his back slapped again. A little dazed, he found the room, closed himself inside.

Quiet, he thought. Silence—or nearly since the noise from downstairs and the corridors was nicely muffled by the door.

Solitude.

He dumped his pack in a chair, dug out the spare socks, boxers, shirt Fiona had instructed him to bring, the travel toothbrush she'd supplied.

On the way to the bathroom he glanced out the window. People continued to mill around. The dogs, obviously too juiced up from the game, trotted after humans or one another.

He didn't find Fiona. He'd lost sight of her minutes after they'd gotten back to base.

He stripped, turned the shower on full and hot. And the instant the spray hit him every cell in his body wept with gratitude.

He might not be an urbanite, Simon thought as he just braced his palms on the tile and let the hot water pound over him, but Mother of God, he worshipped indoor plumbing.

He heard the tap-tap on the bathroom door and would've snarled if Fiona's voice hadn't followed it. "It's me. Want company or do you want to ride solo?"

"Will the company be naked?"

His lips curved as he heard her laugh.

There was solitude, he thought, and solitude. And when she opened the shower door, tall, slim, naked, he decided he much preferred her kind.

"Come on in. The water's fine."

"Oh God." As he had, she closed her eyes and wallowed. "It's not fine. It's bliss."

"Where'd you go?"

"Oh. I needed to feed and water Bogart, touch base with the sergeant, set up the debriefing. We're doing it over food, glorious food."

"I heard. I haven't lived till I eat the meatballs."

"Solid truth." She dunked her head, tipped it back so the water rained on her hair. Then just stood with her eyes closed and a *hmm* of pleasure in her throat.

"I called Syl, told her we'd pick up the boys on our way back."

"You've been busy."

"Things that must be done."

"I've got another one." He turned her to face him.

"Everyone celebrates in their own way."

She sighed her way into the kiss. "I like yours."

TWENTY-TWO

He couldn't argue about the meatballs. As he ate, Simon realized the meal reminded him of one of his family's dinners back home. A lot of noise, interruptions, that situational shorthand again and a stunning amount of food.

But then, he supposed families came in all shapes, sizes and dynamics.

He suspected his pecking order was "The boyfriend"— annoying but predictable—who was still being measured and weighed, but welcomed warmly enough.

He couldn't argue about the charged, happy mood, not when it infected him, too. Watching Kevin hobble toward them after all those hours, all those miles, had struck hard and struck deep.

More than satisfaction, Simon decided, it had been like a revival, like a shot of a really good drug that settled into a sense of pride.

Both Mai and Fiona took notes, and there was talk of documentation, logs, mission reports.

He noticed, in the playback, Fiona deleted her panic attack.

"Anything you want to add, Simon?"

He glanced over at James. "I think Fiona covered it. I was just along for the ride."

"Maybe, but you pulled your weight. He did okay, for a rookie," Fiona added. "He's got endurance, a good sense of direction. He can read a map and a compass, and has a good eye. Some training? He could be ready when Jaws is."

"You're in if you want a shot," Chuck told him.

Simon stabbed a meatball. "Use the dog."

"We'd bring you in at the top pay scale."

Amused, Simon studied Meg as he wound pasta around his fork. "That's goose egg, right?"

"Every time."

"Tempting."

"Think about it," Mai suggested. "Maybe you could bring Jaws to one of our unit practices sometime. See how it goes."

THE MOOD MELLOWED OUT on the trip back, with the dogs dozing in the boat. Lori and James did the same, their heads tipped together, while Mai and Tyson huddled in the stern, fingers linked.

They'd drifted from unit to couples, Simon thought, sending a sidelong glance at Fiona, who sat beside him, reading over her notes. And it looked like he was one of them.

Once they reached Orcas, there were more hugs. He'd never seen people so addicted to squeezing one another.

He took the wheel for the drive home.

"We got dinner out—sort of," Fiona said. "I ate so much pasta I may not eat for days. Plus, as date nights go, it was unique."

"You're never boring, Fiona."

"Well, thank you."

"Too much going on, in your life, in your head, to be boring."

She smiled, flipped open her phone when it signaled. "Fiona Bristow. Yeah, Tod. That's good. I'm really glad to hear it. We all are. You don't have to, we got ours when Kevin and Ella got home safe. Yes, absolutely. You take care."

She closed the phone. "Five stitches and a knee brace for Ella. They hydrated both of them, treated the blisters, the scrapes. Short version, they're both going to be fine, and shortly on their way back to the lodge. They wanted to thank you."

"Me?"

"You were part of the team who found them. How does it feel?"

He said nothing for a moment. "Pretty damn good."

"Yeah. It really does."

"You have to buy all your own equipment. The radios, tents, blankets, first aid, the whole shot." Not that he was thinking about joining up. "I saw you note down what we used. You have to replace it on your own nickel."

"That's part of it. The radio was a gift, and boy did we need it. The parents of a kid we found bought it for us. Some want to pay us, but that's a dicey area. But if they want to pick up some blankets or supplies, we don't say no."

"Give me the list. I'll replace the stuff. I was part of the team, wasn't I?" he asked when she frowned at him.

"Yes, but you don't have to feel obligated to—"

"I don't volunteer to do things out of obligation."

"That's true. I'll give you a list."

They stopped off at Sylvia's, loaded up the dogs, which took twice as long as it might have due to desperate joy. He had to admit he'd missed his own idiot dog, and it felt damn good to be driving home with Fiona beside him and the back full of happy dogs.

"You know what I want?" she asked him.

"What?"

"I want a long, tall glass of wine and a lazy hour in my custom-made porch rocker. Maybe you'd like to join me?"

"I just might."

When she reached over for his hand, he linked it with hers.

"I feel good. Tired, happy and just good all over. How about you guys, huh?" She shifted to look back, rub faces and bodies. "We feel so good. You can play while Simon and I drink wine until the sun goes down. That's what I think. We'll all be tired and happy and just good all over until—"

"Fiona."

"Hmm?" Distracted, she glanced over. The hard set of his face had that happy lift dropping into worry. "What? What is it?"

She swiveled back as he slowed at her drive.

The red scarf tied to the lifted flag on her mailbox fluttered in the fitful breeze.

Her mind emptied, and for a moment she was back in the tight, airless dark.

"Where's your gun? Fiona!" He whipped her name out and slashed her back.

"In my pack."

He reached in the back, shoved her pack into her lap. "Get it out, lock the doors. Stay in the car and call the cops."

"No. What? Wait. Where are you going?"

"To check out the house. He's not going to be there, but we don't take chances."

"And you just walk out there, unarmed, unprotected?" Like Greg, she thought. Just like Greg. "If you get out, I get out. Cops first. Please. I couldn't take it a second time. I couldn't."

She pulled out her phone, hit speed dial for the sheriff's office. "This is Fiona. Someone tied a red scarf to my mailbox. No, I'm with Simon, at the end of the drive. No. No. Yes, all right. Okay."

She drew a breath. "They're on their way. They want us to stay where we are. I know that's not what you want to do. I know it goes against the grain, against your instincts."

She unzipped her pack, took out her gun. With steady hands, she checked the load, the safety. "But if he is there, if he's waiting, he'd know that, too. And maybe I'd be going to another funeral for a man I love. He'd have killed me too, Simon, because I can't come back from that a second time."

"You put it that way to close me in a box."

"I put it that way because it's God's truth. I need you to

stay with me. I'm asking you to stay with me. Please don't leave me alone."

Her need pushed against his. He thought he could have fought hers back if she'd used tears, but the flat, matter-of-fact tone did him in. "Give me your binoculars."

She unzipped another section of her pack, handed them to him.

"I'm not going anywhere, but I'm going to look."

"Okay."

He stepped out of the car but stayed close. He could hear her calming the dogs as he scanned the drive, the trees. Spring had leafed out those trees, forcing him to try to angle through the green and search the shadows. While the pretty breeze fluttered, he took a few steps away to try for a better vantage point, and followed the curve of her drive.

Her pretty house stood quiet before the dark arches of the forest. Butterflies danced on the air above her garden, while in her field, grasses and buttercups barely stirred.

He walked back, opened his door. "Everything looks fine."

"He read the article. He wants me scared."

"No argument. Stupid to leave the marker if he's still around."

"Yes. I don't think he is either. He accomplished what he wanted. I'm scared. The cops are coming. It's all in my face again, and I'm thinking about him. We all are. I called Agent Tawney."

"Good. Here come the cops."

He closed the car door, watched the two cruisers approach. He heard her get out the other side, nearly snapped at her to get back in. She wouldn't, he thought, and it was probably unnecessary.

He watched the sheriff get out of the first cruiser. He'd seen the man around the village a few times, but they'd never had a conversation—or a need for one. Patrick McMahon carried a hefty girth on a big frame. Simon imagined he'd played high school football—maybe a tackle—and likely continued with hard-fought Sunday games with friends.

Aviator sunglasses hid his eyes, but his wide face held grim lines, and his hand rested on the butt of his weapon as he walked.

"Fee. I'm gonna want you to stay in the car. Simon Doyle, right?" McMahon held out a hand. "I'm gonna want you to stay with Fee. Davey and I, we'll go down, take a look at things. Matt'll stay here. He's gonna take some pictures and put that scarf in an evidence bag so we'll have it secure. Did you lock the doors when you left?"

"Yes."

"Windows?"

"I . . . Yes, I think so."

"They're locked," Simon told him. "I checked them before we left."

"Good enough. Fee, how about you give me the keys? Once we clear everything, we'll call on down to Matt. How's that?"

She came around as Simon took the keys out of the ignition, then she peeled off the link that held her house key. "Front and back door."

"Good enough," he said again. "Sit tight."

McMahon got back in the cruiser, swung around Fiona's car and started down the drive.

"Sorry about this, Fiona." Matt, barely old enough to buy a legal beer, gave her arm a little pat. "You and Mr. Doyle get on back in the car now." He glanced down at the gun she held down at her side. "And keep the safety on that."

"He's younger than I am. Matt," Fiona said when she got back in the car. "Barely old enough to drink. I trained his parents' Jack Russell. He's not going to be there," she murmured, running her fist up and down her chest. "Nothing's going to happen to them."

"Did you ask anybody to come by, check on the place while we were gone?"

"No. It was just overnight. If it had been longer, Syl would've come by to water the pots, pick up the mail. God, God, if it had been longer, and—"

"Didn't happen." Simon cut her off. "No point projecting it. Everyone on the island, or damn near, would've known you were on that search by this morning. It's not enough time for him to have pulled this."

Unless, Simon thought, he was already on the island.

"I think it comes from the article—the timing of it—the way he mailed me the scarf after the first one. I guess he wants me to know he can get closer. Did get closer."

"It's arrogant, and arrogance leads to screwups."

"I hope you're right." She stared at the scarf, forced herself to think. Follow the trail, she ordered herself. "Did it rain here last night? Did that storm, or the edge of it, blow through here, too? It was supposed to. The scarf's dry, or dry enough to wave in the breeze. But then, the sun's warm and bright today. He'd want to do that at night, wouldn't he? At night or early enough there wouldn't be much chance of a car going by."

"We've been sitting here twenty minutes and I haven't seen a car go by."

"True, but it's a stupid risk. Not just arrogant, stupid. If he came here at night, he'd need somewhere to stay on the island, or have a boat of his own. But if he came by boat, he'd need a car to get out here."

"One way or the other, he was here. The odds are someone saw him."

A car approached now, slowed, crept by.

"Tourists," Fiona said quietly. "The summer season's already geared up. Coming and going by ferry's the easiest way to disappear. But maybe he didn't come and go in the same day. Maybe he booked a room or a campsite or—"

She jolted when Matt tapped on the window.

"Sorry," he said when she lowered it. "Sheriff says it's clear."

"Thanks. Thanks, Matt."

She studied everything as Simon drove, everything so familiar. Could he have walked here? she wondered. Would he have risked the dogs? Would the need have overridden sense and caution? He might've taken the chance, creeping down, wanting a better look at the house, maybe hoping to see her sitting on the porch or weeding the garden.

Ordinary things, everyday things people do.

Walking down to get the mail, she thought, running an errand, holding a class, playing with her dogs.

Routine.

The idea he might've come before, might've studied her, watched her, stalked her—just as Perry had done—filled her with a sick dread that tasted bitter in the back of her throat.

McMahon opened her door when Simon stopped. "No signs of break-in. I can't see that anything inside's been disturbed, but you can tell me if you see different. We took a walk around outside, and I'm going to have Davey and Matt take another look, go a little farther out while we talk inside. Okay?"

"Yeah. Sheriff, I called Agent Tawney. I felt I should. I don't mean to step on your toes, but—"

"Fiona. How long have you known me?"

She let out a relieved breath at the easy tone. "Since I started coming out to see my dad in the summers."

"Long enough for you to know I'm not worried about my toes. I want you to go in, take a good look around. If you see anything off, you tell me. Even if you just think maybe."

The advantage of a small house, Fiona thought, was it didn't take long to go through it, even when she took the time—obsessively, maybe—to open a few drawers.

"Everything's the way we left it."

"That's good. Why don't we have a seat and talk about this?"

"Do you want something to drink? I could—"

"I'm good. Don't worry about that." He took a seat, continued in the avuncular tone Simon realized was designed to calm nerves and tempers. "I've let Davey take point on this, not because I haven't been involved, but because I figured you'd be most comfortable with him. I don't want you to think I've been brushing this off."

"How long have you known me?"

He smiled at her, the lines at the corners of his eyes crinkling deep. "There you go. What time did you leave yesterday?"

"I logged the call in at seven-fifteen. I didn't note down

the time when we left, but I'd say it was less than fifteen minutes. Just enough time to pass the call to Mai, check the packs, lock up and load up. We dropped the dogs, except for Bogart, off at Syl's, headed over to Chuck's. The full unit was on its way at seven fifty-five."

"That's good response time."

"We work at it."

"I know you do. I know you found those people. That's good work. What time did you get back today?"

"We got back to Chuck's about three-thirty and swung by to pick up the dogs. I called you right away, within a minute after we saw the scarf. Was it wet? Damp? I thought—"

"Are you trying to do my job?" He wagged a finger at her, kept the tone light. "It's dry. We got rain last night. Didn't get hammered as much as you, but it came down pretty hard. Could've dried out by this time, as we've had a nice sunny day. But it wasn't there when Davey did a drive-by at nine this morning."

"Oh."

"You might not've been here, Fee, but we're keeping our eye out. A lot of people get on and off the ferry on a nice day like this. If I had to guess, I'd say he came over today, maybe did some driving around. Sometime between nine this morning and four-fifteen this afternoon he tied that scarf out there. I say drive because you live a good piece out. I can't see him walking out this far, or hitching."

"No," she murmured, "he needs a car." A car with a trunk.

"I've got a couple people I can trust keeping an eye on the ferry, checking out the departures. If they see a man driving on by himself, they're going to get the license plate. The other thing we'll do is check with the hotels, the B-and-Bs, campgrounds, even the rental houses, but it's going to take some time. We'll check out any man traveling alone."

"You're making me feel better," she murmured.

"That's good. But I don't want you to take chance one, Fiona. I'm not just saying this as the sheriff, but as a friend of your father's, and Sylvia's. I don't want you here alone. If here's where you want to be, somebody's here with you. I want your doors locked—day and night," he added, and the warning edge to his gaze told Simon her habit of open, unlocked doors was no secret.

"They will be. Word of honor."

"Good enough. When you're on the road, I want your car windows up and your doors locked. I want you to carry your phone, and I want the name of every new client you take on. Every one of them. If you get another call for a search, I want you to contact me or my office. I want to know where you're going and how to verify it."

"She won't be staying here," Simon told him. "She's moving to my place. Today. She'll pack up what she needs before you leave."

"I can't just—"

"That's a good idea." McMahon ignored Fiona, nodded at Simon. "It changes the pattern. I don't want her there alone, either."

"She won't be."

"Excuse me?" Fiona held up both hands. "I'm not going to be difficult, and I'm not arguing about the need for precautions, but I can't just move out of my house, my place of business. I teach here, and—"

"We'll work it out. Pack."

"What about my—"

"Give us a minute, will you?" Simon asked McMahon.

"No problem." He scraped back his chair. "I'll be right outside."

"Do you know how infuriating it is when you continually interrupt me?" Fiona demanded.

"Yeah, probably about the same level as when you continually argue with good sense."

"I'm not doing that. But good sense has to coordinate with the practical side. I have three dogs. I have a business here. The equipment I need to run that business."

Excuses, not reasons, he concluded. And he wasn't taking any bullshit.

"You want practical? I'll give you practical. I have a bigger house and more room for those dogs. You can't be alone because I'm there. I work there. If he comes looking for you here, he won't find you. If you need the damn equipment, we'll move the damn equipment. Or I'll build new equipment. Do you think I can't build a fucking seesaw?"

"It's not that. Or not just that." She held her hands out, then rubbed them over her face. "You haven't given me five seconds to think. You didn't even bother to ask."

"I'm not asking. I'm telling you to go pack what you need. Consider it a change of pack leadership."

"That's not amusing."

"I'm not feeling funny. We'll get whatever equipment, whatever supplies we can today. We'll get the rest tomorrow. Goddamn it, Fiona, he was under a quarter mile from your house. You asked me to stay, to go against my instincts and what I wanted to do and stay with you back there. Now it's your turn."

"I'm taking that five seconds to think." She spun away from him, fists jammed on her hips as she stalked to the window.

Her place—was that what was wrong with her? Her place here, the first solid building block of the new life she'd created. Now, instead of holding her ground, defending it, she'd be walking away.

Could she be that stubborn, that foolish?

"Time's up."

"Oh, be quiet," she snapped at him. "I'm being driven out of my own home, so give me a damn minute to deal with it."

"Fine. Take a minute, then get moving."

She turned back. "You're a little pissed that you have—or feel you have—to do this. It's one thing for you to sleep here, another for me to essentially live in your home."

"Okay. What's your point?"

"No point, just an observation. I have to make some calls. I can't just pack. I'll need to contact my clients, at least the ones coming tomorrow, and let them know I've moved the school. Temporarily," she added, as much for her benefit as his. "James's number is four on my speed dial. If you call him, he'll come and help us move the outside equipment."

"Okay."

"And I'll need to have calls forwarded to your number—from my house phone. For clients, and in case we get a search call."

"I don't care."

"Yes, you do," she said, wearily now. "I appreciate what you're doing, especially because you're not altogether happy about doing it."

"I'd rather feel a little hemmed in than have anything happen to you."

She let out a half laugh. "You have no idea, you really don't, how sweet that is. I'll do my best not to hem you in too much. Go ahead and tell Sheriff McMahon you won. I'll start putting things together."

He wasn't entirely sure what he'd won as he'd now have four dogs and a woman under his feet, but he stepped outside. McMahon broke off a conversation with his deputies and crossed toward the porch as Simon walked down.

"She's packing."

"Good. We'll still come by here a couple times a day, check things out. When she's going back and forth to hold those classes of hers—"

"She won't be. She'll do it at my place. I'm calling James so he can help me break down and move all that."

Eyebrows lifted, McMahon looked over at the equipment. "Better yet. Tell you what, Matt here's about to go off duty. He's young and got a strong back. He'll give you a hand. Won't take much time. Those are your chairs, right?"

"They're hers now."

"Uh-huh. What I'm wondering is if you do porch gliders. My wife and I got an anniversary coming up next month. I've got a little shop, do some Harry Homeowner stuff, a little this and that. Thought I might try my hand at a glider. I proposed to her on one. I found out pretty quick building one was above my pay grade."

"I can do that."

"Something with those nice wide arms would be good. And she's partial to red."

"Okay."

"Good enough. We'll talk about the details later. You go ahead, get the tools to break what needs to be broken down. I'll get Matt started on what doesn't." He started back, stopped. "Are you really making a sink out of a stump?"

"Yes, I am."

"That's something I want to see. Matt! Haul some of this dog playground business into Simon's truck."

HE ENDED UP calling James anyway, for the third pair of hands and the second truck. And with James came Lori, and with James and Lori came Koby.

Simon's initial annoyance with having so many people and animals swarming around gave way to the realization that sometimes people didn't get in the way, but helped make a necessary and tedious job go smoother.

It wasn't a matter of a couple of suitcases' worth of clothes, not when it was Fiona. It was suitcases, dog beds, dog food, toys, leashes, meds, dishes, grooming equipment—and that didn't begin to factor in platforms, the seesaw, the slide, the tunnel. Or her files—and Jesus the woman had files—her laptop, her packs, her maps, the perishables in her refrigerator.

"The flower beds and vegetable garden are on a soaker hose," she said when he objected to hauling over her flowerpots, "so they'll be fine. But these need regular watering. Besides, we'll enjoy them. And besides besides, Simon, you asked for it."

And that he couldn't argue with.

"Fine, fine. Just . . . go start putting some of this crap away, will you?"

"Any preference to where?"

He stared at the last load and wondered how the hell she'd fit all of that into her Seven Dwarfs–sized house. How had it all tucked in so tidily—and that didn't count what she'd left behind.

"Wherever, I guess. Dump the office stuff in one of the spare bedrooms, and don't mess with my stuff more than you have to."

He walked back to help James put the training equipment back together.

Beside Fiona, Lori rolled her eyes and grabbed a box of files. "Lead the way."

"I'm not entirely sure of it, but I guess we'll take this first load upstairs, find the best spot."

As they started in, Lori glanced around. "Nice. Really nice—a lot of space and light and interesting furniture. What there is of it. Messy," she added as she started up the steps, "but really nice."

"Probably three or four times as much space as I have." Fiona glanced inside a room, frowned at the weight machine, gym equipment, tangle of clothes, unpacked boxes.

She tried another. A stack of paint cans, some brushes, rollers, pans, tools, sawhorses. "Okay, I guess this'll work. I'm going to need my desk and chair. I didn't think of that."

She winced a little at the dust on the floor, the film on the window. "It is messy," she murmured, "and I know what you're thinking. Messy makes me twitchy."

She set down her box of office supplies, turned a circle. "I'll live with it."

And him, she thought. For now.

TWENTY-THREE

She opted to set up her office space first. Which, in this case, meant cleaning the space first. She'd live with messy. It wasn't her house. But temporary live-in lover or not, she wouldn't work in dust and disorder.

While Lori and James set out to get her desk and chair—and lamp, and desk clock—she hunted down cleaning supplies. And, as Simon apparently believed in only the barest of basics, called Lori to add a list from her own supplies.

How, she wondered, did anyone—especially anyone with a dog—live without a Swiffer?

Working with what she had, she cleaned several months of dust from the windows, the floor, the woodwork, and discovered what she'd assumed was a second closet but was actually a bathroom.

One, she thought with a long huff of breath, that surely hadn't been cleaned since he'd moved in. Fortunately, its primary purpose seemed to be gathering more dust.

She was on her hands and knees scrubbing the floor when he came in.

"What are you doing?"

"Planning my next trip to Rome. What does it look like I'm doing? I'm cleaning this bathroom."

"Why?"

"That you would have to ask explains so much." She sat back on her heels. "I may, at some point, have to pee. I find this occurs with some regularity on any given day. I prefer—call me fussy—to engage in this activity in sanitary surroundings."

He stuck his hands in his pockets, leaned on the jamb. "I haven't been using this room or this john. Yet."

"Really? I'd never have guessed."

He glanced around the now dust-free bedroom where paint cans stood in stacks tidily beside sawhorses, rollers, pans and brushes on neatly folded tarps.

"You're setting up in here?"

"Is that a problem?"

"Not for me. Did you wash the floor out here?"

"Damp-mopped. Let me point out, as someone who works with wood, you should take better care of your floors. You need some Murphy's at least."

"I've got some. Somewhere. Maybe." She was making him twitchy. "I've been busy."

"Understood."

"You're not going to go around cleaning everything, are you?"

She swiped a hand over her forehead. "Let me give you my solemn oath on that. But I'm going to work in here. I need a clean, ordered space to work. I'll keep the door closed so it doesn't shock your sensibilities."

"Now you're being bitchy."

Because she heard the amusement in his tone, she smiled back. "Yes, I am. Move back so I can finish this. I appreciate what you're doing, Simon."

"Uh-huh."

"I do, and I know it disrupts your space, your routine, your privacy."

"Shut up."

"I just want to thank—"

"Shut up," he repeated. "You matter. That's it. I've got something to do."

She sat back on her heels when he strode out. *Shut up. You matter. That's it.* Honestly, she mused, coming from him that was practically a poem by Shelley.

By the time she'd arranged her office, with her desk tidy under the window facing the back and the woods, she'd have killed for a glass of wine and a comfortable chair. But her sense of order wouldn't allow her to leave her clothes in suitcases.

She'd scope out Simon's bedroom, then find him and ask how he wanted her to deal with her clothes.

It surprised her to find the bed made—sort of made, she thought. The dog beds had been tossed in a corner, and the doors to the deck stood open to let in the air.

She poked in the closet, saw he'd shoved his clothes over to make room for hers. She'd need a drawer, she thought. Two would be better. She moved to the dresser, opened one gingerly. He'd emptied it out for her. He was one step ahead of her, she thought, then cocked her head, sniffed.

Lemon?

Curious, she crossed to the bathroom, then just leaned on the door frame. She recognized a freshly cleaned bathroom— the scent of citrus, the gleam of porcelain, the rich sheen of brushed nickel. The towels hung in an orderly fashion on rods melted her heart.

He'd probably cursed with every swipe, she mused, but, well, she mattered. And that was it.

She put away her clothes, stowed her toiletries, then went down to find him.

He stood in the kitchen, looking out the back door at the training equipment.

"Some of that should be replaced," he said without looking around. "That platform's crap."

"You're probably right. Did James and Lori go?"

"Yeah. She put stuff in the fridge and wherever, said to tell you she'd call you tomorrow. I offered them a beer," he added, almost defensively. "But they rain-checked."

"I imagine they're tired after all this."

"Yeah. I want a beer and the beach."

"That sounds perfect. Go ahead. I've just a couple things, then I'll come down."

He walked over, opened the fridge for his beer. "Don't clean anything."

She lifted her hand. "Solemn oath."

"Right. I'll leave Newman, take the rest."

She nodded. She couldn't be alone, she thought. Not even here.

She waited until he'd gone out, until she'd heard him order Newman to stay, stay with Fee. Then she sat at his counter, laid her head on it and waited for the tears that had begun to burn in her throat to come.

But they wouldn't. She'd held them back too long, she realized. Pushed them down all these hours, and now they were simply blocked, locked inside, hurting her throat, aching in her head.

"Okay." She breathed the word out, rose. Rather than a beer she chose a bottle of water. Better, she thought. Cleaner.

She stepped outside where the faithful Newman waited. "Let's take a walk."

He bounded over immediately, doing a full-body wag as he rubbed against her.

"I know, new place. It's nice, isn't it? Lots of room. We'll be okay here for a while. We'll figure it all out." Her eye instinctively picked up spots that needed flowers, a good location for a kitchen garden.

Not hers to play with, she reminded herself.

"Still it could use more color, more outdoor seating. I'm surprised he hasn't thought of it. He's the artist." She paused as they came to the drop leading down to the beach. "But then there's this. It's pretty fabulous."

The charm of crooked steps led down to the narrow beach and opened to the dreamy spread of water. Stars winked on, adding to the sense of peace, of privacy. Simon walked along with the three dogs sniffing sand and shale and surf.

He'd missed this, she thought, his solo walks in the twilight where the land met the water. Missed the quiet, the subtle whoosh of the surf at the end of the day, but he'd stepped away from that to be with her.

Whatever happened around them, between them, she wouldn't forget that.

As she stood, looking down, he pulled bright yellow tennis balls from a bag he'd hooked on his belt. He heaved them, one, two, three, into the water—and the dogs charged and leaped.

They'd smell . . . amazing, she thought as she watched them swim toward the bobbing yellow balls.

Even as she thought it, she heard Simon's laugh rise up, over the subtle whoosh of the surf, over the quiet—and the sound of it chased away the demons.

Look at them, she thought. Look how wonderful they are, how perfect they are. My guys.

Beside her, Newman quivered.

"What the hell. Four smelly dogs isn't any worse than three. Go! Go play!"

He charged down the crooked steps, joy in the speed, in the challenging bark. Simon tossed a fourth ball in the air, caught it, then winged it into the water. Without breaking stride, Newman sprinted in.

And Fiona ran down to join the game.

IN HIS MOTEL ROOM near the Seattle airport, Francis X. Eckle read the most recent message from Perry and sipped his evening whiskey on the rocks.

He didn't care for the tone, no, he didn't care for the tone at all. Words like *disappointed, control, focus, unnecessary* popped out of the text and grated against his pride. His ego.

Boring, he thought, and crumpled the paper into a ball. Boring, scolding and annoying. Perry needed to remember just who was in prison, and who wasn't.

That was the problem with teachers—and he should know

because before he evolved he'd been a teacher himself. Boring, scolding and annoying.

But no more.

Now he had the power of life and death in his hands.

He lifted one, studied it. Smiled at it.

He breathed fear at his whim, dispensed pain, eked out hope, then crushed it. He saw all of that in their eyes, all the fear, the pain, the hope and, finally, the surrender.

Perry had never felt this *rush* of power and knowledge. If he had, truly had, he wouldn't constantly preach caution and control—or, as he liked to call it, "The clean kill."

Annette had been the most satisfying kill to date. And why? Because of the sound his fists made when they pounded into her flesh, cracked against bone. Because he'd *felt* every blow even as she did.

Because there had been blood—the sight of it, the smell of it. He'd been able to watch, to study the way the bruises gathered, the way they rose up to stain the skin, and to enjoy the different tones—slap or punch.

They'd gotten to know each other, hadn't they? Taking the time for that, sharing pain, made the kill so much more intimate. So much more *real*.

Thinking about it now, he realized Perry's work had been bloodless, clinical, even detached. There couldn't have been genuine pleasure with so little passion. The single time Perry had deviated, had allowed himself true, bloody violence, he hadn't been able to handle it.

Now he lived in a cell.

That was why this gradual and creative acceleration was superior. Why he was now superior.

It was time, maybe past time, he decided, to break off all contact with Perry. He had nothing more to learn from that source, and no desire to teach.

Remembering himself, he rose to pick up the balled note. He smoothed it out carefully before tucking it into the folder with all the others.

He'd already begun to write a book on his life, his epiphany, his evolution, his work. He'd accepted it would be published posthumously. He'd accepted his inevitable end, and the acceptance made each moment more vital.

Not prison. No, never prison. He'd already lived his life in a self-imposed prison. But glory. In the end, the inevitable end, he would have glory.

For now, he would simply be a shadow, slipping in and out of the light, unnamed and unknown. Or known only by those he chose, those who crossed from life to death with his face caught in their eyes.

He'd already selected the next.

Another change, he thought. Another stage of his evolution. And while he studied her, tracked her like a wolf tracks a rabbit, he could speculate on how it would be between them.

The irony was exquisite, and he knew, already knew it would add to the thrill.

Then before much longer, there would be Fiona.

He took out the newspaper, unfolded it, smoothed his hands over her face. He'd fulfill his obligation to Perry with her, and his debt would be paid in full.

She would be the last to wear the red scarf. That was fitting, he decided. She'd be the highlight of this stage of the work. His crescendo, he thought, with a final homage to Perry.

He was sure already he'd enjoy her most of all. She'd know more pain, more fear than all the others before he was done.

Oh, how people would talk when he took her, when he ended her life. They'd talk of little else. They'd talk and they'd tremble over the man who killed the Perry survivor.

RSKII.

Reading the term made him shake his head, made him chuckle.

Made him preen.

After Fiona lay in the shallow grave he'd force her to dig herself, RSKII would be no more. He would become someone else, something else, find another symbol as he embarked on the next stage of his work.

In a way, he thought, and took another sip of whiskey, Fiona would be the end of him, and the beginning.

* * *

MANTZ HUNG UP the phone and knocked a fist on her desk. "I think I've got something."

Tawney glanced away from his monitor. "What?"

"Verifying residence and employment on prison personnel and outside agencies. There's a Francis X. Eckle, teaches at College Place—English studies, creative writing. He did four stints of instruction at the prison in the past two and a half years. He didn't go back to work after the winter break. Mailed in a resignation, citing a family emergency."

"Did you check it out?"

"He doesn't actually have a family—not a traditional deal. He bumped around in the foster system from the time he was four. He didn't leave any forwarding information at the school. Both the numbers listed for home and cell have been disconnected."

"Let's get more information. Find his caseworkers, some data on his foster homes. No criminal?"

"Not a whiff. No sibs, no spouse, no kids." Though her voice stayed cool, the light of the hunter sparked in her eyes. "Perry signed in for all four of his classes at the prison. I ran a check on Eckle's credit cards. Nothing since January. Not a single charge, but he hasn't canceled them either. That's off."

"Yeah, that's off. He could be dead."

"This one's talking to my gut, Tawney. Look, I know you want to try to get out and connect with Bristow today or tomorrow, but I think we need to check this out, talk to people who know him, face-to-face."

"All right. Let's check his bank accounts, see if you can get more background. An English teacher?"

"Untenured. Single, lives alone, forty-two years old. The administrator I talked to said Eckle just sort of drifted along, did his job, didn't make waves. He couldn't name any particular friends either, and it's a small school, Tawney."

That light sparked in Tawney's eyes, too. "Make the calls. I'll put in for the travel."

*   *   *

SIMON COVERED the nearly finished wine cabinet with a tarp. It made him feel a little foolish, but he didn't want Fiona to see it, or ask him about it. Maybe he didn't want to think too deeply about the fact that he was making it for her, just because she wanted one.

It had been weird enough waking up and knowing she was there. Not in bed, of course, he mused as he added a third coat of poly to his stump-and-burl-wood sink. If the sun was up, so was Fiona. But she'd been there, in his place, his space.

His bathroom smelled of her, just as his kitchen smelled of the coffee she'd brewed while he'd still been in bed.

And the weird thing? He was okay with it. He'd even been okay, after a moment of puzzlement, when he'd opened a drawer for a spoon and found his flatware organized into type.

He'd thought, glancing around, the kitchen was tidier—but since he wasn't sure exactly how he'd left it, that was just a maybe.

By the time he'd been ready to start work, she'd fed the dogs, taken them through a quick training session, showered, dressed and watered her flowerpots.

He heard the cars for her first session and had deliberately angled himself on the shop porch so he could check out who got out.

He'd modulated the volume on his music so he could hear her if she called out—and *that* was a sacrifice. But he remained undisturbed and alone throughout her morning classes.

Even Jaws had deserted him.

Which was fine—better than fine. He didn't have to worry about getting stray dog hair in the poly or ignoring sticks or balls dropped and that pleading look for playtime.

He'd gotten more templates cut out, several pieces glued up and clamped and now, at what the shop clock said was still just shy of noon, he was giving his sink another coat that brought out the rich grain of the wood, deepened the tones.

He caught the movement out of the corner of his eye and paused to watch her and the dog approach.

"Keep them back, will you? This is wet. One shake and they'll have hair all over it."

"Sit. Stay. I just thought I'd see if you want a sandwich or . . ."

She stopped, stared. And he had the great satisfaction of seeing her mouth literally drop open. "Oh my God. Is that the stump? That's my stump?"

"My stump."

"It's amazing!" Instinct had her fingers reaching out to touch. He slapped them back.

"Ouch. Okay, sorry, it's wet. It's upside down. That's how it works. Of course." Sliding her hands in her back pockets to keep them from the reach/slap, Fiona circled the sink.

"The roots form the base, holder, whatever it is for the bowl so it looks like something that grew in a magic forest. Who knew tree roots could look so amazing? Well, you did. But the bowl. What's the bowl?"

"Burl wood. I found it months back. It needed the right base."

"The color's so beautiful. Like glass syrup. It's just beautiful, Simon. I knew it would be interesting, but I didn't know it would be beautiful."

Gushy praise over his work invariably made him itchy. But oddly with her, with that dazzled delight on her face, he felt only satisfaction. "It's not finished."

"What will you do with it when it is?"

"I don't know." He shrugged because he'd caught himself wanting to give it to her. It suited her down to the ground. "Maybe sell it, maybe keep it."

"You'd feel magical every time you washed your hands. I'll never look at a tree stump the same way again. God, wait until people get a load of this!" She laughed over at him. "Anyway, I've got a couple hours until my first afternoon class. If you're hungry, I can make you a sandwich."

He considered it, and her. "Listen, I don't want you to wait on me because if you do I'll want you to wait on me."

She took a second. "You know, I understand that, oddly enough. Okay, how about a trade?"

"What kind of trade?"

"I'll make you a sandwich, and you make me some wood slat things. I wrote down the lengths I want."

She pulled out a list, handed it to him. He frowned down at it.

"What are they for?"

"For me." She smiled.

"Fine. You don't have a width."

"Oh. Hmm. Like this?" She held her thumb and forefinger together.

"About a quarter inch. What kind of wood?"

"The wood kind—whatever you've got around."

"Finish?"

"Jeez, it's a lot of decisions. Just that stuff, the clear stuff. I don't need fancy."

"Okay. I'll run them up when I'm done with this."

"Perfect."

It worked out okay, Simon thought later. He got a sandwich without having to make it, and they stayed out of each other's way during the work. Solemn oath or not, she cleaned up after him—subtly. He saw her sweeping off the porch, and when he realized he'd forgotten to restock his shop fridge and went in for a drink, the gleam inside his refrigerator all but blinded him.

He heard the suspicious sound of the washing machine running.

So fine, they'd trade again. He'd build her some new training equipment when he had the chance.

When he stepped back outside, he saw her pacing the back-yard with the phone to her ear. Something's up, he thought, and crossed to her.

"Yes, sure, that's fine. Thanks for calling. Really. Okay. Bye." She clicked off. "Agent Tawney. He was going to try to come out today, but they've got something else to do. I think they have a lead. He was careful not to say, but I think they have a lead. He sounded too calm."

"Too calm?"

"Deliberately calm." She rubbed the heel of her hand between her breasts as he knew she did when struggling for calm herself.

"As if he didn't want to show any sort of excitement or interest," she explained. "Maybe I'm projecting, but that's how it feels. And he didn't tell me anything because he didn't want me to react exactly the way I am."

She closed her eyes, took a breath. "It's a good thing I have a full afternoon. I can't obsess."

"Yes you can. It's what you do." Reaching behind her, he gave the tail of her braid a tug and tipped the topic to take her mind off her nerves. "Are you washing my clothes, Mom?"

"I'm washing mine." She spoke very primly. "There may be an item or two of yours in there, too, just to fill out the load."

He poked her in the shoulder. "Watch it."

She fisted her hands on her hips as he strode away. "I've already gone radical. I changed the sheets on the bed."

He shook his head, kept walking—and made her laugh.

TAWNEY AND HIS PARTNER took Eckle's last known residence first, a small three-level apartment building within walking distance of campus. Their knock on 202 went unanswered—except for the crack in the door across the hall.

"She's not home."

"She?"

"Just moved in a couple weeks ago." The crack widened. "Young thing, first apartment. What do you want?"

Both agents took out their ID. And the door opened all the way. "FBI!" Her tone might've been the same on *Santa Claus!*

Tawney gauged the woman as early seventies with bright bird eyes behind silver-framed glasses.

"I love those FBI shows on TV. I watch them all. Cop shows, too. Is that little girl up to something? You couldn't prove it by me. She's friendly and polite. Clean, even if she dresses like most of them do."

"We were actually hoping to speak with Francis Eckle."

"Oh, he left right after Christmas. His mother took sick. At least that's what he *said*. I bet he's in some sort of witness protection. Or he's a serial killer. He's just the type."

Mantz raised her eyebrows. "Ms. . . . ?"

"Hawbaker. Stella Hawbaker."

"Ms. Hawbaker, could we come in and speak with you?"

"I knew he was funny." She pointed a finger. "Come on in. You can have a seat," she told them and walked over to shut off the TV. "I don't drink coffee, but I've got some for when one of my kids comes by. That and soft drinks."

"We're fine," Tawney told her. "You said Mr. Eckle left after Christmas."

"That's right. I saw him hauling out suitcases, middle of the day when hardly anyone's around but me. So I said, 'Going on a trip?' And he smiled the way he does that doesn't look you in the eye and said he needed to go help tend his mother, because she'd had a fall and broke her hip. Now, he'd never once mentioned his mother in all the years he lived across the hall. Course he hardly mentioned anything. Kept to himself," she added with a knowing nod. "That's what they say about people who go out and chop people up with an ax. How he was quiet and kept to himself."

"Did he mention where his mother lived?"

"He said, because I asked him straight out, she lived in Columbus, Ohio. Now you tell me," she demanded, pointing her finger again, "if he had a mother out east, how come he never went to see her before this, or how come she didn't come out to see him?"

She tapped the finger to the side of her nose. "Smells funny. And it smells funnier seeing as he never came back. Left his furniture—or most of it from what I could tell when the landlord finally got around to clearing the place out. Not much else, and I know he had cases of books in there—and they didn't go with him. Must've sold them on eBay or something."

"You pay attention, Ms. Hawbaker."

She took Tawney's comment with a sly smile. "That I do, and since most people don't pay much to old ladies, I get away with it. In the past few months, I've seen him go out hauling shipping boxes or stacks of those mailing bags, and coming back empty. So I figure he sold those books, and whatever. Running money, I'll bet. Never paid the rent from January on either. And, 'cause I talked to the landlord about it, I heard he quit his job and cleaned out his bank account. Every penny."

Those bright eyes went shrewd. "I expect you know that."

"Did he have friends, visitors?" Mantz asked. "Any girlfriends?"

Ms. Hawbaker made a dismissive sound. "Never once saw him with a woman—or a man either if he went that way. Not natural. Polite, I'll give him that. Well spoken, but he wouldn't say boo unless you said it first. What'd he do?"

"We're just interested in talking to him."

Now she nodded sagely. "He's what you all call 'a person of interest,' and mostly that means he's a suspect in something bad. He drove one of those little compact cars with the hatchback. That's what he loaded up and drove off in that day. I'll tell you something else, 'cause I'm nosy and I poked in—and the landlord and I talked about it. There wasn't a single photograph in that place, or a letter or a postcard. He never planned to come back, that's what I say. And he didn't go to take care of his mother with any broken hip. If he had a mother, he probably killed her in her sleep."

Outside, Mantz wrenched open the car door. "Now that's an insightful woman."

"I don't think Eckle killed his mother in her sleep, since the records show his mother OD'd when he was eight."

"She pegged him, Tawney. If that's not our UNSUB, I'm a Vegas showgirl."

"You've got good legs, Erin, but I'm looking the same way. Let's track down the landlord, see what we can find out at the college, then I guess we're going back to prison."

TWENTY-FOUR

One day, Fiona thought, she hoped to feel something other than dread when she saw Davey's cruiser come down her drive.

"Uh-oh, we're in trouble now," one of her students joked, and she managed a stiff smile.

"Don't worry, I have connections. Jana, see the way Lotus is circling? What do you read?"

"Ah, she's in the scent pool?"

"Maybe. Maybe she's trying to get a new gauge, work it out. Maybe she's got a cross-scent and she's trying to home in. You need to work it out, too. Work with her. Help her focus. Watch her tail, her hackles, listen to her breathing. Every reaction means something, and hers might be different from, say, Mike's dog. I'll be right back."

She moved off, her heart banging against her ribs with every step as Davey walked to meet her.

"Sorry to interrupt your class—and it's not bad news. How much longer are you going to be?"

"Fifteen, twenty minutes. What—"

"It's not bad news," he repeated. "But I don't want to talk to you with the audience. I can wait. It's my timing that's off."

"No, we would've been done, but this group asked for an add-on cadaver-search cross-training. There're only four of them, and I had the time, so . . ." She shrugged.

"I'll let you get back to it. Okay if I watch?"

"Sure."

"Fee?" Jana signaled, then lifted her hands in frustration. "She's just not getting it, and she seems confused and, well, bored. We nail this at home. She loves this behavior, and we've got it down cold."

Focus, Fiona ordered herself. "You're not at home. Remember, a new place, new environment, new problems."

"Yeah, yeah, I know you've said that before, but if we make it, every time she goes out on a search it's a new place."

"Absolutely true. That's why the more experiences she has, the better. She learns every single time. She's bright and eager, but she's not pulling it in today—and she feels your frustration, too. First thing, relax."

Do the same yourself, Fiona thought and glanced back to where Davey stood watching.

"Go back to where she started to circle and lose interest. Refresh, reward, reestablish. If she just can't get it today, take her to the source, let her find it, reward."

They were a good team, Fiona thought as she hung back. But the human partner tended to want quick results. Still, she put in the time and energy, had a strong relationship with her dog.

She turned to watch Mike and his Australian shepherd mix celebrate the find. The dog happily accepted the food reward and praise before Mike pulled on his plastic gloves and retrieved the cylinder containing human bone fragments.

Well done, she thought. And her third student held both his nose and his tail in the air, which told her he should find his source soon.

One day, she thought, one or all of them might go out on a call, search woods, hills, fields, city streets, and find human remains. And finding them would help give closure to family, help police find answers.

Bodies, she thought, like that of Annette Kellworth. Cruelly posed under a couple feet of dirt, left like a broken toy while the one responsible hunted something new.

Would there be another? Closer yet? Would her own unit be called in to search? She wondered if she could do it, if she could take one of her precious dogs and search for a body that could have been her own.

That would be hers if a man she didn't even know had his way.

"She got it!" Jana called out as she bent to hug her Lotus. "She did it!"

"Terrific."

Not bad news, she reminded herself as she stored her training tools. She got a Coke out of the refrigerator for both of them.

"Okay," she said, "Let's have it."

"The feds have a lead. They think it's a strong one."

"A lead." Now her knees could tremble. She braced a hand on a counter stool to stay on her feet. "What kind of lead?"

"They're looking for a specific individual, one who had contact with Perry inside the prison. An outside instructor. An English teacher from College Place."

"Looking for?"

"Yeah. He quit his job, packed up some of his things and took off between Christmas and New Year's. Cleaned out his bank account, left his furniture, defaulted on his rent. He fits the profile—they say. The thing is, he hasn't had contact—that they can verify—with Perry in nearly a year. That's a long time."

"He's patient. Perry. He's patient."

"The feds are putting pressure on Perry right now. Trying to find out how much he knows. And they're digging into this guy's background. What we got from them is he's a loner. No relationships, no family. His mother was a junkie, so he was in the system even before she OD'd, when he was eight."

"Mother issues," she murmured as hope and fear bubbled up in a messy stew. "Like Perry."

"They've got that in common." Davey took a fax out of his pocket, unfolded it. "Does he look familiar?"

She studied the facsimile photo, the ordinary face, the trim, professorial beard, the ever-so-slightly-shaggy hair. "No. No, I don't know him. I don't know him. Is this really him?"

"He's who they're looking for. They're not calling him a suspect. They're careful not to. But I'm going to tell you, Fee, they believe this is the guy, and they're all over it." He gave her shoulder a quick rub. "I want you to know they're all over it."

"Who is he?"

"Francis Eckle. Francis Xavier Eckle. His age, height, weight, coloring are all listed on the fax. I want you to keep this picture, Fee. He may have changed his appearance. Cut the beard, dyed his hair. So I want you to keep this, and if you see anybody who looks anything like this guy, you don't hesitate. You call."

"Don't worry, I will." Even now his face was burned into her mind. "You said he was a teacher."

"Yeah. His record's clear. He had a rough childhood, but he didn't make any waves—not on record, anyway. They'll be talking to his foster families, his caseworkers. They've already started that, and interviewing his coworkers, supervisors, neighbors. So far, there's nothing in his background that you'd look twice at, but—"

"People can be trained. Just like dogs. They can learn, good behavior or bad. It just depends on the motivation and methods."

"They're going to get him, Fee." Davey put his hands on her shoulders, gave them a squeeze when their eyes met. "You believe that."

Because she needed to believe it, she rushed over to Simon's shop.

He stood at the lathe, music blaring, tool humming as he hollowed and smoothed the pale wood in his hands.

A bowl, she realized, one of those lovely ones he made with a sheen and texture like silk and a thickness that seemed hardly more than tissue.

She watched how he turned and angled, tried to figure out the method to help keep herself still.

He switched off the machine. "I know you're over there, breathing my air."

"Sorry. Why don't you have any of those? You need one about twice that size for your kitchen counter, for seasonal fruit."

He'd pulled off his ear protectors and goggles and simply stood. "Is that what you came in here to tell me?" And looked down as Jaws dropped a scrap of wood at his feet. "See what you started?"

"I'll take them out for a game before my next class. Simon." She held up the fax.

His body language changed. Alerted, she thought. "Do they have him?"

She shook her head. "But they're looking, and they— Davey said—they think . . . I have to sit down."

"Go outside, in the air."

"I can't feel my legs." With a half laugh, she stumbled out, dropped down onto the shop porch.

Seconds later he came out with a bottle of water. "Let me have that." He shoved the water at her, snatched the fax. "Who is this motherfucker?"

"Nobody. Mr. Average Joe, except not really. Where's the rope! Go get the rope!" All four dogs stopped poking with noses and bodies and shot off. "That'll take a few minutes. Davey came to tell me what the FBI told them. His name's Francis Xavier Eckle," she began.

He continued to study the photo as he listened. When the dogs came back—the crafty Newman the winner—Simon took the rope. "Go play," he ordered and heaved it hard and long.

"Don't they check people out before they let them work at a prison?"

"Yes, of course. I guess," she added after a moment. "The point is, there wasn't anything there. Not that they've found so far. But he had contact with Perry, and now he's changed his behavior. Drastically. They probably know more now. More than they told the sheriff's office, or more than Davey could tell me. I'm looking at this because Tawney cleared it. Because he wants me to look at it."

"Teaching at a small college," Simon speculated. "Looking at long-legged coeds all day who probably don't look back. It's still a big leap from ordinary to Perry copycat."

"Not so big if the predilection was there all along, if the drive was in place but he never knew how to engage it. Or didn't have the nerve."

She'd trained dogs like that, hadn't she? Recognizing or finding hidden potentials, exploiting suppressed drives, or channeling overt ones, systematically altering learned behavior.

"You talked about the importance of motivation before," she pointed out. "And you were right. It's possible Perry found the right motivation, the right . . . game, the right reward."

"Trained his replacement."

"He taught there four times," she added, "and Perry signed up for all the classes. He's a chameleon. Perry. He acclimates. He's acclimating in prison, doing his time, keeping his head down. Cooperating. So he becomes, in a way, ordinary again."

"And they don't pay as much attention?" Simon shrugged. "Maybe."

"He's a student of observation. It's how he picked his victims, and how he blended so well for so long. He probably stalked and discarded dozens of women before the ones he abducted. Watching them, judging their behavior, their personality type."

"Moving on if they didn't fit his needs well enough."

"That, and calculating the risk factors. Maybe this one's too passive, and not enough of a challenge, or this one's too chaotic and difficult to pin down."

She rubbed her hand between her breasts, on her thigh—couldn't keep it still. "He knows what to look for in people. It's how he killed so many, how he traveled and engaged others so easily. I understand that. I can usually tell if a dog will respond to advanced training, if the dog and the handler will forge a team. Or if they're better off strictly as the family pet. You can see the potential if you know where and how to look—and you can begin molding that potential. Perry knows where and how to look."

Maybe she just needed to believe it, Simon thought, but she was damn convincing. "So you think Perry saw, we'll say, potential, in this guy?"

"It could be it. It could be this Eckle approached Perry. Nobody's really above flattery when it comes to their work. And killing was Perry's work. But if either of those happened, if these two made that connection, Perry would know how to begin the mold. And, Simon, I think—if this is how it went— that the payment for that training, that molding, is me."

She looked back at the photo. "He'd kill me to repay Perry for recognizing and grooming his potential."

Perry's dog, Simon concluded, who'd want to please his handler. "Perry's never going to collect on that IOU."

"He should've come for me first. They both made a mistake there. I was relaxed. I felt safe, and would've been an easier target at that point. Instead, they wanted me to live with the fear. That was stupid."

He saw it happen, saw the nerves funnel into a steady anger and steely confidence.

"I've lived with fear before, and I'm older and smarter and stronger than I was then. Knowing I'm not invincible and that terrible things happen, that's an advantage. And I have you. I have them."

She looked over as the dogs played a kind of tag-team tug-of-war with the battered rope.

"You're older and smarter and stronger—good for you. But if he tries to put a hand on you, I'll break him to pieces." When she turned her head and stared, he met her eyes with a blink. "I don't say what I don't mean."

"No, I know you don't. It's a reassuring, if occasionally frustrating, behavior. It helps hearing you say it, and knowing you mean it. And I'm really hoping you don't have to follow through. They have his face now, and his name. I'm going to believe that before much longer, they'll have him."

She let out a breath, tipped her head to his shoulder for a

moment. "I have to get ready for my next session. Actually, you might want to keep Jaws in the shop with you for the next hour or so."

"Because?"

"He's not as mature or calm as my boys, and I'm doing a one-on-one behavioral correction session with a rottweiler with aggression issues."

"A rottweiler with aggression issues? Where's your body armor?"

"He's coming along. We've had a couple sessions already, and he's making good progress. Normally I'd go to the source on this sort of thing, but under the circumstances, I asked the client to bring Hulk here."

"Hulk. Perfect. Are you carrying your gun?"

"Stop it. This is what I do," she reminded him. "Or one of the things I do."

"If you get bit, it's going to piss me off. Hang on a minute."

He got up, walked inside. She considered if they kept going down the path they were on now, he'd probably get pissed eventually. She'd rarely been nipped, but it did happen once in a while.

He came out with a box. "Those slats you wanted."

"Oh, great. Thanks."

SHE CAME THROUGH the session unscathed and decided to busy herself in the kitchen for the next hour. And since she had a chunk of time on her hands and was—more or less—confined to quarters, she thought she might make use of what could very loosely be termed Simon's home gym once she'd finished up her kitchen project.

Dogs weren't the only ones who needed to keep up with their training. Pleased with her first project, she emptied one of the kitchen drawers, scrubbed it, measured and cut the liner she'd asked Sylvia to pick up for her. Using the pattern she'd outlined in her head, she slid in the wood dividers—and deemed them perfect.

She'd nearly completed the third drawer when the phone rang. Her mind on organization, she answered it without thinking.

"Hello."

"Oh, I must have the wrong . . . I'm looking for Simon."

Fiona laid spatulas, slotted spoons, serving forks in their allotted space. "He's here, but he's out in the shop. I can go get him for you."

"No, no, that's fine. He's probably got the music blasting and machines running. That's why he didn't answer his cell. Who's this?"

"Ah, Fiona. Who's this?"

"Julie, Julie Doyle. I'm Simon's mother."

"Mrs. Doyle." Wincing a little, Fiona closed the drawer. "I know Simon would want to talk to you. It'll just take me a minute to—"

"I'd much rather talk to you—if you're the Fiona Simon's told me about."

"He . . . really?"

"He may not say much, but I have years of experience prying things out of him. You're a dog trainer."

"Yes."

"And how's that puppy doing?"

"Jaws is great. I hope your years of experience helped you pry out of Simon that he's madly in love with that dog. They're a great team."

"You do Search and Rescue. Simon mentioned to his brother you're training the pup for that."

"He mentioned to his brother?"

"Oh, we e-mail a lot, all of us. But I need a phone conversation at least once a week. The better to pry, plus I'm angling for him to come home for a visit."

"He should." Guilt stewed in her belly. "Of course he should."

"And he will when everything's back to normal. I know you're in a hard situation. How are you doing?"

"Mrs. Doyle—"

"Julie, and why would you want to talk about all of that

with a perfect stranger? Just tell me, are you staying with Simon now, at his place?"

"Yes. He's . . . he's been wonderful. Generous, supportive, understanding. Patient."

"I think I must have the wrong number after all."

Fiona laughed and leaned back on the counter. "He talks about you. Just little things he says once in a while. He's madly in love with you, too."

"The madly's often the key word in the Doyle family."

It was easy to chat. Relaxed, Fiona opened the drawer again and filled it systematically as she and Julie Doyle got acquainted.

When the door opened, she glanced over her shoulder. "Well, here's Simon now, so I'll turn you over. It was really nice talking to you."

"We'll do it again, soon."

"Your mom," Fiona mouthed and offered the phone.

"Hey." He stared at the open drawer, shook his head.

"I've already spent most of the time I have talking to the delightful Fiona. I don't have much left for you."

"You should've called my cell. Some of us work for a living."

"I did call your cell."

"Well, I was working for a living." He opened the fridge, pulled out a Coke. "Everything good?"

"Everything's very good. Simon, you're living with a woman."

"You're not going to send a priest, are you?"

Her laugh rolled through the earpiece. "On the contrary, I'm pleased with this new step."

"It's just a thing because of that other business."

"She thinks you're wonderful, generous, supportive and patient." Julie waited a beat. "Yes, I was speechless, too. Do you know what I see, Simon, with my mother's super-vision?"

"What?"

"I see some rough edges smoothing out."

"You're asking for it, Julie Lynne."

"When I ask for it, I get it. We're good at that, aren't we?"

Amused, he took a swig of Coke. "I guess we are."

"I like the tone of your voice when you talk about her. And that's all I'm saying about it. For now."

"Good."

"I'll give you good, good and proper next time I see you. Do something for me, Simon."

"Maybe."

"Be careful. You're the only second son I have. Take care of your Fiona, but be careful."

"I can do that. Don't worry, Ma. Please."

"Now that's a useless request for a mother. I have to go. I have more important things to do than talk to you."

"Same goes."

"You were always a difficult child. I love you."

"I love you, too. Same to Dad. Bye." He hung up, took another swig of Coke. "You're organizing my kitchen drawers."

"Yes. You're free to disorganize them at your whim and will. But doing this keeps me sane. And you made the clever dividers."

"Uh-huh."

"I enjoyed talking to your mother. I like the way you sound when you talk to her."

Brow creasing, he lowered the bottle. "What is this?"

"What's what?"

"Nothing. Never mind. Turn around."

"Why?"

"I want to see if the rottweiler bit you in the ass."

"He did not bite me in the ass or anywhere else."

"I'll check it out later." He pulled open a drawer at random. "Jesus, Fiona, you lined them."

"I'm so ashamed."

"Let me point out, neither of us actually cooks, so what's the point of having lined, divided, organized kitchen drawers?"

"To be able to find things, whether or not you use them. And what's the point of having all these things in the first place if you don't cook?"

"I wouldn't have all this junk if my mother didn't . . . Never mind that either."

"I can jumble everything up again if it makes you feel better."

"I'm thinking about it."

And she grinned at him, quick and fun. "I'm going to do the cabinets, too. You can just consider it my little hobby."

"That doesn't mean I'm going to put things back where you think they belong."

"See, look how well we understand each other."

"You're sneaky, and don't think I don't know it. I grew up with sneaky."

"I got that impression."

"That's the problem. You're not like her, but you are."

"How about if I tell you I also understand you're not really stewing about me organizing the kitchen drawers, but trying to gauge whether this is a prelude to me trying to organize your life."

"Okay."

"And in the spirit of why fuck around with it, I'll tell you straight I can't promise I won't try, at least in some areas, to do just that. I like to think I know when to back off, give up or adjust, but that doesn't mean I won't irritate you with my deadly sense of order. At the same time"—she held up a finger before he could interrupt—"I think I get that at least part of your creativity feeds on *dis*order. I don't understand it, but I get it. Which doesn't mean that your apparently innate messiness won't irritate me occasionally."

He felt, tidily, put in his place. "I guess that's supposed to be logical."

"It is logical. And I'll tell you something else. The occasional irritation works well for me as a distraction. But then it just fades. I don't hold irritable well for long under most circumstances. But under the current? There's just too much that's bigger to worry about than whether or not you put the corkscrew back in the right drawer or kick your dirty socks under the bed."

"I can't argue with that."

"Good. I want to get in a workout. Is it okay if I use your stuff?"

"You don't have to ask." Frustrated, he stuffed his hands in his pockets. "Don't ask me things like that."

"I don't know where your boundaries are yet, Simon, so I have to ask or . . ." She closed the drawer he'd neglected to. "I'll cross over them." Then she stepped toward him, cupped his face. "I don't mind asking, and I can handle no."

When she walked out, he stayed where he was, hands in pockets, frowning after her.

TWENTY-FIVE

He couldn't figure out if they were fighting. Nothing ever seemed to fall into the nice clear areas of black or white with Fiona—and that drove him a little bit crazy. Because it fascinated him every bit as much as it frustrated him.

If he knew she was pissed and in fighting mode, he could gear up for it, wade into it or ignore it. But the uncertainty kept him off balance.

"That's her point, isn't it?" He wandered outside with the dogs. "I'm thinking about it, and her, because I don't know. It's fucking devious."

He frowned at the back of his house. He could pick out the windows she'd washed. She hadn't gotten to them all, he thought, but she would. Oh, yes, she would. Where the hell did she find the time? Did she get up in the middle of the damn night with a bottle of freaking Windex?

Now, with the way the sun glinted off clean glass, he couldn't ignore the dull, weathered paint on the window trim. And just when was *he* supposed to find the time to paint the freaking window trim, which means painting the door trim?

And once he painted the trim, he knew damn well he'd have to paint the goddamn porches or they'd look like crap.

"It was fine before she cleaned the damn windows, and I'd have gotten to it sooner or later. Go up."

At the command, Jaws cheerfully climbed the ladder of the slide and trotted down again with a hand signal. Simon gave the dog a treat, then repeated the skill a couple of times before moving to the teeter-totter.

The other dogs climbed, tunneled, jumped and navigated on their own, using the training equipment as enthusiastically as kids use a playground in the park.

Simon glanced over as Bogart barked, then watched as the Lab picked his way agilely over a length of board no wider than a gymnast's balance beam.

"Show-off. You can do that." Simon gave Jaws a pat on the head. "Go on up there and do that. What are you, a pussy?" He led the dog over, surveyed the beam. "It's not that high. You can get up there." Simon patted the beam. "Go up!"

Jaws gathered himself, then plopped his ass down. He gave the beam and Simon a look that clearly said, *What the fuck?*

"Don't embarrass me in front of these guys. I'm spotting you, aren't I? Up!"

Jaws angled his head, then his ears pricked when Simon took out a treat and set it on the beam.

"You want it? Come get it. Up!"

Jaws made the jump, scrabbled for purchase, then dropped off the other side.

"He meant to do that." Simon gave the other dogs a cool stare, then leaned down close to Jaws. "You meant to do that. That's your story. Let's try it again."

It took a few attempts, and a human demonstration Simon was grateful no one could see, but Jaws finally managed a landing.

"All right, fucking A. Now you've got to walk. Let's walk." He took out another treat, held it just out of reach until Jaws picked his way to the end of the beam. "Yeah, look at you. Circus Dog."

Ridiculously pleased, he got down to give Jaws a full-body

rub. "Let's do it again. I'd give that one an eight-point-five. We're going for the perfect ten."

He spent the next ten minutes working on the skill, perfecting it before indulging in a wrestling contest in which he was outnumbered four to one. "She's not the only one who can train. We got that one down, didn't we? We— Well, *shit*."

He shoved to his feet as it hit him. He was playing with dogs, working with dogs. He carried dog cookies in his pocket as habitually as loose change and his Leatherman. He was thinking about what color to paint his exterior trim and porches.

He'd made organizers for his kitchen drawers.

"This," he said with feeling, "is nuts."

He strode to the house. Boundaries? She didn't know where his boundaries were? Well, she was about to find out.

He wasn't going to be maneuvered and manipulated, and *trained* to be something he wasn't.

There, he thought, was the black and the white.

He could hear her, breathing hard, as he stomped up the steps. Good, he thought, maybe the workout had worn her out and she wouldn't have enough breath to argue her way out of it.

Then he stepped into the doorway, and just stood.

He didn't notice the clean floor or windows, or that the sweaty shirt he'd peeled off when he'd done some lifting the day before wasn't on the floor where he'd tossed it.

How could he? All he could see was her.

She executed some sort of martial arts routine and looked as if she could kick some serious ass. Lust added the final grip to interest and admiration to choke out temper.

Sweat dampened her face and the skinny tank she'd changed into. Those long legs, highlighted in a pair of snug black shorts, kicked, set, spun while the wiry muscles in her arms rippled.

He'd be drooling in a minute, he thought, as she balanced on one leg, kicked, then landed on the other in a graceful blur.

He must've made some sound because she pivoted, set into a fighting stance—eyes cold and fierce. Just as quickly, she relaxed and laughed.

"Didn't see you there." She sucked in air. "Scared me."

She hadn't looked scared, he thought. "What was that? Tae kwon do?"

She shook her head, gulped from the bottle of water she'd set on the weight bench. "Tai chi—mostly."

"I've seen people doing tai chi. It's like sissy New Age in slow motion."

"First, it's really old age, and the slow moves are about control, practice and form." She crooked a finger. "It's organic," she said, "and about centering your power."

"I'm still hearing sissy New Age, and that's not what I was looking at a minute ago."

"There's a reason many of the moves have pretty names that come from nature. Like Push the Wave."

She demonstrated, slowly, again gracefully pushing her hands out, palms toward him, then drawing them back, palms up. "But if I intensify that same move for defense, it's—"

She shoved him back, knocking him off balance, then pulled him in and past her. "See?"

"I wasn't ready."

Grinning, she spread her legs, bent her knees and gave him a come-ahead gesture.

"Okay, you've seen *The Matrix*," he said, and made her laugh.

"You're stronger than I am, bigger, taller, longer reach. You may be faster, but we haven't tested that yet. If I have to defend myself, I need to be able to center my power and use yours. I used to practice every day, in my obsessive way. Tai chi, power yoga, boxing—"

Interest piqued. "Boxing?"

"Yeah." She put up her dukes. "Want to go a couple rounds?"

"Maybe later."

"I did kickboxing, resistance training, hours of Pilates and whatever else you can think of every week. It made me feel capable and secure. Proactive, I guess. Then I eased off, and I got rusty. I stopped pushing myself until . . . well, until."

"You didn't look rusty."

"Muscle memory. It comes back. And the ever-popular motivation."

"Show me. No, wait. This isn't why I came in here. You did it again."

"I did?"

"Distracted me. Sweaty, sexy body. You don't need tai chi to throw a man off balance."

"Wow." She gave a little shoulder wiggle. "Now I do feel powerful."

"It's that." He pointed.

"It's . . . the window?"

"It's the window. Why did you wash the window?"

"Because I like clean windows. I like to look outside, and it's more pleasant to do that when I'm not looking through a film of dust."

"That's only part of it."

"What's the other part?"

"The other part is getting me to notice the ones you haven't gotten around to washing yet so I feel guilty. And so I see that the trim needs painting."

She picked up her water bottle, uncapped it. "That's a lot of motivation behind some Windex and a rag."

"And there's this." He dug in his pocket, pulled out a handful of dog treats.

"Oh, thanks, but I'm trying to cut down."

"Funny. I put these damn things in my pocket every day. I don't even think about it, I just do it. I just spent a good half hour, maybe more, out there working with the dogs."

All patient attention, she sipped her water. "Because I washed the window?"

"No, but it's the same thing. It's the same thing as the house smelling like a lemon drop or me thinking I should probably pick you up some flowers the next time I'm in the village."

"Oh, Simon."

"Shut up. And it doesn't matter a damn that we've got bigger things to worry about because basic is basic. So . . ."

He strode to the window, slapped the palm of his hand against the sparkling glass. "Leave it," he ordered, pointing at the smudged print he left behind.

"Okay. Why?"

"I don't know why. I don't have to know why, but if I want it gone, I'll wash it off. You leave it alone."

There, he thought. Now they'd get down to it.

She started to laugh, a full-out, up-from-the-gut roll that left her breathless again. She had to bend over, brace her hands on her thighs.

"Listen, it may sound stupid, but—"

Still bent over, she waved him off. "Not entirely, but enough. God, God! I've been up here working my ass off to make myself feel strong, capable of dealing with whatever comes at me so I'm not hiding under the bed trembling, and you accomplish the same thing in under five minutes."

"What the hell are you talking about?"

"You make me feel strong, capable, even ingenious because you just see me that way. I haven't got you wrapped around my finger, Simon—far from it. And the fact is, I wouldn't want you there. But because there's this little part of you that worries I do, or I could, I feel I can take on anything that comes. Anything at all. I feel strong and sexy and capable and ingenious." She flexed her left biceps. "It's heady. I'm drunk on it."

"Well, that's just great."

"And you know what else? That you would do that—that silly thing to make a point." She gestured toward the window. "That you could do that without feeling foolish, but feel just a little foolish because you've spent time out there playing with the dogs? Simon, it just disarms me."

"For God's sake."

"It disarms me and delights me. So I'm disarmed, delighted, strong and sexy and capable all at the same time. And no one has ever made me feel the way you do. No one. That." She pointed to the window again, and let out a laugh that sounded as baffled as he felt. "That right there is why, as ridiculous, as incomprehensible as it is, it's why I'm in love with you.

"Simon." She walked to him, linked her arms around his neck. "Isn't that a kick in the ass?" She pressed her lips to his in a hard, noisy kiss. "So, handprint stays. In fact, I think I'll draw a heart around it first chance. Meanwhile, I can show you some basic moves before I dive into the shower and a glass of wine. Unless you want to yell at me for a while."

"That's it," he muttered, and, grabbing her arm, pulled her across the room.

"That's what? Are you throwing me out of the house?"

"Don't tempt me. I'm taking you to bed. I ought to get something out of this."

"Gosh, what a charming offer, but I really need that shower, so—"

"I want you sweaty." He used the momentum, gave her arm a quick whip and more or less slingshot her onto the bed. "I'll show you some moves."

"I think you just did." She pushed herself up, cocked her head. "Maybe I'm not in the mood." And her breath caught when he yanked the damp shirt over her head, tossed it. "Or—"

"You can pick that up later." He cupped her breasts, rubbed her nipples with calloused thumbs. "You made the bed."

"Yes, I did."

"A lot of good it did you." When she shivered, he pushed her onto her back.

"And you're going to show me the error of my ways?"

"Damn right." He hooked his fingers in the waistband of her gym shorts, pulled.

Smiling, she trailed a fingertip from her collarbone to her belly, and back again. "Then come and get me."

He stripped, watching her watching him.

"I should just keep you naked," he considered as he straddled her. "I know what to do with you when you're naked."

"I like what you do with me when I'm naked."

"Then you're going to love this."

He took her avid, inviting lips with his, roughening the kiss even as he deepened it. He used his weight to pin her as her heart began to gallop, used his hands to exploit her so that hot, damp skin trembled.

Strong and capable she was, down to the marrow, he

thought. It was part of what made her irresistible. But now, just now, he wanted her weak, he wanted her helpless. For him, only for him.

He used his tongue, his fingertips, in long, slow journeys that made her sigh as he felt her body relax into pleasure.

Then his teeth so her pulses leaped.

When his mouth came back to hers, she sighed again, lifting her hands to his face in the way that always disarmed him, then sweeping her fingers through his hair.

Against his mouth her breath quickened when he trailed a finger up her inner thigh, retreated, stroked slowly back to brush, only to brush, the heat.

When she moaned his name, arched her hips, he retreated again.

She ached. Her body quivered, rising toward that lovely release, only to have it denied. Even as she said his name again, he feathered his fingers over her, made her writhe. And his mouth began the same torturous assault on her breasts.

He gave, gave, took her to within a breath of peak. Then eased away to leave her churning.

"I want you. Simon. Please."

Still he played her until her gasps mixed with moans, until her hands pulled at the spread she'd so neatly smoothed that morning.

He drove into her, hard, fast, a shock to her tormented system. The orgasm tore through her, center to throat. She heard her own scream, heard it, felt it deepen into a shuddering moan of release. Her body roared through it, bucking beneath his, nails digging in until her hands simply slid bonelessly to the bed.

He dragged her up so her head fell against his shoulder.

"Put your legs around me."

"I—"

"I want you around me." His teeth scraped over her throat, her shoulders. "It's all I can think about. You around me."

She gave him what he wanted, held on through the storm. Rode it up again, yet again, until there was nothing left.

She all but melted onto the bed, might have lain there weak

as water till morning. But he pulled her over, anchored her so she sprawled over him with her head on his chest over his raging heart.

She dozed off and the next thing she knew she was blinking awake and staring at four furry faces pressed to the deck door. Simon's chest rose and fell steadily under her head, but his fingers played with her hair, sliding through it, twining it, sliding. Everything about the moment made her smile.

"The dogs want in," she murmured.

"Yeah, well, they can wait a minute."

"I'll get them." But she didn't move. "I'm starving. I guess working out followed by working out hones the appetite."

She snuggled in. One more minute, she told herself. Then she'd let the sad-eyed dogs in, grab that shower, and they'd figure out what to toss together for dinner.

She started to stretch, then her gaze landed on the bedside clock.

"What! Is that clock right?"

"I don't know. Who cares?"

"But . . . Did I fall asleep? For an *hour*? That's like a nap."

"Fee, that *is* a nap."

"But I never take naps."

"Welcome to my world."

"Well, God." She shoved up, pushed her hands through her hair. Since it was the closest to hand, she grabbed his T-shirt, dragged it on.

It just covered her ass, he noted. Too bad.

She opened the door, and the room was immediately filled with dogs.

"Sorry, boys. Go on and talk to Simon. I need a shower."

She dashed into the bathroom. And all four dogs lined up on the side of the bed, tails whipping, eyes staring, noses twitching.

"Yeah, that's right. That's right. I had sex with her. A lot of sex. What's it to you? Only one of you has balls, and since everybody's haranguing me, he's not going to have them much longer."

He recognized the gleam in Jaws's eyes. "Don't even think

about jumping up here," Simon warned, but cupped a hand around his own balls, just in case. "Why don't you go get me a beer? Now that would be a useful behavior."

Since none of them seemed inclined, he got up to get one for himself.

Once he got downstairs, he switched it to wine. She'd said she wanted wine, he remembered. He might as well go that route, too. He poured two glasses and sipped the first as he opened the refrigerator to study the contents.

They were going to starve to death, he decided, if one of them didn't think about hitting the grocery store. He poked into the freezer and decided one of her frozen girl meals was better than starvation.

Marginally.

He picked up her wine and, with the dogs trailing him—again—started back for the stairs.

Beside him, Newman let out a quiet *woof* seconds before he saw the woman walk onto his front porch.

She beamed a smile through the screen door. "Well, hello."

Simon took a moment to think she was lucky he'd bothered to pull on his boxers. "Something I can do for you?"

"I hope so. I'd love to talk to you for a few minutes. I'm Kati Starr, with *U.S. Report*. Isn't that Fiona Bristow's car—and her dogs, right?"

Slick looks, slick manner, he thought.

"Here's what I'm going to do for you. I'm going to tell you, once, to turn around, get back in your own car. Go away. Stay away."

"Mr. Doyle, I'm just doing my job, and trying to do it as thoroughly and accurately as I can. My information is there might be a break in the investigation. As I've been told Ms. Bristow's now living with you, I'd hoped to be able to get her thoughts on this potential break. I admire your work," she added. "I'd love to do a feature on you sometime. How long have you and Ms. Bristow been involved?"

Simon closed the door in her face, flipped the lock.

He figured he'd give her three minutes to get the hell off

his property before he called the sheriff and had the satisfaction of pressing charges for trespassing.

But when he got back upstairs, Fiona, wet hair slicked back, sat on the side of the bed.

"I saw her through the window, so you don't have to wonder if you should tell me or not."

"Okay." He passed her the wine.

"I was going to say I'm sorry she came here, started on you, but it's just not my fault."

"No, it's not your fault. She said she had information that there'd been a break in the case. I don't know if she was just fishing or if she's got a source leaking her information."

Fiona let out a muttered oath. "I guess we'd better tell Agent Tawney, just in case. What did you say to her?"

"I told her to go away, and when she didn't, I just closed the door."

"Smarter than I was."

"Well, I considered giving her a quote, but I thought 'Fuck you, bitch' didn't have any real creative zing. And it was all I could think of. If you're going into brood mode, it's going to piss me off."

"I'm not going into brood mode. I'm going into neener-neener mode by calling the FBI and the sheriff's office and tattling on her. And I'm asking for a restraining order after all, just for the fun of it."

He reached out, smoothed a hand over her hair. "I like that mode better."

"Me too. Then what do you say we flip to see who cooks dinner?"

"Buzzing up sissy frozen dinners isn't worthy of a flip."

"I was thinking of the steaks we have in the meat drawer of the fridge."

"We have steaks?" The day got brighter. "We have a meat drawer?"

She smiled and got to her feet. "Yes, we do."

"Okay, the meat drawer probably came with the fridge. How did we get steaks? Do you have a magic cow somewhere?"

"No, I have a fairy stepmother, who delivers. I asked Syl if she'd pick us up a couple steaks, Idahos, some staples I needed. She dropped them off today, including a bunch of fresh vegetables and fruit because she thinks we need those, too. That's why there are fresh vegetables in the crisper. And yes, we have a crisper."

He decided there was no point in telling her he'd looked in the fridge and seen none of those things. There'd just be some variation of his mother's standard crack about Male Refrigerator Blindness Syndrome.

"You make the calls. I'll start the grill."

"Works for me. You do know you're only wearing your underwear."

"I'll put on the pants you've already picked up and folded on the bed you've already made. But that means if we have to have any of those vegetables, you're dealing with them. I'll take the steaks."

"That's a fair trade. I'll make the calls downstairs."

When she went down, he put on the neatly folded work pants she'd laid on the bed.

Before he went downstairs, he stepped into his makeshift gym.

Okay, maybe, like the rest of the house, the room smelled like a lemon drop. But his handprint was still on the window.

It was, he supposed, a strange kind of compromise.

He started down, cursed, walked back up and yanked open a drawer. He pulled on a fresh shirt.

She'd gotten the steaks, he reminded himself.

Steaks, fresh shirt. It was just another kind of compromise.

TWENTY-SIX

Tawney studied Perry on the monitor. He sat at the steel table, shackled, his eyes closed, the smallest of smiles on his face—as a man might when listening to pleasant music.

His prison-pale face, doughier than it had been seven years before, expressed quiet contemplation. Lines carved brackets around his mouth, more spiderwebbed from the corners of his eyes, only enhancing the appearance of an ordinary, harmless man who'd use his senior discount for the Early Bird Special at his local Denny's.

The indulgent uncle, the quiet next-door neighbor who tended his roses and clipped his lawn meticulously. The simple Everyman people passed on the street without a second glance or particular interest.

"He used that the way Bundy used his charming looks and fake arm cast," Tawney murmured.

"Used what?"

"His I'm-somebody's-grandfather mask. He's still using it."

"Maybe. But he's talking to us without his lawyer, and that has to be another device." Mantz shook her head. "What's he up to? What's he thinking? Nobody knows him better than you, Tawney."

"Nobody knows him."

He kept his eyes on Perry's face and thought, He knows we're watching him. He's enjoying it.

"He's good at making you think you do, saying what you want to hear, or expect to hear. It's the layers that trip you up with him. The ones he has already, the ones he adds on to suit the circumstance. You've read the files, Erin. You know it was mostly just his bad luck and the heroism of a canine cop that we caught him."

"You don't give yourself or the investigative team enough credit. You'd have bagged him."

"He stayed in the wind nearly a year, a year after we had his face, his name. Fiona gave him to us, and still, it took months and the murder of a police officer before we took him down."

And for that he'd never completely forgive himself.

"Look at him," Tawney added. "A paunchy man past middle age, chained, caged, and still he finds a way. He found Eckle and lit the fuse."

"You're not getting enough sleep."

"I bet that bastard's sleeping like a baby. Every night, with that goddamn smile on his face just like he has on now. He's got an agenda. He's always got an agenda, a purpose to everything he does. He doesn't need the lawyer to talk to us because he's only going to tell us what he's already decided to tell us."

"He doesn't know we've got a line on Eckle."

"I wonder."

"How could he? And telling him what *we* want to tell him is our leverage. Eckle's screwing up the plan, and that's going to piss him off."

"Well. Let's find out."

When they entered, Tawney nodded to the guard on the door. Perry remained still, eyes closed, the little smile in place as Tawney read the names, date and time into the record. "You've waived your right to counsel during this interview?"

Perry opened his eyes. "Hello, Agent Tawney. Yes, no need for lawyers between old acquaintances. Agent Mantz, you're looking lovely today. It's so nice to have visitors to break up the monotony of the day. We're chatting so often these days. I look forward to it."

"Is that what this is about?" Tawney demanded. "The attention, the break in the monotony?"

"It's certainly a nice benefit. How goes the hunt? I'm hungry for news. The powers that be have narrowed my access to the outside. Understandable, of course, but unfortunate."

"You get your 'news,' Perry. I don't doubt your abilities."

Perry folded his hands, leaned forward a little. "I'll say that before my current situation, I enjoyed the article that bright young woman wrote. Kati Starr? I suspect that's a *nom de plume*, or a clever gift from fate. Either way, I enjoyed her slant, we'll say, and was delighted to catch up a little with Fiona. You'll have to tell her I'm thinking about her."

"I bet you are. It's hard to forget a woman who kicked your ass."

"My face, actually."

"She'll do the same to your apprentice," Mantz put in. "If he's stupid enough to try for her."

"You give me too much credit." Perry's chains rattled as he waved the comment away. "I'm hardly in any position to train anyone, even if I were inclined. Which I'm not. We've talked about this before, and as I said then, you can clearly see from my record in this institution, I've accepted the punishment the courts, and society, meted out. I obey the rules here. Rather than look for trouble, I avoid it. My life on the outside being what it was, I don't have many visitors. My sainted sister, of course. Or maybe you think she's taken up where I left off."

Saying nothing, Tawney opened a file, took out a photo. He tossed it on the table.

"May I?" Perry picked up Eckle's photo, examined it. "Now, he looks very familiar. Give me a minute. I never forget a face. Yes, yes, of course. He came to teach here, several times. Literature and writing. You know how interested I am in books—and I do miss my work in our library. I took his courses. I hope to take more. Incarceration shouldn't preclude education.

"I found him an average teacher. No spark, really. But beggars can't be choosers, can we?"

"I bet he found you a better teacher," Mantz said.

"That's sweet of you. Is that your way of saying you believe I inspired him? That would be fascinating, but I can't be held responsible for the actions of others."

"You don't owe him anything either," Mantz pointed out. "We'll stop him. We'll put him in a cage just like yours, but you have an opportunity, and that should appeal to you. Give us information that leads to his arrest, and we can make things a little less monotonous for you."

A thin shell of hard slid over his face. "What? You'll see I'm served ice cream every Sunday, given an extra hour a week in the yard? There's nothing you can do for me, or to me, Agent Mantz. I'll spend the rest of my life in this place. I accept that. If beggars can't be choosers, I choose not to be a beggar."

"When we catch him, he'll talk. Just like the minister you conned talked," Mantz added. "It didn't take us long to persuade him to admit he smuggled letters in and out for you, for more than a year."

"Correspondence with my prayer group." Perry folded his hands piously. "Reverend Garley sympathized with my need for spiritual comfort—and privacy for my soul, which the system fails to respect."

"Everyone in this room knows you don't have a soul."

"Eckle will roll on you," Mantz continued, "and you've already considered that. When he does, your life in here will get a little more—how did you put it?—narrow. You'll be charged with multiple counts of conspiracy to murder. The years added to your time won't mean a damn, but we'll see to it your time in here is a fucking misery."

Perry only continued to smile at her in his calm, pleasant way. "You think it's not already?"

"It can be worse," Tawney promised. "Believe me when I tell you I'll make sure it's worse. And for what, Perry? For this." He flicked a hand at the photo. "He's a screwup. Impatient, careless. You stayed ahead of us for years. We're breathing down his neck within months. He's not worthy of you."

"Flattery." Perry sighed. "I am susceptible to flattery. You know my weaknesses, Don."

"He tied a red scarf to Fiona Bristow's mailbox." With her eyes trained on Perry's, Mantz saw the quick flicker of irritation in his. There was something he hadn't learned yet. "He'll never get her for you now, never finish it for you."

"That was . . . immature of him."

"You know what he did to Annette Kellworth, beating her half to death before he ended it." Tawney shook his head with a disgust he wanted Perry to see, a disgust he understood Perry would share.

"Not your style, George. Not your class. He's losing control, and showing off. You never stooped like that. If we get him without your help, you're going to pay a heavy price for his mistakes."

"You know my weakness," Perry repeated after a moment. "And you know my strengths. I'm an observer. I observed Mr. Eckle. Took an interest in him as there's so little of interest here. It may be those observations would be helpful to you. I might have theories, speculations. I might even remember certain comments or conversations. I might remember something helpful, but I'd want something in return."

"What flavor ice cream?"

Perry smiled at Tawney. "Something a little sweeter. I want to speak with Fiona. Face-to-face."

"Forget it," Mantz said immediately.

"Oh, I don't think so." Perry kept his eyes on Tawney. "Do you want to save lives? Do you want to save the life of the woman he's stalking even now? Or will she die? Will others die, all for the lack of a single conversation? What would Fiona say to that? It's her choice, isn't it?"

"WE SHOULD PUSH him harder," Mantz insisted. "Dig under his skin. He responded when you said Eckle wasn't worthy of him. It fed his ego."

"It only affirmed what he'd already concluded himself."

"Exactly, so we push that button. Let me do it. I'll work him alone. Flattery and fear from a woman may turn it."

"Erin, he barely acknowledges you." Because it was his turn to drive, Tawney slid behind the wheel. "As far as he's concerned, you're not even part of this. You weren't around during the investigation that brought him down, and this is all about that. All about him. Eckle's just his vehicle, his conduit."

Mantz slammed the buckle of her seat belt into the lock. "I don't like being the ones making the down payment."

"Neither do I."

"Will she do it?"

"A part of me's sorry to say, yes, I think she will."

WHILE THE FBI flew east, Francis Eckle stepped in line a few places behind his prey. She'd worked late tonight, he thought. Just an hour or so, but it pleased him to know she was hard at work. Pleased him that, as usual, she made the stop at Star-bucks for her evening pick-me-up.

Skinny latte, he knew, double shot of espresso.

Tonight was yoga class, and if she hurried, she could fit in twenty minutes on the treadmill in the upscale fitness club she treated herself to.

He'd noted, thanks to his thirty-day trial membership, she rarely did more than twenty, and often skipped even that.

Never touched the weights, never bothered with the other machines. Just liked to show herself off in one of the tight outfits she changed into.

No different from a street-corner whore.

Afterward, she'd walk the three blocks back to work, get her car from the parking lot, then drive the half mile home.

She wasn't fucking anyone at the moment.

Career-focused. Self-focused. Nobody and nothing mattered as much to her as herself.

Selfish bitch. Street-corner whore.

He felt the rage rising up. It felt so good. So good. Hot and bitter.

He imagined pounding his fists into her face, her belly, her breasts. He could feel the way her cheekbone would shatter, smell the blood when her lip split, see the shock and pain in her eye as it swelled and closed.

"Teach her a lesson," he murmured. "Teach her a lesson, all right."

"Hey, buddy, move it up."

His hands shook and fisted as he whirled on the man behind him in line. His rage quivered, and his pride spread as the man took an instinctive step back.

Paying attention now, he thought. Everyone's paying attention now.

You have to blend, Frank. You know how. As long as they don't see you, you can do anything you want. Anything.

Perry's voice murmured in his ear. He made himself turn back, cast his gaze down. He was sick of blending. Sick of not being seen.

But . . . but . . .

He couldn't think with all this *noise*. People talking about him, behind his back. Just like always. He'd show them. Show them all.

Not yet. Not yet. He needed to calm down, to remember the preparations. To focus on the goal.

When he glanced up again, he saw the prey already moving toward the door, her take-out cup in her hand. His face burned with embarrassment. He'd nearly let her walk away, nearly lost her.

He stepped out of line, kept his head down. It couldn't be tonight after all. Discipline, control, focus. He needed to calm down, to calm himself, to box in the excitement until *after*.

She'd have one more night of freedom, one more day of life. And he'd have the pleasure of knowing she was unaware she had already stepped into the trap.

FIONA CONSIDERED a voodoo doll. She could probably get one of Sylvia's artists to make a doll in Kati Starr's likeness. Sticking pins in it, or simply bashing its head against a table, might be childish, but she had a feeling it would also be therapeutic.

Simon didn't seem to be concerned about the latest story with Starr's byline. He was probably right. Probably. But the idea that she claimed to have sources stating the FBI was looking for a "person of interest" in the RSKII investigation grated.

She didn't just pull that out of the air.

Someone was leaking information, and she was confident enough of the source to print it, and to have traveled to Orcas, again.

To have pushed Fiona's name forward, again. And this time linking her with Simon. The *hunky artist who traded Seattle's urban flair for a quiet inlet retreat on Orcas.*

The paper had even printed a sidebar on him, relating his work in the medium of wood, his practical applications with a creative flair, its organic center.

Blah, blah, blah.

She had a few dozen things she'd like to say to Kati Starr, which of course was just what the reporter wanted.

The continued publicity put her in a tenuous position with clients. She couldn't—wouldn't—answer questions, and they couldn't help but ask them.

And because the questions, and the crazies, were popping up on her blog, she had to close the comments section and rerun old entries.

Desperate for something to keep her mind occupied, she focused on a new project. And hunted Simon down in his shop. Whatever he was making involved the lathe and the use of a small carving tool—and looked as though it required precision and focus.

She stood back and kept her mouth shut until he turned off the machine.

"What?"

"Can you make this?"

He tossed the protective goggles aside and studied the photo.

"It's a window box."

"I know what it is."

"It's actually Meg's window box. I asked her to take a picture and upload it for me. Simon, I need something to do."

"This looks like something for me to do."

"Yes, initially. But I'll plant them. If you could make four of them." She caught the wheedling edge in her voice and hated it enough to change tones. "I know maybe you don't actually want window boxes, but you have to admit they'd look good, and they'd perk up the front of the house. You could even decorate them for Christmas with—or not," she said as he only stared.

"Okay, I guess I won't mention an idea for some raised beds on the south side of the house. Sorry. Sorry. One look around here and anyone could see you're already busy enough without me dreaming up more to keep myself occupied. What's that?"

She gestured toward the tarp that covered the wine cabinet.

"That would be none of your business."

"Fine. I'll go clean something and you'll have no one to blame but yourself."

"Fiona."

She stopped at the door.

"Let's go for a walk."

"No, it's fine. You're in the middle of something, and my problem is I'm not. So I'll get in the middle of something."

"So, I'll go for a walk by myself, and you can go in and sulk."

She heaved out a breath before crossing over and putting her arms around him. "I was planning on sulking, but I can put it off." She tipped her face up. "I'm restless, that's all. I'm used to coming and going when I please. Heading off with the dogs, or jumping in the car and driving into the village. Stopping by Sylvia's, or going by to see Mai. I promised I wouldn't go anywhere alone, and I didn't realize how stir-crazy I'd get when I couldn't. So now I'm a pest, and it annoys me. Probably more than it annoys you."

"Doubtful," he said, and made her laugh.

"Go back to work. I'm going to go take some new pictures of the boys and update the website."

"We'll go out later. Go out for dinner or something."

"I feel sanity returning. I'll see you when you're done." She walked back to the door, opened it. Stopped. "Simon."

"What now?"

"Agents Tawney and Mantz just pulled up."

She tried to be optimistic as she walked across the yard. Tawney greeted the dogs, and was immediately offered a rope by Jaws as Mantz stayed several cautious steps back.

"Fiona. Simon." Despite his dark suit, Tawney gave Jaws a quick game of tug. "I hope we're not interrupting."

"No. In fact I was just complaining I had too much time on my hands today."

"Feeling hemmed in?"

"A little. Lie. A lot."

"I remember how it was for you before. We're making progress, Fee. We're going to do everything we can to close this case and get things back to normal for you."

"You look tired."

"Well, it's been a long day." He glanced over at Simon. "Is it all right if we talk inside?"

"No problem." Simon started toward the house. "You've seen the latest in *U.S. Report*," he said. "It upsets her. She doesn't need that added on. You've got a leak to plug."

"Believe me, we're working on it."

"We're no happier about it than you are," Mantz added as they stepped inside. "If Eckle gets the idea we're looking for him, he could go under."

"That answers the top question. You haven't found him yet. Do you want anything?" Fiona asked them. "Coffee? Something cold?"

"Let's just sit down. We're going to tell you as much as we can." Tawney sat and, leaning forward, linked his hands on his knees. "We know he was in Portland on January fifth because he sold his car to a used-car lot on that date. There's no other vehicle registered in his name, but we're checking on purchases in the Portland area on or around that date."

"He could have bought something from a private seller. Not bothered to register it." Simon shrugged. "Or had fake ID. Hell, he could've taken a bus to anywhere and bought a car off Craigslist."

"You're right, but we check, and we keep checking. He needs transportation. He needs lodging. He needs to buy gas and food. We're going to turn over every stone and use every means at our disposal. That includes Perry."

"We spoke with him earlier today," Mantz continued. "We know he and Eckle communicated, using a third party to smuggle letters in and out."

"Who?" Simon demanded.

"The minister Perry bullshitted at the prison. The minister took Perry's letters out and mailed them—they were to different names, different locations," Tawney explained. "Perry claimed they were to members of a prayer group his sister belonged to, and the minister swallowed it. He brought Perry the responses, mailed to him, again from different names and locations."

"So much for maximum security," Simon muttered.

"Perry managed to get a letter out a few days after Kellworth's body was found, but there's been no correspondence *to* him for over three weeks."

"Eckle's distancing himself?" Fiona glanced from agent to agent. "Is that what you think?"

"It plays. Eckle's gone off script now," Tawney added. "And that's something Perry's not pleased about. Now that he knows we've identified Eckle and we're focused on him, Perry's not pleased about that either."

"You told him?" Simon interrupted. "So he'll have a chance to confirm the damn news story with his pen pal?"

"Short of ESP, Perry's not getting any more messages out or in," Mantz insisted. "We've blocked his conduit. He's been locked down, and now he'll remain locked down until we have Eckle in custody. Eckle's not living up to his standards, and Perry's feeling the squeeze of losing some of the privileges he gained through good behavior."

"You think he's going to tell you, if he knows, how to find this Eckle?" Fiona demanded. "Why would he?"

"He wants to cut the cord there, Fee. He's not happy his protégé is making mistakes, going his own way. Perry knows, because we made sure he knows, those mistakes will make it impossible for Eckle to get to you." Tawney waited a beat. "You're still his one failure, and the reason he's in prison. He still thinks about you."

"That's not particularly good news."

"We don't have much to bargain with. Perry knows he's in prison for life. He's never getting out. Eventually, his pride will push him into telling us what we need, or we'll take Eckle without him."

"Eventually."

"He's offered us information. He's careful enough to couch it as observations, speculations, theories, but he's ready to turn on Eckle with the right incentive."

"What does he want?" She already knew. In her gut she already knew.

"He wants to speak with you. Face-to-face. You can't say anything I haven't already thought," Tawney said as Simon surged to his feet. "Nothing I haven't already said to myself."

"You'd put her through that, ask her to sit down with the man who tried to kill her so maybe he might toss you a few crumbs?"

"It's up to her. It's up to you," Tawney said to Fiona. "I don't like it. I don't like asking you to make this decision. I don't like giving him squat."

"Then don't," Simon snapped.

"There are plenty of reasons not to do it. He may lie. He may get what he wants and claim he knows nothing after all, or give us information that sends us in the wrong direction. But I don't think he will."

"It's your job to stop this bastard. Not hers."

Mantz shot him a single hard look. "We're doing our job, Mr. Doyle."

"From where I'm standing, you're asking her to do it."

"She's the key. She's what Perry wants, what he's wanted for eight years. The reason he recruited Eckle, and she's the reason he'll betray him."

"Stop talking around me," Fiona murmured. "Just stop. If I say no, he'll shut down."

"Fiona."

"Just wait." She reached up for Simon's hand, felt the anger through his skin as clearly as she heard it in his voice. "Wait. He'll say nothing. He'll hold out for weeks, maybe months. He's capable of that. He'll wait until there's another. At least one more, so I'll know she's dead because I wouldn't face him."

"That's bullshit."

"It's how I'd feel." She squeezed Simon's hand, hard. "He took Greg to hurt me, and he could do this. He'd like to do it. He expects me to say no. He probably hopes I do until some-one else is dead. It would appeal to him. That's what you think, too."

"I do," Tawney confirmed. "He can wait, and the waiting gives him more time to think. He considers us inferior. We wouldn't have caught him but for a fluke, so he'd calculate Eckle may have time for one or two more."

"There wouldn't have been a fluke if he hadn't killed Greg. He wouldn't have been driven to kill Greg if I hadn't gotten away. So it comes back to me. You need to make the arrange-ments. I want to do this as soon as possible."

"Goddamn it, Fiona."

"We need a minute."

"We'll be outside," Tawney told her.

"I need to do this," she said to Simon when they were alone.

"The fuck you do."

"You didn't know me when Greg was killed. You wouldn't have known me in those weeks, months even, afterward. I shattered. My broods? They're a shadow of it. They're nothing compared to the guilt, the grief, the depression, the despair."

She took both his hands now, hoping to transmit her need through his rage.

"I had help through it. The counseling, sure, but it was friends and family that pulled me out. And Agent Tawney. I could call him, day or night, talk to him when I couldn't talk to my mother, my father, Syl, anyone else. Because he knew. He wouldn't ask me if he didn't believe. That's one."

She took a breath, steadied herself. "If I don't do this, don't try, and someone else dies, I think it'll break something inside me. He'll have won after all. He didn't win when he took me. He didn't win when he killed Greg. But, Simon, God, you can only take so many beatings and get up again. That's two.

"Last. I want to look him in the eye. I want to see him in prison and know he's there because of me. He wants to use me, he wants to manipulate me."

She shook her head, the gesture as fierce as the sudden fury that lit her face. "Fuck him. I'll use him. Maybe, I hope to God, he'll tell them something that leads them to Eckle. I hope to God. But whether he does or not, I'll have used him, and done what I needed to do to live with whatever happens after. I'll be the one who wins. I'll be the one who beats his sorry, motherfucking ass again. And when it's done, he'll know that."

He pulled away, walked to the window, stared out, then walked back to look down at her. "I love you."

Knocked sideways, she lowered to the arm of the couch. "Oh my God."

"I'm so pissed off at you right now. I don't think I've ever been more pissed at anyone in my life. And I've been pissed at plenty."

"Okay. I'm really trying to keep up, but with my head spinning it's hard to focus. You're pissed off because you love me?"

"That's a factor, but not the main thrust. I'm pissed off because you're going to do this, because you, being you, have to do it. I'm pissed off because short of tying you to the bed, I can't stop you."

"You're wrong. You could. You're the only one who could."

"Don't give me the opening," Simon warned. "I'm pissed

at you. And I think you're the most amazing woman I've ever known, and my mother sets a damn high standard for amazing. If you cry," he said when she teared up, "I swear to God . . ."

"I'm having a hell of a day. Give me a break." She got to her feet. "You don't say what you don't mean."

"Goddamn right. What's the point?"

"Tact, diplomacy, but we won't get into that. Simon." Needing to touch, she ran her hands over his chest. "Simon. Everything you just said to me—all of it—there's nothing you could have said or done that could have made me feel better or stronger or more able to do what I need to do."

"Great." A few grains of bitterness came through. "Glad I could help."

"Would you tell me again?"

"Which part?"

She rapped a fist on his chest. "Don't be an ass."

"I love you."

"Good, because I love you. So we're balanced. Simon." She laid her hands on his cheeks, and when she kissed him it was strong and sweet. "Try not to worry. He's going to try to mess with my head. It's the only power he has now. And he can't because I'm going in armed with something he'll never have, and never understand. When I do what I need to do, and walk away from him, I know I'm coming back here. I know you'll be here, and you love me."

"You want me to buy that?"

"I'm not selling it. I'm giving it, and it's truth. Let's go out and make this deal. I want it done and over, so I can come back to the good part."

They walked outside. "How soon can we go?" Fiona asked.

Tawney took a moment to study her face. "We're cleared for tomorrow morning. Agent Mantz and I will see about getting a hotel here on Orcas, and we'll fly out of Sea-Tac at nine-fifteen. We'll escort you all the way, Fee. There and back, and be with you throughout the session with Perry. We'll have her home by midafternoon," he said to Simon.

Over and done and back, Fiona told herself. "I'll have someone cover my classes tomorrow morning and afternoon. You don't need a hotel. You can stay at my place. It's there, it's empty," she added before Tawney could decline. "And it'll save you some time."

"We appreciate that."

"I'll get the keys."

Simon waited until Fiona went back inside. "If he screws her up, you'll pay for it."

Tawney nodded. "Understood."

TWENTY-SEVEN

Normally, though opportunities to travel were few and far between, Fiona liked to fly. She enjoyed the ritual, the people-watching, the sensations, the anticipation of leaving one place and hurtling through the air to another.

But in this case, the flight was simply one more necessary part of a means to an end, just something to get through.

She'd thought carefully about what to wear, and hadn't been able to figure out why her appearance, her *presentation*, took on such importance.

She considered and rejected a suit as too formal and studied. She contemplated jeans, her usual and most comfortable choice, but decided they were too casual. In the end, she decided on black pants, a crisp white shirt and added a jacket in strong blue.

Simple, serious and businesslike.

And that, she realized when she sat between Tawney and Mantz on the plane, had been the importance. What she wore, how she presented herself indicated tone.

Perry thought he was in charge, she reasoned. Though he

currently resided in a maximum-security prison, he'd made a strong bid for alpha position.

He had something they wanted, something they needed, so that gave him power—power she intended to countermand.

The clothes would help remind her—and him—at the end of the day, she'd be the one walking out, going back to her life, to freedom.

He'd be the one going back to a cell.

Nothing he had to trade changed that. And that, she reminded herself, was her power. That was her control.

"I want to go over some of the procedure with you." Tawney shifted toward her. "You'll go through security, and there'll be some paperwork."

She knew by the way he studied her face he wondered if her nerve would falter. "There always is."

"We'll be escorted to an interview room rather than the visitation area. Perry will already be there. He'll be secured with wrist and ankle shackles, Fee. You will never, not for one second, be alone with him. He won't be able to touch you."

"I'm not afraid of him." That, at least, was true. "I'm not afraid of that. I'm afraid all this might be for nothing. He'll get what he wants, get his rocks off on that, and not tell you anything that can help. I hate giving him the satisfaction of being in the same room with me, looking at me. But at the same time I'm getting the satisfaction of doing the same. And knowing I'll walk away, go home—and he won't."

"Good. You keep that in your head. Keep it front and center, and know that if you want to break it off, at any time, it's over. It's your call, Fee. All the way."

He patted her hand as they shimmied through some choppy air.

"He's refused to have his lawyer there, he made a point of it. He thinks he's in charge, in control."

"Yes, I was just thinking about exactly that. Let him believe whatever he wants. Let him get a good long look at me." Her voice hardened, edged with challenge. The turbulence, she thought, was all outside.

"He's not going to see someone who's afraid or subservient. And later today, I'll be playing with my dogs. I'll eat pizza and have some wine, and tonight, I'll be sleeping with the man I love. He'll go back to his cell. I don't give a damn what he thinks, as long as he tells you what you need to know."

"Don't give him anything he can use against you," Mantz added. "No names, no locations, no routines. As much as you can, keep your reactions steady. He'll play you if he can, either to scare you or make you angry—anything to get under your skin. We'll be in the room the entire time, and so will a guard. The entire session will be monitored."

She let their reassurances, their instructions slide over her. No one, not even Tawney, could know what she felt. No one, she thought, could know that in some dark, closed part of herself she reveled in the idea of seeing him again, of seeing him restrained, as she'd once been. When she faced him again, she'd do it for herself, for Greg, for every woman whose life he'd taken.

He couldn't know he'd given that dark, closed part of herself a reason to celebrate.

How could he, when she hadn't known it herself?

She considered it all a journey. The early morning ferry, the plane, the drive. Every leg brought her the comfort that she'd traveled farther and farther from home. That Perry would never know or see what she knew and saw every single day.

Southeastern Washington wasn't just a trip away, but almost another world. These weren't the fields and hills of home, the villages busy with tourists and familiar faces, the sounds and the sea. These weren't her streams and woods and deep green shadows.

The red brick and thick stone of the penitentiary struck her as formidable and intimidating. The square, squat, unadorned block of the Intensive Management Unit that housed him added stark and cold. And that dark place inside her hoped his life had been, would continue to be, equally stark, equally cold.

Every length of iron, every foot of steel added to her comfort, and her secret celebration.

He believed he'd caused her pain and distress by bargaining for this meeting, she thought, but he'd done her an enormous favor.

Every time she thought of Perry now, she'd think of the walls, the bars, the guards, the guns.

She submitted to the security, the search, the paperwork, and thought Perry would never know that by forcing her to open this door he would help her, finally, to close it—lock off even that tiny chink she'd never been able to shut out.

When she walked into the room where he waited, she was ready.

It pleased her she'd worn that deliberate touch of bold color, that she'd worked her hair into a complicated braid and had been meticulous with her makeup. Because she knew he studied her when she came in, knew he took in those details.

Eight years since he'd locked her in the trunk of his car. Seven since she'd sat in the witness chair facing him. They'd both know the woman who faced him now wasn't the same person.

"Fiona, it's been a very long time. You've bloomed. Your new life obviously agrees with you."

"I can't say the same for you and yours."

He smiled at her. "I've managed to find a tolerable routine. I have to tell you, up until this moment, I doubted you'd come. How was your trip?"

Wants to run the show, take the lead, she concluded. Requires a small correction. "Did you ask me to come here for small talk?"

"I rarely have visitors. My sister—you remember her from the trial, I'm sure. And, of course, in recent days our favorite special agent and his attractive new partner. Conversation is a treat."

"If you think I'm here to offer you a treat, you're mistaken. But . . . the trip was uneventful. It's a beautiful spring day. I'm looking forward to enjoying more of it when I leave. I'll enjoy it particularly knowing when I leave you'll be going back into—what do they call it?—segregation."

"I see you've developed a mean streak. A shame." He offered her a sorrowful look, adult to child. "You were such a sweet, unaffected young woman."

"You didn't know me then. You don't know me now."

"Don't I? You retreated to your island—condolences, by the way, on the death of your father. I often think people who choose to live on islands consider the water surrounding them a kind of moat. A deterrent to the outside world. There you have your dogs and your training classes. Training is an interesting endeavor, isn't it? A kind of molding of others into your likeness."

"That would be your take." Lead him, she told herself. Lull him. "I see it as a method of helping individuals reach their potential, in my particular area of interest and expertise."

"Reaching potential, yes. On that we agree."

"Is that what you saw in Francis Eckle? His potential?"

"Now, now." He sat back, chuckled. "Don't segue so ham-handedly when we're having such a nice time."

"I thought you'd want to talk to me about him, since you set him on me. Of course, he's made a mess of it. He's diminished your legacy . . . George."

"Now you're trying to both flatter and annoy me. Did the agents prep you? Tell you what to say, how to say it? Are you a good little puppet, Fiona?"

"I'm not here to flatter or annoy you." Her voice stayed flat, her eyes steady. "I've got no interest in doing either. And no one tells me what to say—or what to do or when to do it. Unlike your situation. Are you a good little puppet in your cage, George?"

"Feisty!"

He laughed out loud, but it wasn't only humor that sparkled in his eyes. She'd hit a switch, she knew, and turned on the heat.

"I've always admired that about you, Fiona. That classic, and clichéd, redhead's spunk. But as I recall you weren't so feisty after your lover and his faithful dog took bullets."

It hurt, brutally, and she held on to the pain.

"You needed medication and 'therapy,'" he added, putting quotes in the air. "You needed your own fatherly special agent to protect you from me, and the drooling press. Poor, poor Fiona. First a heroine through a stroke of luck, then a creature of tragedy and frailty."

"Poor, poor George," she said in the same tone, and saw the temper flash, for just an instant, in his eyes. "First a figure to be feared, and now one forced to recruit the inferior to finish the job he couldn't. Let me be honest. I don't care if you tell the FBI anything about Eckle—a part of me hopes you won't. Because he'll try to finish what you couldn't. You took mine, now I'll take yours. If they don't find him first, he'll come after me, and I'm ready for him."

Now she leaned forward, letting him see it. Letting him catch a glimpse of her will, and the secret inside her. "I'm ready for him, George. I wasn't ready for you, and look where you are. So when he comes for me, he'll lose—and so will you. Again. I want that more than I can say. You're not the only one who sees him as a proxy. So do I."

"Have you considered he wants you to feel so confident? He's manipulating you into this sense of power and security?"

She let out a half laugh as she leaned back again. "Who's being ham-handed now? He's not what you thought he was. Judging character and abilities is one of the traits of a good trainer. Not just teaching, instructing, but recognizing the limitations and the pathology of those you train. You missed that one. You know you did, or I wouldn't be here."

"You're here because I demanded it."

She hoped she pulled off an expression between bored and amused because her heart thumped riotously. She was beating him.

"You can't demand anything of me. You can't scare me, and neither can the vicious dog you've set on me. The only thing you can do is try to make a deal."

"There's no telling who a dog might attack. No telling how many he may bloody along the way."

She cocked her head, smiled a little. "Do you really think that keeps me up at night? I'm on my island, remember? I have my moat. I'll only be sorry if he screws up before he gets to me. Feel free to let him know that—that is, if he's still listening to you. I don't think he is. I think your dog's off the leash, George, and going his own way. As for me?" Deliberately, she glanced at her watch. "That's really all the time I have to spare. It was good to see you here, George," she said as she rose. "It really made my day."

"I'll escort you out." Mantz got to her feet.

"I'll find another. Sooner or later, I'll find another."

Fiona glanced back to see his chained hands fist on the table.

"You're always in my thoughts, Fiona."

She smiled at him. "George, that's just sad."

At Mantz's nod, the guard opened the door. The minute the door closed behind them, Mantz shook her head, held up a hand. "We're going to be escorted to a monitoring area where you can wait."

Fiona held on to her composure, following Mantz's example, saying nothing, keeping her eyes straight ahead. The sound of the thick electronic doors opening, closing, made her want to shudder.

They entered a small room holding electronic equipment, monitors. Mantz ignored them and the officials running them and gestured to a couple of chairs set up across the room.

She poured a glass of water, handed it to Fiona.

"Thanks."

"Do you want a job?"

Fiona looked up again. "Sorry?"

"You'd make a good agent. I'm going to tell you, I had my doubts about this, about bringing you here. I thought he'd play you. I thought he'd twist you up and wring you out to dry, and we'd walk out empty-handed. But you played him. You didn't give him what he wanted, and you sure as hell didn't give him what he expected."

"I gave it a lot of thought. What to say, how to say it. How to . . . Wow, look at that," she said when she saw her hands shaking.

"I can take you out of here altogether. There's a coffee shop not that far away. Tawney can meet us there."

"No, I'll stick. I want to stick, and I know you want to be in there."

"Here's fine. He's not going to take another woman in his face after that. Tawney's better finishing this up without me. How did you know what to say, how to say it?"

"Truth?"

"Yeah, truth."

"I work with dogs, and do one-on-ones with dogs and owners with behavioral problems—some of them fairly severe and violent. You can't show fear—you can't even feel it, because if you do it will show. You can't let them get the upper hand, even for a minute. You don't want to lose your temper, but always maintain the position of power. Alpha position."

Mantz considered a moment. "You're saying you thought of Perry as a bad dog?"

Fiona let out a shuddering breath. "More or less. Do you think it worked?"

"I think you did your job. Now we'll do ours."

PERRY STRUNG IT OUT, dribbling out information, stopping to request a meal, dribbling more. Fiona fought off a rising sense of claustrophobia from being shut up in the small room for so long, and wished—more than once—she'd taken Mantz up on her offer to leave the prison and wait elsewhere.

In for the whole shot, she reminded herself, and sat, sat while Mantz listened on an earpiece, when Tawney came in to confer with her. To wait it out, she thought, refusing an offer of food she wasn't entirely sure she could keep down.

They approached the time Tawney had predicted she'd be home before they left the prison behind. Fiona kept the window of the car open, breathed in the air.

"I can use my phone now? I need to let Simon and Sylvia know I'm delayed."

"Go ahead. I contacted your stepmother," Tawney told her. "I left Simon a voice mail. He didn't answer his phone."

"Between the machines and the music in his shop, he never hears the phone. But Syl would let him know. She's taking my classes this afternoon. I'll wait until we're about to board the plane."

"Erin said you didn't eat."

"Still a little unsteady in that area. You have to tell me something. You have to tell me if this helped."

"You're going to be disappointed."

"Oh."

"Disappointed that Erin's back there on the phone right now, checking out some of the information Perry gave us, coordinating agents to various mail drops Perry said he lined up to contact Eckle over the next few weeks. He gave us locations, trolling sites they agreed on and the two alternate identities Eckle's using."

"Thank God."

"He wants Eckle to go down. One, because he's no longer subservient, no longer obedient. And two—and I believe this cemented it—he doesn't want you to win again. He doesn't want to risk you going up against Eckle and winning. You convinced him not only that you could, that you would, but that you were looking forward to it. Hell, you convinced me."

"I'd just as soon not have to try to prove it."

Mantz returned. "We've got agents on the way to the locations he gave us, and a team to the trolling site, which geographically should be next on Eckle's list. We have another taking Kellworth's college, as that should have been his target for this time frame. He could repeat there if he decides to go back to Perry's game plan."

"I don't see that," Tawney said, "but it's better to cover it."

"We've issued a BOLO for Eckle, including his aliases. And we got a jackpot, Tawney. We have a 2005 Ford Taurus, California plates, issued to one of those aliases. John William Mitchell."

Tawney reached over to lay a hand briefly on Fiona's. "You're not going to have to prove anything."

* * *

MIDAFTERNOON, MY ASS, Simon thought. At this rate, they'd be lucky if she made it home by six. Hearing her on his voice mail helped, but he wasn't going to be able to relax until he saw her for himself.

He'd kept busy, and having Syl pinch-hitting on the classes saved him from a trip to town as she'd hauled off the new stock he'd finished. Plus, she'd made him lunch. Not a bad deal.

He set the last of the window boxes he'd spent most of his day making on its bracket, then walked back into the front yard, surrounded by the pack of dogs who'd rarely left his side all day, to view the results.

"Not bad," he murmured.

He hadn't used the design Fiona cadged from Meg—what would be the point in making something you could buy in a damn catalog? Anyway, his were better. He liked the marriage of mahogany and teak, the slightly rounded shapes, the interest of the Celtic design he'd carved into the wood.

Needed hot colors in the flowers, he decided. And if she tried to do some wussy pastels, she'd have to try again.

Strong, hot colors—nonnegotiable. What was the point in planting flowers if they didn't make a statement?

When the dogs turned as one, he swung around himself. He thought, *Thank God,* when he saw the car on his drive.

He had to force himself not to race to the car, pluck her right out through the window and check every inch of her to make sure she was untouched, unhurt, unchanged.

He waited, with roiling impatience, while she sat, speaking to the agents. They've had you all day, he thought. Say good-fucking-bye and come home. Be home.

Then she got out, walked to him. He barely noticed the car drive away.

He heard her laugh as the dogs surged to greet her, watched color bloom in her cheeks as she stroked and ruffled. My turn, he thought, and moved toward them.

"Back off," he ordered the dogs, then just stood looking at her. "Took you long enough."

"It feels even longer from this side. I need a hug. A really long, hard hug. Crack my ribs, will you, Simon?"

He put his arms around her, gave her what she needed short of snapping bones. Then he kissed the top of her head, her temples, her mouth.

"Better, better." She sighed it out. "So much better. You smell so good. Sawdust and dogs and the forest. You smell like home. I'm so glad to be home."

"You're okay?"

"I'm okay. I'll tell you all about it. I want to shower first. I know it's completely in my head, but I feel . . . I just need a shower. Then maybe we can toss a frozen pizza in the oven, crack a bottle, and I'll . . . You made window boxes."

"I had some spare time today since you weren't around interrupting me."

"You made window boxes," she murmured. "They're so . . . just exactly right. Thank you."

"They're my window boxes on my house."

"Absolutely. Thank you."

He yanked her back into his arms. "Making them kept me from going crazy. Syl and I worked on keeping each other from going crazy. You should call her."

"I did. I called her, my mother and Mai from the ferry."

"Good, then it's just you and me. And them," he added as the dogs sat at their feet. "Have your shower. I'll deal with the pizza." But he caught her chin in his hand, held it while he searched her face. "He didn't touch you."

"Not the way he hoped, no."

"Then I can wait for the rest. I'm hungry anyway."

THEY ATE OUTSIDE on the back porch with the sun beaming through the trees and the birds trilling like mad things. Outside, Simon thought, where it made a point. They were free. Perry wasn't.

Her voice stayed steady as she took him through it, step-by-step.

"I don't know where some of it came from. I'd worked it

out in my head, the approach, the tone, the basic thrust, but some of it was just there, coming out of my mouth before it really seemed to plant in my head. Telling him if Eckle kills other women it has nothing to do with me. I'm usually a lousy liar. It's just not natural to me, so I tend to fumble it. But it just flowed right out, smooth and cold."

"And he bought it."

"Apparently so. He gave them what they were after: locations, mail drops, aliases. They tracked a car and plates with one of the aliases. They've got agents scrambling out to do what they do."

"And you're out of it."

"Oh God, Simon, I really think I am." She lifted her hands, pressed her fingers to her eyes for a moment. "I really think I am. And more, it was so different from what I expected, what I'd prepared for."

"How?"

"He was so angry. Perry. I expected him to be smug, full of himself and his ability to pull all these strings even from prison. And he was, on one level. But under it there was all this anger and frustration. And seeing that, *knowing* that, seeing where he is, how he looks, it felt—feels . . ."

She fisted a hand on the table, studied it. "Solid. It feels hard and strong and solid." She lifted her gaze again, the soft blue clear again, calm again. "It feels over. What was between him and me, still there in the shadows and the dark, it's done now. We're finished."

"Good." He heard the truth of it, felt it—and realized that until that moment, he'd carried those shadows inside him, too. "Then it was worth it. But until Eckle is in the same place, things stay the same here. No chances, Fiona."

"I can live with that. I've got window boxes, and pizza." She unfisted her hand, reached for his. "And you. So." She took a long breath. "Tell me something else. What did you do besides window boxes?"

"I've got a few things going. Let's take a walk."

"Beach or woods?"

"Woods first, then beach. I need to find another stump."

"Simon! You sold the sink."

"I'm keeping that one, but Syl got a look at it and says she's got a client who'll want one."

"You're keeping it."

"Half-bath downstairs needs a bump."

"It'll be fabulous." She glanced over at the dogs, back at Simon. Her guys, she thought. "Come on, boys. Let's go help Simon find a stump."

ECKLE FELT SOMETHING, too. He felt freedom.

A new task, a new agenda. New prey.

He knew he'd severed the strings that held him to Perry, and rather than falling limp, an untethered marionette, he stood strong and vital. He experienced a new sense of self, one he'd never felt before, not even when Perry had helped him reach inside to the man he'd hidden for so many years.

He owed Perry a debt for that, and one he fully intended to pay. But the debt was one of student to teacher. A true teacher, a wise teacher knew the student must step away, must carve his own path once the roadbed was laid.

He'd read, with interest and pride, the article in *U.S. Report*. He critiqued the style, the voice, the content, and gave Kati Starr a solid B.

As he would have done in his other life, he edited, corrected, made suggestions in red pen.

He could help her improve, he had no doubt of it. And he'd considered communicating with her, collaborating, so to speak, to give her series of articles more depth.

He'd never realized how addictive notoriety could be, how *piquant* the flavor once tasted. But his new self wanted more sly licks and nibbled bites before the end. He wanted to feast. To gorge.

He wanted to sate himself on legacy.

As he'd studied his potential student's habits, routines, read her other articles, researched her personal and professional data, he detected in her what he'd often seen in his own students.

Particularly the females.

Whores. All women were whores at their slippery, wet roots.

Bright, clever Kati was, in his opinion, too headstrong, too rash, too sure of herself. She was a manipulator, and wouldn't take instruction or constructive criticism well.

But that didn't mean she couldn't be useful.

The more he observed, the more he learned, the more he wanted. She would be his next and, in a very real way, his first even as she might be his last. His own choice, rather than a mirror of Perry's needs.

She was older, not particularly athletic. More inclined to hours at a desk, a keyboard, a phone than physical pursuits.

Playing in her fancy fitness club so she could show off her body.

Yes, she showed off her body, he thought, but didn't tend it, didn't discipline it. If she lived she'd grow soft and fat and slow.

Really, he'd be doing her a favor, ending it while she was still young and smooth and tight.

He'd been busy during his time in Seattle. He'd changed his license plates twice and had the car painted. Now when he returned to Orcas any cops watching the ferry traffic wouldn't note the return of the car—not that he gave barely educated hayseeds that much credit.

Still, Perry had schooled him carefully on precaution.

He considered the best time and location to take her, then simply waited for Seattle's weather to give him the final element.

KATI SHOT UP her umbrella and stepped out into the drenching rain and gloom. She'd worked late, polishing up some details on her next article. For now, she didn't mind inhabiting a cubicle in a small building in the rainy Northwest.

It served as a stepping-stone.

Her series was gaining her the attention she wanted, not only from readers but from the powers that be. If she could keep the heat turned up, just a little longer, she had every reason to believe she'd be packing her laptop and looking for an apartment in New York.

Fiona Bristow, George Perry and RSKII created and stamped her ticket out of Seattle and into the Big Apple. And it was there she'd shop her book.

She needed to crack Fiona open a bit, she thought as she dug for her keys. And it wouldn't hurt for RSKII to take another coed, keep that flame high—and her byline front and center.

Of course, if the feds broke the case, that wouldn't hurt either. She had sources primed, including the one who'd fed her the information that the Tawney-Mantz team had interviewed Perry again that day—and the fresh, hot juice that Fiona had joined in.

Face-to-face with the man who abducted her, killed her lover. Oh, to have been a fly on the wall in that room. But even without the access, she'd gotten enough from her sources for a solid piece—above the fold—for tomorrow's edition.

She hit the unlock button on her key ring and in the flash of lights saw the flat rear tire.

"Crap. Crap!" She hurried closer to make certain. Even as she turned, digging into her bag for her phone, he boiled out of the gloom.

Out of nowhere, no more than a blur.

She heard him say, "Hi, Kati! How about an exclusive?"

The pain shot through her, an electric bullet that sizzled in every cell of her stunned, seizing body. The rainy gloom burst into blinding white as a scream gagged in her throat. In some shocked part of her brain she thought she'd been struck by lightning.

The white sliced to black.

IT TOOK LESS than a minute to bind her, to lock her in the trunk. He stowed her bag, her computer, her umbrella in the back, for now, carefully turned off her phone.

Filled with power and pride, he drove off into the rainy night. He had a lot of work to do before he slept.

TWENTY-EIGHT

Kati's phone provided a wealth of information. Scrolling through, Eckle carefully copied down all the names and numbers, studied her incomings, outgoings, her calendar, reminders. It fascinated him that virtually every communication, every appointment in her logs—but for an upcoming dentist appointment—dealt with professional interests.

Really, he mused as he wiped the phone clean, he and Kati had a great deal in common: no real connection to family, no particular friends and an absorption with rising in their chosen field.

They both wanted to make a name for themselves, leave a deep mark.

Wouldn't that make their brief time together all the more important?

He tossed the phone in the trash at the rest stop where he'd parked, then backtracked, exited the interstate and drove the wandering twenty miles to the motel he'd chosen for this leg of the work.

He paid cash for a single night's stay, then parked away from the lights. Though he doubted he'd need it, he angled her umbrella to shield his face as he climbed out of the car. People who frequented motels of this type didn't sit around their shitty little rooms looking out the window at a rain-swept parking lot, but it paid to be cautious.

He opened the trunk.

Her eyes were wide open, full of fear and pain with that glaze of shock he found so arousing. She'd struggled, but he'd learned a thing or two and had linked the bindings on her wrists and ankles together in the back, hog-tying her so she could do little more than hump like a worm. Still, it was best to keep her absolutely still, absolutely silent through the night.

"We'll talk in the morning," he told her as he pulled a syringe from his pocket, removed the tip. Her screams were no more than harsh whispers swallowed by the rain as he gripped her arm, shoved up her sleeve. "Sleep tight now," he said, and slid the needle under the skin.

He replaced the tip. She, like the others, wouldn't live long enough to be bothered about any infection from shared needles. He watched her eyes dull as the drug took her under.

After securing the trunk, he got his suitcase and her belongings out of the back and carried them across the broken pavement of the lot to his room.

It smelled of old sex, stale smoke and the cheap detergent that couldn't mask the brew. He'd learned to ignore such annoyances, and he'd learned to ignore the inevitable groans and thumps from adjoining rooms.

He switched on the TV, scrolled until he found local news.

He entertained himself first with a pass through Kati's wallet. She carried nearly two hundred in cash—for payoffs? bribes? he wondered. The money would come in handy, another advantage of changing his target type. The coeds rarely had more than five or ten, if that.

He found the current password for her computer hidden behind her driver's license. He set it aside for later.

He made piles of what he could keep and what he would dispose of from her handbag, and munched on the M&M's she had in an inside pocket, toyed with her bag of cosmetics.

She carried no photos, not his all-work-and-no-play Kati.

But she had a street map of Seattle and one of Orcas, tidily folded.

On the Orcas map she'd marked several routes from the ferry. He recognized the route to Fiona's, wondered about the others. If time permitted, he'd check them out.

He approved of the fact that she carried several pens and sharpened pencils, a small cube of Post-its, a bottle of water.

He saved her breath mints, towelettes, pack of tissues, removed her IDs and credit cards to be cut up and disposed of along the way.

He used the money in her change purse to buy a Sprite and a bag of Lay's potato chips from the vending machine outside the room.

Organized and settled, he opened her computer. As with her phone calls and texts, all of her e-mails centered on work and many were cryptic. But he could follow the dots, as he'd been following her.

While he, Perry and Fiona weren't her only stories, they were, unquestionably, her focus. She'd pushed, and was pushing, for nibbles and bites from numerous sources.

Tenacious, thy name is Kati Starr.

She did well, he thought, digging, digging, digging, amassing details and comments from Perry's past, from Fiona's, from past and present victims.

She had files full of information on Fiona's search unit, on the other members, on her training business, on her mother, her stepmother, the dead father, the dead lover. The current lover.

Thorough. He respected that.

And he understood she'd gathered and was continuing to gather more information, more deep background and areas than a reporter could possibly use in a series of articles.

"Writing a book," he murmured. "You're writing a book, aren't you, Kati?"

He plugged in one of the two thumb drives he'd found in her case. Rather than the novel or true-crime book he'd expected to find, he brought up the file containing her next article.

For tomorrow's edition.

He read it through twice, so engrossed he barely noticed when the couple next door began to fuck.

The betrayal—for he had little doubt Perry had betrayed him—slashed. A whip across the throat that strangled him so he shoved up to pace the miserable little room, his fists clenching, unclenching.

His teacher, his mentor, the father of who he'd become turned on him, and that turning could—almost certainly would—hasten the end of him.

He considered running, simply abandoning the plans he'd so meticulously set in place and driving east. Kill the reporter along the way, he thought, far along the way, out of what he knew the police would call his hunting ground.

Change his looks, his identity again. Change everything— the car, the plates and then . . .

What? he wondered. Be ordinary again, be nothing again? Find another mask and hide behind it? No, no, he could never go back, never be the pathetic shell again.

Calmer, he stood, eyes closed, accepting. Perhaps it was true and right and inevitable that the father destroy the child. Perhaps that formed the circle, brought the journey to its better, bitter end.

And he'd always known it would end. This new life, this sharpness of being was transient. But he'd hoped, he'd *believed* he had more time. With more time he could, and would, surpass Perry, in song and story, thought the teacher, the lover of books.

No, he would not go back, could not go back. Would not hide like a rat in a hole. He'd go forward, as planned.

Live or die, he decided. But he would never, never simply exist again.

He sat and read the article again, and this time felt a sense of destiny. Of course this was why he took the reporter. Everything was happening as it was meant to happen.

He was at peace with that.

By the time his neighbors finished and had checked out to go home to, he assumed, the spouses they'd cheated on, he'd found the book. He read through the draft, noting she worked in what he thought of as patchwork style—scenes and chapters mixed out of order that she'd link and weave together in another draft.

He looked at her key ring with some regret. How he wished he could risk going through her apartment. She'd have more there—files, notes, books, numbers.

He began to read again, this time making some changes, some additions. He'd keep the computer, the drives, and merge her work with his if he survived the next stage.

For the first time in months he felt a bubble of excitement over something other than killing. He'd include the portions of his own book, the draft he'd begun in the first person, with her third-person reporter's point of view. Juxtaposing his parts of the story with hers.

His evolution and her observations.

And with Kati's help, he would create his own song and story. Death, even his own, would be his legacy.

IN THE CONFERENCE ROOM where she and Tawney worked together, Mantz held her phone in one hand and tapped her keyboard with the other. "Yeah, got it. Thanks, Tawney." She set the phone down, gestured. "I just got word that *U.S. Report* is hyping Starr's article for tomorrow. They've got a teaser online. You should see this."

He stepped over to her desk, read over her shoulder.

Under "Sneak Peeks" the headline glared:

FACE-OFF

Fiona Bristow Goes to Prison to Confront Perry

A Kati Starr Exclusive

"Son of a bitch." Tawney murmured it, the low tone more violent than a shout. "The UNSUB will read this and it puts Fee right back in the crosshairs. Front and center."

"And Starr's billing's going up. She's piling up career

capital with this. Whatever she's invested to get information, it's paying off for her."

"We need to find the leak. And we need to see this goddamn story. I'm going to push on her editor, her publisher. She's hampering the investigation by printing sensitive information, information she may have obtained by illegal means."

"Yeah, we try that, and ball it up with lawyers on both sides. I've got a more direct idea. I can move on that while you try the push. I'll try a little face-off myself, with Starr."

"No way she'll reveal her sources." Tawney stalked over to the coffeemaker. "She'll lap it up."

"Yeah. But I'll go see her, now. Off-hours, late. Try to pump her while she's trying to pump me. I might get something." Mantz checked her watch as she outlined the scenario in her head. "Either way, I bring her in, tonight. Obstruction of justice, interference with a federal investigation, harassing a federal witness. I'll pile it on while she makes her noises about the Fourth Estate and freedom of the press."

Tawney sipped his coffee. "Okay, then what?"

"We sweat her awhile. She'll want a lawyer, she'll call her boss, but we might be able to get her to hold off, just a bit. She wants attention, and she wants information. If we make it seem like we have more, she might try to play us. Buy us time."

"For?"

"For letting it leak she's talking. That we're breaking her down."

Considering, Tawney edged a hip onto Mantz's desk. "So her source or sources start to sweat."

"Worth a shot. It's probably a waste of time, but why shouldn't she lose some sleep over this, feel some pressure? She's shortcutting her way through this, Tawney, and using Bristow every chance she gets. We can work with the media. We do. We use them, they use us. That's the way it's done. But she's not interested in cooperation. She's just looking for the byline."

"You're not going to get an argument from me. I'll work from here, play the game with her bosses. You go direct. Let me know if and when you're bringing her in, and I'll set it up."

He rubbed the knots of tension at the back of his neck. "Maybe he won't see the paper. Maybe he'll make a move tomorrow, one of the mail drops, or we'll spot his car at one of the trolling sites."

Mantz nodded as she put on her jacket. "If he's following current events, and we know damn well he is, Starr's telegraphing our leads, or enough of them to put him on alert. The mail drops are a long shot. I think he's done with Perry, and if not, he will be once he knows Bristow went to see him."

She paused at the door. "Are you going to let her know what's coming?"

"Like you said, it's late. Let her get a decent night's sleep. Tomorrow's soon enough for that. Work Starr, Erin, then bring her in and we'll work her harder."

"Looking forward to it."

IT FELT GOOD to be outside, to do something that didn't involve the keyboard or the phone. Mantz didn't mind the rain. In fact, Seattle's weather suited her perfectly. She enjoyed catching sight of Mount Rainier on sunny days, just as she enjoyed the cozy sense of intimacy the rain offered her.

Tonight, she considered it an added bonus. Pulling Starr out of her office or dry apartment into a downpour piped a little icing on the cake.

She really wanted a go at the reporter on a personal level as much as professional. While she wasn't a one-for-all-because-we're-women sort, she saw Starr's barrel-ahead style on this story as a woman climbing over the bodies of other women—dead and alive.

She'd climbed her own rocky cliff to get where she was in the bureau, Mantz thought, but by God she hadn't taken shortcuts, she hadn't stepped on anyone's back to do it.

Those who did deserved to be kicked down a few rungs.

With her windshield wipers swishing and the lights blurring wet on the glass, she drove toward the paper first. Most likely Starr had called it a night by this time, but the building was en route to the apartment. Might as well do a check there.

As she drove she considered her strategy. Go in soft first, she thought, let the fatigue and the stress show. Try the girl-to-girl appeal. Her instincts said that approach would bomb, and Starr would see it as a weakness.

That was just fine. It would add an element of what-the-fuck? when she kicked in, bore down and charged Starr with obstruction, maybe tossed in suspicion of bribing a federal employee.

She'd see how it went.

She turned into the parking lot and lifted her eyebrows when she spotted the apple-red Toyota. A scan of the plate verified it as Starr's car.

Burning the midnight oil? That was just fine.

As she pulled up beside it, she noted the flat right rear tire.

"Bad luck," Mantz murmured and smiled as she parked beside the Toyota.

Even as she reached for her umbrella something tickled in her gut. She sat for a moment, studying the lot, the rain, the building. Dark but for the security lights on the main level, she noted. You'd need a light in your office to burn the midnight oil.

She left the umbrella in the car, hitched her jacket back for easier access to her weapon.

She heard nothing but the rain and the wet whoosh of sporadic traffic when she got out. Traffic light enough, she observed, distant enough so the lot, the position of the car wouldn't be in clear view. And the rain? There was that icing again.

She circled the car, studied the pancaked tire and, going with impulse, tried the door.

That tickle went to a buzz when she found it unlocked.

Following the buzz, she hiked to the building, banged on the locked glass doors. When the security guard crossed the tiled lobby floor, his walk, his body language said retired cop.

Sixty-couple, she judged, and sharp-eyed.

She held her ID up to the glass.

He studied it, and her, then used the intercom.

"Problem?"

"I'm Special Agent Erin Mantz. I'm looking for Kati Starr. Her car's in the lot, rear right tire's flat. It's unlocked. I need to know if she's in the building, or what time she logged out."

He scanned the lot, then her face again. "Hold on."

Mantz took out her phone. She gave her name, her ID number, and asked for the numbers for Starr's home phone, cell and office.

The cell transferred her to voice mail as the guard came back.

"She signed out at nine-forty. There's nobody here. Even the cleaning crew's finished up." He hesitated a moment, then unlocked the doors. "I tried her home phone and her cell," he said as he opened the glass. "Straight to voice mail."

"Did she leave alone?"

"According to lobby security she walked out on her own."

"Is there security video on the lot?"

"No. Stops at the doors, and she walked out the door alone. That's usual for her," he added. "She doesn't travel in groups or socialize much with coworkers. If she had car trouble, she'd have used her key pass and come back in to call for service. No reason she'd have done otherwise. Nobody else signed out within twenty minutes of her, either side."

Mantz nodded, keyed in the number for her partner. "Tawney? We've got a problem."

WITHIN AN HOUR, agents had convinced the building super to open Kati Starr's apartment, roused her editor and took statements from the guard and the cleaning crew.

The editor blocked the request to open her desk computer.

"Not without a warrant. Look, odds are she's following a lead or she's banging her boyfriend."

"Does she have a boyfriend?" Mantz demanded.

"How the hell should I know? Starr keeps her personal life private. So she got a flat tire? Probably called a cab."

"None of the local cab companies made a pickup at this location."

"And you want me to leap from there to foul play? So you can poke around in her files? Not without a warrant."

Mantz pulled out her phone when it signaled and turned away in disgust to answer. "Where? Keep on it. We're on our way there. We got a ping on her cell phone."

"There, see?" The editor shrugged. "With a boyfriend, or out having a drink. She's earned it."

"OUT HAVING A DRINK," Mantz said between her teeth as they stood in the rainy parking lot of the rest stop. She snapped on protective gloves. "He left the phone turned on so we'd get a signal. So we'd come out here."

She waited impatiently while the forensics team documented the scene.

She took the iPhone. "We'll need to dump the data, go through it." She looked over at Tawney. "It's got to be Eckle. It's not a damn coincidence she gets taken from her office lot. He's got her. He grabbed her right under our noses. She doesn't fit his victim profile, but she fits him. Like a glove. We didn't see it."

"No, we didn't see it." He handed her an evidence bag for the phone. "He's got a couple hours on us, but he expected more. A lot more. Nobody would notice she's not around until morning, and even then . . . maybe her editor gets pissed when she doesn't show, but he's not going to call the cops. Maybe not for hours more, until somebody notices and mentions her car's in the lot.

"He figures he's got twelve, maybe fifteen hours on us. He's only got two. We need boots on the ground. Now. I'll drive, you work the phone." He swung toward the car. "We want badges checking every hotel, motel, vacation rental. Focus on out-of-the-way spots first. Cheap. He's used to living frugally. He doesn't need shine. He wants a place where nobody looks too close, nobody cares."

Tawney peeled out. "He needs supplies, food," he continued even as Mantz relayed the orders. "Fast-food joints, places he can pick up road food. Gas. Gas marts would work best, get everything in one stop, move on."

"He's got her computer. She walked out with it, so he has it. Maybe he'll use it. We can trace that. He thinks he's clear, at least until morning. Maybe we send her an e-mail. We set up a name, a URL, send her a message. A tip. I've got information on RSK Two, what's it worth to you?" Mantz flicked Tawney a glance. "He might bite on that. If he answers, we can track it."

"Bargain with him, keep him involved. It could work. Get the geeks working on it."

ECKLE SLEPT ON TOP of the thin bedspread, fully dressed. Still his mind raced. So much to do, so much to relive, so much to imagine. His life had never been so full that even his sleep swirled with color and movement and sound.

He dreamed of what he would do with Kati—bright, sharp Kati. He had the place for it, just waiting for him. The perfect spot—all the privacy he'd need. And the irony of it tasted sweet as candy.

Then when he was finished with her—or maybe not quite—he would take Fiona. While they looked for one, he'd take Perry's lost prize.

Maybe he'd make her watch while he did things to Kati. Make her watch while he turned her from alive to dead. He'd have so little time with Fiona, wouldn't that enhance the brevity?

So he dreamed of two women, bruised and bleeding. Dreamed of their pleading eyes. Dreamed of them begging him, bargaining with him. Doing whatever he told them to do, saying whatever he told them to say. *Listening* to him as no one ever had.

He'd be the single focus of their life. Until he killed them.

He dreamed of a room shuttered from the light, a room washed with red, as if he looked through the thin silk of a red scarf. Dreamed of muffled moans and high, thin screams.

And woke with a jerk, breath wheezing in, eyes wheeling.

Someone at the door? His hand shot under the pillow for the .22, the gun he'd use to put a bullet in his own brain should there be no escape.

He would never go to prison.

He held his breath, listening. Only the rain, he thought. But it hadn't been only the rain. A click, a click, like the turn of a knob, but . . .

His breath eased out again.

E-mail. He'd left the computer on while he charged it.

He pulled the laptop back onto the bed, studied the unopened e-mail. The subject line read RSKII, and reading it sent a thrill over his skin.

Cautious, he checked the sender's address against Kati's contact list.

A new one.

He sat studying the subject line, the sender's name, while the thrill ebbed and flowed like a tide. And he opened it.

Kati Starr:

I've read your stories on RSKII. I think you're pretty smart. I'm smart, too. I have some information on our mutual interest. Information I think you'll want for your next article. I could go to the police, but they don't pay. I want $10,000, and to be reported as an anonymous source. The girl's already dead, so I can't help her. I'll help you and help myself. If you want what I have, let me know by noon tomorrow. After that, I'll send my offer to someone else.

EW (Eye Witness)

"No. No." He shook his head, jabbed the screen with his finger twice. "You're lying. Lying. You didn't see anything. Nobody sees me. Nobody."

Except them, he thought. Except the women he killed. They saw him.

A trick, just a trick. He pushed off the bed to pace the room as the tide over his skin rose high and fast. People were liars. Tricksters.

He told the truth, in the end he told them the truth, didn't he? When he tightened the scarf around their neck, he looked them right in the eye and told them. He gave them his name, and told them who killed them and why.

Simple truth. "My name is Francis Eckle, and I'm going to kill you now. Because I can. Because I like it."

So they died with his truth, like a gift.

But this EW? He—or she—was a liar. Extorting his work for money.

No one saw him.

But he thought of the man in line at Starbucks. Of the pimply-faced clerk at the gas mart whose eyes had passed over him with boredom. Of the greasy-haired night clerk at the motel who'd smelled of pot and smirked at him as he handed over the key.

Maybe.

He sat again, studied the e-mail again. He could answer it, demand more information before any discussion of payment. That's what she'd do.

He poured himself a short glass of whiskey and thought it through.

He composed a response, editing, deleting, refining as carefully as he might a thesis. When his finger hovered over *send*, he hesitated.

It could be a trap. Maybe the FBI was poking a finger in, trying to trap Kati. Or him. He couldn't see it clearly, so he rose and paced again, drank again, thought it through again.

Just in case, he decided. Safety first.

He took a shower, brushed his teeth, shaved the faint shadow over his skull, his face. He stowed all his things in his duffel.

Moments after he hit *send*, he left the room. He bought a Coke at vending for the caffeine jolt, but realized he didn't need it.

The idea of being seen, the vague possibility of being tricked, energized him. Excited him.

In some secret part of his heart he hoped he had been seen. It made it all the more worthwhile.

He gave the trunk a little pat as he passed it. "Let's take a drive, shall we, Kati?"

"JESUS, HE ANSWERED IT." Mantz leaped toward the tech. "He bit. Can you track it to the source?"

"Give me a minute," the tech told her, tapping keys.

EW,

she and Tawney read:

I'm very interested in good information. However, I can't negotiate any sort of payment without more data. Ten thousand is a lot of money, and the paper will require a show of good faith on your part. You claim to be an eyewitness. To what? You'll have to give me some details, of your choosing, before we can go to the next step.

I can meet you, in a public place—again of your choosing—if you don't want to put those details in writing or on the record at this time.

I'm eager to discuss this.

Kati Starr

"Smart enough to know she wouldn't jump without having more," Tawney commented. "But curious enough not to ignore it."

"And not mobile," Mantz added. "He has to be holed up somewhere with Internet access. Awake but not moving. It took him less than an hour to answer, and he'd have thought about it first. He was on top of her computer when we sent it."

"Got him." The tech gestured to the screen.

They set it up on the move. Agents, snipers, hostage negotiators—all with orders to surround, to go in silent.

"The agent who roused the night clerk said four single men have checked in tonight," Mantz relayed as they raced through the night. "Two paid in cash. He's got no holdovers from yesterday, or any day. He can't make Eckle from the photo, didn't see any of the cars and can't say if any of them went into the rooms alone. Basically, he's stoned and could give a rat's ass."

"Let's get a team in rooms next to the four check-ins. Hold positions. There's always the chance he took her in with him."

They parked in the lot of the all-night diner next to the motel, donned their vests. As Tawney assessed the lay of the land, he nodded to an agent.

"Cage, give me the word."

"We've got it down to two rooms. The other two have dual occupancy of the consenting kind. One's got a couple banging like it's the Fourth of July, and the other's got a woman ragging on a guy about leaving his bitch of a wife. Teams said the walls are like paper. It's like being there."

"The other two?"

"One's got somebody snoring loud enough to peel the paint off the walls." He paused, held up a finger to his earpiece. "Just heard a woman's voice saying, 'Shut the fuck up, Harry.' I'd say that leaves the one. Number four-fourteen. Corner room, back, east side. Team on that says it's dead quiet. Not a sound."

"I want the other rooms covered, and the parking lot blocked off. He doesn't slip through."

"Affirmative."

"Desk clerk have a problem with us taking down the door?"

"He's stoned to the eyeballs. Said do what we got to do— and probably went back to his bong and porn."

Tawney nodded as they walked. "I want to take it down fast. I want lights in there the second it goes down. Blind his ass. The team's in there and on him like a wolf on a deer. How about the car?"

"None matching the description or plates on the lot, or in the diner lot."

"Could've switched it," Mantz put it. "She could be in one of these. Any of them."

"She won't be for long."

He had to hang back, let the take-down team move into position. He wanted to take the door, wanted it like he wanted breath. But he wanted it done clean and fast and safe just a little more.

It went exactly as he'd ordered. With his weapon drawn, he moved forward as the sounds of *Clear! Clear!* rang out of the room. His stomach dropped. That wasn't the response he'd wanted. He knew before he reached the door that Eckle had already slipped through their fingers.

TWENTY-NINE

Fiona slathered cream over her damp skin and hummed a tune that got stuck in her head in the shower. She couldn't quite pin down the song, the lyrics, but the cheery melody suited her mood.

She felt she'd turned a corner and closed a door. She liked the philosophy that by closing one she could—and maybe already had—opened another.

Maybe it was naive, but she had every confidence the FBI would track down Francis Xavier Eckle, and quickly, with the new information. Information she'd helped generate.

She'd kicked her way out of the trunk again, she decided.

Still humming, she stepped into the bedroom. Her eyebrows lifted in surprise when she saw the bed empty. Usually she'd find Simon sprawled in it, pillow over his head as he clung to those last minutes of sleep—until she went down and made coffee.

She liked the routine, she thought as she dressed. The easy give and take of it. Liked knowing the dogs were outside for their morning romp, and that Simon would stumble downstairs, with uncanny timing, when the coffee was ready so, in this lovely weather, they'd have it and whatever food came readily to hand on the back deck.

She supposed the siren's call of coffee had been too loud for him to resist that morning, or she'd taken too long to suit him in the shower.

She pulled on her army green Chucks, then spent a few minutes on her hair, her makeup in anticipation of her morning classes. There was a window in the afternoon, she calculated, just wide enough for a trip to the nursery.

If she couldn't go alone—not yet—Simon would just have to go through the window with her. She wanted to plant her window boxes.

She jogged downstairs, the tune in her head juggling with geraniums and petunias and the planned session of obstacle training.

"I smell coffee!" Her voice danced into the kitchen a few steps ahead of her. "And I've got a yen for Toaster Strudels. Why don't we—"

She knew the moment she saw his face, and the shadow blocked her sun. "Oh God. Goddamn. Say it fast."

"He took the reporter. Kati Starr."

"But—"

"I said it fast." He pushed the coffee he'd poured into her hands. "Now take this. We'll sit down and I'll give you the rest."

She made herself sit. "Is she dead?"

"I don't know. They don't know. Tawney called while you were in the shower. He'd hoped to get out here, tell you in person, but he can't get away."

"Okay, that's okay. They're sure?" She shook her head before he could speak. "Stupid question. He wouldn't have called if they weren't sure. I'm trying to shut up, let you tell me, but words keep shoving into my throat. She's not the right type. She's five years out of the age group, at least. She's not in college, not the right body type. She's—"

For the second time, she shook her head. "No, I'm wrong. She's not *Perry's* type. He's already shown he wants to make his own mark, hasn't he? He's tired of doing it Perry's way.

Boy's all grown up now and wants his own. And she—the reporter—she's made him a star, she made him important. She gave him a name. She knows him, wouldn't he think? That makes it more intimate and exciting. More his."

She took a breath. "Sorry."

"You're the behavioral specialist, not me. But that's how I see it." He studied her face, judged her ready to hear the rest. "He grabbed her last night, from the parking lot where she works."

She bit back the urge to interrupt as he took her through it.

"They nearly had him," she murmured. "They were never that close with Perry, not so soon after an abduction. She's still alive. She has to be. Do they think he knows?"

"They're going on the theory that he was just being careful, or he was planning to leave the motel before morning anyway. They sent another e-mail claiming they'd seen him burying the last victim while they were camped illegally in the park. He hasn't responded. Yet."

"She's still alive. The dogs are at the door, wondering what's taking us so long. Let's go out. I could use the air anyway."

She rose, left her untouched coffee where it was.

Sensing her mood, the dogs whined, pushed against her legs, shoved noses in her hands.

"I have such a violent dislike of her," Fiona told him. "It's still there, just as intense even though I'm sick knowing what she's going through right now. It's a weird tug-of-war."

"It's natural. What she's going through doesn't change what she is."

"Oh, it will." Briefly, she pressed her fingers to her eyes, then let them fall. "If she lives, it will. She'll never be quite the same. He'll hurt her more than the others because he's got a taste for that now. Like a dog who bites and gets away with it. If he answers the e-mail, they'll be able to track him again, even if he keeps moving. They'll do that stuff they do. Analysis, triangulating, calculating. So she has a better chance than the others. She'll need it."

"They have a little more. They interviewed everybody at

the motel, and there was one guy who saw him. He was keeping an eye out for the woman he was meeting and looked out when he heard the car. Mostly he noticed because Eckle parked across the lot, and it was raining hard so it seemed weird."

"He saw Eckle? He saw his face?"

"He didn't really get a look at him. Eckle had an umbrella, had it angled so his face was behind it—and the guy only glanced out for a few seconds. But he's sure the car was a dark color—black, dark blue, dark gray—too hard to tell in the rain."

"He changed cars, or the color anyway. More they know that he's unaware of."

"The guy's going to work with an FBI artist. He's even agreed to try hypnosis. Apparently, he's into it. They're working the desk clerk, too. They're pretty sure he's ditched the beard."

"Okay, that's as good as it gets." She tried not to think about the miles of back roads and interstates a beardless man in a dark-colored car could travel or the acres and acres of parkland he could wander.

"What do you want to do?"

"I want to go pull the covers over my head, brood and curse God. What I'm going to do is take my morning classes, then drag you to the nursery this afternoon so I can pick out flowers for the window boxes."

"Crap. If we're doing that, I'm going to stop and pick up some lumber and drop some designs off at the Inlet Hotel."

"Fine. I have to be back by four."

"Then we'll be back by four."

She worked up a smile for him. "Let's go by and rent a movie while we're at it. Something fun."

"Can it be porn?"

"No. You have to buy porn movies off the Internet so they come in plain mailers and nobody on the island knows for sure you're watching porn. Those are the rules."

"I'll settle for nudity and adult language."

"Deal." She laid a hand on his cheek. "I have to prep."

He covered her hand with his before she could step back.

"We're stuck now because you wheedled me into falling in love with you. So we get through whatever there is to get through." He kissed her. "With or without porn."

"If I could needlepoint, I swear I'd make that into a sampler." She kissed him back. "Come on, boys, it's time for work."

ECKLE BOUGHT A COPY of the paper to read at his leisure on the ferry. He'd given Kati another dose that morning before she'd fully come out from the first.

He needed her nice and quiet and peaceful. That was one of the mistakes Perry made that he hadn't—and wouldn't. Perry had wanted them at least semi-aware while they were trapped—and that's how Fiona had beaten him.

Eckle liked the idea of Kati unconscious and helpless in the trunk, appreciated the fresh terror she'd experience when she woke in a different place entirely. As if by magic.

But for now, he'd just enjoy the ride on the ferry busy with tourists and summer people. He might have preferred to sit in his car the entire way, but he understood that might rouse some suspicion if anyone paid attention. Besides, wandering, mingling, even speaking to people here and there was good practice, and better cover.

He made a point of talking to a pair of hikers who'd boarded the ferry on foot. In preparation for his time on Orcas he'd studied the trails and parks and campgrounds, and had already visited several on previous trips. So he was able to speak knowledgeably—and gained their gratitude by buying them coffee.

He waved it off. "I know what it's like to be your age and hitting the trail. I've got a boy about your age. He's coming out with his mother next week."

"You baching it till then?"

Eckle smiled. The hiker's name had nearly escaped him. He saw them both as tools to be used. "That's right. Just me, some peace and quiet and a six-pack."

"I hear that. If you decide to hit the trail today, we're going to start at Cascade Lake."

"I might. But I think I'm more inclined to . . ." He knew the expression. What was it? What was it? He felt the back of his neck start to burn as the boys looked at him oddly. "Drown some worms," he said, imagining pushing both their heads underwater. "Listen, if you're heading for the lake, I can give you a lift as far as Rosario. Save you the boot leather."

"Seriously? That'd be cool." The boys looked at each other, nodded.

"Thanks, Frank."

"No problem at all. We're nearly there. Why don't we go ahead, get your gear in the car?"

He was Frank Blinckenstaff from Olympia. A high school teacher with a wife, Sharon, and a son, Marcus. Of course they hadn't asked him about Sharon and Marcus—they were too self-involved, too egocentric to care about him. He was a means to an end—but so were they.

"Trunk's loaded," he said with a bright, bright smile that sent a skitter of ice down one of the boys' spines. "But there's room enough in the back."

The boys hesitated, then shrugged.

In the end he drove off the ferry and passed the vigilant gaze of the deputy checking cars, looking, he imagined, like a father heading out on a little vacation with his two sons.

Nobody saw him, he thought again. And that was perfect.

HE DROPPED HIS PASSENGERS off and forgot them. They were ghosts, like the students who'd passed in and out of his classroom. Transient, insubstantial, meaningless.

His more important passenger would be stirring soon, he thought, so he'd have to keep on schedule if he wanted to have her, and himself, all settled in before she regained full consciousness.

It was time for the next act.

Excitement frothed in his belly. No one would see him. They would see only Frank Blinckenstaff from Olympia. He drove through the busy village, along the twisting roads and into the park. He had to wipe damp palms on his jeans as he thought of Fiona. So close now, nearly close enough to touch.

He could've told the watchful deputy at the ferry she had a few days left. Days to eat and sleep and teach. Days left to wonder. Days left before he repaid his mentor, and made both her and Perry other ghosts who'd passed in and out of his life.

And once that was done, he'd fully become. His own man, at last.

Live or die, his own man.

He navigated the winding roads, easing carefully on the switchbacks, and smiled as the trees thickened. Like curtains, he thought, green curtains he'd keep snugly closed as he worked.

He turned into the narrow drive—wound his way back as his excitement grew till his hands wanted to shake.

He spotted the car in front of the picturesque cabin shrouded by those green, green curtains. His landlady waited, as promised.

He noted the windows were open—airing it out for him. There were planters of flowers on the porch. He'd have to remember to water them, in case she slipped by to check.

As he parked beside her car, she stepped out. He had to repeat her name over and over in his head to make her real.

"Mrs. Greene!"

"Meg," she reminded him and walked down to offer her hand. "Welcome. Smooth trip in?"

"Couldn't've been smoother. I can't tell you how happy I am to be here." He kept his smile pasted on his face as the dog trotted up to greet him. "Hey, boy, how's it going!"

"Xena and I spruced the place up for you a little."

"Oh now, you shouldn't have bothered. It's just going to be me for a few days. Wait till Sharon and Marcus get here. It's going to be love at first sight."

"I hope so. Now we've laid in some basics for you. Don't say we shouldn't've bothered. It's part of the package. Why don't I help you in with your things, show you through again. Xena! Come on away from there."

"She must smell my fishing tackle," Eckle said as the dog

sniffed around the trunk of the car. His voice went flat. He imagined kicking the dog bloody, strangling its master. "I'll get my gear later. No need to show me through again, Mrs.— Meg. I think the first thing I'm going to do is take a long walk, stretch out my legs."

"If you're sure. I left the keys on the kitchen counter, and there's a list with all the numbers you should need right on the refrigerator. Booklet in the living room has all the information on the cabin, restaurant menus, shops, park information. Now you're sure you don't want the cleaning service?"

"We'll be fine." He would kill her if she didn't leave him *alone*. Yes, he would kill her and her sniffing dog if she didn't leave within one minute. Really, he'd have no choice.

"Well, if you change your mind, or you need anything, you just call. Otherwise, enjoy the cabin, and the quiet. Good luck with your writing."

"What?"

"Your writing? The travel piece you're going to do."

"Yes, yes. My mind was wandering." He let out a *heh-heh-heh*, the closest he could get to a laugh. "Not enough coffee this morning."

"There's a fresh pound of beans in the freezer."

Thirty seconds, he thought. Live or die.

"Appreciate it."

"I'll let you get to your walk. Come on, Xena."

He waited and, because his fingers had begun to tremble, slipped his hands in his pockets while the dog followed her to the car. He watched the dog look back at the trunk, nose quivering.

Kick you bloody, then carve you up and bury you with the bitch who owns you.

He spread his lips in a smile, pulled his trembling fingers out of his pocket to answer Meg's wave.

And he breathed and breathed, the air charging out of him like an engine as she drove down the lane and disappeared into the trees.

Nosy bitches better stay away.

It took him time to get settled. All the windows had to be

closed, locked, the curtains drawn. In the cozy bedroom his chatty landlady had shown him on his previous visit and deemed perfect for his imaginary son, he covered the bed with plastic.

He unpacked, tidily arranging his things in the closet, the dresser, on the bathroom counter while he enjoyed the quiet and the generous space. He'd gotten too used to tiny motel rooms, shabby beds, ugly sounds and smells.

This was a treat.

Satisfied with his preparations and his privacy, he walked back outside. For a few moments he simply stood basking in the quiet, in the peace.

Then he opened the trunk.

"We're home, Kati! Let me show you to your room."

She trembled toward consciousness, ill, aching, confused. She felt as though she was floating in some freezing river with slabs of jagged ice scraping and stabbing along her skin. Red and black dots spun in front of her eyes, tilting sickeningly. Through the rush of blood in her head, she heard someone humming. A sudden burning pain in her arm brought on a shocked gasp, but the air wouldn't come.

As she began to struggle, as her eyes wheeled, the humming stopped.

"So, awake at last. You slept right through your bath. Believe me, you needed it. You'd made a mess of yourself and stank to high heaven. No wonder that idiot dog was sniffing around."

She tried to focus on the face over hers, but everything about it was too hard, too bright. The eyes, the smile. She cringed away.

"I didn't have time to introduce myself before. I'm Francis Eckle. But you can call me RSK Two."

Fear drenched her like sweat, and as she shook her head in denial that bright, hard smile only widened.

"I'm a big fan! And I'm going to give you an exclusive interview. It's the story of your life, Kati. Just think of it. You'll know everything, experience everything." He patted her cheek. "I smell Pulitzer! Of course, it's going to cost you, but we'll talk about that. I'll leave you to settle in."

He leaned down close to her ear and whispered, "I'm going to hurt you. I'm going to enjoy it. Think about that."

He leaned back, beamed that smile again. "Well, all this excitement has worked up my appetite. I'm going to go down and have some lunch. Want anything? No?" He laughed at his own joke while tears leaked down her cheeks. "See you soon."

IT FELT GOOD to do something normal, something fun. Better yet, Fiona thought, to wander around the nursery and stop and catch up with neighbors. It struck her just how isolated she'd become over the past week, tethered to the house.

She missed outings, she realized, and errands and the bits of easy gossip gathered up at routine stops.

She'd even enjoyed the interlude with lumber and hardware.

Simon spent his time vetoing choices or shrugging his assent. Until she dawdled over dahlia.

"Pick one. They all have stems, leaves, petals."

"This from a man who just spent half a lifetime over drawer pulls."

"The drawer pulls won't die in the first hard frost."

"Which makes the choice of dahlia more important, as its time's brief."

"This one." He snatched one at random. "I can't live without this one."

She laughed even as she grabbed two more. "Perfect. Now I want some of that blue stuff." She gestured toward a flat of lobelia. "Then we'll be— Hey, hi, Meg, Chuck."

Her friends turned, with Meg's hands full of dianthus.

"Hi! Oh, aren't those pretty." Meg beamed at Simon. "You must've built those window boxes."

"Yeah," he confirmed as he and Chuck exchanged brief yet long-suffering glances over the women's heads.

"Are you putting in another bed?" Fiona asked.

"No. I had to run over and open the cabin for a new tenant, and Chuck stayed back, started cleaning out the shed."

"If I try it when she's around, nothing gets thrown away."

"You never know, do you? He was going to toss this old washtub."

"Piece of junk," Chuck said under his breath.

"It won't be, once I fill it with these and put it in the yard. I'm thinking of sort of digging in one end, so it looks like it just got tossed there. It'll be a bit of lawn art instead of a piece of junk."

"Meg's always figuring out how to repurpose things." Fiona set the flowers in the cart.

"I hate waste."

"I guess it saves us in the long run," Chuck put in. "She mostly furnished the cabin out of thrift store and yard sale junk she fixed up."

"So you've got a tenant," Fiona said as she picked through the lobelia.

"A two-weeker. Husband's down by himself this week. His wife and son are coming down next." Meg picked up some lobelia, held it next to the dianthus and deemed it good. "The boy's got some swim meet or some such thing he didn't want to miss. The dad's a teacher and writes travel articles. We're hoping he does one on the cabin and Orcas. It couldn't hurt. Kind of an odd one," Meg added as they wandered through. "He came in a couple months back, asked to see it. Wanted a quiet place, private, so he could write."

"That's natural enough, I guess."

"I guess he likes his solitude because he sure gave me the bum's rush this morning. Wouldn't have the housekeeping service, so I'm already feeling for his wife. But he paid cash, up front and in full, and that buys a lot of washtub flowers."

"What kind of screening do you do on tenants?"

Meg blinked at Simon's question. "Oh, well, there's really not much you can do there. Most people take a week or two, or even a weekend off-season. You take a security deposit and hope for the best. We haven't had any serious problems there. Are you thinking of buying a place for rentals?"

"No. Do you get many who pay cash?"

"Not a lot, but it happens. Some people just feel uncomfortable giving us their credit card number."

"What did he look like?"

Meg glanced at Fiona, who'd gone uncharacteristically silent. "Ah, he's . . . Oh my Jesus, you're thinking he might be . . . God, Simon, you're freaking me out. He's, well, he's in his mid-forties somewhere. I've got his driver's license on file because we ask to see ID, but I can't remember the birthday. He's clean-shaven, bald as a hard-boiled egg. He's well spoken, friendly enough. He talked about his wife, and how his boy was going to love the place. He even asked if his boy could bring a friend with him for a few days if he wanted."

"We're all just a little jumpy." Fiona rubbed a hand up and down Meg's arm.

"Do you want to go by the place, check him out?" Chuck asked.

"We can't check out everybody who's rented a place, or who's camping or spending a few days at one of the hotels or B-and-Bs," Fiona pointed out. "They're watching the ferry."

It had to be enough.

She waited until they were in the truck, heading back. "I forget, or don't always realize, how worried you are. Don't shrug it off," she said when he did just that. "This thing has been there almost from the start with us. Like a shadow in the room, all the time. And I'm so busy thinking about it, or telling myself not to think about it, I can forget it's weighing on you, too."

He said nothing for nearly a mile. "I didn't want you. Got that?"

"Simon, I hold that sentiment close to my heart."

"I didn't want you because I knew damn well you'd get in my way, and you'd find a way to make me like it. Need it. And you. So, now I do. I keep what's mine, and I take care of it."

She lifted her eyebrows. "Like a puppy?"

"Like however you want to see it."

"I'll have to think about that."

"Cops, feds, that's all fine. They do what they do. But no-body's getting through me to you. Nobody."

This time Fiona fell silent, stayed silent until they made the turn to his house. "You know I can and will take care of myself. No, wait—you know that. And because you know that, hearing you say that to me, knowing you mean it, it makes me feel more cared for than I have in a very, very long time."

She drew a breath. "So I'm going to plant window boxes, then I'm going to teach my evening class. And I'm going to hope with everything I've got they find Kati Starr, alive, and that soon—really soon—we'll be rid of the shadows so it's just you and me."

"And a pack of dogs."

She smiled. "Yeah."

ECKLE STEPPED OUT of the bathroom, freshly showered, in clean boxers and a T-shirt. On the bed, Kati whimpered be-hind the tape as her eyes, the left nearly swollen shut, ticked in his direction.

"That's better. I wasn't sure how I'd feel about rape as I've never found sex to be particularly important. But I liked it. It was an entirely new experience for me, and every new experi-ence is important to the whole—thanks for that. With rape, all the pressure's off as there's just no need to worry about pleasing the whore spreading them for you."

He pulled the little desk chair over and sat beside the bed. "I like giving pain. I always knew it, but since it's not accept-able under the *rules*"—he gave the word quick air quotes—"I buried the urge. I was not a happy man, Kati. I was just going through the motions, living a life in the gray. Until Perry. I owe him for that. I owe him Fiona for that. But this, all the rest? You? That's mine, entirely. Now."

He tapped the mini tape recorder he'd taken from her bag and set on the nightstand. "I'm going to turn this on, and we're going to have a conversation. You're going to tell me everything you know, everything your source or sources have leaked to you. If you scream, even once, I'll put the tape back on and I'll start breaking your fingers. There's no one to hear you, but you're not going to scream. Are you, Kati?" As he asked her he reached up and bent the pinkie of one of her bound hands backward until her face went bone white. "Are you, Kati?"

She shook her head, arching up as if to escape the pain.

"Good. This is going to hurt." He ripped the tape away, viciously, nodded with satisfaction as she bit back the scream. "Very good. Say thank you."

Her breath shuddered out, in, her chest trembled with it, but she managed a barely audible whisper. And licked her dry lips. "Please. Water. Please."

"This?" He held up the bottle. "I bet you're parched." He pulled her head up by the hair, poured water into her mouth so she choked, gagged, wheezed. "Better? What do you say?"

She said thank you.

THIRTY

They had more than he'd expected, but not more than he'd prepared for.

Tawney and his partner had been to College Place, though Kati couldn't confirm they'd gone to his school or apartment. Even when he broke two of her fingers she couldn't give him the exact locations. Her source hadn't given her the data, or hadn't had the data to give.

But they'd been there, he was sure of it. They'd pawed through his things, through the daily life of the person he'd once been. Not that it mattered, he thought. They weren't his things any longer. They belonged to another life—the gray life.

They were, as he'd expected, watching the ferries. And Fiona had moved into her lover's house. She was never alone.

He'd taken care of the first, and had plans for the second complication. The centerpiece of that plan lay unconscious on the plastic sheet.

He thought of the e-mail. A trap, just as he'd suspected. He was sure of it now. They thought they could trick him, outwit him, but he was much too smart for that.

He considered, briefly, tossing the reporter back in the

trunk and taking the morning ferry back to the mainland or one of the other islands. But that would leave Fiona undone, and a debt was a debt.

More, the student would surpass the teacher when he killed Fiona. Correcting Perry's mistake would be part of his legacy.

His song and story.

The pity was he could no longer take his time with Kati, no longer risk two or three days with her as he'd hoped. It left him little time for their collaboration on the book.

He'd need to do the lion's share of that himself as he had to start the next phase sooner than originally planned.

He studied her, shrugged. Really, there wasn't much more he wanted to do with her.

He decided he'd study his maps again, then get a few hours' sleep, fry up a good breakfast. He'd want to get started well before dawn.

As he went out, he decided it was a good thing he'd broken her fingers instead of her toes. He didn't want to carry her the whole way.

SIMON KEPT HIS MUSIC turned off and found work he could do on the shop porch. That way he could see, and hear, who came and went.

Just something else he owed Eckle, he thought. The fact that he couldn't focus on his work, couldn't blast his music.

He'd already decided to give it one more week, then whatever Fiona's schedule, he was taking her away for a while. Nonnegotiable. They'd go visit his parents in Spokane, which would kill two birds as his mother would stop nagging him about meeting Fiona every time they talked on the phone or e-mailed.

He'd already selected the hammer to drive home that nail. He'd sacrifice his dog's balls. Fiona wanted Jaws neutered— and kept leaving information about it all over the house. He'd give her that; she'd give him this.

Sorry, pal, he thought.

Then they'd drive—the whole pack of them, if she wanted—to Spokane. He'd rent a damn van if he had to. Driving took time, the more the better as far as he was concerned.

If Tawney and Mantz couldn't run Eckle to ground by the time they got back, they didn't deserve their badges.

He glanced up at the sound of a car, then set aside the brush he'd been using to stain a pair of bar stools when he saw the police cruiser.

He hoped to hell it was good news.

"Davey." Fiona stepped out of the house. "You've got the timing down. My last clients left ten minutes ago. The next aren't due for twenty." She pressed her knuckles between her breasts where the breath wanted to stick. "Is she alive?"

"They haven't found her yet, Fee."

She just sat down where she stood, on the porch steps. Her arms went around dogs as they crowded around her.

"They sent us a picture. The best they could get from the two witnesses at the motel. I brought you a copy."

He took it from the file he carried, offered it.

"It hardly looks like him—or like he did. The eyes, I guess. The eyes do."

"The witnesses were shaky there. They've done a composite."

"His face looks . . . beefier, and he looks younger without the beard. But . . . the cap covers a lot, doesn't it?"

"The night clerk was next to useless—that's the word we got. The other guy, he did his best. But he barely saw Eckle. He left prints in the motel room—Eckle did. They matched them with prints from his apartment. He's not biting on the e-mail again, at least not so far."

He nodded to Simon as Simon walked up. "They don't think he will now so they're releasing his name and this sketch to the media this afternoon. It's going to be all over the TV and the Internet in a couple of hours. Somebody's going to make him, Fee."

Simon said nothing but took the sketch out of Fiona's hand to study it.

"We're going to plaster those on the ferries, at the docks,"

Davey continued. "Starr's paper's offering a quarter-million reward for information that leads to her or Eckle. It's blowing open in his face, Fee."

"Yes, I think it is. I only hope it blows hot and fast enough to save Starr."

HE'D MADE HER WALK. Even with the speed and the protein drink he forced down her throat it took a full three hours. She fell often, but that was fine. He wanted to leave a good trail. He dragged her when he had to, and enjoyed it. He knew where he was going and how to get there.

The perfect spot. Brilliant, if he said so himself.

By the time they stopped, her face was filthy, purpled with bruises, hatchmarked with scrapes and nicks. The clothes he'd washed and put back on her were little more than rags.

She didn't cry, didn't fight when he lashed her to the tree. Her head just fell forward, and her bound hands lay limp in her lap.

He had to slap her several times to bring her around.

"I have to leave you here awhile. I'll be back, don't worry. You may die of dehydration or exposure, infection." He lifted his shoulders in a what-can-you-do? gesture. "I hope not because I really want to kill you with my own hands. After I kill Fiona. One for Perry, one for me. Jesus, you smell, Kati. All the better, but phew. Anyway, when this is done, I'm going to write the story for you, send it in, in your name. You'll get that Pulitzer. Posthumously, but I think you're a shoo-in. See you soon."

He popped one of the black pills himself—he needed the kick—and started off in a brisk jog. Without the dead weight, he calculated he could make it back in under half the time it had taken to drag her pitiful ass alone. He'd be back at the cabin before dawn, or just after.

He had a lot of work to do before he made the return trip.

SIMON WATCHED HER push herself through her next class, and decided enough was enough. When he'd done what he needed to do, he waited until the last car pulled away and she walked back into the house.

He found her in the kitchen running a cold can of Diet Coke over her forehead. "Hot today." She lowered the can, popped it. "It feels like the sky's dropped down a few thousand feet so the sun's pressing against the tops of the trees."

"Go take a shower, cool off. You've got time," he said before she could answer. "Sylvia's coming over to take your last two classes."

"What? Why?"

"Because you look like hell and probably feel worse. You got fuck-all for sleep last night, and I know because I was the one trying to sleep beside you. You're wound up and worn out. So take a shower, take a nap. Brood, if you need to, as long as I'm not around. I'll order some dinner in a couple hours."

"Just hold it." She set the can aside, very deliberately. "My classes, my business, my decision. You don't get to decide when I'm capable of running my business or when I need a goddamn nap. You're not in charge."

"You think I want to be? You think I want to take care of you? I damn well don't. It's a pain in the ass."

"Nobody asked you to take care of me."

He grabbed her arm, dragged her out of the kitchen.

"If you don't let go of me I'm going to deck you."

"Yeah, you do that." He shoved her in the powder room, pushed her in front of the mirror. "Look at yourself. You couldn't deck an unconscious toddler. So be as pissed off as you want because I'm right there with you. And I'm bigger, I'm stronger and I'm meaner."

"Well, excuse the hell right out of me for not looking my best. And thanks so much for not sparing my feelings and letting me know I look like warmed-over crap."

"Your feelings aren't my priority."

"Oh, *there's* news. You do your work, and I'll do mine, and I'll do you a favor. When I'm done I'll take myself off to your slobfest of an excuse for a spare room and sleep there so I don't disturb your beauty sleep."

He recognized by the pitch of her voice she jiggled midway between fury and a crying jag. It damn well couldn't be helped.

"If you try to run this next class I'll make a scene and you'll lose every client in it. Believe me, I'll make sure of it."

"Who the hell do you think you are?" She shoved him with considerably more strength than her pale face advertised. "Giving me ultimatums, threats, blackmail. Who the *hell* do you think you are?"

"I'm the one who loves you. Goddamn it."

"Don't use that on me."

"It's what I've got." Stupid, he realized. He'd let temper bump aside sense—and strategy. This wasn't the way to handle her, and he knew it. "I can't stand it." He gave her the truth, harder for him than the threats. "I can't stand seeing you like this." He pulled her in. "You need a break. I'm asking you to take a break."

"You weren't asking."

"Okay. I'm asking now."

She sighed, hugely. "I look like shit."

"Yeah, you do."

"But that doesn't mean I can't handle my work, or that you get to call in the reserves without asking me."

"We'll make a trade."

"What?" She pulled back. "A trade?"

"You take the break, Mai gets to cut off Jaws's balls." An ace in the hole, Simon figured, needed to be used sooner rather than later.

"Oh! That's ridiculous. That's wrong. That's . . ." She fisted her hands at her temples. "Low. You're using my belief in responsible pet ownership."

"A couple hours down for you, a lifetime of never knowing the thrill of a woman for him. You get the shiny end on this."

She shoved him back, strode out of the bathroom. Then she turned and scowled at him as he leaned against the door-jamb. "You're going to do it anyway."

"Maybe. Maybe not. Part of me figures he ought to at least have a shot at a couple of willing bitches first. A guy should have some memories."

"You're stringing me." But he only shrugged, let the silence hang. "Damn it. You'll call Mai now, today, make an appointment?"

He opened his mouth and swore he felt his own balls shrink up. "No. You do it."

"Okay, but no backing out."

"What do you want, a pinkie swear? A deal's a deal. Go take a shower."

"I will, after I call Mai—and give Sylvia the roundup for the classes she's taking."

"Fair enough. You know how they have those weird-ass dog spas and dog salons and boutiques?"

She huffed, struggling to settle . . . somewhere. "Not everyone thinks they're weird-ass, but yes."

"They ought to have dog bordellos for times like this. A guy could at least have a bang before he becomes a eunuch."

"You ought to look into that. There are enough people who think like you do that you'd probably make a fortune." She glanced toward the front door as the dogs gave the alert. "That's Syl now."

He moved to the door ahead of her, checked for himself.

"Are you that worried?" she asked him.

"I don't see any reason to take chances. Meg's with her."

"Oh." She stepped out. "Hi. First, sorry, second, thanks."

"First, don't be sorry. Second, you're welcome. It was my afternoon off, and Meg and I were doing a garden exchange. I'm overrun with daylilies and she's got extra purple coneflowers."

"So, I tagged along." Meg spoke with calculated cheer. "You've got co-instructors."

"And Simon's right. Honey, you do look tired."

"So I've been told," Fiona said, shooting him one burning stare, "in less tactful terms. Come on in. I'll give you the overview for the classes—and we've got some sun tea."

"Sounds good." Sylvia walked onto the porch, rose to her toes and kissed Simon on the cheek. "Good job."

He smirked at Fiona over Sylvia's head.

"Don't encourage him." Fiona went inside. "The first is a

beginners' class, and we're working on the basics. You're going to want to keep the sheltie mix away from the Goldendoodle. He's determined she's the love of his life, and he'll hump her every chance he gets. There's a border collie," she continued as they reached the kitchen. "She's honor-bound to try to spend the entire class herding everyone."

"Any snappers?" Sylvia asked while Fiona got out glasses.

"No. They run in age from around three to six months, so there's short attention span and some screwing around, but pretty good temperaments. In fact there's . . . Meg?"

Fiona paused when she caught the stunned look on Meg's face. "What's wrong?"

"This is him." She pressed a finger to the sketch on the counter. "The guy in our cabin. This is Frank."

The glass started to dissolve in Fiona's hand. She set it down before she dropped it. "Are you sure? Meg, are you sure?"

"It's him. It's not perfect, but it's him. The eyes, the shape of the face. I know this is him. It's a police sketch, isn't it? Oh my God."

"This is a police composite of what Eckle looks like now?" Sylvia's voice was utterly calm and seemed to come from inside a wind tunnel. "Fee!"

"Yes. Yes. Davey brought it over earlier. Tawney sent it in to the sheriff."

"Meg, go out and get Simon. Right now. Right now. Fee, call Agent Tawney. I'm calling the sheriff."

But before she called the FBI, Fiona went upstairs and got her gun.

WHEN SHE CAME DOWN she'd found her calm, and ignored the quick look of distress on Sylvia's face when her stepmother saw the gun strapped to her belt.

"The sheriff's on his way."

"So's the FBI. They'll coordinate with the sheriff en route. Everything's under control." Fiona laid a hand on Meg's shoulder as her friend sat at the counter.

"I was alone with him in that cabin. I showed him through it last spring, chatted with him. And yesterday . . . Oh sweet Jesus, that poor woman was in the trunk while I was making small talk. That's why Xena kept sniffing all around it. I should've known—"

"Why? How?" Fiona demanded. "Let's just be grateful you're okay, and you're here, and you recognized the sketch."

"I shook his hand," Meg murmured, staring at her own. "And that makes me feel . . . God, I have to call Chuck."

"I already did." Sylvia moved behind Meg and began to rub her shoulders. "He's coming."

"You may have saved that reporter's life," Fiona pointed out. "You may have saved mine. Think of that. Simon." She walked out of the kitchen to the living room, kept her voice low. "I know what you want to do. I can see it. You want to go over there, drag him out of that cabin and beat him to a pulp."

"The thought crossed. I'm not stupid," he said before she could speak. "And not willing to risk even the slim chance that he'd get away from me. I know how to wait."

She took his hand, squeezed it. "He doesn't. Not like Perry. It was wildly stupid to come here like this, and to bring her— he must've brought her."

"Stupid, yeah, but if he got away with it? A big splash if they found the reporter dead all but in your goddamn backyard. Perry just wanted to kill. This guy wants to be somebody."

"He'll never get away." Still, she rubbed her arms to warm them as she checked through the front window again. "He won't get off the island. But he's had her for two days now. She may already be dead."

"If she's got a chance, it's because of you."

"Me?"

"You're not stupid. He brought her here to unravel you, to hurt you. He's boxed himself in, and he may have hurt you, but he hasn't unraveled you."

"I like having you around."

"It's my house. I have you around."

She didn't think she could laugh, but he brought it out of her. And with it she put her arms around him and held on until the sheriff pulled into the drive.

When they stepped out to meet him, Sheriff McMahon didn't waste time.

"We've got the road to the cabin blocked off. Davey was able to get close enough to get a look through binocs. The car's there, all the windows in the cabin are closed, the curtains drawn."

"He's inside. With her."

"It looks that way," he said with a nod to Fiona. "Feds are coming in by chopper, and I called in for some backup. Ben Tyson over on San Juan's heading in now with two of his deputies. Feds don't want us moving in, but I'm going to argue some on that. It would help us out, Simon, if we could use your place here as a base for now."

"It's yours."

"Appreciate it. I need to talk to Meg, and keep the line open with Davey and Matt. They're watching the cabin."

Fiona felt the minutes dripping like syrup, so slow, so thick.

No movement, the deputies reported, again and again. Each time she imagined what moved inside, behind those shuttered windows.

"The problem is, there just aren't enough of us, and goddamn it, Matt's still green." McMahon scrubbed his fingers over his head. "We can keep watch, but I can't argue with the feds that if we go in, he might get through us. It doesn't sit well, I can tell you, but sit's what I have to do. At least till Tyson gets here."

"I've got a shotgun." Chuck stood, his arm around Meg's shoulders. "We could have half a dozen men here in ten minutes willing to help out with this."

"I don't need a bunch of civilians, Chuck, or to be worried about maybe having to tell somebody's wife she's a widow. He killed the others where he buried them—I can't argue that fact, either. Odds are she's alive, and we're going to get her out the same way."

He pulled out his phone when it signaled and walked outside to take the call.

"He'd have her up here, wouldn't he?" Fiona gestured to the printout of the floor plan they'd gotten off the cabin's website. "In one of the bedrooms. Not downstairs, just in case somebody got in. But where he could lock her in. So they not only have to get into the cabin but up the stairs—if he's with her."

She tried to think of it as a search and applied the same principles of most likely behavior. "The master has the little deck off it. I don't think he'd keep her there. He'd use the smaller room, the one with less access. But they could get men on that deck from the outside, and they could go through the slider, into the cabin on the second floor. Then—"

She broke off when McMahon strode back in. "Chopper just landed, they're on the road. And Tyson's on island, on his way. I'm going out to meet them. I need all of you to stay here. Right here. I'll keep in touch best I can."

FROM HIS PERCH in the trees on the rise well beyond Simon's house, Eckle watched the sheriff through his field glasses. The third time the man paced the back porch, with the phone at his ear, Eckle knew they'd made him.

He pondered how. The e-mail he'd composed wasn't set to send for another two hours. Maybe there'd been a glitch.

It didn't matter, he told himself. Things would just get started sooner. He heard it, faintly—the whir of a helicopter.

The gang's all here, he decided. The chances of his escape, of going under long enough to write the article, finish the book, dropped dramatically.

He'd most likely die on Fiona's island.

That didn't matter either. If formerly pretty Kati wasn't dead by now, she'd likely be before they found her, so he'd have had his own.

And while they were looking, he'd find Fiona and accomplish what his teacher never did, never could.

* * *

THEY WENT IN much as she'd imagined—fast, silent, covering every door and window. As one unit rushed through the first floor of the cabin, another rushed the second.

Tawney swept into the second bedroom steps behind the team.

He didn't need the calls of *Clear!* to know Eckle had moved out, and taken Starr with him.

"He's on his own script now. He's tossed Perry's and he's on his own."

"The trunk's empty." A little breathless, Mantz joined him. "He had her in there. It's lined with plastic, and it's blood-stained. Jesus," she added with a murmur when she saw the plastic, and what stained it, covering the bed.

"He left us plenty of her scent."

He wondered why.

Fiona wondered the same as her search unit reported to the cabin. She listened to the theory speculating he intended to come back, clean up, clear out—he'd left clothes behind as well—after he'd killed and buried Starr.

She didn't argue. Her unit had a job to do, and the focus was to find the reporter.

"We'll use the buddy system," she said. "None of us goes in alone. Meg and Chuck, Team One; James and Lori, Team Two; Simon and me, Team Three. Two people, two dogs per team."

She took a breath. "There are going to be armed police and federal agents swarming everywhere. You'll keep in regular contact with Mai, and with Agent Tawney. They're running the base. We've got about three hours before we lose the light. There's a strong chance of a storm hitting before dusk. If we don't find her before dark, we call it until morning. Every-body's back to base at dusk. We don't risk ourselves or our dogs."

She glanced toward Tawney. "We all heard what Agent Tawney told us. Francis Eckle is a killer. He may be armed, he's certainly dangerous. If any of you want to opt out of this search, it's not a reflection on you or the unit. Just tell Mai, and she'll recoordinate."

She stepped aside as Mai signaled. "I don't like you going in, Fee. You're a target. He's fixed on you already, and if he got any sort of a chance—"

"He won't."

"Can't you convince her to take the com on this?" she said to Simon. "I'll take Newman in, go with you and Peck."

"I'd be wasting my breath, just like you, and Tawney, for that matter. But she's right. He won't get the chance."

Mai swore, then caught Fiona in a hard hug. "If anything happens to you—anything—I'm going to kick your ass."

"Fear of that alone will keep me safe. Let's get started," she called out. Signaling the dogs, she moved off toward her sector.

"Aren't you supposed to give them the scent?" Simon asked her.

"Not yet," she murmured. "I need you to cover me here. I'll explain."

When she judged the distance enough, she drew the scent bag out of her pack. "We've got four experienced search people and dogs looking for Starr—and cops and feds. They'll find her, or they won't."

She looked up into Simon's eyes. "We're not going to look for her. We're going to look for him."

"That suits me fine."

This time she blew out a breath. "Good. Okay, good." She opened the bag. "This is his. He wore this sock and it hasn't been washed. Even I can smell him on it."

She gave both dogs the scent. "This is Eckle. It's Eckle. Let's find Eckle. Find him!"

As the dogs scented the air, noses twitching, heads lifted, she and Simon followed.

THIRTY-ONE

As they covered the first quarter mile, Simon swore the dogs consulted each other. Ear flicks, tail wags, a duet of sniffing. The temperature eased down under the cover of trees, along ground soft with its bed of needles, and rose again in the open, through wild grass and juts of rock.

"If he brought her this way," Simon wondered, "why didn't he use the road, keep her in the trunk until he found his spot? And if he did that, why is the car back at the cabin, and the cabin empty?"

"He didn't bring her this way. At least I don't see any sign of it." Fiona trailed her flashlight over the ground, over brush and branch. "He left tracks, he wasn't being careful. But I don't see any that could be hers. It doesn't make any sense, but I know damn well we're following his route. His solo route."

"Maybe he spotted the cops, or got wind of them somehow and got out. It could explain why he left everything."

"Panicked, ran." She nodded. "We've only been on a couple of searches where the person didn't want to be found. A pair of teenage lovers, and a guy who stabbed his wife during an argument when they were here on a camping trip. The teenagers had a plan, such as it was, and covered their trail, hid out. The man just ran, and that made him easier to find. I wish I knew which category Eckle falls into. If either.

"I have to check in with Mai."

Simon watched her take out the radio. "Decide yet what you're going to tell her?"

"We're still in our sector, so I'll tell her the truth. Just not all of it yet." She stared at the radio in her hand. "I should tell her all of it. I know that in one logical part of my head. Tell Agent Tawney or at least the sheriff. I could tell Meg to tell Sheriff Tyson. We could pull a couple of the deputies in on this trail."

"You could," he agreed. "And spend time arguing with them when you're told to go back to base."

Which wasn't an entirely bad idea, Simon considered. "Can any of them—Davey, McMahon, Tyson—handle the dogs on a search?"

"Davey might. That's a maybe. The reality is he hasn't had much more training or experience than you have. Which isn't enough, not without an experienced handler on the team. I know how to read my dogs. I can't guarantee any of them can."

"I guess that's the answer."

She called in, gave their location. "I've made some tracks," she told Mai, "and the dogs have a good scent."

"Tawney wants to know if you've spotted any blood trail, or any signs of struggle."

"No, none of that."

"James and Lori found blood, and strong signs of someone falling, possibly being dragged. Their dogs have multiple alerts. I'm working on narrowing the sectors."

Fiona looked at Simon. "I'd like to follow this for now. I don't want to confuse the dogs when they're alerting."

"Understood, but . . . hold on. Stand by."

"I gave the dogs Eckle, and they took his route. It must be fresher than the trail James and Lori picked up. I can't lie to Mai, to any of them," Fiona told Simon. "The unit's built on trust."

"So give it to her straight. Argue it out. You're still going to do what you have to do."

Even as she nodded, the radio crackled. "All teams, Agent Tawney's just relayed that Eckle sent a timed e-mail from Starr's computer. They're speculating that he wanted it traced, wanted the authorities to find the cabin. Fee, he wants you to head back, now. They think this might be a lure to get you out there."

"I am out here," Fiona responded. "And we're tracking him. Eckle, not Starr."

"Fee—"

"The dogs are alerting, Mai, and I'm not coming back in while the rest of my unit is out here. I'll stay in contact, but I need a minute to think this out."

She shoved the radio back onto her belt, turned down the volume. "I have to see this through."

"I'm standing right here," Simon pointed out. "That makes it we. Where are we in connection to James and Lori's area?"

"Give me a minute." She pulled out her copy of the map. Okay, okay," she murmured as she studied. "They're east of us, here. Plenty of places off the trails or on private property. But if they've got the scent, and found blood, he had to cross this road."

"So he had to do it at night. He'd need the dark, and the relative assurance he wouldn't be seen."

"Yeah, but we're here. Well west. In fact, he veered west all along, which is more like panic, more like trying to distance himself from wherever he took her. But . . ."

"New element," Simon put in. "If he sent the e-mail to bring the cops in, and to bring you out, where's he going? He thinks you'll be following Starr's scent, not his. If he's set a trap for you, it's not here."

"You think she's bait," Fiona murmured. "He brought her here, to my place, even used the cabin of a friend, a partner. God, of course she's bait." How, she wondered, did that make it worse? "He walked her, dragged her, left a blood trail because he wanted to lead us—or me—to wherever she is. But he can't be sure I'd be the one to find her."

"He'd need a place where he could watch. If you're the one who finds her, he takes or kills you there. If you're not, he moves over to your location, does the same."

"But . . . No, I see. He doesn't need to abduct me, to string it out. He just needs to kill me. I'm Perry's. I'm payment." She stared straight ahead, spoke calmly. "We need to water the dogs."

He crouched down with her to fill the bowl. "Fiona, you don't have to be a cop or a shrink to figure out this guy's gone over an edge. Once he slipped over, changed Perry's agenda, method, criteria—whatever the hell—for his own, he went over."

"Yes."

"Starr had information, some she'd printed, some she probably was still trying to confirm. He probably knows they've got his name, his face, everything there is about him. He probably knows Perry turned on him."

"Yes," she said again. "And she'd have told him anything, I imagine, anything he wanted to know if he told her he'd let her live. Maybe he didn't need to ask. He had her laptop, her phone. He knew the FBI was closing in."

"Where does he go, Fiona? When he's paid his debt to Perry, where does he go? How does he get off the island? Steal a boat? A car? How does he get through all the search teams to manage that? Long odds. Even if he did it, how does he get through more cops to get on the ferry or get a boat off the island?"

"He doesn't." She picked up the empty bowl, stowed it. "It's not panic, it was never panic. Maybe, back in April when he rented the cabin he thought he could get to me, take care of it and move on, but all that changed when he took Starr. When he brought her here knowing I'd gone to see Perry, when he read her article. It ends with me, one way or the other. Maybe he tries to kill the dogs, and you. Maybe as many as he can manage. But he knows it ends with me."

"Blaze of glory."

"He's never had it." She took out the scent bag. "But he's tasted it now. Starr gave it to him, so he made her part of it.

This is Eckle," she said, forcing enthusiasm into her voice as she freshened the scent. "Let's find Eckle! Find him!"

As they started again, she turned up her radio, winced at the chatter and the demands that she respond.

"Let me do it." Simon held out his hand. "You need to focus on the dogs."

He was right. There wasn't just one life on the line but many. Starr was either alive or she was dead—that depended on Eckle's whim.

Her unit, her friends, they were subject to that whim, too. As Greg had been to Perry's.

But for Eckle it had never been about her, she realized. Despite the taunts, the terrorizing. She was no more than an IOU, and his twisted sense of honor demanded he pay that debt before the ugly new life Perry had given him was finished.

"He's cutting back east now." She flagged the next alert. "If he keeps the direction, he's going to cross into James's sector. I need to—"

"I'll do it. You missed that." He took another flag, marked a discarded candy wrapper. "You're letting yourself get distracted. Stop it."

Right again, she thought, and paused for a moment. She shut her eyes, let herself hear, scent, feel.

Orcas was a small island, a lot of ground to cover, yes, but limited. If his goal was to lure her into a trap, he'd have to have cover, and a vantage point.

"His route had to cross with the route he took with Starr. Somewhere he has to cross it, or parallel, but crossing from this direction . . ."

She had the map in her head, but took the one from her backpack to study again. No chances.

"Perry took high ground when he killed Greg. That was another kind of payment."

"Perry got caught, put in prison. I don't think Eckle is looking at prison as an option." Over Fiona's shoulder, Simon scanned the map, the trails, the routes. "Neither does Tawney."

"He's got work to do first," she murmured. "He's traveled in an arc—a wide curve, rounding west, now rounding east.

Taking himself away from Starr, moving back toward her. Not to her. That doesn't make sense. But near enough to watch. Maybe even hear the dogs, the radios when they get close enough. And in this direction, he's going to start running into houses, Gary and Sue's farm."

"I don't have your sense of direction, but your place is before the farm. How far are we out?"

"From my . . ." Her breath caught. "My place. You said it before. My own backyard. He's taken everyone, even Starr, from their own place—school, routine area, work. He's never deviated from that."

She gripped Simon's hand as certainty, and urgency, coursed through her in fast streams.

"Not just the island, my home. It's empty, my house, because I'm out here looking for him. Or maybe he knows I'm at your place. Either way, he'd have the woods for cover."

"And if he could get you inside, a place to take that last stand. How far, Fiona?"

"Maybe a half mile. Less. It depends on how far he circles, which point he's picked for his hide." She scanned the shadows, pools of gray and green. "The wind's picking up, and that'll affect the scent cone. We're going to be crossing into James and Lori's sector if we keep going east. We have to make the dogs stay in the trees, even if the trail goes into the open. We have to keep them quiet. And once we contact base, we have to turn the radio off."

He considered telling her to stay there, but she wouldn't. Considered telling her they'd both stay where they were and give Tawney her best guess of Eckle's location. He knew the answer to that, too, but gave it a shot.

"We stay here, call it in, give Tawney the information."

"And if Eckle changes direction? We can't tell them where he's going until we're sure. We can only theorize."

"That's what I figured. Take out your gun. It's in your hand from this point on." He took out the radio. "Mai, put Tawney on."

"They're alerting again." Fiona moved forward to flag the location.

"He wants to talk to you." Simon passed her the radio.

"This is Fee. Over."

"Fiona, I want you to listen to me. Stay where you are. We've triangulated your route with the other two search teams. We believe he's on your property, or close. We're dispatching a unit to your house, and pulling officers off search to join you and your unit. Do you copy?"

"Yes, I copy, Agent Tawney. Do any of your men know this area, have dogs who are giving stronger and stronger alerts? We're just crossing into Team One's sector. I see one of their flags."

Getting closer, she thought and her blood pumped hard.

"He crossed here, too, crossed the area where he took her. James and Lori could . . . He could kill them. Simon and I are approaching from what should be his blind side. Send the cavalry, please God, but we're following the dogs. I have to turn off the radio. We can't risk him hearing us."

She turned it off, handed it to Simon. "James won't hold back. He might argue with Lori and convince her to wait, but he won't. Not when there's a chance he could find Starr alive. And I can't wait, Simon, and take the chance someone else I love gets killed because of a vendetta against me."

"Who's arguing?"

It settled her, she realized, that faint edge of irritation in his tone. "We need to leash the dogs. Keep them close. And quiet."

She glanced up when thunder rumbled. "We're going to lose the light. It's nearly dusk anyway. The wind's good cover. Rain would be better. But both are affecting the scent. We're all going to be going on instinct soon."

"I want you behind me. That's my instinct," he said before she could object. "I need you to respect it."

"I'm the one with the gun," she pointed out.

"That's right." He kissed her lightly. "And I'm the one who's counting on you using it if you need to."

They continued in silence through air that cooled with the wind. The rising surf of wind through the trees made good cover, and would—she hoped—mask their approach. But she couldn't hear over it either. And every sigh and shake of the trees caused her heart to jump.

They used hand signals, for each other and the dogs.

They came to the edge of the clearing where Simon found the stump. She saw the young sapling he'd planted without telling her. It made her galloping heart calm.

She touched her fingertips to him, just a brush of thanks.

She spotted another flag, and when the dogs wanted to cross into the open, she ordered them back.

Her blood froze when she heard the crackle of the radio, but even as her gaze flew to Simon's belt she realized it wasn't theirs.

James, she thought. Closer than she'd realized. She couldn't make out the words, not all of them, but the excited tone translated. As did the happy bark.

"They've found her," she whispered.

And a shadow moved in the shadows.

Her breath stuttered in her throat. He'd been sitting behind a tree, she saw, on the far side of the clearing. And now he used the wind, the gloom, those first quick patters of rain to mask his movements.

Simon laid his hand over her mouth, leaned close to her ear.

"You stay here. You keep the dogs right here. I'm going to circle around, cut him off. Stay here," he repeated. "He won't get past me. Cops'll be here in minutes."

She wanted to argue; couldn't risk it. She ordered her confused dogs with a down and stay, a firm, angry hand signal that had their heads drooping, their eyes casting up at her whining with hurt feelings.

The game wasn't over. The prize was right there, lurking in the shadows. Her unexpected anger had them letting out low whines until she silenced them with a furious look, a jabbing finger.

Satisfied, she eased out a little to look, and saw the gun in Eckle's hand. His head cocked to the side—listening—as he turned slowly in the direction Simon took.

She thought, very simply, *No*. And stepped out into the clearing.

. She held the gun up and aimed. Cursed that it trembled as he completed the turn and looked into her eyes.

"Drop your gun, Francis, or I swear on every life you and Perry took, I'll shoot you." She would live with it, could live with it. Had to live with it.

"He told me not to underestimate you." As she did, Eckle held the gun up and aimed. But it didn't tremble. He smiled as he might at the unexpected appearance of a friend. "You know when I kill you, your partner will rush in this direction. Then I'll kill him, too. His dog. Yours. Where's your dog, Fiona?"

"Put the gun down. You know the police and the FBI are coming. They're spread all over this area. You'll never get through them."

"But I've finally lived. In a few short months I've lived and experienced more than I did in all the years before. All those gray years. I hope Tawney's with the ones who come. If I have a chance to take him, it would be like a parting gift for Perry."

"He betrayed you."

"But first he freed me. I wish we had more time, Fiona. Your hand's trembling."

"It won't stop me." She drew a breath in, prepared to kill.

Simon charged out of the trees, his body low and between hers and Eckle's. He rammed Eckle's right side, making Fiona think briefly, crazily, of a speeding train.

The gun fired, the bullet digging a trench in the soft earth an instant before the gun flew from Eckle's hand.

She rushed forward, grabbed it. Even as she aimed both guns she heard James shouting, and thrashing through the brush. Just, she thought, as Eckle had predicted. When he broke through, she shoved the guns at him.

"Hold these."

"Fee, Jesus. Jesus."

She simply dropped down beside Simon as he viciously, methodically battered Eckle's face with his fists.

"Stop. Stop that now." She struggled for the firm, no-nonsense tone she used with misbehaving dogs, and nearly succeeded. "Simon, stop. He's finished."

He flicked one furious glance at her. "I told you to stay under cover. I told you he wouldn't get past me."

"And he didn't." She took one of his balled fists, the knuckles bruised and bloody, and laid it on her cheek as her dogs shoved against her. "I told them to stay, but they didn't. We all protect each other. That's how it works."

She barely spared Eckle a glance. "Is she alive?" she asked James.

"Yeah. But I don't know if she's going to stay that way. She's in bad shape. I have to get back to Lori. You scared the shit out of us."

He, however, took a long study of Eckle's battered, slack face. "You do nice work, Simon. Here." He handed the guns back to Fiona. "I hear the cops, or feds. Whichever. We've got to get the victim out and to the hospital. We're going to do some serious talking in the debriefing," he added, then shoved through the brush.

"I didn't know if you saw the gun," she told Simon. "I couldn't be sure. I couldn't take a chance."

"You're lucky he didn't just blast away at you. What if he hadn't wanted to chat for a minute?"

"I'd have shot him." She put her own gun back in her holster, then Eckle's in her belt. "Another fraction of a second . . . I'm glad I didn't have to. Glad you broke his goddamn face instead."

She let out a long breath, then crouched. "Good dogs! You're such good dogs. You found Eckle."

She had her arms around the dogs and her head on Simon's chest when the cops rushed the clearing.

IT TOOK HOURS MORE, hours that seemed like days. Questions, reports, more questions, the briefing.

Mantz walked over to shake her hand. "I still say you'd make a good agent."

"Maybe, but I'm really looking forward to the quiet life."

"Good luck with it." Bending, she petted Newman, who'd yet to leave Fiona's side. "Good dog," she said, and when

Fiona cocked a brow, laughed. "I guess they've changed my mind about the species. See you around."

From Tawney, she got a hug.

"Don't wait until there's trouble to come see me," she murmured. "Because I'm done with trouble, but not with you."

"You gave me a whole new patch of gray hair today. I'd say take care of yourself, but you already do. We're going to need to do some follow-ups."

"Anytime."

"Go home." He kissed her forehead. "Get some sleep."

Since she nearly dozed off on the drive home she didn't think that would be a problem.

"I'm going to have a shower, then I'm going to eat whatever's in the refrigerator, then I'm going to sleep for twelve hours."

"I've got a couple things to do, then we'll both eat whatever's in the fridge."

She started out, stopped. "Would you check, see if there's any update on Starr's condition? I know it looks bad for her, but maybe . . . We hate losing one."

"I'll check. Have your shower."

She wallowed in it, basked, lingered. Then, tying her wet hair back in a tail, pulled on cotton pants and a soft, faded tee. Comfort, she thought. She wanted nothing but comfort.

And the start, please God, of her quiet life.

She picked up the little penknife she'd set on her dresser, pressed it to her cheek. "You'd be happy for me," she murmured. Setting it down, she studied herself in the mirror. She looked a little tired, she thought, but she didn't look like hell.

She looked, she thought with a smile, free.

As she started downstairs, she frowned at the quick toot of a horn. She loved her friends, but God, she just wanted to eat and sleep. No more talk.

But she found Simon in the kitchen, alone with the dogs.

"Who was here?"

"When? Oh, James. I needed a hand with something. Here." He shoved a cracker with a thin slice of cheese on top into her mouth.

"Good," she managed over it. "More."

He shoved a second in. "That's it. Now you make your own. Here." He pushed a glass of wine into her hand.

"Did you call the hospital?"

"She's critical. Exposure, dehydration, shock. She's got broken fingers, a broken jaw. There's more. He had considerable time to pound on her, and he used it. She's got a decent shot."

"Okay."

"Eckle's got a few problems of his own." He glanced at his own bandaged hands.

"He earned them." She took those bandaged hands and made him mutter to himself when she kissed them.

"He was writing a book."

"What?"

"You took a long shower," Simon pointed out. "Davey filled in some blanks. She was, too. It looks like Eckle did some editing on hers, added some material."

"God." Closing her eyes, she pressed the wineglass to her brow. "You were right. He wanted to be someone."

"Still does. According to Davey, he waived a lawyer and hasn't shut up. He wants to talk, wants to give details. He's proud of himself."

"Proud." She repeated the word, gave in to one shudder.

"And he's finished. He's done. Like Perry."

"Yes." She opened her eyes, lowered the glass. She thought of the prison walls, the bars, the guns, the guards. "He didn't get that blaze of glory, not the kind he wanted. I think we should sit outside, watch the dogs, drink this wine, then eat like maniacs. Because we can."

"Not yet. Bring the wine. I want to show you something."

"Is it more food?"

He took her arm and pulled her into the dining room—where the table, she noted, was sadly empty of food. "Okay. I really hope you don't want fun on the dining room table because I don't think I've got it in me tonight. Now tomorrow—" She broke off as she spotted the wine cabinet. "Oh!"

She rounded the table in a flash. "Oh, it's *wonderful*. The wood's like chocolate silk and heavy cream. And the doors? Those are dogwoods. It's just, oh . . ." She opened the doors, danced in place. "It's just absolutely fabulous. Every detail. It's charming and fun and beautiful."

"It suits you."

She spun around. "Is it *mine*? Oh my God, Simon—"

Before she could rush him, he held up a hand. "It depends. I'm thinking a trade. I'll give it to you, but since it's going to stay here, that means you stay, too."

She opened her mouth, shut it again. Picked up the wine she'd set on the table, sipped. "I can have the cabinet if I live here, with you?"

"I'm the one who lives here, so yeah, with me. This house is bigger than yours. You've got the woods, but I've got the woods and the beach. The dogs have more room. And I need my shop."

"Hmmm."

"You can keep doing your classes here, or you can move them back. Keep the house for the business. Or sell it. Or rent it out. But if you want that, you stay."

"That's some interesting bartering."

"You started it." He slid his thumbs into the front pockets of his jeans. "I figure we got through some of the worst anybody gets through. And here we are. I don't see the point in wasting time. So, you want the cabinet, you live here. We should probably get married."

She choked, managed to swallow the wine. "We should probably?"

"I'm not coming up with some fancy proposal."

"How about something between we-should-probably and fancy?"

"Do you want to get married?"

Now she laughed. "I guess that's between. Well, I want the cabinet. I want you. So . . . yeah, I guess I want to get married."

"It's a good deal," he said as he stepped to her.

"It's a very good deal." She laid her hands on his cheeks. "Simon."

He pressed his lips to her right palm, then the left. "I love you."

"I know." She slid into his arms. "It's the best feeling in the world, knowing. And every time I look at that cabinet, put a glass in, take a bottle out, I'll know it. It's an incredible gift."

"It's a trade."

"Of course." She laid her lips on his, lingered.

She was free, she thought, and she was loved. And she was home.

"Let's go tell the boys," she murmured.

"Right. I'm sure they'll want champagne and cigars." Still he took her hand to walk out. "Let's make it fast. I'm starving."

He made her laugh, and that, she thought, was another very good deal.

Keep reading for a special excerpt from
the exciting novel by Nora Roberts

CHASING FIRE

Caught in the cross hairs of wind above the Bitterroots, the jump ship fought to find its stream. Fire boiling over the land jabbed its fists up through towers of smoke as if trying for a knockout punch.

From her seat Rowan Tripp angled to watch a seriously pissed-off Mother Nature's big show. In minutes she'd be inside it, enclosed in the mad world of searing heat, leaping flames, choking smoke. She'd wage war with shovel and saw, grit and guile. A war she didn't intend to lose.

Her stomach bounced along with the plane, a sensation she'd taught herself to ignore. She'd flown all of her life, and had fought wildfires every season since her eighteenth birthday. For the last half of those eight years she'd jumped fire.

She'd studied, trained, bled and burned—outwilled pain and exhaustion to become a Zulie. A Missoula smokejumper.

She stretched out her long legs as best she could for a moment, rolled her shoulders under her pack to keep them loose.

Beside her, her jump partner watched as she did. His fingers did a fast tap dance on his thighs. "She looks mean."

"We're meaner."

He shot her a fast, toothy grin. "Bet your ass."

Nerves. She could all but feel them riding along his skin.

Near the end of his first season, Rowan thought, and Jim Brayner needed to pump himself up before a jump. Some always would, she decided, while others caught short catnaps to bank sleep against the heavy withdrawals to come.

She was first jump on this load, and Jim would be right behind her. If he needed a little juice, she'd supply it.

"Kick her ass, more like. It's the first real bitch we've jumped in a week." She gave him an easy elbow jab. "Weren't you the one who kept saying the season was done?"

He tapped those busy fingers on his thighs to some inner rhythm. "Nah, that was Matt," he insisted, grin still wide as he deflected the claim onto his brother.

"That's what you get with a couple of Nebraska farm boys. Don't you have a hot date tomorrow night?"

"My date's are always hot."

She couldn't argue, as she'd seen Jim snag women like rainbow trout any time the unit had pulled a night off to kick it up in town. He'd hit on her, she remembered, about two short seconds after he'd arrived on base. Still, he'd been good-natured about her shutdown. She'd implemented a firm policy against dating within the unit.

Otherwise, she might've been tempted. He had that open, innocent face offset by the quick grin, and the gleam in the eye. For fun, she thought, for a careless pop of the cork out of the lust bottle. For serious—even if she'd been looking for serious—he'd never do the trick. Though they were the same age, he was just too young, too fresh off the farm—and maybe just a little too sweet under the thin layer of green that hadn't burned off quite yet.

"Which girl's going to bed sad and lonely if you're still dancing with the dragon?" she asked him.

"Lucille."

"That's the little one—with the giggle."

His fingers tap, tap, tapped on his knee. "She does more than giggle."

"You're a dog, Romeo."

He tipped back his head, let out a series of sharp barks that made her laugh.

"Make sure Dolly doesn't find out you're out howling," she commented. She knew—everyone knew—he'd been banging one of the base cooks like a drum all season.

"I can handle Dolly." The tapping picked up pace. "Gonna handle Dolly."

Okay, Rowan thought, something bent out of shape there, which was why smart people didn't bang or get banged by people they worked with.

She gave him a little nudge because those busy fingers concerned her. "Everything okay with you, Farmboy?"

His pale blue eyes met hers for an instant, then shifted away while his knees did a bounce under those drumming fingers. "No problems here. It's going to be smooth sailing like always. I just need to get down there."

She put a hand over his to still it. "You need to keep your head in the game, Jim."

"It's there. Right there. Look at her, swishing her tail," he said. "Once us Zulies get down there, she won't be so sassy. We'll put her down, and I'll be making time with Lucille tomorrow night."

Unlikely, Rowan thought to herself. Her aerial view of the fire put her gauge at a solid two days of hard, sweaty work.

And that was if things went their way.

Rowan reached for her helmet, nodded toward their spotter. "Getting ready. Stay chilly, Farmboy."

"I'm ice."

Cards—so dubbed as he carried a pack everywhere— wound his way through the load of ten jumpers and equipment to the rear of the plane, attached the tail of his harness to the restraining line.

Even as Cards shouted out the warning to guard their

reserves, Rowan hooked an arm over hers. Cards, a tough-bodied vet, pulled the door open to a rush of wind tainted with smoke and fuel. As he reached for the first set of streamers, Rowan set her helmet over her short crown of blond hair, strapped it, adjusted her face mask.

She watched the streamers doing their colorful dance against the smoke-stained sky. Their long strips kicked in the turbulence, spiraled toward the southwest, seemed to roll, to rise, then caught another bounce before whisking into the trees.

Cards called, "Right!" into his headset, and the pilot turned the plane.

The second set of streamers snapped out, spun like a kid's wind toy. The strips wrapped together, pulled apart, then dropped on the tree-flanked patch of the jump site.

"The wind line's running across that creek, down to the trees and across the site," Rowan said to Jim.

Over her, the spotter and pilot made more adjustments, and another set of streamers snapped out into the slipstream.

"It's got a bite to it."

"Yeah. I saw." Jim swiped the back of his hand over his mouth before strapping on his helmet and mask.

"Take her to three thousand," Cards shouted.

Jump altitude. As first man, first stick, Rowan rose to take position. "About three hundred yards of drift," she shouted to Jim, repeated what she'd heard Cards telling the pilot. "But there's that bite. Don't get caught downwind."

"Not my first party."

She saw his grin behind the bars of his face mask—confident, even eager. But something in his eyes, she thought. Just for a flash. She started to speak again, but Cards, already in position to the right of the door, called out, "Are you ready?"

"We're ready," she called back.

"Hook up."

Rowan snapped the static line in place.

"Get in the door!"

She dropped to sitting, legs out in the wicked slipstream,

body leaning back. Everything roared. Below her extended legs, fire ran in vibrant red and gold.

There was nothing but the moment, nothing but the wind and fire and the twist of exhilaration and fear that always, always surprised her.

"Did you see the streamers?"

"Yeah."

"You see the spot?"

She nodded, bringing both into her head, following those colorful strips to the target.

Cards repeated what she'd told Jim, almost word for word. She only nodded again, eyes on the horizon, letting her breath come easy, visualizing herself flying, falling, navigating the sky down to the heart of the jump spot.

She went through her four-point check as the plane completed its circle and leveled out.

Cards pulled his head back in. "Get ready."

Ready-steady, her father said in her head. She grabbed both sides of the door, sucked in a breath.

And when the spotter's hand slapped her shoulder, she launched herself into the sky.

Nothing she knew topped that one instant of insanity, hurling herself into the void. She counted off in her mind, a task as automatic as breathing and rolled in that charged sky to watch the plane fly past. She caught sight of Jim, hurtling after her.

Again, she turned her body, fighting the drag of wind until her feet were down. With a yank and jerk, her canopy burst open. She scouted out Jim again, felt a tiny pop of relief when she saw his chute spread against the empty sky. In that pocket of eerie silence, beyond the roar of the plane, above the voice of the fire, she gripped her steering toggles.

The wind wanted to drag her north, and was pretty insistent about it. Rowan was just as insistent on staying on the course she'd mapped out in her head. She watched the ground as she steered against the frisky crosscurrent that pinched its fingers on her canopy, doing its best to circle her into the tail wind.

The turbulence that had caught the streamers struck her in

gusty slaps while the heat pumped up from the burning ground. If the wind had its way, she'd overshoot the jump spot, fly into the verge of trees, risk a hangup. Or worse, it could shove her west and into the flame.

She dragged hard on her toggle, glanced over in time to see Jim catch the downwind and go into a spin.

"Pull right! Pull right!"

"I got it! I got it."

But to her horror, he pulled left.

"Right, goddamn it!"

She had to turn for her final, and the pleasure of a near seamless slide into the glide path drowned in sheer panic. Jim soared west, helplessly towed by a horizontal canopy.

Rowan hit the jump site, rolled. She gained her feet, slapped her release. And heard it as she stood in the center of the blaze.

She heard her jump partner's scream.

THE SCREAM FOLLOWED HER as she shot up in bed, echoed in her head as she sat huddled in the dark.

Stop, stop, stop! she ordered herself. And dropped her head on her updrawn knees until she got her breath back.

No point in it, she thought. No point in reliving it, in going over all the details, all the moments, or asking herself, again, if she could've done just one thing differently.

Asking herself why Jim hadn't followed her drop into the jump spot. Why he'd pulled the wrong toggle. Because *goddamn it* he'd pulled the wrong toggle.

And had flown straight into the towers and lethal branches of those burning trees.

Months ago now, she reminded herself. She'd had the long winter to get past it. And thought she had.

Being back on base triggered it, she admitted, and rubbed her hands over her face, back over the hair she'd had cut into a short, maintenance-free cap only days before.

Fire season was nearly on them. Refresher training started in a few short hours. Memories, regrets, grief—they were bound to pay a return visit. But she needed sleep, another hour before she got up, geared up for the punishing three-mile run.

She was damn good at willing herself to sleep, anyplace, anytime. Coyoteing in a safe zone during a fire, on a shuddering jump plane. She knew how to eat and sleep when the need and opportunity arose.

But when she closed her eyes again, she saw herself back on the plane, turning toward Jim's grin.

Knowing she had to shake it off, she shoved out of bed. She'd grab a shower, some caffeine, stuff in some carbs then do a light workout to warm up for the physical training test.

It continued to baffle her fellow jumpers that she never drank coffee unless it was her only choice. She liked the cold and sweet. After she'd dressed, Rowan hit her stash of Cokes, grabbed a power bar. She took both outside where the sky was still shy of first light and the air stayed chill in the early spring of western Montana.

In the vast sky stars blinked out, little candles snuffed. She pulled the dark and quiet around her, found some comfort in it. In an hour, give or take, the base would wake, and testosterone would flood the air.

Since she generally preferred the company of men, for conversation, for companionship, she didn't mind being outnumbered by them. But she prized her quiet time, those little pieces of alone that became rare and precious during the season. Next best thing to sleep before a day filled with pressure and stress, she thought.

She could tell herself not to worry about the run, remind herself she'd been vigilant about her PT all winter, was in the best shape of her life—and it didn't mean a damn.

Anything could happen. A turned ankle, a mental lapse, a sudden, debilitating cramp. Or she could just have a bad run. Others had. Sometimes they came back from it, sometimes they didn't.

And a negative attitude wasn't going to help. She chowed down on the power bar, gulped caffeine into her system and watched the day eke its first shimmer over the rugged, snow-tipped western peaks.

When she ducked into the gym minutes later, she noted her alone time was over.

"Hey, Trigger." She nodded to the man doing crunches on a mat. "What do you know?"

"I know we're all crazy. What the hell am I doing here, Ro? I'm forty-fucking-three years old."

She unrolled a mat, started her stretches. "If you weren't crazy, weren't here, you'd still be forty-fucking-three."

At six-five, barely making the height restrictions, Trigger Gulch was a lean, mean machine with a west Texas twang and an affection for cowboy boots.

He huffed through a quick series of pulsing crunches. "I could be lying on a beach in Waikiki."

"You could be selling real estate in Amarillo."

"I could do that." He mopped his face, pointed at her. "Nine-to-five the next fifteen years, then retire to that beach in Waikiki."

"Waikiki's full of people, I hear."

"Yeah, that's the damn trouble." He sat up, a good-looking man with gray liberally salted through his brown hair, and a scar snaked on his left knee from a meniscus repair. He smiled at her as she lay on her back, pulled her right leg up and toward her nose. "Looking good, Ro. How was your fat season?"

"Busy." She repeated the stretch on her left leg. "I've been looking forward to coming back, getting me some rest."

He laughed at that. "How's your dad?"

"Good as gold." Rowan sat up, then folded her long, curvy body in two. "Gets a little wistful this time of year." She closed ice blue eyes and pulled her flexed feet back toward the crown of her head. "He missed the start-up, everybody coming back, but the business doesn't give him time to brood."

"Even people who aren't us like to jump out of planes."

"Pay good money for it, too. Had a good one last week." She spread her legs in a wide vee, grabbed her toes and again bent forward. "Couple celebrated their fiftieth anniversary with a jump. Gave me a bottle of French champagne as a tip."

Trigger sat where he was, watching as she pushed to her

feet to begin the first sun salutation. "Are you still teaching that hippie class?"

Rowan flowed from Up Dog to Down Dog, turned her head to shoot Trigger a pitying look. "It's yoga, old man, and yeah, I'm still doing some personal trainer work off-season. Helps keep the lard out of my ass. How about you?"

"I pile the lard on. It gives me more to burn off when the real work starts."

"If this season's as slow as last, we'll all be sitting on fat asses. Have you seen Cards? He doesn't appear to have turned down any second helpings this winter."

"Got a new woman."

"No shit." Looser, she picked up the pace, added lunges.

"He met her in the frozen food section of the grocery store in October and moved in with her for New Year's. She's got a couple kids. Schoolteacher."

"Schoolteacher? Kids? Cards?" Rowan shook her head. "Must be love."

"Must be something. He said the woman and the kids are coming out maybe late July, maybe spend the rest of the summer."

"That sounds serious." She shifted to a twist, eyeing Trigger as she held the position. "She must be something. Still, he'd better see how she handles a season. It's one thing to hook up with a smokejumper in the winter, and another to stick through the summer. Families crack like eggs," she added, then wished she hadn't as Matt Brayner stepped in.

She hadn't seen him since Jim's funeral, and though she'd spoken with his mother a few times, she hadn't been sure he'd come back.

He looked older, she thought, more worn around the eyes and mouth. And heartbreakingly like his brother with the floppy mop of bleached wheat hair, the pale blue eyes. His gaze tracked from Trigger, met hers. She wondered what the smile cost him.

"How's it going?"

"Pretty good." She straightened, wiped her palms on the

thighs of her workout pants. "Just sweating off some nerves before the PT test."

"I thought I'd do the same. Or just screw it and go into town and order a double stack of pancakes."

"We'll get 'em after the run." Trigger walked over, held out a hand. "Good to see you, Hayseed."

"You, too."

"I'm going for coffee. They'll be loading us up before too long."

As Trigger went out, Matt walked over, picked up a twenty-pound weight. Put it down again. "I guess it's going to be weird, for a while anyway. Seeing me makes everybody . . . think."

"Nobody's going to forget. I'm glad you're back."

"I don't know if I am, but I couldn't seem to do anything else. Anyway. I wanted to say thanks for keeping in touch with my ma the way you have. It means a lot to her."

"I wish . . . Well, if wishes were horses I'd have a rodeo. I'm glad you're back. See you at the van."

SHE UNDERSTOOD MATT'S SENTIMENT, couldn't seem to do anything else. It would sum up the core feelings of the men, and four women including herself, who piled into vans for the ride out to the start of the run for their jobs. She settled in, letting the ragging and bragging flow over her.

A lot of insults about winter weight, and the ever-popular lard-ass remarks. She closed her eyes, tried to let herself drift as the nerves riding under the good-natured bullshit winging around the van wanted to reach inside and shake hands with her own.

Janis Petrie, one of the four females in the unit, dropped down beside her. Her small, compact build had earned her the nickname Elf, and she looked like a perky head cheerleader.

This morning her nails sported bright pink polish and her shiny brown hair bounced in a tail tied with a circle of butter-flies.

She was pretty as a gumdrop, tended to giggle, and could work—had worked—a saw line for fourteen hours straight.

"Ready to rock, Swede?"

"And roll. Why would you put on makeup before this bitch of a test?"

Janis fluttered her long, lush lashes. "So these poor guys'll have something pretty to look at when they stumble over the finish line. Seeing as I'll be there first."

"You are pretty damn fast."

"Small but mighty. Did you check out the rookies?"

"Not yet."

"Six of our kind in there. Maybe we'll add enough women for a nice little sewing circle. Or a book club."

Rowan laughed. "And after, we'll have a bake sale."

"Cupcakes. Cupcakes are my weakness. It's such pretty country." Janis leaned forward a little to get a clearer view out the window. "I always miss it when I'm gone, always wonder what I'm doing living in the city doing physical therapy on country-club types with tennis elbow."

She blew out a breath. "Then by July I'll be wondering what I'm doing out here, strung-out on no sleep, hurting everywhere when I could be taking my lunch break at the pool."

"It's a long way from Missoula to San Diego."

"Damn right. You don't have that pull-tug. You live here. For most of us, this is coming home. Until we finish the season and go home, then that feels like home. It can cross up the circuits."

She rolled her warm brown eyes toward Rowan as the van stopped. "Here we go again."

Rowan climbed out of the van, drew in the air. It smelled good, fresh and new. Spring, the kind with green and wildflowers and balmy breezes, wouldn't be far off now. She scouted the flags marking the course as the base manager, Michael Little Bear, laid out requirements.

His long black braid streamed down his bright red jacket. Rowan knew there'd be a roll of Life Savers in the pocket, a substitute for the Marlboros he'd quit over the winter.

L.B. and his family lived a stone's throw from the base, and his wife worked for Rowan's father.

Everyone knew the rules. Run the course, and get it done in under twenty-two-thirty, or walk away. Try it again in a week. Fail that? Find a new summer job.

Rowan stretched out—hamstrings, quads, calves.

"I hate this shit."

She glanced over at Cards as he did a little running in place, and judged Trigger as correct. Cards hadn't taken off all the winter weight.

"You'll make it." She gave him an elbow in the belly. "Think of a meat-lover's pizza waiting for you on the other side of the line."

"Kiss my ass."

"The size it is now? That'd take me a while."

He snorted out a laugh as they lined up.

She calmed herself. Got in her head, got in her body, as L.B. walked back to the van. When the van took off, so did the line. Rowan hit the timer button on her watch, merged with the pack. She knew every one of these men—had worked with them, sweat with them, risked her life with them. And she wished them—every one—good luck and a good run.

But for the next twenty-two and thirty, it was every man, and woman, for themselves.

She dug in, kicked up her pace and ran for, what was in a very large sense, her life. She made her way through the pack, and as others did called out encouragement or jibes, whatever worked best to kick asses into gear. She knew there would be knees aching, chests hammering, stomachs churning. Spring training would have toned some, added insult to injuries on others.

She couldn't think about it. She focused on mile one, and when she passed the marker, noted her time at four minutes and twelve.

Mile two, she ordered herself, and kept her stride smooth, her pace steady—even when Janis passed her with a grim smile. The burn rose up from her toes to her ankles flowed up her calves. Sweat ran hot down her back, down her chest over her galloping heart.

She could slow her pace—her time was good—but the stress of imagined stumbles, turned ankles, a lightning strike from beyond, pushed her.

Don't let up.

When she passed mile two she'd moved beyond the burn, the sweat, into the mindless. One more mile. She passed some, was passed by others while her pulse pounded in her ears. As before a jump, she kept her eyes on the horizon— land and sky. Her love of both whipped her through the final mile.

She blew past the last marker, heard L.B. call out her name and time. *Tripp, fifteen-twenty.* And ran another twenty yards before she could convince her legs it was okay to stop.

Bending from the waist, she caught her breath, squeezed her eyes tightly shut. As always after the PT test she wanted to weep. Not from the effort. She—all of them—had faced worse, harder, tougher. But the stress clawing at her mind finally retracted.

She could continue to be what she wanted to be.

She walked off the run, tuning in now as other names and times were called out. She high-fived with Trigger as he crossed three miles.

Every one who'd passed stayed on the line. A unit again, all but willing the rest to make it, make that time. She checked her watch, saw the deadline coming up, and four had yet to cross.

Cards, Matt, Yangtree—who'd celebrated, or mourned, his fifty-fourth birthday the month before—and Gibbons, whose bad knee had him nearly hobbling those last yards.

Cards wheezed in with three seconds to spare, with Yangtree right behind him. Gibbons's face was a sweat-drenched study in pain and grit, but Matt? It seemed to Rowan he barely pushed.

His eyes met hers. She pumped her fist, imagined herself dragging him and Gibbons over the last few feet while the seconds counted down. She swore she could see the light come on, could see Matt reaching in, digging down.

He hit at twenty-two-twenty-eight, with Gibbons stumbling over at a half second behind.

The cheer rose then, the triumph of one more season.

"Guess you two wanted to add a little suspense." L.B. lowered his clipboard. "Welcome back. Take a minute to bask, then let's get loaded."

"Hey, Ro!" She glanced over at Cards's shout, in time to see him turn, bend over, and drop his pants. "Pucker up!"

And we're back, she thought.